Mountain Calling

Carol Cole O'Dell

FIRST EDITION

ISBN: 9780979648915
Library of Congress Control Number: 2008940356

Fiction denotes invention. Names, characters, places and incidents are fictitiously placed in the realms of authors' license and thus products of imagination. Any resemblance to actualities is coincidence.

Printed in the United States of America.

WARNOCK PRESS
P.O. Box 846
North Fork, CA 93643

Visit us at www.warnockpress.com

Cover and book design by G.C. O'Dell

Editing by Carlene O'Dell
                Amber Castillo

Carol Cole O'Dell is a pseudonym for Glenwood "Carol" O'Dell and Jeremy "Cole" O'Dell
A father and son writing team.

Visit the authors at www.gcodell.com

"To my wife, lover and best friend."

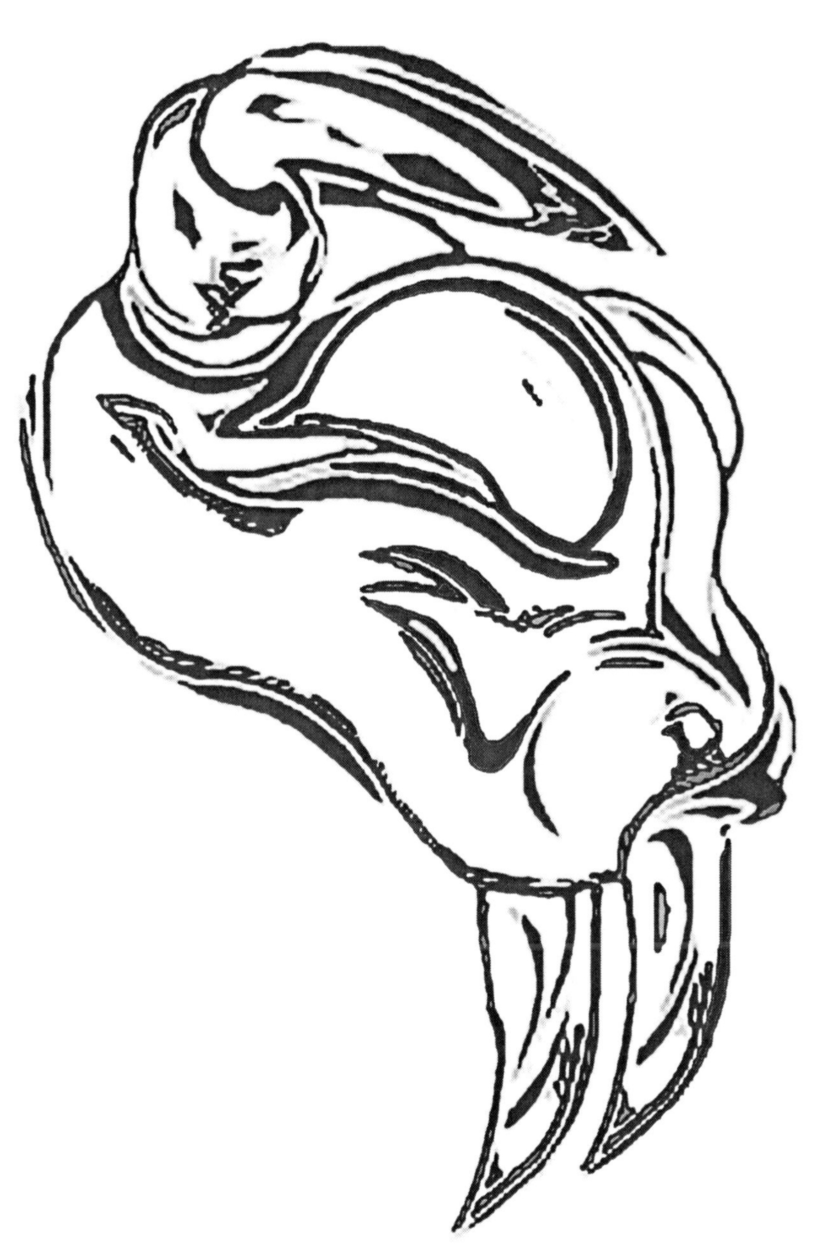

Mountain Calling

Carol Cole O'Dell

PROLOGUE

The old man gradually melted away from reality. His rhythmic chant— a repetitive prayer— softly resounded through the smoke filled chamber, centering the mystic on the quest for understanding as he gave himself over to the calling. Steam and ash rose from the fire as the man splashed water on the flames then sprinkled a fine powder over the amber coals. White smoke, mushroomed forth, clouding the small room in a blanketed shroud. And the low, recurring mutterings continued: "Hi-ya-hu-ya...hi-ya-hu-ha..." as sweat beaded over the man's face and chest. The mantra helped in the focus for the vision, bathing the one seeking in the dream world of the spirit messengers. From this place the riddles could be revealed. The future seen. The outcome foretold.

Eyes-of-an-Owl took a long pull from his sacred pipe and exhaled as he lifted his offer to the four winds. Presenting the instrument of tobacco was a measure of respect to the spirits and a silent request: please,— lead me on this journey. He had come to this secret world often in his many years of guiding his people. The spirits directed, but the visionary had to interpret the signs. From this realm what would be seen could be hidden: hazy, not full clear, drifting aimlessly... then centered; but the meaning always obscured by the disconnection of sights. The secrets to be revealed were there to be interpreted to one on the same plane as the guides; and the old man longed for that plane.

"Hi-ya-hu-ya...hi-ya-hu-ha..." The chant continues as the fog of reality lifted and the visionary drifted into the hallucinogen. Following the path of the unknown. The dream-world of the future, the past, the present. To which would the signs lead? What truths would the spirits tell?

The smoke of the chamber and the heat of the fire consumed the old man as he passed into the corridor of change. Like a blank canvas the visionary was incased in a void. Meaningless space of endless horizons unmarred by any distinguishing facets, but white. Mist shifted before him as the babbling of a brook trickled in the background. The fog began to lift. In the distance Eyes-of-an-Owl could see the white man — trappers... then settlers. Buffalo grazed an endless plain. The prairie was green from spring rains, but then one by one the buffalo vanished. At first gradually they disappeared, then faster,— faster as the meadow turned brown under the harsh sun, bleaching bones left scattered, and picked clean by scavengers.

The wind lifted the dust and blew the view away. In the wake were the dead. Lodges, broken and burned,— smoldering in the morning sun,— and bodies littered the ground: his children. The visionaries sacred lands...his people... laid waste. Snow began to fall, burying all and with it came the blinding wind. The old man closed his eyes, then blinked.

The haze of the trance continued to unfold as fog billowed at his feet. Reaching out he touched a wall, hot to his stroke, but smooth and hard. He had been here before. Recognition like deja-vu questioned the sign as he felt both sides of a narrow passage.

The air was musty, thick with the smell of animal rot: death was in this place. He walked down a narrow corridor that opened into a larger chamber. Ghostly shadows emerged then disappeared in the heavy vapor that swirled and shifted with the eddies of passage.

"*The Gatherers,*" whispered a soft memory — the spirits were talking. "*The Gatherers...*"

Eyes-of-an-Owl fumbled with his perception. He had seen this before as he looked at the ghastly features of the dark demon's face. The piercing red evil eyes glimmered as the creature peeled the skin from a live human. The man screamed in agony as the war god seemed to relish in the suffering of the lost soul. Rolling its head as if laughing the demon continued the torture. Long taloned fingers worked swift and skillfully as the scaly muscular forearms flexed and rippled under the metallic skin.

"*Death's Shadow...,*" whispered the haunting voice. The visionary was pulled as if falling down a dark hole. Balance was gone. Spinning aimlessly the man's heart raced as he again found himself in a tunnel — a cave.

Shadows moved cunningly through the misty dark crevices and corridors. Ammonia burned his eyes and seared his sinuses, yet the phantoms kept shifting,— darting. Polished black figures, drifting and moving in the dark like spirits in the night. A sharp squeal erupted as a jagged row of teeth came out of the gloom. Savage canines salivating for flesh. Then death stepped from the shadows. Organs and rotting flesh hung from massive bones. The ghoulish specter, a mutant skeleton, appeared laughing as it reached for him. Eyes-of-an-Owl stepped back, but ebony talons kept stretching foreword.

"*Death's Shadow...,*" the voice whispered and the old man fell backwards down a dark shaft. Spinning, twisting, then floating, the panorama below opened up. A young woman groaned in the throes of birth. Under the moaning pains of delivery she rubbed her abdomen. Rocking her head back she screamed as her chest bulged and her frame contorted. With every ounce of her strength she pulled herself upright then fell back into convulsions. Gagging on blood the woman surged once more then her skin began to peel from her ribs. The transformation had begun as flesh melted from bone. Out of the pool of human residue the new organism rose from its chrysalis. Rising erect the unnatural life lifted its head in triumph. A giant, living skeleton, greased to a glossy sheen in the puddling remains.

The terrified woman's distorted features laid twisted in the liquid mass like a mask; the last remnants of the human cocoon the creature was wrapped in.

More bodies appeared confined within walls. The stockade,— fencing of the white man,— concealed in the trees near the forking of several rivers. Scattered over the grounds: men and women— with gaping wounds where death was delivered. The infestation was coming.

"*Death's Shadow awakened...*" the voice whispered, "*...the Gatherers....*"

Eyes-of-an-Owl focused on the realization. It was the beginning.... Marking: "The harvest's coming."

"*Death's Shadow*...," whispered the voice again.

The dark chamber snapped to reality as the old man took a deep breath of the stale air and stared at the bark walls of his den. The amber coals of the fire shifted in intensity as each in turn consumed the depleted oxygen from the small room offering the only light to the shrouded interior. The vision was gone, but Eyes-of-an-Owl continued to sit. The thin layer of sweat over his weakened frame glistening like shellac in the faint glow of the dying pit. His expression revealed nothing as he sat motionless.

The plague was coming. The time of change to arrive.

"Hi-ya-hu-ya...hi-ya-hu-ha..." Eyes-of-an-Owl raised his pipe to the four winds. More was needed,— his time of quest,— incomplete.

*** Chapter One***

Broken-Toe's Honor

From the heavens will fall, a poisonous seed

The Mountain's Call, there will be no peace

Vengeance yearns, a cry for blood

But the ear can't learn, when death stalks alone

A sprout will grow, The Awakening at last

But the stones won't hear, The Destroyer pass

*　　*　　*

An alien giant stood over his bridge; his command in a shambles. Lights flickered and sparks arched across air and apparatus, in vain attempts to maintain their connection or transfer the power they still held before the reactors exploded. The ship rocked at additional impacts as many of the crew were knocked off their feet, but the giant Guardian managed to hold his stance; the twisted and damaged toe on his right foot was no deterrent to his balance. Broken-Toe was locked to his perch on the deck plating. The large muscular talons flexed like biting anchors with each trembler as the giant ordered the third wave of counter blasts amid the continuing barrage of plasma cannons. His transport vessel and crew had born the brunt of the pirate vessel's salvos with courage and grim determination: pride was a powerful force among his clan. But feelings of anger and disgust passed through the giant's mind as he stared at the vile enemy ship; a craft that held a pack of the dishonorable. These were more than criminals,— galactic scum. Thieves that traversed the heavens in search of someone else's livelihood. This clan of rejects from their own race had done the unspeakable: abandoning the Guardianship, perverting the creed of his people. Broken-Toe snarled with disgust. His red orbs burned beneath the glossy black visor of his war helmet. In dishonor they stalked their own; preying and pirating on their own kind. Unseasoned and unskilled Podjows. Rejects from the academies and enemies of the state.

Broken scanned his busted bridge. His young crew of unseasoned troops, many first year cadets, were ill equipped to face the evils of the Transaque clan. They were not even full marshals yet. Not one of them was a warrior. Most lacked any military training at all. Only Broken had the experience of live combat. But today what little training they had would be taxed to the limit.

Broken-Toe couldn't believe the degradation of the pirates in their raid. This rogue clan had waited to attack when he and most of his squad had gone to complete the finial cleansing and reclaiming of the abandoned planet. His team had been on the last leg of their sterilization before they continued their mission to transport one of the parasites to their home planet for study. An antidote was desperately needed for the deadly bug before any other colonies faced the ravaging death unleashed by a still unknown terrorists group. Broken's young team had been chosen for the controlled Yet-Tat: the extraction or destruction of an infestation; but now the giant wondered if fate had cast him in the path of the terrorists group responsible for the savage outbreaks of the plague across the many diverse sectors.

To the Guardian's young crew the Yet-Tat was a— Right-of-Passage; it was a triumph of trust placed only on the best. A marking of the bravest of marshals in obedience to the Center Counsel's command as they walked through an inferno that would purge any weakness granting the victors the full rank of Guardian. The Yet-Tat could take many forms, but the Counsels letter and decree were the finial label to any challenge. To survive such a challenge was an honor few would ever hoped to attain.

This mission to capture the parasite required great skill and the Counsel had hand selected Broken-Toe to lead the Yet-Tat. But seasoned marshals were on short supply due to eruptions across the empire, so the giant was forced to draw from fresh recruits that had just completed their training. It was a dangerous gamble, but the Counsel had no choice. One parasitic Queen with her hanging ulcers had been released on the Sig-zaw by a rogue terrorist group and the colony was totally engulfed in mere days. Any planet the terrorist might dump such an abomination would be devastating, sending ripples across the empire, and fear through the entire galaxy. And what fear? In hours a parasite queen builds her nest while infecting hosts. No indigenous inhabitants of any world is safe. Her viral seeds seep into the blood of the contaminated. Using the host's cardiovascular system infection dispenses throughout the body rewriting the very DNA of the victim.

Transformation is swift; in one day the new life breaks through shedding the now useless skin of the former animal. The bone mass grows as an exoskeleton of the new being. Organs and tissue of the old animal gradually fall off as the useless rotting evidence of previous life dissipate with time. Only a queen carries the mucus ulcers that drop like eggs giving birth to the beginning larva of the parasite. All other hosts develop into workers, like a horde of ants that support the queen in one common goal:— to multiply.

If the Queen on Sig-zaw were let on her own the entire planet would have soon been completely overrun. But the code of The Guardian could never allow that to happen. The battle for Broken's trainees became a life and death match to kill all the parasite's offspring and recapture or kill the queen. If the Queen couldn't be taken alive a larva needed to be saved. Finding an antidote was the empire's top priority.

Broken's strategy was simple. Secure a few shed ulcers first. Quarantine them then destroy the nest. It would be a difficult battle with her horde of mindless drones, driven on by the telepathy of their leader and their own instinct, for a worker would sacrifice all to protect its royalty.

And the Queen herself could display an uncanny intelligence. Driven by survival, her cunning, and viciousness was unpredictable in the course of battle. That trainees would die in the venture of a Yet-Tat was expected by the empire, but Broken-Toe was a wise leader and as of yet never lost a cadet in any other Right-of-Passage.

The Pirates had waited like cowards, hitting the giant's ship when it was virtually deserted because of the Yet-Tat — stealing and killing everything in sight. The Parasite larvae, that Broken-Toe's troops had recaptured from the hive, stored in the cargo hold of the transport vessel, were stolen. The needless carnage and destruction had filled the giant's heart with anger. It had taken his crew hours to get his damaged ship into somewhat of a working order: enough to get it into space and begin pursuit. The ion trail and faint gases left in the wake of the pirate ship's passing had dispersed, but not enough to hide their course from Broken-Toe. As a skilled marshal he was trained to stalk his prey in whatever environment his game was hiding. Whether some distant planet at the outer reaches of the galaxy or in the empty void of space, Broken-Toe could read the signs and find his quarry. And he was driven to succeed, driven by honor, driven by pride; the dead cried out for justice and the giant planned to continue his quest until the last drop of his blood spilled from his veins. If victory was his he would lengthen the punishment rent upon his vanquished until their life's-fluid painted the decks of their ship and drenched the bulkheads of his own.

The two frigates had been playing a deadly game of hunter and prey for the better part of a week; the roles changing, back and forth, between hunter and hunted, as they dodged through solar systems and danced around stars. Each encounter brought a wave of fire and more damage to both of the crippled ships, but still Broken-Toe pressed on. He would not lose this match. To much was at stake.

This latest encounter had turned out to be an ambush. The pirate ship was hidden in an asteroid field in a solar system containing one inhabited planet. The planet was familiar to Broken. He had walked its violent and savage terrain before. It sat third from the sun and held a warrior species. Hunters, savages, beings that could track and kill with skill beyond any other aliens he had ever confronted. He himself had to fight them just to survive and found them to be a true challenge. A prison break years past had trapped him on that violent world. And today his fate had come full circle. Hunting for criminals he had returned to this solar system. But today he was not hunting for escaped convicts. Today his hunt was for vengeance. Today he would kill for lost honor.

The enemy had used the asteroid field skillfully. Hidden by the heavy metals of the fields undefined ores and the random gravitational forces that sent ghost images to the stalking sensors, Broken had approached too close and unprepared for the swift execution of a surprise lunge at their rear. The first salvo had taken out the ships steering thrusters and port weapons before the giant could even fire a shot. In the counterattack one of Broken-Toe's gunners actually missed the enemy frigate and hit one of the asteroids that contained a high concentration of hydrogen. Luckily the ensuing explosion swallowed up the pirates' ship and disabled its engines enough to equal the match.

A growl and a few short clicks from a nearby crew member told Broken what was left of their weapons were locked on target. The honored giant raised his closed fist and opened his clawed hand: a sign of the hunt meaning to engage. He could have voiced the order, but this was a Yack-Taw and he felt like treating it as such.

The wounded and limping enemy craft had taken a severe pummeling over the chase and the final blow of the asteroid rendered it virtually dead. It was in no condition to continue to try and run; its battered hull and damaged engines left it unable to propel itself at light speed any longer. The last thrust it fired, cast it adrift in the void of space at a virtually uncontrollable speed as it passed by the stalking ship almost helpless. With limited steering and useless engines it floated aimlessly; the only source of repair parts floating in the massive hulk still firing on its weakened frame from behind. With its damaged reserves of power the vessel turned to face its enemy. A boarding party would have to take the ship.

Broken-Toe felt a sense of amusement at the sign of life. So they've had enough running and now they're going to stay and fight. His ship shook as the diminished weapons aboard his craft fired on the fast approaching vessel. Even in the onslaught the enemy ship continued to employ breaking thrusters set for a collision as Broken-Toe's craft continued forward carried by the last momentum of its final thruster fire. *"Perhaps they do have some honor left,"* Broken-Toe clicked and chirped under his breath.

Alarms flashed all around him warning of an unexpected power up in the oncoming ship. The pirate frigate surged toward Broken's vessel: veering starboard at the last minute. The action led to their ships scraping across each other. The impact sent Broken Toe and his crew off their feet. Further rumbles shook his ship as explosions sounded throughout the interior.

From underneath, the enemy vessel fired large grappling hooks at point blank range. Strong ionized liquid steel cables shot through space as their clawed ends grappled with the damaged hull of the pursuing ship, tearing through the outer skin and locking onto any supporting structure. The sheer power of the boarding weapons welded their supports to the enemy's craft, as specters in heavy space armor launched across the void, shot by personal cannons: boarding tubes that could propel the infantry through the emptiness of space to the opposing ship. The attacking party quickly torched entry holes in the thick plating of the Marshal vessel's outer skin.

The sound of metal tearing at near ear shattering volumes gripped the structures as the crafts heaved: the two frigates colliding under the drag of the tow cables pulling their frames together. Alarms for hull breaches were heard on the bridge. Broken-Toe gave the order for the breaches to be sealed and for zero-gee armor to be donned by all the crew. The battle was now reduced to hand-to-hand amid the emptiness of space. Survival for the victors would come only if the needed parts for their own ship could be salvaged from that of the vanquished pirate vessel.

*   *   *

Three Spots stood guard as four other pirates guided the boarding tubes manually aiming their soldiers to the hull of the Marshal's ship. Two others of The Lost stood near him. His warriors were ready for battle, waiting for the chance to wet their blades with the blood of the empire's police. Three Spots held the position of point man, — a place of honor given to the most proven warriors. Many guardians had fallen by Three Spots hand. He was proud to have taken their weapons from their cold death grip. How he longed for the glory of battle. He stood proud, holding the spear that had pierced his skin and had given him his name. During a fierce confrontation a warden years earlier had thrust this very lance through his chest and scarred his hide. The double bladed weapon sheared his flesh and ripped a wound of two large round scars that matched a birth mark on his left shoulder. He had killed that assailant with his bare-hands, wrenching the lance from his chest and thus earned his name.

Three Spots was proud of the name for it showed he was a true warrior, unlike the arrogant guardians. Those stupidly proud clans tried to force their honor code on everyone. Any that rebelled earned The Mark of Lost Honor. How Three Spots hated The Guardians, their code, their self-righteousness. Using their laws on honor to raise themselves above every other vocation among the hated empire; how the daft among them longed for the glory of their arrests, the Yack-Taw. Yes, he despised The Guardians and loved killing them. And oh, how he relished the fact that he would soon get the chance to wet his blades once more in their hot blood.

Three Spots hit the hull of the enemy ship with a thud as his gravity boots locked onto the heavy metal plating. His Second hit the casing nearby as The Cutter landed at his feet and began immediately torching an entry to take the ship. Scattered across the floating hulk were numerous parties at work; the lasers spewing sparks and molten metal into the emptiness of the dark void of space as warrior pirates watched in earnest for victory.

The first wave of Boarding Repelers rounded the contours of the dead frigate amid the eruption of plasma cannons and laser weapons. Streaks of light sliced the darkness of the backdrop as flames bounced off armor and deflected against the hulls surface. The pirates defended their position, launching their salvos to protect The Cutters. In the wake of the onslaught both sides casualties', rendered helpless by injury, were ripped from their anchors and floated haplessly along with the dead hulk, as the suspended battlefield drifted near the speed of light on a collision course with a blue orb fast approaching. Soon the gravitational pull of that planet would grab at the battered vessels and end any hope of salvation. Both sides were working for a speedy victory.

Three Spots stepped forward ready to meet the assault, firing his mask cannon as the enemy moved in close to stop the pirates boarding action.

A wall of armored marshals swinging weapons and darting blows, hit the intruders line as swords, lances and staffs flashed in a wave of fury. Each combatant skilled in the use of his weapon of choice: bent on extermination of the opposing force. The measure of one's prowess reduced to kill or be killed.

Three Spots deflected the savage arch of a long sword with the double-bladed end of his quarterstaff-lance as he brought the butt around to catch his opponent across the helmet. The enemy stopped the swing with a second sword and shot a burst from his mask cannon at Three Spots' right hand to dislodge his weapon. Most of the power of the blast was deflected by the heavy gauntlet protecting the appendage, but the effect still burned, weakening his grip. The pirate spun and returned a shot from his mask cannon at his assailant's first sword arm, catching a weakness at the joint. It cut through the space armor and severed muscle and tendon. The creature let go of his sword in pain as the weapon simply floated where it was released.

Three Spots jumped forward driving his shoulder into his opponent's chest, then sidestepped swiping downward with the double edged side of his staff. The marshal deflected the blow with his second sword and reaching up with his weakened hand grasped the sword still floating in space and jabbed it at the knee of the pirate. The thrust was weak because of the injury, but the blade was sharp and pierced the armor, cutting tissue and scraping Three Spots' thigh as the weapon was extracted. The ice cold vacuum of space froze the wound, but the pirate ignored the discomfort and punched the enemy with his left hand under the helmet. The force knocked the marshal's head up and backwards as the pirate then spun, kicking his opponent in the chest with his right foot. The blow dislodged the guardian's gravity boots from the hull of the ship and sent him floating uncontrolled into the void. Three Spots turned just in time to block the attack of a second enemy when he saw his Cutter drop through the hole now completed: finishing the first phase of their mission. The pirate twisted and swept the back end of his lance peeling the defender from the ships surface. As the officer drifted helplessly, Three Spots shot a burst from his mask cannon. The impact did little against the heavy space armor, but the force of the shot pushed the enemy further from the skin of the drifting battle platform. The pirate then made his way to the newly cut entrance and climbed down to the decks below.

Life support and artificial gravity were obviously off-line as Three Spots looked up and down the corridor he had ascended into. His Cutter was already halfway down the hall. The pirate took up pursuit. Life depended on salvaging the needed engine parts and protecting his technician was a priority at this juncture. It wouldn't be long before the gravitational field of the planet they were approaching would suck them in and pull them all to their deaths. The pirate was sure his ship had just enough power to sustain an orbit of the planet, but not enough to hold the marshal's ship with it. If they didn't get the parts they needed now their clan would be stuck in orbit without a way to escape. Other pirates followed Three Spots into the frigate as throughout the surface of the ship Cutters opened additional holes, but none of the guardians pursued.

*   *   *

Broken-Toe engaged the escape pod and watched as the tube cleared the ship on a course for the planet. He had set the homing beacon on the vehicle to call others of his clan to this solar system for rescue, but first he planned to destroy the remaining pirates. After he was sure the pod was well on its way he turned to the engine room. The strategy was to wait until the enemy was aboard then blow the transport vessel's reactors. Even now his crew would be crossing the void, climbing to the pirate ship by means of the grappling cables.

Broken slipped down the corridor, determined to reach the reactors before the enemy. The walls were changing colors as he walked: the cold vacuum of space draining the heat from the ships interior. Environmental controls were beyond repair as were most of the ship's systems. Essentially their vessel was nothing more than a derelict, but the power core could still be used to unleash a devastating explosion. It would determine victory or defeat and Broken had no intention of losing. As he reached the engine room door the panel was jammed shut by a metal obstruction welded into position by an earlier shot from the attacking frigate. Somehow a missile had blown through the heavy bulwark of the outer construction and fused some of the ships framework to the entryway. That explained why the bridge lost contact with engineering, this direct hit to the port side must have killed everyone instantly.

Broken bent his giant strength at the blockade as the metal framework began slowing giving way. Laser fire erupted around him as a mine floated by, magnetically locking to the wall. The Marshal turned off his boots and jumped against the wall then pushed himself deeper down the corridor. The blast behind blew a hole in the structure; the ensuing flame pulled what little oxygen was yet free floating in the hall, generating a vacuum that sucked Broken back through the new opening and his continuing momentum carried him deep inside the chamber almost on top of one of the reactors. The giant clicked on his boots locking himself to the framework and busted open the control panel.

The enemy hit the opening behind and the room quickly turned into a light show as mask cannon fire sprayed the interior. Broken aimed and shot his mask weapon into a key area of the control panel then jumped deeper into the chamber while again switching off his boots. The blast from his weapon began a chain reaction as explosions began erupting throughout the rooms machinery. The giant hit the far wall reengaging his gravity gear and made his way to an escape pod, still intact. Climbing through the portal tube he slammed the ejection lever before even shutting the door as the vehicle sparked to life and shot out of the launch sleeve. The pod barely cleared the pirates vessel as gravity from the planet pulled the small life boat towards its upper atmosphere. Broken tugged the hatch shut and locked its mechanism, trying to prepare the vessel for entry, when the transport ship's reactors blew. The explosion tossed the little pod as it spun out of control slamming The Guardian violently around the interior.

The unforeseen misjudgment of Broken-Toes plan suddenly played out as the frigate split in two. The force of the blast pushed the grappled side of the police ship into the pirate's craft, knocking out all the thrusters on the enemies starboard side and destroying any chance of the vessel remaining in orbit. As the contorted metal frame grated across the surface of the enemies hull, the impact fractured the super structure and ripped through the bulkheads causing the ship to erupt in a series of explosions. Death would come swiftly to all as the entire conglomerate of twisted debris and helpless passengers raked the outer atmosphere of the planet and began to plummet earthward. Broken-Toe cried out in anger as he watched. The destruction of his own ship was premature. There was no way his crew would survive.

Chapter Two

New Start

Verse from: The Fallen's Song

The Destroyer will cometh

Their calling gave no warning

Pass through their midst and strike

Let not thy eye sorrow nor thy heart compassion

Take thy weapon for smashing, to ruination thou must march

Order of the King

*　　*　　*

Jake stood scanning the horizon. The setting sun hung like a glowing ember in the evening sky, casting the last dark shadows of day before night would swallow the waning torch of light. The large stone face to the west was doing its best to speed up the process as the man marveled at the vibrant reds and deep yellows, mirrored across the smattering of thin clouds, that almost appeared to be on fire, against the backdrop of purples and greens of the distant peaks. This was truly a beautiful land, full of the wonders that spark imagination and the venture of life.

Jake took the reins of his mount tighter as the animal came up beside him. "God sure knows how to paint fer the soul don't he Cass?"

The horse whinnied as if answering. Jake patted then rubbed the animal on the forehead.

"We'll be just fine on our own again." Jake put his left foot in the stirrup and pulled his long, lanky form into the saddle. He had come west at the tail end of the fur trade and ended up as a guide to many with aspirations — beckoning the Oregon movement. His heart was saddened by the changes he had seen with the increase of settlers, but he himself had ventured west for opportunity — how could he slight others with similar dreams?

As he seated his right foot, he slid his rifle — just acquired permanent from the detachment he quit — into its boot and sat back in the saddle. With a sigh, stroking his long graying beard, he again marveled at the glory of the ending day. "This is God's country with plenty... We don't need no yellow Northerner tellin' us what's what... right Cass?"

The horse seemed to appreciate the conversation and responded to the man with an exhaust of its large lungs and a rumble of its lips.

Jake patted the animal on the neck then scratched the withers. As a scout, the military would frown on the man's decision to leave on his own with a government issued repeater, but Jake didn't view his agreement to help Lieutenant Oswalt as an enlistment. He just said, "he'd be takin' them to the fort at Twin Forks by the shortest route," through the increasingly hostile Indian presence. With that done so was Jake's job...or so he thought — with that ill tempered, rat-faced, little man — barkin' orders like he was some all important cuss — when Jake was sure the man couldn't find his butt with both hands on his ass. How the military made promotions to lead was beyond him. It was as if all that was needed for promotion was a big ego, and no common sense.

Of course Jake didn't feel that way about all officers. He had served under some of the best during the war. He walked through hell with them and carried the scars of near fatal misses that ripped through his garments and cut his flesh. Men had fallen around him in untold numbers as they walked deaths ridge only to surrender on reaching the goal. Jake's uniform had been slit to shreds by as many as thirty near misses as he would often tell of the rags he wore... torn and slashed as ball and bullet devastated their offensive that ended his military career and any threat the south might have mustered for morale. Jake's own view of the battle and the war itself diminished with time as he returned to the North Western Territory — where life was all about new beginnings and forgetting the pain that follows a man over the choices made.

As Jake eased Cass down the soft sloping ridge a thunderous roar echoed over the rolling terrain spooking the horse.

"Easy boy!" the man exclaimed trying to bring his mount under control. The deafening sound increased as Jake caught a glimpse of an immense fireball overhead while his horse circled then reared. The object appeared to be heading right for them.

Spurring Cass the horse bolted for the nearby trees at the top of the ridge from where they had just come. The flaming ball topped the wood line, igniting the upper terraces as it passed, and plunged into the valley floor ripping a trench that uprooted trees and threw debris in its wake.

The ground literally shook from the impact causing Cass to lose his footing and go down as rubble, thrown into the air from the impact, almost buried horse and rider.

Jake, pinned under his mount, pulled himself forward as Cass rolled to his belly in a panic trying to regain footing in the choking cloud of the dust filled air.

Grabbing the saddle high on the bridge the man managed to balance himself as Cass rose on all fours and again bolted away from the unnatural occurrence. Jake, hanging precariously from the right side of the horse, worked to regain center. The man's right ankle, still in its stirrup, was hurting and offered no support as Jake tried to pull himself back into the saddle. Branches and brush resisted his effort, working to remove him the rest of the way from Cass.

The horse whinnied and abruptly turned to the right as a

fiery branch dropped from the upper terraces blocking their path. The swift move aided Jake, shifting him back center of the saddle, as Cass continued his flight at a right angle to the new obstruction.

Jake ducked low on his mount and found the left stirrup and let Cass choose the best course of escape as he hung onto the saddle bridge with his left hand and retained his hold on the reins with his right.

Fear was in full control as both horse and rider cared little for anything but self-preservation and at this point safety was all about distance. Cass was well lathered when Jake finally eased the horse to a stop on the top of a higher ridge in an open meadow overlooking the disaster below. Patches of fire dotted the landscape, but didn't appear to be spreading as the man studied the scene trying to determine what had happened. He had heard of stars falling from the sky before and had seen streaks in the sky of the telltale sign of the truth of such an occurrence, but never had he heard of one actually falling on someone. Jake squinted trying to make out what the star looked like, but after some strain figured it must have been buried by the impact. He had seen craters left behind by cannon balls on the battlefield, but this impact was huge. He was intrigued.

Could this fallen object be of any value? This could be a discovery beyond any known to man.

Curiosity has been a driving force behind many a downfall, and Jake knew that, but the drive is strong in a man. The scout turned Cass back to the spot that just a moment before they had fled with abandon.

The horse for its part is not a curious animal and Cass was no different having little desire to venture back so soon to that fearful place of noise and fire, but Jake talked soothingly to his companion, patting and coaxing the animal against its better judgment. At first they walked the top of the ridge studying the wreck below, but after several hours of observation the flames began to die down and Jake started the slow descent back to the valley of the star. It was well into night before they reached the basin floor, lit by the numerous pockets of flaming brush and small trees, still burning the green fuel of living matter, as the consuming blazes rumbled and cracked over a wide area of the ridge and valley. The canyon carved by the falling object reminded the scout of a city road, wide enough for ten or more carriages to travel abreast and the walls on either side of the gorge were so tall Jake thought he was riding into a tunnel. As he continued down the sloping hole he came to what looked like a man-made opening. A large square door rested bent and damaged against a pile of debris, half obscuring a dark cave behind. Jake was mystified. The door and frame appeared to be out of some type of metal.

A bluish, glowing webbing crackled and sparked, weaving an intermittent, translucent mesh, over the metallic surfaces of the opening, reminded Jake of lightning as it systematically pulsed and sizzled in a gradually diminishing pattern. It was almost mesmerizing as Jake dismounted and walked closer to the phenomenon still holding Cass by the reins.

Reaching out with his left hand to touch the spectacle, Cass snorted and jerked his head backward, pulling the man off-balance and away from the wonder, but Jake's attention was undeterred as he retained his grip on the animal.

"Easy boy,— just needs me a look-see," the man said, as he again moved his hand near the blinking web. The hair along the man's arm began to standup and tingle and his hand felt a pulsing burn before he actually made contact, which was enough of a warning to go no farther. Jake pulled back his hand. "Some things I guess are best not experienced," he said with a chuckle as he looked back at Cass whose eyes were wide with fear. "It'll be OK. You were right."

Jake patted the horse on the forehead. "It's good one of us has horse sense," he said laughing.

The doorway was wide enough for the two of them to walk through as the large interior opened up to a sizeable cavern, lit by the same flashing of blue webbing around the interior, and pockets of fire that sparked and popped in little explosions of showering orange and white lines throughout the chamber.

"What the hell is this place?" Jake asked as he stepped deeper into the sweltering chamber and surveyed the expanse. It reminded him of a cargo hold in a wooden vessel used for transporting goods across the ocean. What looked like metal containers were strung around the compartment, some with flashing round knobs, and others just solid boxes. It was confusing to the man who knew all of this came about by the impact of what he thought was a star. Was this some kind of underground cache that the falling object had struck? But then where was the star? It was hard for Jake to believe that the room itself could have fallen from the sky. How could something this large and that looked man-made come out of the sky?

Jake began to work his way through the interior, weaving around the clutter thrown about in disarray, marveling at the apparent construction of the cave. It looked as though a huge explosion had ripped the place apart, scattering the loose items, but the walls were still intact, showing very little damage. The air had a strange scent to it and a thin mist floated low to the ground, which left a haunting aura to the enclosure, but Jake pressed on suppressing the disquieting thoughts telling him to leave. The fog and smoke limited his vision some as sweat, beading up over his forehead, dripped into his eyes; the salty fluid stung and momentarily blinded him. Jake stumbled over something and accidentally bumped into one of the containers, burning his forearm.

"Damn!" Catching his balance, he rubbed the injury softly, but the distraction brought his attention to a mass of purple glowing matter splattered around one portion of a wall among a mass of tottered objects. As Jake moved nearer he saw what looked like a man's leg, badly burned and contorted, smashed in-between a pile of debris. The leg looked metallic green in the minimal light which couldn't be right the man thought, but on closer inspection found the foot was oddly shaped with long clawed talons off each toe and had an almost scaled look. Purple phosphorous fluid was everywhere around the limb and still oozing from a cut above the knee.

This was the most unnatural thing Jake had seen to date. The scout went to push some of the wreckage away from the body, but finding it hot retrieved some leather gloves from his saddle. The object were heavy and scorching, but he managed one by one to push them aside.

The strange creature uncovered caused the man to back away in shock as he stared. "What in the hell are you?"

Jake studied the body then pulled it the rest of the way free. The uncanny light made full recognition difficult, but the scout could tell it was some type of giant. A regular Goliath or perhaps one of them Nephilim come down from heaven.

Heavily roped locks crowned the ghoulish head, reminding Jake of a warrior's headdress. Large insect eyes that reflected the man's image were inset low on the almost nonexistent forehead, appeared unnaturally out of balance with the small ugly features. But the most mesmerizing aspect about the demon's face was the horn like protrusions at either side of the eyes that curved gracefully upward then twisted forward. Jake reached down and felt the metallic appendages and was amazed at the smooth contours and cold hardness of the savage antler attributes when the tip burned through his glove and scorched his hand. He jerked it back cursing and pulled off the glove that was still smoldering, slapping the spark out on the ground, he cursed; but then resumed his inspection after the short interruption.

Running his hand over where he guessed the heart would be he felt a faint beating.

Whatever this critter was, it was still alive. The scout contemplated what to do. The thing wasn't a man. "I don't think yer from these here parts,— partner." Jake signed, "You friend or foe?" The man knelt low when a red glow appeared deep within the reflective contours of the eyes. A powerful hand shot out and grabbed Jake by the neck.

Cass reared back and stumbled as the choking man pulled his long knife from his boot and drove it into his assailant's neck. The demon coughed as phosphorous purple fluid gurgled around the wound, but the death grip at Jake's neck remained. Reaching up with his left hand the scout tried to pry the creature's hand away, at the same time cocking his head toward Cass.

The horse was trying to regain its footing in the confined area when something buzzed by Jake's ear and took another pass darting at Cass. Its sound startled the scout. Like a unexpected covey of quail the fluttering noise flew by his head again. It reminded the scout of a humming bird defending it source of nectar.

Jake gagged at the vise grip choking his life and pushed the knife deeper. *Feud-d-d-d,* the strange fluttering sound stopped as it impacted on Cass. The horse reared as the thing burst against the animal's ribcage; moments latter Cass again jumped, tossing sideways and fell kicking. Black tarry ooze plastered the horse's midsection.

The scout managed to pull free from the death grip as the demon weakened and then proceeded to plunge his blade into the creature's chest again and again. Glowing purple blood spewed forth as Jake rolled free and watched the demon's life signs fade.

Turning his attention to Cass, Jake stumbled over to his horse dropping his knife and tried to wipe the tarry ooze from his suffering animal. The fluid adhered to his hand and burned causing him to shriek out in pain. The man tried to wipe off the acidic tar on his leather pants, but the substance immediately began to eat away at his leggings. The leather smoked and Jake coughed on the fumes as he was again buzzed by an unseen apparition. "What the hell are you?" he screamed, shaking as the black tar seemed to be spreading over his forearms. Jake saw a puddle of what looked like water and jumped for it splashing the liquid over his arms and legs.

Feud-d-d-d-d, flapped a second almost invisible creature. This time Jake got a glimpse. Perhaps an immense beetle or funny looking bird. The man swatted at the critter, but it seemed undeterred as it dive-bombed into the man's chest. The splatter painted his abdomen as the burning increased. Wet from the puddle, the tarry ooze seemed to spread quicker as Jake fell backward with tremors. He looked at his hands shaking, but the thick fluid was dissipating. It was being absorbed by his skin. His extremities were unscarred, but the burning increased as the pain turned inward. Bone and muscle felt on fire as he rolled on the ground in agony.

On the floor of the chamber next to him Jake saw a quivering mass changing shape. As an amphibian's eggs transform first into tadpoles the gooey heap began to morph into the strange flying creature that flew into Cass and himself. Jake was loosing consciousness because of the pain, but the sight and speed of the transformation was mesmerizing.

"Damn..." The man muttered as he tried to roll away. The creature took to flight. The man swung his arm batting at the bug, but he was to weak and delirious to truly defend himself. It dodged and flew a short distance away and landed. With the darting movements of a bird studying its surrounding, the eyeless bug identified its target and launched itself at the alien the scout had stabbed. Gagging, Jake dropped into unconsciousness.

Chapter Three

The Buffalo Soldier

July 1866 Congress Establishes All Black Regiments

In July of this year Congress laid to rest the question of whether former slaves would continue to serve in this country's military. Over 180,000 blacks served in the Union Army during the war. As many as 33,000 died defending the call for freedom. This summer, legislation approved the formation of two mounted and four of our infantry regiments made up almost entirely of men that served in all black units during the war. It's rumored the Cheyenne have nicknamed these new patrolling forces,— "Buffalo Soldiers." This paper looks forward to the continuing news about the 9th and 10th Cavalries and their work defending and taming of our American frontier.

Independence News

*   *   *

Titus sat on his haunches, his black hands slowly combing the underbrush. Some light gray cloth had caught hold of a jagged twig to tell Titus the way the horse thieves had gone. Not that the hoof tracks weren't enough, but the pieces of fiber told Titus the type of men he was dealing with. He had seen the fabric plenty of times when he scouted for the Union looking for the gray coats during the war. Gently he rubbed the remnant between his fingers until it began to fall apart in his hand. Sometimes he wished he could unravel life's mysteries just as easily. Mysteries like: why he was targeted by horse thieves when the Indians nearby would trade one of their finest ponies for a few simple beads or meager quantity of goods from back east. Even the mining operation in the next camp over the distant ridge had three fine mares, but they were white men. Why the horse thieves had taken his animal when they each had a horse was telling. He knew these men had begun a mining operation just north of him a few days ago, he recognized two of the men's horseshoe prints and saw their camp while hunting; but he didn't realize they were southerners then. Why were men filled with such hate because of a man's color?

The gray material told him he was dealing with some good old boys; the type that probably still blamed, *"his kind,"* for the war. He knew the probable outcome. He had dealt with many such twisted bastards during his stint in the military. Men who killed for the fun of it. He hated men like that, more than those who hated him for his skin color. Titus never killed for pleasure, but in the war he did what was required. It was duty. It meant stopping injustice, and Titus was good at it. When necessary, the formidable ebony soldier could deal death swiftly; as a cobra's strike, his incisive vision and agile muscles formulated into an unstoppable tool of the military. Sharp eyes put him in a position as sniper on the battlefield and his wilderness skills, a scout to his detachment. Many times he had held men's lives in his hand. Like a god with the power of judgment in his finger all he had to do was squeeze his trigger and render verdict, crushing the unfortunate in his sights. His lieutenant would joke at nights to other officers about his very own, *"Black Death,"* the son of slaves under his command that could drop men that appeared as mere specks on the field. The lieutenant had often preyed on the pride of his fellow white officers,— betting money that his buffalo soldier,— his *"Black Death,"*— could outshoot any marksmen their companies could muster. Titus took no pleasure in his commander's games, but he did what he was asked under the officers prodding — guised as pride for his people. In reality the lieutenant had little respect for Titus as a man, or for that matter his brothers of the 10th. The officer even appeared to resent the position the military had assigned him to. A graduate of West Point put in charge of black soldiers? But he did at least mask his prejudice and demonstrated a decor of fairness to those under his command.

The lieutenant, after an especially lucrative transaction, won against an extreme bigot, gave Titus the gift of a Henry rifle and two navy colts. The present in itself seemed to demonstrate a measure of respect, but the true reason was probably more tied to a mocking slap to the losing lieutenant's face as Officer Erwig made sure the loser saw the gestures.

Titus brushed his fingertips against the ivory hilt of one of his colts. The weapons had saved his life too many times and yet had cursed him. To see the faces of those he killed in his dreams, plagued his conscious and burned his waking thoughts; but putting aside the security the pistols offered in the cruel and dangerous world in which he lived generated a greater fear of what could happen without the ability to exercise his honed lifesaving skills.

With one graceful motion Titus stood and moved on through the jackstraws; his cavalry blues masked in the shadows of the thick brush. Eyes always sweeping: scanning the wood, searching for clues, watching for danger. The four thieves seemed to know how to move in the forest,— probably from their own time in the war. Titus had the feel that these men were raiders. Clues left behind marked them as experienced thieves. The Missouri border raids of the 1850's began the training that had extended over the decades for many southern guerillas. A way of life that followed the trail and hid among the brush. However, their span of years was nothing compared to the life the buffalo soldier had spent growing up in the Missouri wilderness: a runaway.

The world had given the youngster a mentor with a matchless knowledge of survival skills. At first Titus was scared of James. Here was another white man: a loner,— hardened by a life that offered little in the means of monetary gain. A runaway slave could go a long way in enriching one's pockets, but James seemed to have little interest in the laws of the white man. To Titus who was short for his young age when they first met, the elderly weathered giant was stoic in his demeanor. Long thick black hair, dusted with gray, hung full under a bowler hat, but his leathery face spoke of a man that could make harsh decisions without concern for others. A man who chose a life of solitude after the beaver trade died out. A man that had no desire for the trappings of civilization. James was half Iroquois. And although his father was white: a British officer and a well educated man, James had little interest in his English heritage and chose to wander and live off the land as an Indian. It was this heritage that the Iroquois warrior passed on to his adopted son Titus, and the young man was ever thankful for the blessing of James, the adoptive father that was such a big part of his teen years.

The surrounding brush and trees of this northern landscape were a kind of home to Titus, but as he moved through the wilderness a look of dismay dotted his brow. The hoof tracks had changed. His horse appeared to have come up lame. The men had shown little regard for the animals as they traveled over this rough terrain. Titus was well aware of men like these. Men that lacked respect for anything they dominated. Men that justified slavery.

Titus was born into this world a slave. His earliest memory was of following his mother around the house as she did her chores. Soon after when he was big enough he had chores of his own. At that time the master had wanted him out in the field, but the mistress of the house wouldn't have it. She had become attached to Titus and enjoyed his smiling face and questioning eyes. The young boy's mother told him it was because the mistress had lost her own son when he was Titus' age, but whatever the reason the woman latched onto the child in her grief and treated him with favor; even teaching him how to read and write,— which was strictly forbidden. Titus enjoyed the lessons and especially the hugs that came with his advancement, a welcome retreat from working the fields and the lonely drudgery required under brutal task masters.

Titus was an avid student with a bright young mind ready for the secrets of the written page. He was also quick to learn the language the mistress spoke to her friends when they came over. One day she was having tea with her sister and a few southern ladies when one asked if the master Mr. Brigwing had gone to town. Titus overheard the question and told the ladies in the same dialect, "The master was out overseeing the fields." Later he learned the language was French.

Then the worst and probably the most pivotal event occurred in his young life. Soon after he turned ten he heard a disturbance coming from the basement. When he went down the stairs and came across the master pummeling his mother in a forcible rape. Fear and anger overcame him and he pulled the master's gun from his discarded holster thrown haphazardly over a chair. The firearm was heavy and he was inexperienced, but he pointed the weapon and fired. The trigger jerked hard and the gun kicked causing the shot to merely injure the master: a minor flesh wound. Angered by the disruption and offence by the child slave, the master grabbed the gun and brought it to bear on Titus. The young boy's mother came rushing to her son to shield him, but the bullet struck her in the chest and pitched her backward. Titus fell to his mother's side as the master paused briefly at the realization of his mistake, but the young boy paid him little heed. Titus' last memory of his mother was her weak form, crumpled on the dirt floor, whispering through blood stained lips, "Run my child!"

The master's outrage exploded. Shrieking some racial slur he pressed the pistol to Titus' forehead. The young boy, resigned to his fate, simply looked up with hate filled eyes of defiance. Death was to come at the hands of his mother's killer and he was powerless to stop it. The master smiled viciously and pressed the barrel harder into Titus' forehead. However, when he saw the lack of fear the coward paused.

The mistress of the house had heard the commotion and the gun fire coming from the cellar. Not knowing what was happening she grabbed a hot fire poker and moved quietly down the stairs to find her husband standing over the dying, partially clothed house servant and a pistol buried in the forehead of her young charge. She swung the rod, crushing the head of her husband as the pistol fired uselessly into the air.

Titus watched the man crumple to the floor, but his attention was pulled back to his mother who smiled weakly as she slipped away: her son was safe.

The mistress dropped the poker and rushed to Titus' aid. "My boy!" She cried, "my boy," as she cuddled the limp form lost to the world around him. Titus knew the mistress loved him. In truth she was almost like a grandmother to the young boy. The fact that she would kill her own husband to protect him would be a memory he would carry with him for the rest of his life. She may have been white, the wife of the master; but her love for Titus transcended all barriers of race. She saw Titus as a son and as a mother she would have given her life in his behalf.

After tears and comfort were shared on that dirt floor with the lifeless form in the young boy's arms; the realization of the danger Titus was in overcame the mistress. She crawled over her dead husband's body and sifted through pockets pulling out a small wad of cash which she placed in Titus' hand along with the man's revolver.

"Titus you must run," she cried. "Run Titus and never come back." She then embraced him and whispered, "If you don't they will kill you — and — and I could never live with myself knowing my son had died." She took his small head in her hands and kissed his forehead. Tears ran down her cheeks as she looked tenderly in his eyes, "Please — please you must run."

Titus did run. For weeks he ran, following rivers and roads, heading northwest, until the roads disappeared. He had no idea how far he had traveled. All he could remember was running as hard and as long as he could. If it weren't for James finding him he didn't know what he would have done. Well,— more like James catching him. Titus had accidentally walked onto a trap James had set for a wolf. He soon found himself hanging in the air with a rope looped tightly around his ankle. Titus fought and grunted as he scrambled and pulled at the branches trying to free himself; but the rope held and the boy couldn't reach his freedom. Fear that the whites would hang him by the neck kept him struggling as the noise of his confinement, although he remained verbally silent, could be heard for quite a distance. It wasn't long before an old man barked, "Quiet boy. Your going to scare off the wolf that trap was meant fer." The fiery gray eyes of the stranger were piercing as he steadied the snared, swinging by the rope. "He'll pay fer food fer months if I can catch him."

James cut down the runaway and took Titus in. Treated him well, all the while teaching him everything he knew about living in the woods: how to track, hunt, how to avoid being seen. When Titus was 16, the pair heard rumors of war, but the world of the white offered little interest until rebels came knocking finding their hidden camp. At the time Titus was away hunting. The whites had heard in town that a half-breed was hiding a runaway somewhere in the hills and a large party of men went out searching for the duo. When Titus returned to their small trapping cabin, he discovered it burning and James killed: apparently tortured, staked to a post and butchered.

Titus joined the Union as a scout after that. Re-enlisted in 1866 with the formation of the Buffalo Soldiers regiments, but took his leave of the military in 1871 when the wages for a private dropped from $16 to $14 per month. Gold was the cry of the Dakota territories and Titus was ready to turn his endeavors to new pursuits. Now almost ten years after his first enlistment as a soldier he was hunting down gray coats again, but this time it was personal.

The thick matting of fallen timber worked as a detriment to the progress of the thieves as the horses could not travel as swiftly over the maze of dead trunks and jagged stumps, but Titus on foot and unhindered by any four legged animal, gained ground, moving through the jackstraw, jumping logs and running across the artificial bridges the downed trees formed over the haphazard landscape.

Voices ahead brought the scout to a stop. Men were arguing, but the heavy woods muffled the words spoken. Titus ducked behind a large fallen trunk and worked his way along the makeshift wall as he crept nearer the commotion. Sitting in a narrow clearing blanketed by a smattering of downed wood, two old men bickered in a heated discussion; but neither man appeared interested in standing or taking action on the others insults. It was a peculiar sight that almost caused Titus to laugh as he stepped from his hidden perch and approached the duo. Both men paid no heed to the intruder until Titus' sudden appearance startled them as they realized he was in their company.

"Shit,— where the hell did you come from?" Barked one of the two, obviously shaken by the strangers silent approach.

"I heard you talkin', thought you might be able to help me." Titus smiled, trying to pass off as friendly a demeanor as he could muster.

"If yer here to rob us yer too late." Yelled the second man, apparently somewhat deaf by the volume chosen. "Some fellers already relieved us of everything but our clothes."

"How long ago?"

"Just before you got here." The volume didn't diminish.

"Shit, you can't listen to him. Last week was a few minutes ago to him."

"You were robbed last week?" Titus asked, scratching his head.

"Shit no. We were robbed a few minutes ago."

"But you said..." Titus was cut off.

"Son, I don't have time to sit here and shoot the breeze with you. We was just robbed."

Titus shook his head and wiped his hand over his brow in frustration. "I was robbed also, maybe we could help each other?"

The two old gents pulled their pistols with amazing speed and trained them on Titus in one smooth action. "I told you those fools left a trail right back to our camp."

Titus raised his hands slowly in surrender. "I want no trouble from you two. I just want my horse."

"Son, — you should have left well enough alone," came a third raspy voice from behind a stand of trees. Titus noticed three more rifles aimed at him as the parties came forth from their hiding. "Now you dead."

"Drop your weapons," entered a command from the opposite side of the encampment. "Nobody move," as two more rifles poked out from a varied radius, behind the surrounding cover.

"And just who might you be?" The raspy voiced man spoke trying to make out the new opponents.

"Drop da belchers befores we'z plug da lods of ya."

A young wild eyed kid among the bushwhackers turned and fired at the hidden enemies, initiating the fire fight, as Titus pulled his colts shooting and ran for cover. The youngster dropped dead before he could pull his trigger a second time, but the remainder of the men secured concealment afforded by the abundant jackstraw and brush around the clearing. The standoff continued with a volley of useless gunfire, before the gruff voiced man called out to the intruders. "What business you fellers have with the blacky?"

"We're here after a kid named Bill,— a horse thief."

"Well ya done plugged him first thing, but he just joined our camp today. Didn't know about no horse thievin'." A reprieve in the battle opened as weapons could be heard loading. "Take him and go we don't want no trouble with you gents."

"Soldier?" Came the voice that first spoke, delivering Titus from the ambush. It took a second before he realized the call was for him.

"Yeh?"

"What business you have with these men?"

"They took my horse." Titus stayed low as he listened trying to pinpoint the position of the spokesman for the ambushers.

"We don't know nothin' about the blackey's horse." The

raspy voice barked back. "That Billy kid must have takin' it."

"They're lying," Titus yelled back. "I followed the trail of four men to here."

"Billy came with three others, but they rode off shortly." The gruff man's bark changed slightly and Titus knew the man was smiling. "Stoled our provisions they did. Thought that blackey was with um."

"Whad horse dat kid come in on?" Came the stuttered question of the second man that was after Billy.

"A mare down below us. Had a cavalry saddle it did."

"I suggest you leave the horse and get then." The command gave no quarter. It was obvious the negotiations were over.

"How do we know you fellars won't shoot us in the back?" Stalled the gruff voiced leader.

"Don't show us your back if-in yer worried, but git. I got no reservations about shootin' horse thieves."

Titus could hear the ambushers working their way down the ridge, careful to stay hidden. He popped his head up to see the retreat. Two men dressed in buckskins slipped from the opposite side of the clearing and moved to follow the enemy. Titus worked his way along the fallen trunk to give support, flanking the thieves.

One of the men fired his rifle at the ambushers. "We'z said leave da mare."

"Just trying to get around her," responded the spokesman.

Titus made the ridge as the men rode off down a rocky canyon. "Young feller," came the butchered cackle of the older of the two men that had just saved his life. "Dat your girl?"

"Yes sir." Titus answered, his years in the military showing.

"Lucky we happened along when we did," the younger of the two stated as he approached Titus with his hand extended. "Names Zeb,— and this old coots,— Claude."

"Old coo',— I'll skin yer blistered hide fer dat un, youz snapper."

The retired soldier smiled, taking the offer with a brisk shake. "Titus,— glad to meet you gents."

"Pleasures ours." The younger buckskinned man's expression suddenly got serious. "There's a bounty on that kid over yonder. You lookin' fer a three way?"

"How'd you find him? I was trackin' and never spotted you two." Titus scratched his head.

"We was followin' them other fellers."

"So he was travelin' with them?"

"Yeh, but the bounty was only on that feller over yonder. No sense killin' scum until wez can make uz a good markup on their hide."

"Dare's a $500 re—ward on dat kid. Youz deserve a piece."

Titus paused, considering the offer.

"You handled them six guns pretty good. How abouts joinin' us. We could use another man."

Titus wasn't real interested in becoming a bounty hunter. Besides he had just struck a small vein the other day and needed to get the nuggets to town to cash them in. He couldn't take these stranger back to his mine, but when his horse was stolen he had rushed off, forgetting to secure his claim. "I thank you gents, but I have to be getting back to my camp."

"You be headed toward town anytime soon?"

"Maybe tomorrow."

"Tell you what. The sheriff there is a good man. We'll leave your share with him. You can pick it up when you come into town."

"That's mighty fair of you two." Titus said with a renewed smile. "I'm good friends with the deputy there. If you mention my name he'll see to it you have no problems."

After a few parting pleasantries they separated company as Titus, with a renewed respect for his new acquaintances made his way back to camp.

Chapter Four

The Need

Trapper's Correspondence

Dear: Daniel

I'm sorry so much time had passed since my last letter. I hope Martha and the kids are doing well. Last I heard you were a grandfather twice over: congratulations. I know you wanted me to come home, quit my wanderings and find a wife; but I could never be happy in a world away from these mountains.

I wanted you to be the first to know I have found peace at last in the arms of a Sioux princess. Her beauty gives my life meaning and my heart soars every time I look into her deep dark eyes. My only regret is how much time has passed since I last saw you and the family. Maybe next spring if the weathers right I'll swing your way after the buffalo return. Give the family my love and best wishes.

Your Brother

Isaac

*   *   *

Isaac kissed his wife then mounted his large buckskin mare, saddled for the hunt. His young Sioux bride smiled with pride as she walked up beside the Golden haired mountain man. Her piercing black orbs seemed to search right through his soul as she put her hand on his thigh. "Winter will come early this year my husband, but the Great Spirit is smiling down on his children." She looked out over the empty prairie. In past years the bison literally covered the landscape; the rolling plains — black with the coarse haired bulls and cows grazing the green meadows. "The buffalo have left us, but the deer have returned to the land.... The hunt will go well with you today."

Isaac nodded in agreement as he covered her hand and stared at the lovely features that captured his soul the previous spring. Her long silky hair flowed gracefully over her leather dress enhancing the soft curvature of her form as it also framed her dark complexion and strong cheekbones, augmenting her glowing smile. To think, if he would have stayed back east, he wouldn't have met this beautiful creature that was now his wife. Isaac was a mountain man at heart, but after the beaver trade died out he had returned to Independence, Missouri for a time and lived with his brother Daniel. Even then it just never felt like home. Then the border wars erupted and the chaos that followed dividing family and friend; Isaac felt even more distant than ever to what man called civilization. It's true he had his share of run-ins with hostile Indians when he trapped in the North Western Territory, but Isaac saw no hypocrisy in how the Indians dealt with invaders. The white man's world however, was so two-faced that he longed for the simpler ways of the mountains.

When war divided the nation, Isaac was living far from the canon's call. What little he knew of the conflict came in bits and pieces by word of mouth from the occasional traveler he happened on or when trade brought news with his needs. For the most part, though — he had little interest in what was happening back east and even less about a war that both sides clamored to arms centered around a call for freedom.

Isaac's search for his freedom had at last found rest. Life with the Sioux was simple. To hunt, provide for his family and roam this beautiful land brought a sense of peace he couldn't explain even though his world was filled with violence. And now life had even greater meaning, for last night his love had revealed that she was expecting.

The mountain man leaned over and kissed his wife tenderly. "I'll be back in two days."

"We'll be waiting," Sashtee said with a smile as she placed her hand over her stomach.

Isaac smiled as his mount moved off sideways and began to prance, approaching the gathering of braves assembled for the hunt.

"You still act like newly-weds, uncle." Laughed a young warrior that didn't look Sioux. "It's been almost a year."

"How would you know, Reuben?" Isaac looked back at his wife watching dutifully. "Your dad still looks at your mother like a bride."

"I should be so lucky." Reuben replied as his eyes drifted over to a young woman moving their way. Ta-shawn-nay's eyes looked sad as they met the young half-breed's, but Reuben smiled back with confidence. Her father had rejected Reuben's bride price of a week ago. "Two horses are not sufficient to purchase my daughter," he had said. "Five strong horses is the price." Tun-ka-nay-haut-tue never really accepted Reuben as part of the tribe. He wanted Ten-cun to be his son-in-law: the offspring of nobles. He knew it would be difficult for the stranger to come up with so many animals, but by Tun-ka-nay-haut-tue inadvertently upping the price Ten-cun appeared to lose interest in Ta-shawn-nay. Now because of pride his daughter was without a tribal suitor. Reuben's heart, although crushed at her father's rejection, was unchanged. He didn't know how, but he was determined to win her love.

Isaac noticed the glimmer in his partner's stare and joked. "You have expensive taste brother. Didn't her father already turn you down once?"

"He didn't turn me down... Uncle." A big grin doted the younger man's face. "He just upped the ante."

Isaac wasn't really Reuben's uncle, but for a time the blond was Ben and Aiyana's trapping partner. The couple had taken Isaac, as a young fledgling, under their wings, teaching him the ways of the mountains when Isaac first came west during the invasion and defeat of the Sky Hunters: the mystic demons from the heavens that by freak circumstance brought the unusual family together. Reuben was born about five months after Broken-Toe (the perceived teacher and leader of the Shy Hunters) rewarded Ben with a trophy. The prize was given after the mountain man had conquered one of the creatures in hand-to-hand combat.

Reuben grew up with Isaac as family and even returned with his adopted uncle to Missouri in the late 1850's. The two men were almost indivisible and even looked about the same age although twenty years separated their life's experiences: a strange after effect of contact with the Sky Hunters — so named by the Sioux. That connection seemed to keep all of them from aging. Isaac was at a loss to figure how he didn't age. And what added even greater confusion was Reuben's youthful appearance. He was still in Aiyana's womb when the creatures left in the big metal bird. Isaac had thought he had guessed why fate had granted extensions to the men that fought the creatures, but for whatever reason the strange twist to normalcy granted opportunities to Reuben,— confused him. He was grateful for the opportunities: the blessings long life granted and that were only now beginning to be fully appreciated by Isaac, but it didn't fit the pattern of magic he accredited the mystery to. The time he had spent with his younger counterpart created a bond of friendship that was never severed throughout their journeys together. It was only natural for him to think, after so much time, that life would continue as such forever, but the question still nagged him: Why?

Reuben heeled his mount away from his partner and toward the young woman. "Good morning Ta-shawn-nay," he said in the Sioux language.

The young woman's sadness ripped at Reuben as she looked down at her feet, remaining silent.

"I will pay the price my love. We will yet be married."

Ta-shawn-nay lifted her head; tears welled, and ran down her cheeks. "I have faith in you Ree-bin," she said, but her grief revealed her lie. The young half-breed's perception was blinded by his captivated heart, as is the case often with young men; he only heard her words, not feeling their desperation. So with a smile he turned his mount, "When I get back then."

Ta-shawn-nay couldn't help but exhale a small laugh at his confidence: a cheerful glimmer sparking a light in her sorrowful plight. Maybe he would achieve the impossible. She watched with renewed hope as the party of about thirty braves rode out over the meadow amid the brilliant blue hues of the early morning horizon, doted with white billowing clouds, floating lazily above the still distant trees. With the dawn of a bright day perhaps the future wasn't so dismal.

Sashtee approached and wrapped her arm around her younger childhood friend while considering her saddened state. "We will be sisters soon." She smiled. "You will see," as the married bride lovingly shook her companion and then raised her eyes watching their men ride off.

Ta-shawn-nay responded in like, resting her head on her confidant's shoulder. *Everyone else had such conviction, maybe things would work out.* She felt better as they turned back to the village.

Chapter Five

Fort Fever

14 May, 1852

Untitled

The old chief whispered of legends bygone

His death bed mutterings of warnings to come

The ways of the past would fall like the leaves

Of life as it's been, forever to change

The buffalo will vanish, the deer taken flight

The woods will be silenced, when sins come to light

Can it be stopped? Watch for the sign

When death comes calling and the gathering declined

Trapper's Poem

*   *   *

The world had changed for the men of buckskin. The fashion and desire for beaver goods passed with the advent of fad,— the whimsical nature of man with his view on stature. The wilderness over which they traveled was disappearing. Settlers brought west by the lure of a new and better life now populated the vast expanse that Jefferson claimed at purchase would last a thousand years. It saddened Ben as he watched in years past the covered wagons that stretched out for miles on their slow journey to the Oregon territory: the sickness and death that followed as the number of people unaccustomed to the riggers of this difficult and harsh land never experienced their dream that moved them for change.

The gold rush of California had brought its share of travelers set on greed and the call for gold, but now after the war, many were moving north to get their own piece of sod, transforming this territory once dominated by the Indians and vast untamed expanses to that of farms and towns where people flocked as civilization continued its push to dominate like a cancer that grows without mercy. The very thing that moved Ben so many years ago to take up the life of a mountain trapper was forever going to vanish. Like an unwanted stalker bent on destroying everything in its path, man would never be happy until there wasn't a blade of grass that didn't have claim, or an inch of ground that wasn't plowed.

The small caravan traveled light. The man was dressed in buckskins with a new Winchester repeater resting across his saddle. A young Crow woman followed close behind on a beautiful appaloosa with three other horses in tow carrying a small assortment of supplies.

A large mountain lion walked abreast the man surveying the landscape without concern or purpose as its soft padded feet fell lightly on the grassy plain of the green meadow. Experience would dictate that neither case was true, but the cat's non-challenging nature exposed its comfort with its surroundings and its security in choice of company.

The value of skins left little power for trade in this day, but the mountain man had learned to adapt to the changes of his environment. Early on money was the force that moved many a man to chase beaver like the gold of California drove people after that elusive metal for riches and the power they envisioned came with wealth. But in the end the fortunes paid to the trappers for their plews were spent on the inflated goods needed for the following years effort. The only people that made it rich in the years of the beaver were the merchants and businessmen that bilked the mountain men of any hope of profit.

For most of the trappers, the way of life that was adopted by the men in buckskin was imprinted on their souls — like a tattoo that doesn't wash away. To this breed of man: the freedom to go forth without the restraints that civilization carves into the hearts of its sheep, or the chains that bar a man's reach because of law — based on the opinion of some ego — would never set right in the soul of those who refused to bow to the will of another.

For Ben the way of the mountains was ingrained. Taking the trail as a nomad he lived off the land and avoided people, except for the occasional trade for the essentials: coffee, tobacco, sugar or ammo. Life was all about freedom and with each passing year Ben was watching his recede. So it was with mixed emotions Ben spied the fort ahead. He would make camp outside the fort for trade, perhaps spend the night; but by the following morning he planned to distance himself from the double-edged grip of civilization. The provisions were necessary: granted only by the availability of progress that spread its hated encroachment with a continuous growing evolution of change. And Ben despised that change.

Dusk would come quickly so with the carefree ease of one not obligated to any schedule Ben decided to make camp some distance from the fort knowing the cat's discomfort around people. Ben understood the feeling because it was a shared experience with his nomadic denizen companion. Trade could easily be carried out after they settled or early in the morning but either way Ben's plan,— *lone gone before the sun's zenith on the morrow.*

Camp was set up quickly as Ben tended the horses and worked on a small lean-to. Perched on a large rock near her chosen spot for the fire pit, Aiyana started the small flames to cook the evening's meal. As she cut steaks from a large elk roast, Missy came purring and lay next to the woman,— watching with keen interest the skillful work at hand.

Ben paused and smiled at the scene as he reflected fondly on the encounter long ago: Aiyana and Missy's first meeting. He was himself just learning who Aiyana was back then.

Missy's head turned lazily toward Ben then bobbed back to the fire. *It's funny how things come-about*, Ben thought to himself. *How strange the hunters from the heavens, and their murderous ways brought us all together.* He at first believed, *the war gods Long-Claw, Broken-Toe and Three-Spots among others,— devils incarnate...* after witnessing the handy-work of one of the *demon creatures in* action against *the* ill-fated *ambush* by the Blackfoot, that desperate night, *so long ago.* Ben recalled how just a week or so earlier he, *happened on the giant of a man,* Jacob, nicknamed *Grizz, — butchered in the same fashion...* as the creature performed that night on the Blackfoot war party.

The image of Grizz still haunted him as pictures,— imprinted like stills, flashing through his mind. *The huge lifeless mass, void of skin, rocking gently in the icy breeze with long trails of blood, curled and frozen from the mountain winds, extending like claws from each finger.* It was as if a sleeping demon from hell was guarding the trail as an imposing statue of the future. Destiny led Ben in a search of information about the Sky Demon to the cave were Grizz lived. Missy either returned there after Grizz was killed or perhaps had stayed behind when Jacob went out hunting the elusive Sky Hunter. Either way, when Ben and Aiyana arrived at the little valley Grizz called home,— Missy was there to greet them. Ben laughed inwardly as he remembered how, *the cat spooked the horses causing Aiyana to almost shoot the lion.*

It was a rocky relationship in the beginning. Aiyana had no desire to share the cave or the cabin they later built with the large feline, but now the woman and cat were almost inseparable. *Yes, its truly funny how things worked out,* Ben thought as he smiled.

Aiyana completed the cooking and the fresh, fatty elk steaks were washed down with the last of the coffee,— brewed into a strong black bitter potion that Ben loved and savored.

Missy preferred her meal raw and carried her portion off to the relative quiet and solitude of the nearby trees.

Aiyana ate in silence as she scanned the surrounding woods with an eye of suspicion that made Ben uncomfortable.

"What's wrong with you today woman?" A subtle note of concern in his voice, "You haven't said two words all day."

Aiyana's piercing black orbs met her husband's gaze. "We should not be here."

Her reply was firm and level, but her eye's told of her anger at being ignored. She voiced her concerns earlier and Ben had weighed those words carefully, but they were in desperate need of supplies. It was a difficult choice for Ben, for he had learned to trust

Aiyana's intuition. Her uncanny perception, a gift she seemed to inherit from her father, Eyes-of-an-Owl. The old visionary had the habit of knowing events before they happened and apparently passed on his legacy to his daughter after his death about ten years back. He spoke to Aiyana and Ben then, "Of another coming... *The Gatherers*." Even related events that would supersede their arrival. The mountain man could never forget those strange warriors from the heavens. *Hunters with the power to become invisible. To kill without sound. And their stealth...* was almost unmatched when it came to the game,— almost mystical in their prowess. But the ominous tone as the old man spoke of the dark demons left little doubt to Ben, *that this time would be very different. This time the whole world was in danger by some type of infestation.*

Ben had a pretty good understanding of the Crow language, but some of the details were muddled in his interpretation. He knew, *death was stalking* and "Like locusts, the swarm would come... unless it could be stopped." Those words, spoken by the old man, were burned into Ben's mind as a brand would singe the hide permanently. The spirits had revealed the clues and Aiyana was now voicing her revelation. Somehow she knew the time had arrived and this wasn't the place to be. But Ben felt fate could not be tampered with. *If destiny brought...* him, *face-to-face with death...* there was no way he could change that. He *would* meet the confrontation head on and if he was to *die,* he would do it *fighting.*

"I'll get in and out of there now, before the day's completely spent," Ben replied trying to show his wife he put weight to her words. He moved over to Aiyana and sat down wrapping his arms around her and tried to nuzzle her cheek. "Ifin' them critters do show up, I's expects it's up to me to bump blade with them again. After all your father selected me to stop them last time."

Aiyana leaned her head away from her husband's, but didn't pull free from his arms. "One does not charge the buffalo without first preparing for the battle."

Chapter Six

Town

Dear Sir:

The articles submitted for publication recently have met with a general skepticism and warrant further proof before we could consider further negotiations. I appreciated your candor during our last meeting, but Indian myths mean little to my superiors and the public's view of fantasy must at least depict a sense of realism in order to procure a profit. I have arranged for you to meet personally with Mr. Warnock at our next appointment. Please be prepared for hard questions if you wish to sell your tale.

I remain your obt. servant,

Samuel Denten, Editor

Warnock Press, New York

*   *   *

It was a quaint western town. A few weathered residences dotted the single narrow street amid a general store, saloon, bank and stables. The barbershop / dentist office, next to the Land Survey and Registration building seemed to be the center of attraction as the new, painless tooth drill was being demonstrated on a poor soul strapped to a chair — screaming. Among the spectators stood a tall graying sergeant, probably in his fifties. With a broad smile at the comment of a fellow observer the soldier turned laughing only to stop as he made eye contact with one of two strangers ambling by on horseback with three other animals in tow. One of the heavily armed men in buckskin looked familiar, but the soldier couldn't place why. He scanned the large, but younger of the two men trying to place the familiarity. "Bounty hunters?" he mumbled to himself as his attention focused on a bagged body draped over the third horse in tow. *Did I have dealings with them before?*

The younger rider noticed the soldier's stare and tilted his head in a nod of recognition: the unspoken "Hi" as he passed.

The soldier responded in like, but curiosity moved him off the wooden walk and into the street behind the pair. The buckskin dressed mountain men continued on a course straight for the jail house at the end of the narrow dirt lane running through town. The sergeant followed casually, moving to the opposite side of the road in front of the saloon and leaned up against a support post to watch the coming transaction; collecting bounties was a grizzly occupation and these two men didn't fit the usual profile of gun-slingers.

The bounty hunters probably spent fifteen-minutes in the office after a deputy came out and roughly lifted the head of the dead body to get a look at the face. The whole time the soldier watched in earnest for them to again step outside. The heavy wooden door of the Sheriff's Office cracked open amid a conversation as one of the mountain men made a reappearance with his back to the street. That was the observers cue as he made his way over to the jail. The men came out onto the walkway still talking to the marshal as the sergeant stepped onto the raised porch. "Hello," the curious soldier said as he paused.

"What'ch ya need friend?" The older man asked with a note of suspicion in his squinting slits for eyes.

The sergeant faced the younger man ignoring the older and extended his hand, "Name's Lloyd."

The mountain man looked at the offer without response then

back to the soldier.

"You look mighty familiar Sir. Was your father's name Zeb? Zeb Shaffer?"

Zeb thought about that question carefully. Here was someone he had had past dealings with, yet he couldn't place the face. It was curious that the man was asking Zeb about his father? Zeb was near seventy, but looked in his twenties. A strange after-effect of their experience with the magical creatures that came from the heavens in that big metal ship. Superior hunters... actual demons... they came from off world, and had amazing abilities. Zeb had witnessed them transform personally; turning invisible in a blink of an eye. They hunted Indians and trappers alike; killing and butchering the victims in their deadly game. Zeb had killed one in hand-to-hand combat as did his brother Ben. The younger looking mountain man attributed his greatly reduced aging along with the other men that also vanquished one of the super beings to their personal victories. He assumed that by killing a creature — a magical spell was put on the victors extending their life. Claude, Zeb's traveling companion, was the only one who knew the real reason for their longevity. The older man with the speech impediment had discovered the truth when he killed one of the creatures at Yellowstone. Claude never revealed his secret, so his partners continued to guess and wonder without growing old. But the fact that they didn't age made them nervous as to what others might think. How would people respond if they found out? Zeb studied the soldier. "My dad's name was Eber Shaffer...friend. Sorry I can't help you."

"You still must be related." The man was waving his hands excitedly. "The same last name and the family resemblance is remarkable."

"Where'd ya met Zeb?" Claude asked.

The soldier relaxed a bit, "In 26 he brought my half brother's belongings back east. Shawn, my brother, was killed not far from here in the early 20s." The soldier pointed to the northwest as he talked. "Even named the place after him." The soldier then returned his attention to Zeb. "He was a trapper who traveled with Zeb. It's funny you even dress like him." The man smiled, but the confused expression on his face told he was trying to piece together a puzzle. "I was ten when Zeb came east and stayed with my family a while. Became like an older brother."

Zeb stood silent, listening. He had no intention of telling Lloyd that he was the man that ventured east and lived with him and Willie's dad for a time. It did bring back fond memories just the same. He remembered Lloyd as a boy: full of vigor. Even tried coming with Zeb on his return out west. It took some work, but Zeb convinced Lloyd he needed to stay and help the family. But it did make Zeb kind of curious as to what became of Cathryn. Shawn, or Willie as Zeb called him, talked about Cathryn all the time. While Willie was out west she married a store keeper: near broke Willie's heart. Zeb understood why after he met her in '26. She was one beautiful lady. Her husband had died shortly after their marriage and when Cathryn found out Zeb had traveled with Willie she began spending a lot of time with the tall mountain man; at first wanting to know everything about her childhood friend and how he had lived. But the more time they spent with each other the greater the attraction grew. Zeb, for his part was a man whose soul was still captive by his first wife's love. He lost her to smallpox almost ten years prior to meeting Cathryn, but still couldn't let go of the loss. Cathryn was the one woman that might have helped him put the past behind him, but he knew in his heart that she wasn't cut out for a life in the wild. His experiences with city life were pleasant, but the call of the mountains burned strong in his soul — so after a year he again headed west amid the gentle tears of yet another lost love. With the memories came a smile that Lloyd took notice of.

"Was Zeb a cousin or something?"

Claude chimed in, "Dat sounds like dat uncle you's named after, rit Zeb?"

"Your name's Zeb?"

"Zeb Shaffer friend." The young looking mountain man extended his hand and the sergeant took hold briskly. "Any friend of my dad's brother is a friend of mine."

"I'm glad to hear that." The soldier was grinning from ear-to-ear. "Could I buy you two a drink?"

"I'z mighty parched son," Claude said patting their new acquaintance on the back. "Lead da way."

"I didn't catch your name."

"Names Claude... Nows hows bout dat drink?"

The sergeant paused studying the older man.

"Is dare ah prob-slem son?"

"My brother also used to ride with a man named Claude."

"I's sez dat mus be ah good omens. Let'z all have dat drink to Willie."

The sergeant gave a half chuckle and then froze. "How'd you know they called my brother Willie?"

"You called him that," Zeb said as he stepped off the walkway.

"No... I said Shawn."

The two mountain men started off for the saloon laughing. The sergeant followed moments later catching up.

"How'd you know?"

"My uncle used to talk about Willie all the time. Told us a lot of funny stories too."

"Where's your uncle now?"

"Injuns done lifted tis hair ah few back," Claude replied as they walked. He caught a glimpse of Zeb who was frowning at his latest revelation. The older then injected as an after thought, "Made good accounts of tis self dough."

Taker's Saloon was a multi-story inn with a large tavern. Tables filled the large hall and a surprising number of patrons were busy playing cards, drinking or mulling about — considering the time of day, the towns size and its location — being in the middle of nowhere.

Zeb and Claude entered the establishment scanning its interior and absorbing the atmosphere.

The bartender was a plump gentleman with a handle-bar mustache and wavy red locks of coarse hair. The wide part down the middle of his oily scalp caught the light of the overhead lamps, reflecting a glow in his shinny patches of white. His gruff, weathered face belied his current occupation. He placed glasses down on the counter and poured drinks with hands, callused and scarred, more suited to one experienced with rope and sail. He barked a rough, salty greeting that lacked the signature of a friendly business owner.

"Bess yuz kind sir," Claude returned with a smile, then swallowed the shot of amber liquid. Wiping his mouth on his leather sleeve he sighed with pleasure. "We'll be dakin' dat indire boddle off yer hands good Sir."

"That's two dollars," came the harsh reply.

Lloyd slapped two coins down and picked up the bottle, "Lets find us a table."

Working their way to a more secluded corner the men sat

and began to drink their prize.

"So, what brings you to town soldier?" Zeb asked as he pulled a wad of tobacco from a leather pouch.

"We got word of a desertion yesterday from one of our patrols. The man also stole a rifle. The Captain in charge dispatched a letter asking for assistance. My commander sent me to town to find a tracker."

"Any reward?"

"Not as of yet, but I'm sure you'd be paid. You interested?"

"We'd be knowin' hows much?"

The sergeant stood, "Let me find out. I'll be back in a few hours."

"Sounds a plan," Zeb replied.

Lloyd left the two men as they continued to work their bottle. Claude took another swig and slammed his glass briskly to the table. "What youz say we'z mosey down to Momma's Cradle and pick uz some flowers."

Zeb's steely glare never cracked a glimmer. "I'm afraid those ladies are more wiltin' than buddin'."

"Com'on Zeb, we's got's fresh coin burnin' and I got's me ah awe-full tall hankerin'. The older man gave his companion a friendly pat on the back. "Fifty year's much too long fer any man's to be pinin'."

Zeb shook the gesture off abruptly standing and turning angrily on his friend. Claude just looked at him with sad forlorn eyes. The younger checked his burst of hostility, realizing his friend meant no disrespect. He paused for a moment in thought. "I guess I'z could use me a meal. Momma's can burn a good piece of hide as well as another."

"Dat's da spirit," Claude said with renewed zeal as he stood. "I'z race ya."

"Momma's ain't goin' nowhere," Zeb replied, slowly picking up the bottle, already regretting his decision.

Claude was already on the move to the door. "Would's ya gets dat tail burnin', dems flowers ain't gettin' younger."

*   *   *

Five riders in long coats and dirty from the trail rode into town, heading straight to the Sheriff's Office. The apparent leader was a coarse looking gent with hard weathered wrinkles and a rugged knife scar across his left brow that extended down his cheek to the corner of his graying mustache. His right hand was missing two fingers, including their knuckles, and the smaller portion of his palm as he gripped the reins with a relaxed hold of confidence despite the handicap. The four other men were younger, but carried similar healed injuries: the signs of men that had seen their share of violence — more by choice than accident.

At the jail they dismounted and entered the building amid the sound of jingling spurs and the hollow footfalls on wooden planks.

"What can I do for ya?" The marshal asked, looking up from a chess game with his deputy.

"We're lookin' fer a couple bounty hunters. Look like mountain men," replied the leader. His voice was raspy. Damage to the larynx was a possibility, but a scarf tied around his neck concealed the savage scar that would of exposed the truth.

"And you would be?"

"Friends trying to hook up." Came the whispered lie from the icy glared rider.

The marshal studied his visitors with the suspicious eye of a man of law enforcement.
"I believe they headed over to Taker's."

"That would be?"

"The saloon," the deputy chimed in.

The lower fold of the leaders coat parted as the man pulled a pistol. The marshal fumbled for his, but was too slow as the shot caught the officer in the forehead.

The Deputy was quicker, but two of the followers fired throwing him backward off his chair and against the wall. Blood leaked from the deputy's mouth as he coughed, his stomach filling with fluid; his hand trying to cover the dark flow leaking from his abdomen. The mortally wounded man groaned and tried to move as one of the two men that shot him stepped over and kicked the man face-up, pointing his cocked gun at the deputy's head.

"Should I make it quick Cap?" The younger man turned his head to his leader. His sadistic sneer magnifying his steely wild eyes.

"Let the Yank bleed slow Lieutenant." Came the raspy whisper. "Liver and gut shot, he ain't long anyway." The older man turned from the carnage to his men. "Bobby, Johnny, you two find a rear entrance to the saloon. And watch yer back. These aren't green pegs." The raspy man holstered his weapon. "We'll take the front. It's time to show them boys — you don't mess around with one of our own."

50

Chapter Seven

The Awakening

10 Sept. 1871

Before first lite i approached the camp real quiet like to spi me out their number when i hears me a sound in the brush by the crick. I pulled me my blade and crept up to the bank looking over the ridge and heres this youngen. Probable not more than 15 squattin by a big tree naked as the day is long. She never i'd me as i watched and danged if not one sound but her breathin did i heres until that baby pushed its way out and wimpered in the cold air.

Scout's log entry

*   *   *

The eerie glow of the dim chamber light left Jake disorientated when he came to. Turning his head in a weak effort to regain awareness, he saw another quivering gelatinous mass. The recent memory — the dream he thought he was waking up from, flashed its nightmarish imprint as he rolled away and scrambled to his feet in panic. Dizziness wavered his posture, but he balanced his stance with his right hand on a large metal container, looking around the room in fear.

Cass snorted behind him as Jake noticed the horse calmly standing near the entrance of the strange room. Jake stumbled toward his animal kicking another one of the unusual gelatin eggs that had a more leathery feel to the sole of his boot than it appeared. The action brought him to a standstill. He paused, kicking the object again. The lifeless form showed no aggression. Jake picked the thing up and studied the bag vaguely remembering the unusual bird that transformed from the egg just moments ago and the black tar painted on his horse's side. *What was happening?* What had happened to him? He looked at Cass again then the lifeless thing in his hand. Was this some type of strange dream? Scanning the room Jake noticed the dead giant that tried to kill him covered in glowing purple blood. He suddenly didn't feel so good. His bones tingled. His stomach was churning. He felt his neck and forehead with his free hand. He was running a high fever. He vaguely remembering the burning, the tar, was it real? He couldn't put it all together.

Jake dropped the object that bounced rippling and he scrambled for his horse. It was time to go and he wanted to put as much distance between himself and this chamber as he could.

Cass seemed to share the scout's attitude, as the horse needed little encouragement to flee the area as quickly as possible. Horse and rider bolted over the valley floor and up the opposite ridge from their entrance under the light of a full moon. The fires scattered around the area had burned themselves out and Jake noticed little smell of smoke, which had been almost gagging when he first approached the strange cave. The scout's mind was racing as he tried to piece the puzzle of recent events together — things just didn't add up.

At the top of the ridge Jake reined his horse to a halt and scanned the valley below. Cass was unsettled by the pause, stomping and rearing as the horse circled trying to continue its flight.

"Easy..." Jake said to settle his mount. "We'll be out of here soon enough."

The valley below was still — no sound... no fires... nothing. It was then that Jake looked at the moon. The full moon wasn't due until tomorrow. "What the hell is going on!" The scout yelled in frustration, aggravating the pain of his joints and the tingling of his muscles.

Cass, still spooked was fighting Jake to leave as his powerful hooves pounded the earth with each lunge the animal made in its effort to convince his rider to go.

Jake eased off the reins and Cass took flight. With remarkable speed the animal traversed the open ground of the high mountain meadows under the soft light of the harvester's aid. For a good hour the animal kept up the pace with Herculean effort before Jake slowed Cass to a trot; a pace that would eat up the miles they both wanted to distance from the valley of the star. The wee hours of the morning found Cass heavily lathered and exhausted from his escape still trudging forward over a snow covered hillside dotted with trees.

Jake was sore, tired and sick — dropping in and out of a delirium that he didn't understand. He dismounted and walked his horse for a time, but an almost unbearable cramping began to affect each footfall on the ice-encrusted earth. Although the night was brisk the scout had begun to sweat in cold chills. He decided to camp and unsaddled Cass and set about to make a big fire to warm himself.

Shaking and stumbling he managed to get a good blaze going as Cass began to put up a fuss. Knowing the danger of hostiles, Jake guessed intruders were approaching and retrieved his rifle that was by his saddle. The fire cast its flickering beams across the sparse landscape, but showed no sign of an enemy as Jake scanned the surrounding terrain. The scout ducked behind one of the few trees for cover — away from the fire and to the side of his horse. Moments later Cass hit the ground kicking and snorting in some kind of twisted convulsions.

"What the hell?" The man muttered to himself as he moved closer to his animal staying low to the ground to avoid being shot. *Why would someone shoot his horse?* But wait: Jake hadn't heard the report of a rifle.

The horse began coughing and choking as the animal puked up a white foaming substance. Jake backed away as Cass tried to right itself, but the horse's skin began to contort and bulge. Distorted way beyond anything the scout had ever seen before the animal lifted its head and screeched. Jake lifted his rifle to put his companion out of its misery when an earth shifting crack erupted and the horse's ribs exploded through the animals thin hide. Its legs enlarged as skin and muscle tissue fell away from the thickening vertebrate and blood shot across the white snow carpet reaching Jake's boots. The scout backed away even further startled by the appearance of the horse's darkened skeletal mass rising out of the scattered pile of abandoned flesh and organs. Long wiry legs of enlarged bone matter walked out onto the snow giving the appearance of a insect pushed free of its chrysalis.

"What the hell?" Jake barked as he stared at the walking frame; an elongated and living contorted skeleton of his former horse. The eyeless heavily plated face turned to the man as the beast screeched, but Jake's hesitation was only a split second. Aiming his ready weapon he shot the thing. The bullet impacted, hitting the forehead and launched the creature over the top of the horse's remains and spun it onto the snow kicking. Jake cocked his rifle again and fired... again and again as the lead seemed to be absorbed into the hard bony frame doing little damage. But the new life squirmed and protested under each shot until it rose to its hooves again and charged the man. Jake dropped his rifle and dodged rolling across the snow to his saddle and pulled his lariat from its strap as the animal turned and reared, kicking. The scout jumped to his feet slapping the animal across the neck with the rope and avoided a lunge. One of the elongated ribs jabbed at the man, but he sidestepped and lassoed the front legs tripping the beast up. With a thud the monster fell into the fire as sparks lit up the night sky. The animal tried to kick free of the rope, but the flames began to engulf the ready fuel of its flammable structure.

Jake ran to his fallen rifle as the strange beast broke free of the fire trumpeting in anguish. The scout pulled a branch from a nearby pine and charged the creature swinging the heavily laden needles through the raging pit lighting it as a torch. "Burn you devil's spawn," he cried and shoved the pyre into the animals open ribcage. His aim proved true, but the creature kicked striking him in the forehead knocking him back. It was a grazing blow but dazed him. Jake rolled over as the beast tried to trample him pinching his left hand to the earth and snapping off his index finger. Lifting his rifle with his right hand he shot the monster in the eyeless face as a heavy hoof pounded his right leg. Jake yelled out in pain as the bone snapped and blood flowed out through the exit wound of the fracture. Jake dragged himself backwards, crawling with his elbows and shoulders as the flame totally engulfed the demon.

The crack of the repeater echoed twice more in rapid succession as the last shot pushed the charcoal gray colored walking death into the fire pit. With an ear-piercing scream the beast tossed in the coals; its bony casing popped then ruptured as the blue flames appeared to be consuming the thing from within. Jake shot at the creature again as it spun out of the fire and rolled across the snow. The movement now appeared to be death-throes. Flames licked across its body and in-cinerary streaks broke through segments of its joints sending rays of white light from numerous pockets all over the seams of the plate like structure of the creature's outer shell.

The acidic smell of the burning carcass stung Jake's eyes as the man gagged on the putrid odor. Blinking he covered his mouth and nose with his sleeve and crawled forward to poke the lifeless heap with the end of his rifle to make sure it was dead, but then decided against it as a severe cramp brought him wrenching forward. Jake held his upper abdomen and looked over at the piled remains of his dead companion. Cass' putrid mass of flesh and organs laid still on the frozen earth, his skin pulled from the bone like a cleaned carcass. A pool of blood had spewed forth under the mass, already melting the white icy hard pack under the evisceration. The strange skeletal creature that burst from the horse's being and was smoldering and steaming amid the melting snow directly in front of him. The heat of the dying embers were amazingly intense.

Jake staggered to get his good leg supporting his weight with his rifle as a crutch; fear was taking hold: fear of the unknown, fear of the condemned. Jake was panicked. He had faced many life and death situations in his course of living. He had walked through the pounding artillery and wave upon wave of infantry fire in a charge against unbearable odds, but fate had never dealt him a blow like this. Alone, sick... miles from aid — he knew he was going to die. Paranoia grabbed at his soul and sent him wandering. There was no logic, no reasoning, just moving — he had to leave. He needed to hide. To get away... far away — and so he staggered across the moon swept plain. Over the snow covered hills he trudged, limping for hours until he came to an outcropping of rock miles from his previous camp. Under the pain of his played out leg, the agonies of his burning chest and left hand, he finally collapsed. Head buried in the snow; he gasped for air as his chest wrenched — tossing him to his back. His abdomen was burning and contorting as the man choked on a fluid pushing up through his esophagus. Coughing he rolled to his stomach and crawled toward the rocky outcropping which partially hid the mouth of a cave. As he entered the dark opening his ribs pushed through his chest. Sparks shot through his brain as he heaved then burst under the cracking of bone and tearing of flesh.

The grossly contorted eyeless frame emerged screaming. It appeared to be filling its lungs deep within the enlarged exoskeleton with air. Hauntingly the new life then disappeared down the dark cavern and into the security its tunnels would afford.

Chapter Eight

Fall From Heaven

Dear: Mr. Denten

Thank you for your recent correspondence and help in arranging a personal audience with Mr. Warnock about my book. I regret to inform you that I will not be able to make said appointment at this time. My wife has take very ill and would be unable to make the long train ride to New York. To leave her unattended in her current condition would not be possible. I deeply lament not being able to meet with Mr. Warnock personally, but I assure you that the eyewitness accounts about these creatures are reliable and the mystical powers they possess are real. The Indian legends about these living breathing mysteries are based on facts and although bizarre, these stories will play on the imagination of your readers and spark the curiosity of people for generations to come.

Sincerely,

Daniel Gibson

*   *   *

The intense heat of entry cooked the exterior of the small pod. Broken-Toe could not isolate the malfunction in the thermal skin as the missile shaped escape vehicle plummeted through the earth's atmosphere, spiraling out of control. The powerful giant was helpless against the forces pulling and spinning his small craft as he strained to reach the small control panel with his right hand while trying to manipulate the steering with his left. The interior temperature of the compartment would soon reach critical levels shutting down all systems if the giant could not flush the thermal skin barrier quickly. A resounding thud shook the craft causing the creature to lose his grip: his only current control as the pod struck a piece of falling debris — residue of the recent battle in space.

A second impact twisted the vehicle suddenly thrusting Broken-Toe's forehead into an upper console ripping the tough hide across his brow. His right elbow was pushed through a monitor on the lower panel at the same time, short circuiting some of the controls; but inadvertently triggering the thermal flush. The exterior shell began to cool, but the interior levels were burning the giants skin as phosphorous purple fluid covered his face and clouded his vision. Broken-Toe knew he was going to pass out. If that happened his chances of survival were minimal. With the Herculean effort of self-preservation the giant pulled his fractured forearm from the damaged panel and slammed his broken fingers against the mechanism that controlled the wing deployment. Metal groaned under the strain of the engaging function as the parts pushed against the wrecked and twisted superstructure, but the flight directional aids forced through the damaged section and banged into place. Consciousness was fading as the ship began to stabilize; Broken-Toe locked onto the falling pirate ship and tried to calibrate the directional pilot to track the vessel, but passed out before completing the cycle.

The pod's rapid descent plunged it into the upper terraces of the northern woodlands as the breaking thrusters fired, and the wing flaps flared automatically; the craft detecting the lower altitude. Branches ignited as the vehicle busted through the dry fall growth leaving a burning trail in its wake until the craft plowed into the snow covered terrain coming to an abrupt stop in an immense icy drift.

Broken-Toe awoke hours later to the smoke filled tomb — tangled in the wreckage of the crash. Cut, burned and bruised he fought desperately to pull himself free, but with the limited use of his right arm and weakened condition because of loss of blood he resigned himself to doctoring what injuries he could buried and trapped in his metal cage. Opening a compartment at his side he removed a cylindrical tube and cracked it onto a flat surface in front of him. A pasty gel leaked from the container as the giant pulled a second sleeve and sprinkled powder over the goo. It began to smolder. Broken-Toe stabbed a paddle into the mess and stirred it, then smeared the putty on the gash deep in his forehead. An agonizing yell resounded as the creature shook from the pain. The wound smoked, sealing the slash like a chemical bandage.

The giant then lifted his right arm to examine the damage. A splintered bone protruded through the skin in the middle of the meaty muscled tissue of his forearm with a heavy amount of blood congealed around the injury. Pulling an odd metal clamp from his med-kit Broken-Toe strapped the device above the wound and twisted it. The fractured extrusion began to recede under the pressure bringing another earth shattering scream. Running a small box over the break an image of the injury was transposed to a damaged screen in front of him; but enough of the picture was available to determine the necessary adjustment to the clamp, aligning the severed bone. The pain was intensive, yet the creature continued the procedure even after passing out twice during the operation. When the bone was again aligned according to the screen the creature took a straight strap of an unusual metal and pushed it into his skin and beside the break, along side the bone. Passing the box across his arm again to see the repair he pushed a button on the viewing apparatus and watched dazed, as the strip appeared to burn itself into the bone fusing the fracture.

After a forced sleep due to near death Broken-Toe passed the night in delirium. At midday he again awoke. This time he examined his right hand. Fingers were dislocated, but he realigned each joint respectively. Then with renewed vigor he worked himself free of his entrapment. The Pod was a disaster, but the creature salvaged a few choice weapons from the storage compartment and was able to discern the general direction of the pirate ship's descent.

He had a lot of miles to travel in his weakened condition, but his course of action had been predetermined by honor. Cyst eggs were stolen from his ship's cargo hold and were now in that pirate's vessel somewhere on this planet. By now the infestation had probably started. A full-blown nest could grow in a matter of days. To allow a planet to be overrun by the parasites would forever disgrace his name among his clan. He knew in his weakened condition, and alone, his probability of failure was ultimately imminent; but that would never stop him from his duty. The Guardian lived for challenge. The more dangerous the encounter, the greater the prize, but the need to stop the spread of the infestation was even more important than personal pride. Broken-Toe set the self-destruct sequence on the pod and then with the stealth of a trained bounty-hunter, silently melted into the surrounding landscape like a phantom not wishing to be seen.

*   *   *

Darkness had blanketed the land changing the color of the backdrop in which the creature walked. The heat signature of each respective object established the pattern of sight for the being unhindered by a change in light as it walked, determined in its course of action. Ahead the telltale sign of intense heat spoke of the presence of the natural inhabitants of this planet. Fire was a source of heat and light that the Sentients used often in this violent world. He had heard the sound of battle earlier in the evening as he followed the river in the direction of the noise, but now as he neared the site of the conflict the silence was absent and any sign that the Sentients were still present had vanished.

Broken-Toe bent over and studied an empty camp he had come on some distance from the habitats of the Sentients ahead. A fire-pit had been doused hours ago — at a time most from this planet would have been settling in for the night. The tracks were of three. One of the Sentient's tracks were smaller than the other, but what intrigued the Marshal the most was the large animal print of a four legged-hunter that was traveling with the Sentients. He was familiar from past experience with both these types of predators.

Many years ago Broken-Toe was stranded on this planet while hunting escapees from a prisoner transport ship. The criminals he was after were homicidal sadists of his own race that were being moved to a more secure planet away from the growing danger of the revolutionaries. He knew the four footed animal's normal habit was to live and hunt alone, but he had witnessed a Sentient of extraordinary skill that traveled with such a companion during his

60

last visit to this world. It was so long ago, the probability was negligible that it would be the same beings, but Broken-Toe's curiosity was stirred as he learned what he could from the spot.

He then found the tracks and followed the larger of the two legged creature to the buildings where the fires were burning. As he neared he could detect no sign of life. At the entrance were two dead Sentients. Their bodies had been mutilated and their heads removed. Scattered throughout the remainder of the site were bodies: about thirty dead, with the same decapitation and their chests brutality opened up and ripped apart. But what surprised the giant the most as he examined the battle site was the six parasitic infested hosts killed before the transformation could take place. *How did the Sentients know of the infestation? Had they had contact with the parasites before?*

It was obvious — *they killed everyone* — the Sentients couldn't tell who was or wasn't infected. But still Broken-Toe was amazed. He would learn all he could from this site before he moved on, but a sense of awe still captivated him. The abilities of these Sentients should never be underestimated. Although their body structure was relatively fragile, the Sentients were fierce in battle, fearless in the face of death, and had extraordinary skill in hunting and tracking. Truly these were creatures of legend. But today the giant wasn't here fighting Sentients while capturing criminals. Today he was here to recapture his honor stolen by the pirate clan. He would reap vengeance on his enemy and stop the infestation of the parasite. This day Broken-Toe was on a crusade, — a crusade to save this planet.

Chapter Nine

Titus Goes to Town

Sept. 1870

War Department Washington D.C. Stop. To Commander Northern Division. Stop. Supplies en route. Stop. Support troops required. Stop. Protecting shipment the up most priority. Stop. Acknowledge receipt by telegraph immediately. Stop.

*   *   *

After returning to his mine, Titus cached his small treasure of harvested metal in a more secure location and hid the mouth of the main shaft with brush and a few big rocks. The tunnel had been started a few years earlier, but was abandoned. Someone must have killed the original miners: probably after spilling their find to the wrong person, the killer / killers not learning the location of the claim before the untimely deaths, or perhaps the disappearance was related to the Indian hostilities that had increased as of late. Titus knew the men had to be dead, for no one would leave a mine with an active vein still exposed in its walls.

The private had come on the opening, seeking cover from a harsh summer storm while scouting for the military. He knew the cave was man-made after crawling through the small entrance; the tools: pick axes, shovels and oil lanterns were stored neatly in one corner of the main room where the men apparently lived. The scout used one of the lamps and followed the shaft a short way, surprised to find the bright color of gold amid the sparkle of quartz wedged in the rock face of an exposed granite outcropping. Carefully he hid his discovery and returned after his five year reenlistment was up. He had been planning a departure from the Cavalry anyway; the government had lowered the monthly salaries for the enlisted, so he saw no point in signing up for another five years for less money. The mine enlivened his prospects of retirement as he stumbled onto his new future only one month before his discharge.

Titus ended up spending the night in a camp not far from his claim. At first light he started for town. It was late afternoon by the time he reached the small smattering of buildings that marked the settlement, growing due to the clamor of gold. Something was wrong as the street was still and the wood walks along the establishments were vacant. The retired scout made his way straight for the jail, tying off Sam at the trough. The office door creaked as it swayed under a light breeze, unnerving Titus at the haunting abandoned feel the open door generated.

"Blake,— you in there?" Silence didn't seem right as the scout jumped up the steps and entered the office. "Blake!—" Titus first spotted the sheriff sprawled out on the floor, then heard a moan from behind the wall leading to the jail. "Blake!" Titus cried out as he ran to his friend's side and knelt. "What happened?"

"Five men came lookin' fer a couple of bounty hunters. You must know somethin' about um." The man coughed, spitting blood and tried to gasp for air.

"The hunters,— dressed in buckskins?"

Blake nodded his head affirming what Titus already knew. "They left you a cut." The man coughed again as the scout lifted his head on his lap to help him breathe.

"Who shot you?"

"Gruff man. Spoke in almost a whisper.— Had a big scar down his cheek." Blake gagged again, the blood choking his air. After a long pause, "Titus could you find the doc?"

"I'll be right back." The scout whispered as he set the man's head down gently on the wood floor. "You hang in there."

"I'm hurtin' bad Titus."

"Doc." Titus yelled as he ran from the jail towards the dentist office. Not quite the medical practitioner called for in this emergency, but he would have to do. Why no one was around was still a mystery as he pounded on the locked door of the Doc.'s business. "Doc,— I need your help."

A little man peek through a closed window obviously panicked. "What do you want?"

"A man's been shot. I need your help."

"Did those men that were shooting up the town leave?" The little man made no motion for the door.

"Yes, yes,— they're gone,— now hurry!" Titus heard the sound of numerous horses coming into town. Turning he spotted a detachment heading up the only street. The scout ran out waving his arm. "Help, help,— the deputy's been shot."

The Captain held up his arm bringing his men to a stop as the dentist stepped out onto the walk. "Sergeant,— see to the injured."

"Thank you sir." Titus pleaded. "He's at the jail." The scout ran back up the street as the little man, carrying a small bag followed.

Lloyd and the captain's physician followed suit as the commander dispatched his men to scout the town and secure it as safe.

Chapter Ten

Deserter

Rider's Dispatch

Sir:

Upon arrival at The Forks for provisions to continue pursuit of the renegades ~ our Scout has abandoned his post in possession of a military issue Repeater among other pilferage. Please be advised, I have dispatched men in pursuit. I request additional troops and trackers to continue main mission, but also to retrieve deserter and said property.

I remain your obt. servant,

Franklin Oswalt Captain,

16th U.S. Cavalry

*   *   *

"What!" yelled the robust captain as a heavy hand pounded the makeshift desk. "I'll have that Virginian's — desertin' southern ass on the spit by nightfall."

"Sir," replied a young lieutenant in a calm voice as he poked and pushed the contents of the cast iron wood burner in the corner of the cabin. "I don't believe we could make such charges stick."

"Buffalo droppin's," the captain spit as sweat beaded up over his brow although the room was still frosty. Pulling a hanky he wiped away the moisture and then passed the cloth across his bushy white mustache covering his mouth as he cleared his throat. "The man was under the employ of the US Cavalry... and he's stolen a military issue rifle to boo...."

The deep hacking cough that erupted cut the captain off as he leaned forward trying to catch his breath. A high fever had plagued the man for several days, along with dysentery, and a terrible sore throat. Five of the small contingent of 25 men on mission, scouting hostiles for the last ten days, had come down with the same sickness: causing the decision to hold up at the Forks Trading Post and Stockade. One man died of the disease — probably brought on by bad water and Captain Oswalt was feeling the weight of command under the adverse effects of weak joints and a draining high temperature. His aged pale clammy face looked even more puffy under the dim light of one oil lamp hanging from a post in the wall. The gray hues of morning were sifting through the small window marking the beginning of day as the weighty man's attack subsided. He stood, knocking over the chair on the rickety wooden floor. "Send word to the 25th... Tell Captain Blancher we'll need some support and a couple of good trackers."

The young lieutenant let out a sigh as the potbelly stove cracked and popped under the fresh fuel that the young officer placed within its hearth.

"Captain Oswalt,— Sir,— we'll probably need more than a couple of good trackers. That southerner was a cunning scout and knows these parts well."

The lieutenant turned to look at his commander without standing. He wasn't overly fond of the older man. Oswalt had served with volunteers during the Civil War and earned a commission shortly after the surrender when the military, for the most part, was being reduced in size.

The barrel shaped captain with the swollen red nose: an

inflamed, veining attribute — due to his indulgence in whiskey — had worked his way up through the ranks without a formal education. Lieutenant Chapmen was a recent West Point graduate. Oswalt felt the pencil-pushing pup lacked the experience necessary for Indian fighting. Nothing was ever said directly by the captain of his distain for the formal training his younger officer had received, but his gruff treatment was interpreted by the lieutenant as jealousy.

"I believe we'll have trouble no matter who we find to track him," the younger man continued.

"Then we have no time to waste," rasped the still choking walrus. "When did he set out of here?"

"Some time before dusk the men said,— not quite sure."

"He probably set up for the night then. I doubt he's traveled far." The robust captain righted his chair and paced the small office. "Send out a scouting party. That Sergeant Scott has some trackin' experience... send him."

Lt. Chapmen stood shutting the door of the stove. "Yes, Sir."

*   *   *

Six men on fresh mounts let out of the stockade shortly after noon. The trail could have been marked with road signs for all the good it would have done Sergeant Scott, but from the beginning they were at least headed in the right direction from talking with some of the locals who had witnessed the scout's departure. The falling star that grabbed the attention of many at the post the night before aimed the party in the general path Jake had taken, but the pace set by the *"tracker"* and his uncanny abilities left them at nightfall camping way off course. Circling aimlessly miles from the valley where the star hit, they passed up the scene of the previous night's collision. As the group of enlisted men sat around a large campfire, joking and laughing, while eating the sorry excuse for rations, the sound of nearby gunfire disrupted the dinner. Sound carries in the mountains, but to the untrained ear the direction was hard to determine. The sergeant made haste kicking out the fire. The party saddled up under the light of the full moon and headed north, opposite the actual occurrence of the shots — straight toward the site of the fallen ship. By midnight they topped the ridge above the crash site. One of the men spotted the eerie glow of the hidden doorway in the carved canyon of the impact and the entire party made their way to the valley floor to investigate.

Leaving Samuel at the entrance to watch the horses, the remainder of the hunting party moved inside with rifles ready. A white mist lingered at the floor and swirled around the legs of the men as they walked. The dim hue of the interior cast little shadows of the unusual chamber as the men fanned out in the unnaturally humid cavern. Panels with flashing lights appeared to be the source of the illumination, but none of the men had ever seen anything of the kind.

"Sergeant Scott!" cried out a soldier who had worked his way to a far wall.

"What is it Wilkins?"

"You have to see this."

The sergeant made his way around the clutter of haphazard metal containers reaching the private who was holding his rifle aimed at something in a pile of debris.

The sergeant poked his muzzle at what looked to be a burned and contorted leg sticking out of the heap of jumbled boxes and apparatus of some unknown origin. When no movement was detected the man stepped in closer for a look. The grotesque features of the dead creature caused him to step back. "What the hell?"

"What is that thing Sarge?" Came the excited panicked voice of Wilkins as he waved his weapon in fear.

The sergeant regained his composure studying the ghoul and the phosphorous purple fluid smeared and splattered over the wall and corpse. He moved closer again pushing the end of his repeater at the massive wound, opening the creature's chest. "I don't rightly know, but this injury looks brutal."

Kneeling, the sergeant tried to lift one of the creature's arms. The body was stiff. A heavy metal gauntlet covered most of the immense forearm, but the man was unable to pry the appendage free due to rigormortis. The other arm was still buried under the debris. Scott grabbed at a horn protruding by the oversized eyes and tried to pull the creature free as two more of his men approached. The body was just too heavy to move.

"What do you think it is?" asked one of the two.

"I think it came up from hell," laughed the other in a shaky reach for humor.

"You think this is the doorway to hell itself?" asked another in a tone much too serious for a joke.

"What,— you think hell is purging itself of undesirables?" the jokester sneered back.

"Quiet,— all of you and help me." The sergeant ordered looking at the debaters.

All three set down their rifles and started working to free the body from its trappings. The giant wasn't burned after all. The light and its unfamiliar skin tones gave the appearance of scorching. As they strained, dragging the corpse into the open they all stared in amazement. Large reflective eyes, glazed over with a white film, still cast a menacing stare from their round sockets. Scales covered the body and the horns on either side of the bulging eyes looked like a bulls', jetting forward. Thick knotted hair, jointed as the legs of an arachnid, laced the round head and appeared as knobby appendages with thick joints except for the multiple branches that webbed off each main protrusion.

Wilkins pushed at the hair with the butt of his rifle. "Looks like a twisted mass of spider legs."

The tentacles resisted the pressure of the wood stock. "What you make of this insect, Sarge? It has human form."

"It's a locust of the abyss," barked one of the men as recognition caused his face to go pale.

"What are you talking about?" coughed another.

"The locust of the bible book of Revelation. This is one of the locust that comes forth from the abyss to plague mankind."

"Go to hell," Wilkins said kicking the dead beast.

"I'm telling ya... we're at the mouth of the abyss."

The rest of the men in the chamber circled the corpse in silence.

"We're all as good as dead," continued the Bible thumper.

"Shut-up Blake," spat the Sarge.

"I'm tellin'..."

"I said shut-up."

The somber mood of the men was obvious. Most were at least superstitious. The demon lying on the ground before them was unfathomable. Blake's explanation was taking hold as most had read the Bible or at least heard sermons and looked at Blake as knowledgeable on the subject on account of his reading the book all the time. After all he was raised the son of a minister.

"Let's get out of here Sarge!"

The Sergeant looked up then shook his head. "This critter's dead... Ain't goin' to hurt no one." Then pointed at a wounds almost opening the creature's chest. "Those cuts were made by a knife blade. Whatever this critter is, it was carved on, and kilt by a man." He scanned his men trying to regain control. "We're U.S. Cavalry damn you. And we'll act like soldiers in the face of whatever enemy we're called upon to fight."

A few of the men dropped their heads in shame and all began regaining their nerve.

"What should we do with Lucifer there?" asked Wilkins snickering.

"That's not funny," Blake barked.

"Let's take him with us. I think it's time to report back to the Captain. John,— Frank," barked the Sarge, "grab his legs. Jim, Bob you two help me." He continued, standing and taking hold of the creature's shoulder.

They all set to work finding places to set down their rifles to help when Jim paused, "What's that?"

A large gelatinous mass quivered near where one of the men had placed his weapon. Jim grabbed his rifle back as the glob transformed and spanned out its wings and took to flight aimed to hit Jim. The soldier instinctively blocked the attack with his repeater batting the creature to the ground, but it immediately rolled and jumped back at the Bible thumper who again moved his rifle to impede the eyeless bug. Blake tripped in his panic, simultaneously knocking the winged thing away as he fell next to another quivering egg sack.

Frank was the quickest to respond to the sudden events, retrieving his repeater and cocking the rifle in one smooth motion he shot the beast in midair. A ghastly shriek issued forth as fluid splattered from the wound and spilled on Jim, burning his arm and causing him to drop his weapon with an agonizing scream. The black ooze painted his face and drenched his clothing.

John was working his way through the obstacle course of the chamber trying to get a shot at a new thing when another egg sprang to life and powerful wings launched it into the man.

Bob, the closest to John, dropped his rifle and pulled his long knife and ran to his friend who had fallen over a metal container.

"It burns, it burns," John cried.

Grabbing John's shirt Bob tried to cut the sizzling fabric from the man's back, but the tar cooked into his own hands. The dark ooze stained his blade and almost seemed to melt over his sweat laden skin seeping into his pores. Bob ripped John's shirt free and threw it aside as both men were screaming in pain. Bob dropped his weapon shaking as a partially hidden blob next to the men shimmied and sprouted wings launching yet another tar bag onto the now defenseless John.

Jim sat up to scramble out of his predicament when the feud-d-d-d-d of fast beating wings buzzed by his head. He tried to bat the nuisance away but the fluttering sound flew closer undeterred. Lifting the butt of his rifle he tried to block the winged menace, but it slammed into his face and pushed through his gaping mouth and down his throat choking him.

Sarge, aware several of his men were already down, yelled orders to his troops, but continued to try and fend off the attack. Taking two shots at a flying creature, hitting it once, and it came to a rest along the nearby wall leaking its black bodily fluid. His immediate attention was focused on the strange eyeless bird as it screeched at him. With a shrill cry the thing darted under a pile of debris. The Sergeant ran forward, kicking and pushing items out of the way in his endeavor to finish it off.

Frank was coming up beside his leader when he spotted one of the eggs spilled out on the floor of the chamber nearby. Without thinking he started shooting the object. Acidic liquid splattered from direct hits and landed onto the lit panels causing sparks and flashes as the whole room blinked from the dim light to complete blackness repeatedly.

Samuel, standing outside with the horses, tied off the animals and was standing guard when he heard the commotion and ran inside to help. What he took for a large black rat darted behind an obstruction as he entered the door momentarily distracting him, but another gun shot quickly directing his attention to the sergeant and Frank chasing something along the far wall. He again noticed motion to his right when the lights went out. In seconds what felt like a huge impact struck his face and forced him back out the doorway, knocking the wind out of him as he hit the ground. He pulled at the strange tar, gasping for breath as another bird slammed into his mouth and down his throat — everything went black.

"Sarge — to your left!" Shouted Frank as darkness

enveloped the two.

"Shoot the damn thing!"

"I can't see it."

The Sergeant backed up and yelled, "Sh..." as the lights came back on.

Like the huge talons of a bird of prey the splat wrapped like tentacles around the head of the leader causing him to fall backward. Frank watched in horror as the man kicked and struggled trying to wipe the burning menace off. Frozen in fear he looked on, then around the dimly lit room. All off his companions were now lying quivering and comatose, scattered throughout the interior. The creatures had won and now Frank stood alone, lost in the devastation.

The lights went out again. Darkness shrouded the room. Frank tried to feel his way out. The obstacle course made it hard to keep his footing as he stumbled around the chamber. At one point he kicked the body of one of downed soldiers then tripped over something and landed on the man's chest. The man was still breathing and shaking. "What's happening?" he cried. Climbing to a sitting position on his comrade's stomach he became determined to remove the strange tar suffocating his companion. The translucent glow of the room flicked momentarily then stayed on as Frank went to work pulling his knife and scraping the mass from the man's face.

"Skee..." Began an ear piercing scream.

Frank turned to face the blob, perched next to him as its wings sprung outward and without warning jumped at his chest. The burning ooze painted his skin and burned his flesh as it seeped into his pores. He could feel the etching of thousands of needles piercing his tissue as the intensity grew bringing on the delirium. Then the trembling coma gripped his soul as he slipped into darkness.

Chapter Eleven

Return

WAR DEPARTMENT WASHINGTON D.C. STOP. TO THE COMMANDER OF THE NORTHERN DIVISIONS. STOP. INDIANS TO PROCEED TO THE DESIGNATED RESERVATIONS. STOP. PRESIDENT ISSUED NO TOLERATION POLICY. STOP. ACKNOWLEDGE BY TELEGRAPH IMMEDIATELY. STOP.

*   *   *

Sergeant Scott came to, dizzy and sore, draped over a metal crate. His throat hurt something terrible, as he climbed off his precarious perch and stood on shaky legs. Every joint in his body ached and he felt a dreadful fever to his very bones. His men were lying about the chamber: that looked the remnants of a bar fight. The smashed and broken interior of the cavern took on new dimensions as the light of day filtered in the doorway and the mist that had lingered around the floor the evening before had diminished substantially. The room had dropped in temperature drastically and the musty smell had dissipated, but the sergeant was in his own personal fog as to what had happened the previous night or even the passage of time. As he looked around trying to get his bearings his men began to awaken.

Frank was the nearest so the sergeant started to work his way over to his corporal kicking what looked to be a huge dried up black leather bag. He picked up the gelatinous object mystified. The strange bag quivered. He swung it down on the edge of a broken metal crate smashing it between palm and steel. The object popped spreading black inky tar across the hard surface. Then the goo slowly began to congeal back to its original form as he studied the phenomenon momentarily. "What the hell?" Something was familiar about the unusual substance, but he couldn't place it. Looking at his hand none of the contents of the residue was present. Scott shook his head and cast the search for recognition aside and continued toward Frank who was now sitting up supporting his head. Scattered about the room by his other men he noticed more of the strange gelatinous goo.

"I'm hurt Sarge," Jim said as he stood holding his right forearm that was missing a good chunk of skin and muscle tissue.

"Where are we?" Responded John looking around the room as he slid off a pile of metal crates.

Frank picked up his rifle as he stood up when Bob let out a scream.

All eyes turned to the man who was still sitting, but holding his right arm at the elbow — minus the hand. The appendage laid under a corner of a metal box that must of fallen and severed it.

"What in hell happened here? Does anyone remember?" The sergeant barked turning to move toward his injured men.

"Some kind of battle." Replied Frank as he cocked his rifle studying his weapon. "I've fired this recently and repeatedly." He then looked at the others. "I vaguely remember shooting at something in this room."

"I think it was this thing," Jim said picking up a gelatin like bag lying next to him with his good hand while holding his forearm against his abdomen.

The sergeant knelt down next to Bob who was sobbing franticly staring at his stump. It looked as though it had been snapped clean off hardly crushing any of the bone. The man's arm was quivering in spasmodic movements of uncontrollable tremors as Bob supported the appendage with his left hand.

All worked their way to the crying man. John Wilkins helped Jim up and was supporting him. Samuel came in through the doorway where he had been lying.

Frank, who was the farthest away paused, "I remember this guy," the corporal said in a raspy voice pushing the corpse at his feet with the end of his rifle. He then knelt down by the giant sprawled out on the floor blocking his path. "We were going to take this guy back to the post with us."

John looked over his shoulder at Frank and then the giant. "Yeh... that was one of them locust," without any of his sarcasm from the previous night as he looked back at Jim who he was helping.

"We have more important concerns." The sergeant stood. "You two help Bob out to his horse. Frank; gather up their rifles. Does anyone else feel feverish?"

All his men shook their head in affirmation.

"Let's move before we die here of this fever." He then turned to Samuel. "Why aren't you with the horses?" Perturbed his order hadn't been followed.

"I...I don't know?" The man stammered back. "I guess I thought I could help."

"Well then help,— Bob," the sergeant snapped trying to regain control of the situation.

"Sarge, I don't feel so good. I'm not sure I can travel." John whined as the two men reached the side of their leader.

"I don't believe any of us are feelin' cockerel private." The Sergeant looked over his hurting men as he felt the burning pain in his own joints and body. "I'm feeling weaker by the minute. Let's get our asses back to the post while we still can."

The horses were pointed in the general direction of the post as the men mounted up and within a few hours the animals — left to their own sense of direction — brought their sick charges back to the Forks Trading Post.

*   *   *

The late afternoon sun was nearing the purple crests of the western ridges as the search party, headed by Scott, somberly entered the stockade and dismounted at the command cabin to report in. Ben looked on — taking note of the two injured men and the sickly condition that the entire party of returnees cast: with an appearance of scarecrows, in a haunting imitation of near death. The captain that came out to meet them appeared no better as he hacked and coughed up phlegm while struggling to regain his composure.

Ben tethered his animal to the hitching rail in front of the general store and untied his trade goods. His wife's words were vivid as he considered forgetting the supplies he had come for and leaving the fort that moment, but better judgment was pushed aside as the mountain man assured himself that the swap would only take a few minutes. White man's sicknesses in the past had devastated Aiyana's people. But his wife's current apprehension was dreading something much greater than smallpox. Ben studied the soldiers as his own fears were taking hold. With renewed speed the trapper stepped through the door of the civilian-trading store.

The Forks Trading Post Stockade wasn't an official US fort. The military presence at the establishment was a convenience due to its location because of recent Indian aggression. The military built additional barracks, stables, and residences for officers amid the private business enterprise after the war without objection from the owner. The increased protection the symbiotic relationship entertained benefited both parties although no official posting was assigned to the civilian fort. But the military often used the small convenience as a resting place during scouting missions and today was no different.

Ben walked up to the clerk, setting his furs on the counter.

"What we in need of today sir?"

"I be needed some coffee, ta-back-ee and some rounds for my rifle here," hefting the weapon up with his left hand.

The clerk eyed the military issue repeater with suspicion; few men not under the employ of the service had the ability to afford or the resources to acquire such a relatively new, lever action piece. Most of the enlisted soldiers were still carrying carbines. "Where abouts you headed?"

"Didn't come fer small talk sonny: just trade."

"Just tryin' to be pleasant," the man commented in a friendly tone regardless of Ben's short return as he examined the high quality furs. Raising a questioning eye from his work he noticed the mountain man's apparent interest in the returning scouting party across the way. The trapper was watching the soldiers through the large window that faced the command cabin across the street. Normally a trader would be more interested in the evaluation of his goods, watching a clerk with an eye of distrust, but this man seemed overly concerned about the meeting taking place outside. "They're returning from a search for a deserter."

"Looks, they weren't successful," Ben sneered back without turning.

The clerk looked again at Ben's rifle without moving his head, then raised up to deal with his client direct. "Man let out of here two days ago. Captain Oswalt might be in need of a good tracker."

"Oswalt?" Ben repeated with a note of sarcasm in his voice.

"You knows him?"

"I've had dealin's. Nothin' directly."

"He's determined to get that southerner," the clerk continued.

"I'll bet," Ben mumbled under his breath.

"The scout's name was Jake. Maybe you know him. The captain would probably pay you well."

"Ain't interested in no military career," Ben's icy glare met the clerk's with a stressed note of finality. "I've had my full share, — no more."

The owner looked away, but his eyes fell on the mountain man's rifle again.

Ben noticed the attention.

"I'll pass your message onto the captain."

Ben didn't like the sound of that. Who did this clerk think he was anyway? "If yer so interested in catching this deserter why don't you join up with Oswalt and go after him yerself?"

"Oh no, no, no... I'm just a store operator not a soldier," a half crooked smile broke the shyster's demeanor as he backed up shaking his hands and head. "No experience with that."

Ben put both hands on his rifle and slammed it down on the counter in front of him and leaned in menacingly. "Well then let's get busy with what yer good fer."

Ben left the store and promptly began to tie his acquired supplies to his second animal. The store clerk came out shortly behind him and crossed the street to the officer's cabin. The meeting there had adjourned, but the captain was still standing on the porch with what looked like a lieutenant. The clerk was swift in striking up a conversation with the two officers.

Ben saddled up with rifle in hand and headed for the gate. He was moving in a leisurely pace to avoid attention, but deep down he felt like spurring his animal into a run.

"Sir,— Sir," came a voice behind him. Ben ignored the call and moved through the gate.

"Just one moment Sir," offered the command of one of the two privates at the exit, stepping into Ben's path. The one speaking pointed behind the mountain man, "Looks like you're wanted."

Ben glanced back and saw the lieutenant coming his way.

The trapper turned back to the young guard and spit a wad of tobacco almost on the man's boot. "Son, my business is done here. Get out of my way."

"I can't do that sir. The lieutenant wants you."

Ben ignored the man and with a slight twist of the reins and a nudge of his mount started again moving between the sentries.

The man who had done the speaking reached up grabbing the horse by the bit and pulled, but with lightning speed Ben's right foot slipped the stirrup and caught the soldier full in the face knocking the guard backward. With the butt of his rifle he caught the other man across the bridge of his nose breaking the already crooked masterpiece.

"I'm kind a in a hurry," Ben barked as a dark wad of chew splattered on the first man's leg, but before he could heel his animal into a run two cavalry riders came up beside him with rifles aimed. The lieutenant ran up pistol drawn. "What the hell did you do that for?" He yelled, frustrated. "We just wanted to ask you a few questions."

"My business done here Yank. He gots in my way."

"Well now you're under arrest."

Ben leaned over and spat, the brown saliva puddling in the

soft loom at the officer's feet. His unwavering icy stare locked on the lieutenant's, ignoring the man's weapon as he leaned over in the man's face, "Son,— I said my business was done here."

*   *   *

Ben stood silent looking at what he was sure was a walking dead man. The pale complexion of his features magnified the red hue of the veined protrusion that was the focus of attention you couldn't help but stare at. Years of heavy drinking burst the blood vessels and engorged the man's nose into a masterpiece of over indulgence. The color was such a contrast with his white cheeks that it jumped out like a target from the round jowls and balding forehead of the plump face that circled it.

The captain wheezed into a hanky, "I need your name sir."

Ben ignored the officer.

"I could have you shot tomorrow and no one would know the better," the man continued as he stood.

"The butcher."

"Say what?" The captain sneered with notable anger.

"Isn't that what they called your grandfather?"

"Just what do you think you know about that?" The captain snapped as his eyes narrowed on the man now on trial.

"A ruthless butcherer, your grandfather."

"Mind your tongue sonny or I'll cut it off."

"It wasn't enough to just kill those Injuns... was it?" Ben's icy glare — stared down the captain's. "I met the dog."

The officer burst out in laughter, then coughed, hacking. It took quit some time to regain his composure. "Sonny,— I don't know where you got your info, but my granddaddy probably died before you were born."

Ben went silent as he pondered that. Since his contact with what he took as the Gatherers (the mystical Sky Demons from the heavens that hunted men) he didn't seem to age. Nor had any of those in his party that had killed one of the mysterious creatures gotten older. As he thought about it he wondered what people would do if they knew the truth about his age or his friends for that matter. The captain looked and probably was all of fifty. Ben was over eighty, but looked thirty. At the notion Ben smiled. *Life can be so cruel*, he laughed as he focused on the man's nose.

"Besides his family was killed by those thievin' reds."

"Mine were killed in the same massacre."

"So that explains it," the captain said with a smile. "We've got somethin' in common in our ancestry,— you and me. Now what you say — you help me out and tell me what you know about Jake Clintlock."

Ben's glare was uncompromising, "Say what,— Butcher."

"You stubborn fool, I ain't my grandfather."

"The acorn don't fall far."

"Lieutenant!" The captain called out.

The young officer entered briskly.

"Our guest here will be spending the night. Show him to his quarters."

"Sir."

*   *   *

Aiyana, uncomfortable with her husband's departure, waited nervously for his return. When darkness covered his delay, she broke camp and packed up the animals. Something was wrong and she was determined to find out what had happened. With uncanny stealth Missy and Aiyana moved nearer the fort. She tied the horses, concealed in the trees, hidden from view of the stockade. Moving along the tall wooden wall of the outer barrier she found a tree with branches, although small, draped over one edge of the picket. Climbing the tall cottonwood she found a comfortable crotch and perched herself in the fork as Missy climbed up beside her. Spying out the grounds lit by lamps at various strategic positions about the long yard, she carefully examined the layout-taking note of guards at a few points; but was amazed to see a few people walking the streets that didn't appear to be military. She noticed two men by the stables and could hear laughing burst forth occasionally from a large room with many lights. As she looked on, her husband was led out of a small cabin by two men with rifles.

Missy perked up with a muffled growl as Aiyana patted the feline. "Shu…, we'll get him out," she whispered. Both watched intently as Ben was pushed into a tiny wooden building and a thick plank was placed, barricading the door. Aiyana had seen enough. Her husband was in trouble and she needed to help.

"Keep an eye on the horses. I'll be back shortly."

Missy stood up on the branch an shook her head like she was

80

shaking a mane.

"Stay here, everythings fine."

Missy sat back on her haunches and yawned. Aiyana smiled then worked her way out on the small limbs and made a jump for the tall fence landing lightly on its top and swung down to the ground below with a soft thud. Squatting silently for a moment she listened then made her move toward the stables through the dark corridors between the many scattered buildings. Missy watched with keen interest as her mistress moved into the shadows. Aiyana stopped beside the stables and looked around the corner at the door to the large barn.

Two men who had apparently finished their conversation were at the entrance. One saluted as the other turned and started back to the building down the center of the street with all the lights and noise. Aiyana leaned back against the stable wall and pulled her heavier coat off and laid it over a nearby barrel. Loosening the lacing joining the front of her garment down to her navel, she straightened her hair. She then looked around the corner at the man still standing in the light of two lamps beside each of the big doors of the barn. He was smoking a pipe and seemed fairly relaxed. Aiyana stepped out casually into the light and approached the man with a smile. At first the soldier brought up his rifle.

His assessment of the interruption quickly changed as the woman spoke.

"Whisky?" The half-giggling enticement whispered.

"Say what?" The private asked with a partial smile through his two black eyes and swollen cheeks.

"Trade for whisky?" The shapely young beauty continued as she pulled lightly on the rawhide cord loosening her garment a little more.

The man's hand rubbed across his mouth as he contemplated the weight of her suggestion with a smile.

"So you'd like some whisky?" He said with a big grin.

The young woman beamed as she nodded her head.

"Come with me darlin' and we'll see about gettin' you what you want." The man extended his hand and Aiyana took it as the soldier pulled her without resistance into the barn. The interior was well lit as the soldier led his tall shapely prize to the back of the building over the hard dirt floor.

Aiyana spotted Ben's horse unsaddled and stabled in a

corner stall. The packhorse was on the opposite side busy eating from a pile of hay and his saddle was over a rail nearby.

The guard noticed her interest in her surroundings as he led her along. "You wouldn't be lookin' to steal from old Carter... would ya?"

Aiyana turned back to her companion with a blank grin. "Whiskey?" Came out the mindless response.

The man chuckled, "Right back here," pulling Aiyana gently into a darkened stall; he let go of her hand and leaned his rifle against the gate. "Now let's see what you got to trade," he said reaching out and taking hold of her garment by each shoulder and began to slip the leatherwear down her arms.

Aiyana playfully pulled away giggling and backed along the wall. "Whiskey."

"We'll get to that. I promise," the man said with a mimicked frown.

Aiyana laughed and sauntered close holding her wrap up with her left hand and rubbed the man's cheek with her right.

"You're a playful one," he joked.

Aiyana shifted suddenly driving the palm of her hand into the man's swollen nose. The loud crack signaled a significant blow as the soldier fell backward blinded by the smashed cartilage of his already damaged bridge.

"Damn-it!" he screamed out through tearing eyes. "I said I'd get you the whiskey." The wounded sentry rolled over and tried to get up. Aiyana picked up his rifle and struck the man across the jaw with the butt and the soldier dropped back unconscious.

Quickly straightening her garment some, she covered her victim with hay and then ran with the newly acquired rifle to her husband's horse. A heavy hickory ax handle hung on the wall and Aiyana grabbed the item and slipped it into her belt like a scabbard sword at her side. Saddling Ben's animal and gathering the packhorse she led them to the door and cautiously looked out. The street was empty. With a push she brought the animals out and to the side of the stable, retrieving her coat and tying it to the pack animal. She then slipped the rifle into the boot on Ben's saddle and noticed several horses were tethered to a rail at the building across the street. Aiyana added hers to the assortment of saddled animals and then moved off into the shadows toward the jail.

The light was less pronounced in front of the four by eight-foot confinement with one guard watching the door. Aiyana's earlier rehearsal worked well so, with a tug on her leathers she parted her wrap and pulled the hickory makeshift club from her belt. Moving carefully along the wall she paused, leaning her wooden weapon out of sight against the building near the front corner.

The alert guard heard the noise and snapped to the ready. "Who goes there?"

Aiyana stepped from the shadows with a smile, tugging lightly at her dress. "Whiskey?" She giggled as she thought how gullible men were.

The guard thought the laugh was for an entirely different reason.

"I don't have no whiskey," the man laughed.

"Trade... Whiskey," Aiyana insisted pulling at her buckskins and motioning the man to come.

The soldier looked around nervously. Good judgment is a virtue with its own rewards, but to this man the promise before him outweighed responsibility. He moved toward the young sun bronzed beauty — forgetting all about duty.

Aiyana backed around the building smiling as the man followed. She stopped when they were out of sight of the street.

"We'll have to make this fast darlin'."

Aiyana could tell the man was grinning by his words and giggled.

"My name's Steve," he said as he turned and bent down placing his rifle against the wall.

A loud thud resounded as the heavy hickory handle struck the man on the back of his head. He fell to his knees groaning. "Shi..."

Aiyana swung her makeshift bat with a powerful upward swing, catching the man across the cheek with a loud crack. The man flipped, landing on to his back as he expelled his lungs with a thud.

"Nice meeting you Steve," Aiyana replied in clear English as she dropped the broken handle next to the prone man. She squatted looking to see if anyone heard the commotion then worked her way around the building. The street was still empty. Slipping over to the door Aiyana tried to lift the heavy rail. "My love... are you in there?" She whispered,— half groaning under the load of the barricade. The large bar fell out of place and the door slid open.

"I thought I heard your voice," Ben said stepping through

the partially offset entrance and looking at his wife. "What took you so long?"

"Next time you don't listen to me you can rot in that little room."

"I'm sorry," the man replied sheepishly.

"You wouldn't believe what a girl has to do to free her man."

Ben studied the angry expression of his wife in the pale light. Her hair was tussled and the front of her garb was half open. A wave of jealousy flashed over the man, but Aiyana spun and moved off around the building. The three-quarter moon popped out from behind a cloud and bathed the shadowed alley as Ben almost tripped over the still body. He paused staring at the broken ax handle lying in a pool of blood. The mountain man knelt down and found the prone man was still breathing.

Aiyana, a short distance ahead turned back and came up crouching by her husband. "He tried to take advantage of me."

"Remind me never to make you angry."

"Too late," the woman spat with a smirk and continued to sneak along the wall. Ben followed.

Aiyana paused as she reached the stables and spied out the street. Everyone was apparently settling in for the night.

'I'll get the horses," Ben whispered.

"They're tied over there," Aiyana pointed.

"Anybody at the front gate?"

"Two men."

"How did you get in?"

Aiyana directed Ben's attention across the opening to a large cabin. "Over the wall behind that building."

"Let's get to the horses."

Both stood and slipped across the dirt road and pushed their way in with the animals. Untying their mounts they worked their way back into the alleyway where Aiyana had entered.

"You work your way near the gate. I'll get them to open it."

"Be careful my love."

Ben took his wife's head in his hand and tenderly kissed her. "I will this time." With that he pulled his rifle and climbed to the back of his horse. Standing he reached for the top of the stockade and pulled himself over.

Aiyana took the animals and started toward the gate.

"Let me in!" Called out the voice beyond the gate. Pounding shook the heavy door.

"Who goes there?"

"Jake Clintlock... Now open the gate fool — and let me in. I have news for Captain Oswalt."

"It's the deserter," the second guard said moving to lift the locking brace.

"I ain't no deserter. Now open the gate. I've been scouting. Found that renegade."

"Hurry... help me." The guard continued, trying to open the door. With both men pushing at the door it swung out easily and the scout walked in aiming his rifle at the two shocked men.

"Sorry boys, came back for my wife. Now I'd be obliged ifin's you'd drop them belchers."

A young scantily dressed Indian woman leading two horses walked by as the two men set down their weapons.

"Kick um over here."

The men complied. Then the scout and woman mounted the saddled mare. "Tell Captain Oswalt I'll remember his hospitality." And with a wave of the repeater the two fugitives made a break for the trees. Both men ran for their weapons, but froze in their tracks as a large mountain lion appeared from the shadows with a roar. When the two escapees disappeared in the folds of the woods the cat also turned and melted into the darkness of the night leaving the guards scratching their heads in amazement at the strange occurrence — having no idea how they were going to explain this to their commander.

Chapter Twelve

Renegade

Sir:

I feel it is my duty to report with misgivings my failure to round up the few rogue bands still roaming the plains. I fear more men will be needed to accomplish this task. We tracked a small party for three days, but lost their sign while running out of water and provisions. We know not the land nor can we match the speed of the enemies mounts for their ponies are fleet. Lost two men on account of bad water and as many animals. Returning to the post for supplies and will await your orders.

Your obt. servant

Jeffery Kain

1st Lieutenant

*   *   *

As the sun dropped over the crest of Stone Face Peak extending the shadows of dusk under its lofty summit, thirty braves waded silently through the icy water upriver of the Forks Trading Post and Stockade under the direction of Chulk-na-tu-ka, the infamous Cheyenne War Chief. The U.S. Cavalry had been searching diligently without success for the renegade guerilla leader who's self proclaimed war against the western expansion was gradually gaining a voice with the rest of his nation.

Raised the only son of the medicine man, Tal-kee-da-toe, Chulk-na-tu-ka at a mere fifteen successfully killed six Blackfoot Indians raiding their small village when most of the tribe's young men were off hunting. The prestige won by this act of valor positioned the small boy among the warriors of his tribe at an early age and gained him the respect of his nation. Inheriting the abilities of his father, Chulk-na-tu-ka was gifted with vision and leadership qualities necessary to inspire men who shared similar views. But he began preaching war after the death of his father. Tal-kee-da-toe's foresight recognized that the white man would keep coming until the land was overrun, but felt peace was necessary because regardless of action the outcome would be the same. His views spoken often as a man of peace whispered to the call of the inevitable, proclaiming: "Better to live."

But his son took a different path. Declaring war on the white man, Chulk-na-tu-ka with fifteen men of similar disposition began raids on the white man's movements, outposts and homesteads causing a wave of hostilities among settlers and soldiers alike. The cavalry was having little success in tracking the elusive leader whose abilities to disappear without sign was becoming legendary. The young chief's following had spanned out across tribal barriers as men from the Sioux nation also joined themselves to his call for war causing his numbers to double in the recent months of aggression.

His gift of prediction enhanced victory and he came to be called by his followers: "The Seer,"— due to this uncanny knowledge of the future.

But plagued by recurrent dreams of the coming, The Seer now recognized the danger his people faced. Ancient Indian prophecies spoke of Death's Shadow and the plague that would follow, sweeping the land. Nothing would remain in the wake of the Black Death if it wasn't stopped. In the past these visions were interpreted by some as white men, but as of late The Seer was granted signs of its beginning. The infestation was coming and the renegade chief was set on his course — a crusade to cheat fate.

Without a sound the small raiding party crept to the frontier post under the cover of darkness spanning out around the fortress. True to the word of their leader the front of the stockade was open. Two riders were just escaping the fort and under the direction of The Seer the guerillas left them alone, unmolested. The followers did not fully understand the reason for allowing the flight of the man and woman when the instruction was that all others must die, but his loyal warriors obeyed the command and watched as a mountain man and Indian woman disappeared into the surrounding trees.

Two soldiers appeared at the entrance of the fort in pursuit of the escapees, but the silent death of swift arrows dropped them in their tracks. The invaders then filtered through the unguarded door.

A woman's scream alerted the post as men filtered out of the barracks to a full-blown battle. The captain running from his cabin spotted his second. "Lieutenant,— fall back to the stables... sound retreat. We'll form an offensive fr..." But he never completed the sentence as three arrows lodged in his chest. Amid the war cries of the enemy a brave then tackled the commander and began stabbing the dying man repeatedly in the upper abdomen busting open his rib cage and spilling out the captain's organs to the earth. Then he removed the head.

The lieutenant witnessing the butchery was horrified. Drawing his colt to intervene while running, he pointed his weapon at the enemy, but was struck in the forehead by a war ax pitching him spinning to the hard dirt street.

A weaponless private, dazed, his face covered in blood, stumbled through the doors of the stable barn only to crumple two paces from the entrance as an arrow lodged in his neck cutting off his wind pipe.

The bugler's "Call to Arms" echoed over the moonlit night amid the whoops and howls of the enemy, but the attack was so swift and well planned that the defensive, made up of numerous civilian settlers and the few cavalry, crumbled to the lesser numbers of the savage invading guerillas.

Fires erupted throughout the walled town amid Cheyenne and Sioux victory cries as the Indians fell on the carcasses of the slain, mutilating and decapitated fallen.

The Seer walked down the wide stretch of the compound

examining the carnage. The flickering lights of the flaming structures washed over the bronze skin of his small thin frame causing his war paint to stand out in glowing patterns of haunting mysticism. His long black locks, held to the side of his smooth young face by a single strap of narrow leather,— with a circular badge picturing a fiery bird,— centered his forehead and held his thick braided hair in an even part bordering his pronounced features. His short stature belied his authority as every man in his company obeyed his commands without question. A proven leader that was respected regardless of his size, The Seer inspired his brothers with wisdom beyond his age.

The Seer paused, as several of his men approached waving captured rifles above their heads while screaming wildly. Raising his war lance high he yelled, *"Make a through search. Desecrate the bodies. No remains must stay intact."*

Immediately the warriors scattered in obedience with war cries announcing the power of the victory.

At the front gate a mere child arrived leading some of the parties' horses. The animals were kept back on the other side of the river, but now following the advanced direction of their leader the boy brought them to the fort.

"Noooo...." Came the distant scream of a woman from across the stockade as the last remnants of opposition dissipated.

Warriors filtered out from the surrounding buildings and the Cheyenne War Chief motioned six of the braves nearby to come to him with simple hand gestures. Circling their leader, he spoke softly, *"The two that fled on horseback, hunt them down. They must die."*

No questions were asked as to why they were let go in the first place. No doubts were expressed of the decisions made during the siege. The warriors turned as one and took to the trail of the escapees, for all knew the spirits were directing their leader.

Chapter thirteen

The Queen

Song of the Priestess:

"Whispers on the Wind"

Like a shadow a cloud blankets the land

Locust that swarm, an evil to dread

Hard shells their skin, armored and strong

The plague has awakened, the quest, the run

The call will be answered, are the winds wrong?

Who will come? is the mountain's song

Translated 1850s

*   *   *

The smell of dung and rotting flesh hung heavy in the air, but the small creature seemed oblivious to the odor. Deeper into the black recesses of the cave the newborn fled: seeking solitude. Guided by instinct, by a will to survive as it matured over the next few days of life. Growth came in spurts: within hours its hard skeletal legs enlarged, its frame doubling, then tripling, quadrupling... until it towered in the confines of the caverns it was making home. Eyeless it roamed the dark tunnels: a maze carved by water and time under the shelter of the mountains.

The creature could sense its surrounding. As a bat uses radar, the being walked the corridors. Images of the formations deep underground transposed to its mind, imprinting better than vision, a map of the twists and turns of the cavern's subterranean recesses; but its ability to perceive its surroundings was not limited to the power of seeing with its mind's eye. The creature could hear by means of vibrations. Even the most minute quiver was detected and isolated to the position on the mental map. Movements of the air,— felt. Sounds touching the walls and ground,— identified. Even smells were cataloged in the small mind and recorded for future use. Pheromones, chemicals,— elements, living or lifeless matter — nothing was hidden from the creature's sensory pores.

Unlike the indigenous animals of this world the small parasitic growth's senses functioned and adapted to the new environment with amazing speed. The need to evolve over millenniums was never even a question as it embraced this new world ready to dominate. But this viral creature was different than its ancestors. Perhaps the stasis chambers it was stored in malfunctioned, or the plummet that brought its spore to this planet, teaming with life, caused a ripple in its own DNA. But for whatever reason this creature's development didn't follow the norm. The legs that grew weren't as mobile. Its features deformed. Birth defects had changed the normal patterns of growth, yet it was still far superior in its will to survive than the beasts indigenous to this planet.

A large amphitheater unfolded at the bottom of a shaft as the creature circled the place it would make its nest. Shedding its exoskeleton several times during its spurts, the empty shells were added to the framework of the structure that would house its final resting place: its very life would be transformed into a larva growing machine. Regurgitating a thick gooey slime it began plastering the walls and floor in preparation of the nursery. Her minions soon to come would continue the work she started, transforming the cave into a living hive.

The queen was born as if fertile. Cyst production was a matter of cell division. This creature's sole purpose in life; but the cycle required a host for the larva. The symbiotic development of the young was linked to the availability of other living beings,— mandatory to awaken her hive. Before her complete transformation, before the ulcerated cysts would fully multiply: she would need to secure at least one host to assure success. The emergent drone would be the beginning of her hive. A mindless extension of her presence. Almost a complete DNA copy of her, a living virus, her drone would venture forth to gather subjects and return them to the nest. From there the cycle would continue. Thousands, millions,— the growing creatures had no checks or balances. No natural predator limiting the size of the swarm. To grow,— to dominate,— to consume, the living culture of the parasite had no equal in its natural ability to overrun a planet.

The preparation of the hive caused changes in the dark recesses of the cavern. The walls glowed with an eerie hue as the regurgitated slime cooked into the limestone and rock. Humidity climbed, as the temperature inside the cave rose due to the chemical changes transforming the walls and ceiling. Armored plates of composed bone were shed by the queen and added to the foundation and structure supporting the interior of the nursery. And through it all the queen could sense the life around her. With an enhanced ability to reach out with its mind it knew this planet was blanketed with life. A kind of telepathy that allowed it to read the electrical synapses in brain activity. Not that she understood the thinking process of other species, but the noise of their presence could be felt. It was by this same gift that the creature could reach out and control her offspring.

Somewhere nearby a drone had transposed its host and had heard her call: sensed her presence. The new creature would sacrifice all in obedience to its royalty. Its only purpose in life to serve. Joining the hive it would extend the queen's reach. Then more would follow. The cysts would drop from the queen's back. The beginning larva needing only a host. Her children would continue to multiply. Shedding their molting armor and adding it to the structure as they in turn matured. All the parasitic life during their growth would work to extend the hive. Regurgitating the thick acidic bio fluid that would digest the walls slowly over time: generating heat and raising the humidity of the home. And all the while her young would swarm forth. Without end they would multiply, consuming the world around them.

The queen nestled into her chamber. A giant amid the amphitheatre now dwarfed in her presence. Her humped back fully developed, her ulcerated cysts developing across its wide extension of viral division; she was ready. The gelatinous sacks containing the first phase of the parasitic life cycle began their formation. Round orbs quivering in the gelatinous fluid flushing the creature's spores off her back and into their new world. Within hours the amphibian looking egg clusters littered the floor of the nursery; constantly quivering, growing, transforming.

Life had been detected when the queen originally entered the cave. The first of her hatchlings morphed from their lair. Like disembodied bugs their wings stretched out across dark recess of the cave. The strange eyeless birds scooted back up the dark tunnels that brought its mother to this place. Somewhere near the aperture of the maze slept a giant. A massive warm blooded form that seemed to be dormant. The winged bugs were drawn to this animal. The soothing sound of the hibernating beast's snoring resonated like a call, and the hatchlings responded. Oblivious to the smell of ammonia they fluttered and weaved as they neared the target. Huge white teeth resting inactive on the soft floor of the cave offered no resistance as the winged virus rounded a rock barrier that covered the mouth of the hole hiding the sleeping goliath. The bear spasmed momentarily as a creature slammed into the animal's midsection, then the beast simply fell back into the rhythmic breathing of a comatose rest.

Chapter Fourteen

Momma's Cradle

TO MARY CLEVENGER. STOP. DID DAD HAVE A BROTHER NAMED CLAUDE CLEVENGER. STOP. I HAVE RECENTLY MET A MAN WHO SAYS HE IS MY UNCLE. STOP. TELEGRAPH PLEASE ROBIN. STOP.

*   *   *

The large foyer with a cathedral ceiling and wide spiral staircase enhanced the spacious parlor, decorated with the delicate trappings of eastern finery. Several couches lined the walls of the open room with a hardwood floor and throw-rugs.

"Fewooo... You boys ain't favoring any of my ladies until you've bathed."

"What?"

"Git..." The haggard old buxom woman barked, pointing to the graceful spiral staircase. Her wrinkly aged snarl partially concealed the dark mustache favoring the corners of her mouth as she reemphasized her gesture with the shake of her hand. "Up those stairs and clean yourselves now."

"I just came fer a steak," Zeb coughed.

"I don't care if you just came to sit. You'll give my patrons a bad taste. Now git!"

"I...."

"Git!"

Claude was already halfway up the stairs with a big grin on his face before Zeb started on his way.

The bathroom was a big converted, un-partitioned bedroom with six metal tubs, more like horse-troughs, spaced out evenly along the walls. A wood burning stove was stoked and glowing in one corner of the bath, keeping the relative temperature and humidity overly comfortable. Water was carried continually up a back set of stairs, by a young mistress, to be boiled: supplying the bathers with hot water.

Claude was enjoying the luxury of the warm soothing water while resting back and puffing on a cigar: one of the perks included in the price of the service.

Zeb was busy scrubbing with brush and lye several months of the trail from his person.

"Dis iz da life," Claude said as he sighed with pleasure after expelling several smoke rings from his dime cigar.

"Thinkin' about takin' it up permanent like?" Zeb laughed.

"Ah man'z of my calber dezerves somedin' bedder."

"Thinkin' of a career change? Maybe mindin' a house?"

"I'z could be livin' worse."

"Like the last sixty years? I'm hurt."

Claude grinned, puffing on his cigar as the mistress entered carrying another bucket which she sat on the stove. Water slopped down the front of her undergarments adding transparency to a portion of her apparel and Claude winked at Zeb with the revelation. The young blonde picked up the other bucket, now boiling, with a leather glove. "Could I freshen anyone's bath?"

Claude removed his cigar like a king in all his regal splendor. "Darlin' you'z could freshin's me'z anytimes."

"What's your name, doll?" Zeb asked as she came toward them.

"Robin," the woman replied with a sly whisper.

"I'z could use me with Robin's the Cradle."

The women dumped the hot water over Claude's head, laughing. The older mountain man coughed and hacked, choking on some fluid he inadvertently sucked into his lungs.

Zeb chuckled at his partners misfortune looking over the young girl with renewed pleasure. Her blonde hair enhanced her dark eyebrows and fiery blue eyes. Strong cheekbones reminded Zeb of someone as he studied the contours of her nose and wide broad lips. "What's your full name darlin'?"

Robin was still giggling, "Clevenger."

"Claude isn't that family?" Zeb continued as he began to notice a family resemblance between Claude and Robin.

Claude stuffed the soggy cigar back in his mouth. "What's of id?" He mumbled from the corner of his doused ego. "Lod's of Clevengers."

"I need to get some more water for you two."

"What was your father's name doll?"

"Why all the questions?" Robin asked continuing with her duties.

"Just curious."

"Tom." She seemed apprehensive as she opened the door and looked back. "Tom was my dad's name."

"You know of a Tom, Claude?"

The older man shook his head.

"What about your Grandfather's name?"

"What's this all about?" The young woman replied stepping back into the room.

"Please?"

"Frank."

Claude's left eyebrow raised. "Frank Clevenger... from da Shenandoah Valley?"

"How'd you know?" Robin said in surprise.

"Yer ers families."

"What?"

"That would make you an uncle," Zeb laughed as he threw a towel at his friend.

"Dis can'd be."

"Makin' the moves on yer niece?"

"Shudup!"

"I'll just be getting you two some more bath water." The young woman said not sure what to make of any of the current conversation. She slipped out of the room amid the uncomfortable dialogue.

Claude leaned up wiping his face with the towel, "I'z got's to git hers outs of here."

"I thought you wanted to run this place?" Zeb laughed. "It could be a family business."

"Shudup!"

"You wanted a career change, I'm sure your niece could put in a good word."

"Dis ain't funny."

"I never had designs on a niece. What's that like?"

"Yu'z pushin's."

"Maybe fifty years has been long enough. Robin sure is a cutie."

Claude threw the towel back at Zeb. "Don'd you'z even dink id."

*   *   *

Robin entered the back door and made her way toward the steps. She could hear voices coming from the front parlor, but the usually commanding volume of the madam seemed different. Setting down her bucket she slipped silently to the cracked hall door and peered through the gap.

Five rugged men, heavily armed, stood at the entrance — the tallest one talking in a raspy tone to the owner.

Her demeanor appeared shaken as she muttered, "I don't know," repeatedly.

The tall man then grabbed the haggard old woman and struck her with the back of his hand; she fell violently to the floor as

97

another of the party pulled a pistol aiming it at the madam. "Two men in leathers. I know they're here. Tell me, and Johnny here won't have to shoot ya."

The woman covered the cut on the side of her mouth with one hand still shaking her head no.

The speaker nodded at the man with the pistol. Without a blink Johnny shot the defenseless woman in the temple.

Robin turned away from the door in a panic holding back a scream as she rocked against the opposite wall. She knew these men would kill everyone here if they weren't stopped. Quietly she worked her way to the stairs trying to avoid the creaky planks of the old wooden steps. The men in the bath were hunted and outnumbered, but she figured they were the house's only hope. When she burst into their room, Claude and Zeb were standing, unclothed, at opposite sides of the bath with rifles trained on the door.

"What's going on?" Zeb whispered, as he motioned Robin to move away from the entryway.

"Five men are here looking for you. They just killed Inez."

"Where's our britches?"

"We sent'um to the laundry!"

Both men's jaws dropped.

She got a blank look on her face as she shook her hands in panic, "They stood on their own. Whad you expect us to do?"

"Damn, what you got fer us to wear?"

"There's some winterin's in the next room."

Zeb nodded to his partner. "I think your right about that career change."

"Yeas... dese places brings un-savories."

"What about a saloon?"

"I'z got no mind fer dose kinds of figers."

Glass broke as a chair launched through the window from the exterior balcony. The man outside made only a brief appearance at the opening, firing a shot at the younger mountain man; but Zeb dropped him with one shot between the eyes. Re-cocking his rifle briskly, he grinned. "That's one. Your gittin' slow in your old age."

"I'z didn't haft ah clear dat ones."

Zeb turned to Robin, "That balcony exit to the next room?"

"Nod dyin' wid-oud da skivies?"

"I ain't losin' no hair tonight."

Claude slipped his boots on, over his wet feet.

"That's a good look for you," Zeb said picking up his boots and moving toward the door.

"Nod daken da win-der?"

"I think they'll be waiting there," Zeb pushed open the front entrance to the room and peeked out. Several underdressed women were scrambling down the hall. He checked both ways, amid the panic, then slipped out along the wall of the corridor and moved to the next room. Claude entered behind him with Robin closing the door. "Where's those skivvies?"

"Inez keeps them here to sell to patrons," Robin replied, dashing to a wardrobe and fumbling through the draws. "These should fit." She pulled out two red woolens and threw them at the men.

They began dressing quickly, keeping one eye on the door.

"Who are those men?" Robin whispered as she watched.

"How should we know?" Zeb pulled the one piece over his shoulders and began buttoning it.

"Prob-bly a piss-off reladive."

"And they'd be mad at you because?"

"Our line of work tends to anger those on the wrong side of the law."

"I'd never pictured you two as lawmen."

"Bounty hunters," Zeb responded with a grin, picking up his rifle and stepping back to the door. Claude followed as both men forgot about closing the breezy portion of their backsides.

Robin smiled as she looked down. "You—"

"Whad?" Claude sneered at the distraction.

She decided not to tell them. "You might want to make your way to the back stairs from the other room. I don't think they knew about that entrance to the bathroom."

Female screams disrupted the trio's conversation as the breaking of glass was heard on the first floor. A few other male patrons scrambled for the stairs while trying to dress as rifle shots plastered them to the decorative wall coverings amid more panic. The smell of smoke abruptly alerted all to a new foe.

"Trapped like rats on a sinking ship!" Zeb snarled as he watched the dead men sink down the steps.

"The back stairs — quick."

Women were running back up the hall as Zeb and Claude

stepped out of the storage room.

"We're trapped — we're trapped!" Yelled one of the panic stricken residents.

"What about the back stairs?"

"The whole first floor is in flames," cried the naked girl. "We're going to burn to death."

"Let's get to the balcony off the bathroom."

Claude pushed into the room and brushed by the window. A shot whistled through the broken glass just missing him.

"Dare wa-chin's da win-ders Zeb — ain't no good — we're drapped!"

The pounding of hooves resounded from the street below. "Now what?" Zeb skirted the window and glanced outside. Armed men were running for horses. Zeb's eyes drifted to the reason for the stampede; down the street, what looked like a full division of cavalry was storming up the road. "Talk about perfect timing."

"Wad is id?" Claude asked trying to peer through the busted glass and avoid getting shot.

"Looks like the whole US Cavalry's come," Zeb watched their antagonist flee as several of the troops were ordered to pursue the fugitives. The remainder dismounted and began toting buckets from the nearby well. In moments a fire brigade was formed passing pail after pail in the useless battle.

Zeb and Claude helped the women with them out onto the balcony over the flames and down to the street below. Claude hit the ground first and turned to help his partner, but hesitated to lend a hand when he saw Zeb's backside peeking through the open flap of his skivvies.

"Sergeant, — Are these the men?"

Zeb spun as he hit the ground; Lloyd, Titus and a captain were approaching swiftly. "Yes Sir."

"Gentlemen — who were those men that fled as we rode up?"

Claude and Zeb stood silent, but looked at each other bewildered. Zeb was the first to speak. "Don't rightly know."

"You've had no contact with them before?" The captain appeared suspicious.

"Spec's wez add a loss, never got's a look see."

The captain sized up the two men standing in their woolens. Zeb went to scratch himself and realized his flap was open.

"Damn!"

Claude snickered then noticed his was dropped also.

As the men fumbled for their dignity the captain continued, "I've been told you could track down a deserter for us?"

Zeb pulling at his woolens coughed, "Could be, what's the pay?" Not looking up as he got one button snapped on his exposure.

"You'll be under the employ of the US Military."

"We don't work for no pittance."

"Ain'd lookin' fer no career change neither."

"I assure you both — it will be just temporary. Gentlemen your government needs you."

The two bounty hunters sheepishly averted their eyes as Zeb sneered at Claude, "You wanted a damn change."

"I'z been dare. Add my fill."

Zeb met the captain's icy glare, but noticed Lloyd's wanting. He considered the task thinking of the young boy, full of vinegar, he had abandoned so long ago. Could he owe a debt here? His pause was minimal, but his mind raced. "We'll help you find your man, Captain. Then we'll be on our way."

"Fair enough," the captain said as he turned back to his command. "Sergeant get these men some clothes."

"Yes Sir," Lloyd saluted, smiling from ear-to-ear.

Chapter Fifteen

The Track

Sir:

The locals reported a renegade band east of here. They killed a family of settlers, stole their horses and burned the wagons. Our Osage scouts believe the war party was made up of about 15 braves. Hostilities have continued to increase. We have followed the trail for two days, but will need to re-supply by Thursday. Request fresh horses and provision for rendezvous at Snake Junction. Corporal Wiggins is familiar with the territory and the most direct route.

Your obt. servant

Jeffery Kain

1st Lieutenant

*   *   *

The previous day's hunting proved less than successful as the warriors gathered to the morning fire. One of their number earlier in the week happened on a herd of mountain goats in the surrounding hills, a days ride from the village. The party had hoped to replenish the meat supplies before the pending winter hit the lower elevations, but a two-day-old snowfall had hidden all traces of the herd. The white carpet blanketing the frozen woods dampened the spirits of some of the men, desperate not to return home empty-handed.

Isaac had arisen early and started the fire to make himself some coffee. Only Reuben shared his love for the bitter swig on this chilly morning as most of the tribe were feeding on "pemmican" for breakfast and munching on snow to wash it down. It was decided to divide into five groups to better cover the area, so Isaac, Reuben and four others, including Tencun, headed north with first light.

The chill of a stiff breeze whipped down the valley as they rode heading for a distant ridge lined with pines. Isaac was the first to notice patches of burned brush and scorched tree trunks scattered randomly about the frozen landscape. It was extremely unusual considering the time of year and the haphazard scars of a fire that seemed to pick its fuel carefully without even touching kindling so close to anyone of the fires that a spark should have spread the blaze over the entire basin. Curiosity moved the men to examine the phenomena more closely. The charred trunks were only surface marks, apparently singed by a heat source without flame; but chunks of bark were missing in the center of the scorched patches where objects had struck the trees. Digging into the snow near one of the burns, Reuben found a black rock that appeared to have been molten at some point, but was now solidified.

"Uncle, look — this rock had to be what struck the tree. By where it landed it had to of come from the sky like this with a lot of force," Reuben made motion with the rock and demonstrated the angle of impact. Without knowledge Reuben was exhibiting a practical understanding of physics. Isaac said nothing, but scanned the horizon in thought.

The mystery deepened as the men moved further into the site and found a huge epicenter of fallen timber scattered in a circular pattern with an immense crater right in the middle. It was like a massive canon ball had exploded leveling the area.

Isaac felt uneasy... out of control. He remembered vividly,

as if it was yesterday, the battle with the Sky Hunters. The storm that swept over that valley when the floating ship fired on the earth. The whole valley shook that day. The explosion that mushroomed forth was beyond anything capable by man as the shock wave blew over trees and rained down debris for miles. This spot had all the feel of that fateful day about fifty years ago.

"What could do this Uncle?"

"Only one thing in my experience," Isaac answered, rubbing the pouch at his belt, his own answer to an Indian medicine bag. The mountain man now carried a necklace he used to wear in the pouch. A bear claw trophy given to him by the man Jon, who taught him how to shoot. Between the long curled grizzly daggers systematically spaced on the rawhide band was the mummified finger of a long dead Sky Hunter: his only relic of their previous visit. Isaac had shot the digit off himself in his first confrontation with one of the creatures and later tracked it down and killed it. "I think they're back," Isaac's mood was grim. He knew the danger they were all in if it were true, but he needed proof. "We need to look for tracks."

"What kind of tracks?"

"Like nothing you've seen before."

Isaac got everyone to span out and search. Within minutes Tencun had located the unusual print. The long taloned imprints with an offset toe were unmistakable proof that the creatures had returned. As all gathered to see, the blonde mountain man knelt and examined the evidence. "I know this one."

"What?"

"See this portion that looks like a dewclaw?" Isaac said pointing to the unusual offset toe on the instep.

"Yes."

"Notice on this foot how its twisted. This varmint was here fifty years ago. He's the one that gave your father that funny looking bow with the pulleys on it."

"You think this is Broken-Toe?"

"We tracked this very critter fifty years ago."

Everyone's attention was suddenly drawn to a disruption on the opposite side of the clearing. They relaxed as one of the other hunting parties entered the site; then a second. They had seen the strange site also from a distance and came to investigate.

Reuben returned to business and stood, walking off, following the trail of the creature for a short distance. "This doesn't make sense Uncle. This track looks a week old..." The young looking half-breed knelt and pushed his finger into hardened ice formed in the sole of the print. "But this snow is just a few days."

"That's because that's a fresh track. Those critters are hotter than men. If I didn't know better, I'd guess they're from hell itself."

Isaac understood the nature of tracking and was no novice, but he lacked the true skill involved when it came to reading a trail. As with most talents there's an art to understanding, seeing, and reading sign left behind by the hunted. Reuben however, like his father could examine and interpret great detail from the obscure marks left in something's passing.

"Whatever this creature is... it's hurting Uncle."

"What do you see?"

"For one thing it's favoring its left side. Notice this scrape in the snow, intermittently, and the distance is shorter in the stride here." The younger man pointed along the trail at what to him was obvious but Isaac just nodded in agreement, not truly recognizing the significance. "He's also carrying something relatively awkward." Reuben, while looking at a small bush, knelt, studying the surroundings. "He stumbled here. Whatever he's carrying raked over this shrub and caused him to lose his balance."

Isaac squatted by his friend and put his hand on Reuben's shoulder, "I think we should round up the others, and get out of here fast."

Reuben looked shocked. "Uncle... this critter's weak: probably disoriented. We could hunt him down and kill him."

"You don't know what you're dealing with here. There could be more than just this one," Isaac was shaking his head. "This one could be bait. These critters are nothing to trifle with. They can turn invisible. Move at speeds that defy nature. And they're powerful. More than a match for any man, or group of men." He ran his right hand over the side of his face. "They live to kill, and they're good at it. We need to warn the others and get back to the village." Isaac stood surveying his surroundings.

"Uncle... I can't believe you'd pass up this opportunity. You've hunted them before and won. Let's take this critter," Reuben was clenching his fist, gesturing victory.

"My brother... Please... " Isaac again placed his hand on his friend. "This creature's the devil himself. I have no wish to lose you or anyone else to this demon." The blonde's gaze dropped to the ground. "I lost too many last time." Isaac then stared hard at Reuben. "Please listen to me — My main concern is my family — my friends. I want them safe. We need to leave this place,— now."

"Then hunting and killing this demon is the best way to protect them from this devil!" Reuben dropped his voice to a whisper. "I want the prestige it would give me before Tunkanayhautue."

"There's no prestige if you're dead," Isaac whispered back. "Besides, these beasties might be part of a pack."

Reuben was saddened by his uncle's cowardice. He had always looked up to Isaac as a slayer, a stalker of the Sky Hunters. Now when face-to-face with the challenge he wanted to turn tail? "I want to hunt this thing. Like my father before me..." Reuben was shaking as he returned his friend's stare. "Uncle we could take this critter. I want this challenge."

Isaac turned walking back to his mount contemplatively and deeply saddened. The four other braves watched in silence not sure what to do for a moment, then fell in behind Isaac as the mountain man mounted his horse..

"Uncle,— do you wish me to go it alone?"

Isaac's head sunk low. Perhaps Reuben was right. Following the thing might be the only way to insure the safety of the tribe. The blonde turned back to whom he viewed as a younger brother — his family. "We need to at least warn the other's first."

"Yes!" Reuben declared jumping after his confidant. "They can't be far. We can round them up and meet back here."

"That critter could be watching us right now."

"Then a few of us should start tracking it and send the others to gather all to some rendezvous."

All were told what they were up against. A plan was discussed and agreed to. The two groups that came to the site after the initial investigation went out after the remaining hunting parties. Isaac's original band set off after the creature with, Reuben setting the pace.

*   *   *

"Riders coming," sounded the alarm.

A tall graying man stepped from his tent watching as the young corporal and an Indian scout neared the camp. Running a

106

weathered hand through his thinning top-not the 1st lieutenant centered his hat comfortably and removed his gloves from his belt. "Let's see why the corporal is back so soon."

"Yes sir," barked a heavy set sergeant.

The young corporal broke through a line of curious, gathered non-commissioned troops and reined his mount to a halt directly in front of the lieutenant, leaving the Osage scout at the edge of the encampment. "Sir," the man saluted after slipping from the saddle, his horse obviously agitated at the sudden stop. "Indians hit a group of wagons just north of here," he panted out between his gasps of excitement. "Looks like several families,— women and children sir."

"How the hell are we suppose to keep the peace," the officer spat in disgust, "when the rumor of gold brings every sort of white trash imaginable, regardless of the danger?"

"Sir," the corporal interrupted hesitantly. "They appeared to just be settlers."

"Nonsense corporal: the allure of hidden wealth is what brought them. Gold does that to people. Makes any man feel invincible, ignoring certain death. Greed overcomes reason and will continue to draw every sort of rif-raf to this God forsaken land to gain what isn't even here. Sergeant," the Lieutenant ordered in is commanding tone, "Have the men mount up, we'll have a ride ahead of us."

"Sir," the corporal interrupted again. "The most terrible atrocities were perpetrated on the victims."

"Of course they were corporal, didn't our scout there know which tribe was responsible?"

"Alls he would say Sir,— was that the demons have returned."

"Well, we need to find these red-devils before anymore bloodshed occurs."

Chapter Sixteen

Old Friends?

Tears of the Trail

The winds whip briskly — the night of change

the seasons of time — cry too late

Too many moons have passed — silence beckons

so stirs the beast's — the mountain's call to awaken

Asleep so many falls — the sands will not count

death has a name — but to learn it

Means sorrow

Sioux chant

*   *   *

Ben and Aiyana hit the trees enveloped by the darkness. Missy snarled and screamed a warning somewhere in the rear, but the two companions slowed only because the light of the moon could not break through the dense canopy above.

"This way my husband," Aiyana said, pointing in the direction of their other tethered animals: near where she had jumped the stockade wall.

Ben heard Missy hit the brush behind and he let out a screech that mimicked perfectly the haunting cry of a panther. The horses spooked momentarily. Ben patted his animal's neck and whispered soothing words of comfort to his startled mount as Aiyana kept control of the one in tow. Missy would find them shortly, chasing Ben's call.

The mountain man reined his mare in the direction Aiyana directed and nudged his mount forward. The heavy brush proved a difficult obstacle, but as they moved deeper into the foliage the ground cover thinned allowing the horses freer movement. With little effort they found the tethered animals as Aiyana dismounted from behind Ben and acquired her own ride and prepared the supply animals to follow in a train.

Missy snarled on entering the rendezvous; partially lit by beams filtering through the thinner canopy covering the small clearing.

"Glad you could make it," Ben chuckled, as he watched the big cat sit on its haunches and start cleaning itself in its nonchalant manner. "We better get a move on — those soldier-boys ain't goin' to take to kindly to my leavin' their accommodations."

A commotion coming from the fort dictated the need for a quick departure. Aiyana finished with the pack animals and mounted her pony. The three traveling companions then moved off deeper into the woods until they hit water. Walking into the shallow swells by the shore, they turned upstream washing their passing over the gravelly bed, in the steady current of the wide river. The bright round of silver, lit their course, reflecting off the rippling surface that cast a sparkling path of glitter to an otherwise black backdrop. The haunting beauty was almost mesmerizing as the party pressed on in the cold shallows of the timeless stream. It was as if silver flakes of metal were guiding their way in a hidden world of imagination. A dream, beckoning them in a world shrouded in darkness: "Come to the light! — This is the way."

Ben was a man hardened by a life of experiences that would make most men shake; but he still marveled at the beauty of a world so cruel, yet full of wonder as to astonish the eye and move the heart. Tonight he escaped prison and now he exhilarated in his freedom. What more could one ask than to be free: free to explore a world ready for any willing to grab life and play it to the full, free to wander on a path lit by the gods — on a trail that would lead to where? Men of his caliber never asked. Life was meant to be experienced — and fate was never questioned. Only to live free was worth the price he paid and he never looked back on his choices, but the trail sometimes forces one to glance behind.— Gunfire erupted from the fort.

"What's going on my husband?"

"We appeared to have stirred up a hornets nest.— We need to move!" as he quickened the pace.

Ahead the dull white of granite stood out against the darker mat of vegetation. The incline of rock situated like a wall amidst the rumbling of falling water somewhere in the distance spoke of an obstacle forged by time itself.

"We need to cross here." Ben turned in the saddle to face his wife. "You wait here... I'll see if it's safe."

Ben heard the whicker of a horse from the trail behind and paused, distressed that anyone could have found them. His horse whinnied in response as he tried to get his bearing and determine how much of a lead he had. "Sssh..." Ben whispered to quiet his mare. "Make sure I'm across then follow."

Aiyana nodded as Ben reined his animal into the wide crossing at the bottom of the mouth of the swifter moving current. The river was still somewhat lazy at this point and shallow with a small delta blocking the opening of the canyon ahead. Ben avoided the softer sands of the delta and easily reached the opposite shore. The moon was full and high, lighting the opposite shoreline as Ben motioned his wife to follow.

Aiyana nudged her animal out across the water, but dropped into a deeper pocket of the lazy stream. The icy cold lapped at her thighs and wet the fringes of her wrap, but she continued without a shiver.

Missy plunged in behind, only her head visible as she tailed her companions. On reaching the other side she shook her large frame like a dog, trying to dry the chill of the cold night air from her wet fur.

Ben and Aiyana stayed together along the water line of the shore on up past the small sandy island then exited the river onto an outcropping of granite. From here the terrain turned into terraced cliffs and rocky projections interwoven with brush and small trees.

Ben was hard pressed to put as much distance as possible between himself and those following, but the landscape proved extremely treacherous, forcing them to travel at a crawl long into the night. Their course up the relatively steep incline, mostly barren of tall trees, continued to give them a panoramic view of the sizeable valley below; the large moon bathing the shadowed woods and wide river with a luminous glow, spawning haunting silhouettes that stood masking the topography and changing the perception of the world they had just passed through.

Ben's mare lost its footing briefly as the ground cover turned to shards of slate. He dismounted and turned to his wife, "We'll have ta walk fer a ways. This spot wouldn't even be safe to cross in the day."

Aiyana slid gracefully from her saddle; her attention drawn to their trail behind. Along the river where they crossed she could see lights bobbing up and down the shore line. "They are gaining on us."

Missy looked back and snarled, as if sensing the danger.

Ben stepped over to his wife and paused watching the events below. "These un's are good," he said in a grim tone as icy as the cold wind around them. "To track the course we took, and at night."

"How could they have followed our trail in the river... and so quickly?" Aiyana asked, somewhat unnerved at the rare abilities being demonstrated below.

"Perhaps they're part of a larger group that split up, — up and down the river looking' fer sign." Ben pulled his wife close, wrapping an arm around her. "No doubt they'll find where we crossed and exited. It was the last probable place before the rapids. We done did the predictable. The water we splashed up on that rock surely wouldn't have soaked into that granite yet."

"They must of found some brave ta scout for um."

"Maybe,— ain't like any other soldier boys I've met before," Ben replied in his nonchalant, matter-of-fact manner. He shook his wife's shoulder with affection and pulled her attention back to the path ahead. It was like a field of slate scattered all over the hillside.

"We'll git out of this darlin', but we need to get a move on. I think this ground cover will help hide our trail."

Ben bent over and picked up a piece of the flat rock as if weighing the shard, then looked across the face of the hill. "We'll change our course across this," he said tossing the stone. "No one can track across slate." Ben turned back to his wife and smiled, her black orbs shadowed in the soft glow of the moon. "Not even me."

Aiyana chuckled, but looked back at the men following. They were crossing the river, three lanterns moving lazily over the water. She tied the pack animals to her horse. Taking the reins of her ride she turned her attention to her husband. Together they began the treacherous walk across the loose footing afforded by the flat stones. Each step shifted the flat rock under foot as they slipped and stumbled along the sloping hillside. A short distance into the field they changed course heading down instead of up. Walking down the slope proved a little less difficult than trying to parallel the incline, but the danger of falling and rolling all the way to the bottom was still a hazard to avoid. The safest course would have been to go up and around the dangerous slide area, but from this point on Ben was bent on doing what was the least likely.

The mountain man was sure the trackers following them were part of a larger party. The river was the best possible place to hide a trail so these men took up pursuit by going straight to the water and split into two groups. One heading down river and the other up. This assembly behind had no doubt heard his horse whicker and knew they were going in the right direction: finding where they crossed was just a coincidence. It had to be. Ben had waited to the last possible point to cross the river. So had these men. He looked back at the lights now moving up the hill. If he could keep the animals quiet from this point on they'd be home free. The shards of slate would hide any trail. The shifting of the ground cover would cause no pattern. No indentation could be detected in passing. The flat rocks would slip and find new points of rest: stacking randomly, in an indeterminable pattern. The new locations just as unstable and just as indefinable as the original positions before movement. Without dogs, no scent could be detected to follow the trail — and Ben heard no canines behind. The important thing now was to remain quiet and slip away in the night.

The escapees dropped out of the shards after about twenty minutes and took to the woods. Missy disappeared in the thick brush as Ben and Aiyana mounted up behind the cloak of bark and branch. To circle back to the river could bring them into contact with the balance of the party Ben was sure was after them, but to turn straight away from the mountain would keep them in the valley come morning and the probability of being found would be heightened by patrols the fort would establish after an escape.

"My husband... if we circle back I know a pass opposite that island at the river fork. Its a narrow trail of rock and cliffs, but it will hide us and take us north out of the reach of our enemy."

"How is it you know of this trail?" Ben said with a smile of pride at his wife's ingenuity.

"When I was young, my brother took me on the cliffs to scare me. I ran from him and got lost. Our people were camped where that fort was and I was able to find my way out of those hills by means of that passage."

"Well our trackers certainly won't be expectin' us to walk right by them and past their backdoor."

Aiyana's lips cracked into a sly smile as she eyed her lover. "They will never see us as we slip by my husband."

Morning found the trio miles from the fort, heading north on the narrow passage of Aiyana's youth. The hard rocky soil left little sign of their passing and the nature of the trail made pursuit by a large number of soldiers impractical due to the limited space afforded for fighting: putting a charging advance at a great disadvantage because the attack would have to take place one at a time. Ben was still nervous about the possibility of chase, but during the remainder of the wee morning hours saw no such evidence behind: no bobbing lights, or sounds of horses weathering their course. As they reached the peak of the tall ridge overlooking the entire valley below Ben turned to his wife with a smile of success. The panoramic view of the majestic wooded plains and rolling rivers took form under the gray hues of dawn as the shadows of dark waned in the new light. Fog drifted lazily about the waterways and concealed much of the vista, but the mountain man could see the distant walls of the stockade and was surprised that there appeared little activity at the fort. "That's strange, the post looks deserted."

Aiyana looked back then at her husband, in shock and dismay, "Somehow they found us."

"What!" Ben dismounted and stepped behind a barrier of vegetation, where he could view their previous path, but remained completely concealed to the ones following. Through the winding pass about an hour behind horses were climbing the steep sloping contours leading up the cliffs. "Who are these yanks?" Ben spat under his breath. "How could they follow us over slate rock and water... catch a circle back and not lose time on top of it?" Scratching his coarse beard while studying the terrain and the enemy, he thought hard. "If I didn't know no's better, I'd think my brother was on my tail ready to fester a debt."

"You think Zeb follows us?" Aiyana asked, perplexed.

"No, darling... But I did never know no other that could track like him, — until now."

Ben studied the deep dark eyes looking into his: eyes of trust and faith. Beautiful eyes that beckoned at his heart and fired his soul, but today those flames fanned his fear. Fear of the danger those lovely orbs were in. Fear of what the men behind might be capable of. That his wife could take care of herself, he had no doubt; but the soldiers outnumbered them. They could send for reinforcements, or just pin them down in these rocks: surrounding them like beaver in a trap, and wait. Ben thought long and hard then spoke in his matter-of-fact manner, revealing none of his worries to dispel her trust or shake her faith. "We can make a stand in these here rocks. It's a sound defendable spot, or we can continue to run. Which do you think my love?"

"If we stay we'll be trapped. We will continue to a better place to make our stand."

Ben couldn't help but smile at the confidence his wife expressed. She was fearless in the face of danger. Wise in a pragmatic way that throughout their years together still amazed him. "Then we best be on our way."

As they cleared the top of the cliffs, a rolling wooded plain tapering downward, spanned the horizon for miles. The two riders melted into the trees with supply horses in tow; the large cat bringing up the rear. The forest was relatively open and the trio made good use of the terrain, trotting their animals at a pace that would eat up the miles in a minimal amount of time without overworking the horses. They would increase their lead by many miles before the enemy would reach the crest of the mountain plain and Ben would use every minute to advance the chase with obstacles that would limit their pursuer's ability to track. The soil was frozen solid and the ground cover was a mixture of hardpan and barren granite that covered wide swaths of the wooded landscape: impenetrable to paw or hoof. Ben was confident that no sign of their passing was recorded on the mountainous plateau for the trackers behind to follow.

Crossing several large clearings, they bolstered their mounts to greater speed then again dropped to a trot at the forest's crest. An hour into the ride the small party reached the border of an immense canyon that cut across their path forcing a course change that skirted the natural barrier. As they followed the twisting contours of the deep ravine the topography of the landscape continued to climb to higher and higher elevations giving them a clear view of the plateau behind, although the ground cover concealed their position from any that might be searching for them. To Ben's amazement he could see riders moving across one of the eminence glens they had sped over a short time earlier.

"How in the hell are these guys following us so easily?"

Aiyana turned to see the small party dogging them; the deep blue of military garb standing out in strong contrast to the brown terrain and green backdrop of the high plateau. It was unnerving that the men appeared: not only tracking the exact course, but they seemed to be narrowing the gap. "How they gainin'?"

"I don't know, but it looks like we're gonna have to make a stand." Ben scanned the horizon ahead for a strong defensible spot to lay an ambush. "We need to distance ourselves from this canyon. Don't want to be trapped with no place to fall back." To the fore and left of their position was a jagged ridge that afforded plenty of rock cover and a defendable hill that would be difficult to approach by the enemy. Ben looked back at the party following to try and ascertain their numbers. "There's only about six. I say we move up there and put a stop to this runnin'." The mountain man pointed out his decision and Aiyana quickly turned her lead to the direction indicated. It took them about ten minutes to reach their posting, dismount and secure the horses; but to Ben's dismay the riders had already moved into the heavy brush, concealing their approach.

"They couldn't of seen us." Ben studied the tree line to try and determine the most likely point they would attack from.

"Who are these guys?"

"Ain't like no other soldier boy I've come across before."

Missy growled in discontent at the chosen camp and the apparent duress her human companions were under, but found a shaded rock crevasse and hid to rest from their strenuous run.

Ben and Aiyana pulled their rifles and readied themselves behind a large outcropping of granite. The surrounding woods were quiet. Aiyana strained to hear the enemies approach when she caught sight of movement along a break along the clearing — nothing more than a shadow really. She detected no presence, but the brushy slope of a parting in the woods seemed to flicker in an unusual motion: not from wind but from a distortion of light and shade, silhouetting the pines. Aiyana squinted as the ethereal apparition took form, then was lost to an indeterminate shape, tangled against the multi-colored backdrop. The flickering darted in and out around a fallen stump then disappeared completely amid the twisted roots.

Aiyana blink and strained, trying to make sense of the site when she again saw the faint glimmer further down the tree-line. This time the phantom distortion took on a human form,— froze momentarily, as if peering into the forest then disappeared. "These woods are haunted," Aiyana whispered to her husband as she motioned to the wraith.

Ben's gaze followed his wife's finger looking intently at her observation, but could see nothing.

"We have entered Ik-tom-i's domain... He will play with us, then kill us."

"Shhhhh... What are you seeing woman?" Ben was distressed at his wife's nonsense when the apparition moved and the mountain man recognized the silhouette. Ben ducked pulling his wife low behind the rocks. "Shit... what's that thing doing here?"

"You saw Iktomi?"

"That wasn't Iktomi," he whispered. "That was one of those damn critters from the flaming bird."

It had been a long time, but recognition melted over Aiyana's face. "They've returned?"

"It does look that way." Ben slid up the rock carefully to get a better look, but the image was gone. "I wonder if he saw us?"

"He saw us."

"Then why hasn't he attacked?"

Aiyana peeked over the concealment, scanning for the creature and spotted the blue uniform of a soldier crawling through the underbrush. "Maybe he's more interested in those following."

The crack of a rifle sounded as a bullet smacked the granite throwing debris into Aiyana's face. She ducked brushing away the dust then fired back.

Ben popped up over the boulder and fired at the enemy. "Careful, I've got no interest in you gettin' hurt." Several bullets pounded the barrier, but Ben stayed atop long enough to see four of the group working their way through the limited ground cover on their way up the ridge. "I can take care of myself," Aiyana spat shifting for another shot.

"Our company's on the move. I wonder where our invisible friend got off to," Ben's sarcasm dripped as he fired two quick rounds one hitting his target. The body was thrown backward across a small bush giving Ben his first clear view of the enemy. "Them's not soldier boys, them's Injuns."

Aiyana spied the dead man then turned to her husband, "Where'd they come from?"

The warrior was wearing the cavalry coat of a sergeant with a blue bandana tying back his long black hair.

"Maybe he's the scout," Ben fired again at the men in the trees trying to pin them down when the Indians began yelling their war cries and raised the level of the gunfire.

"Looks like they're Sioux." Aiyana scored a hit winging one of the warriors in the trees.

"The Sioux wouldn't be helping no soldier boys."

"Maybe we fell onto a small war party."

"No... these boys have been trailing us all night," Ben could see the men charging the hill and they were making progress possibly working their way behind. "Looks like things are going to get ugly." The mountain man quickly assessed the encampment's weakness. "Missy watch our backs!"

The large cat, at the first few shots, had worked her way into the large crag ready to pounce. At Ben's warning she carefully crept out of the mouth of the crevasse and slipped along the stone wall watching for any enemy that might enter the camp from behind. She was quiet... vigilant; ready to defend.

Ben looked over at the lion, knowing she would sound a warning and attack if any tried to sneak in from the rear. For an independent feline she had an uncanny knack of understanding her companions and on more than one occasion saved their lives. The mountain man had over the years put a great deal of trust and faith in her ability to read danger and know what to do. Today their lives would depend on her once again.

*   *   *

The warriors sent out by The Seer dogged their quarry all night long. By the light of lanterns stolen from the fort the tracker found where the stalked moved into the water and followed the clouded disturbance lifted from the bottom of the slow moving stream, upriver. Tri-cha-nan-tu could track. He was a man in tune with his surroundings and understood his quarry. Half of the work of tracking men came from understanding how they think. The small signs left clues; but to the one who stalks men, a knowledge of human nature and the ability to read how the quarry will react to any given stimulus, aids in the interpretation of those clues. And Trichanantu knew this prey was smart when it came to avoiding an enemy and hiding its trail. He could comprehend much of his intended game, but he realized that the true test would come once they caught this enemy. That he would find them he had no doubt; but the one leading this small party was sly and well versed in avoiding pursuit. The danger of cornering any vicious animal would raise the stakes of a conflict tenfold; but when the coming battle involved men of the caliber he was now tracking, casualties would hang for a certainty, and a slip in vigilance would mean death.

This enemy used many obstacles to hide their trail. The way the game had used the river would have cause a tremendous loss of time if they hadn't taken up pursuit immediately after the victory at the post. Trichanantu never questioned The Seer's decision to let this quarry escape from the fort. If they had tried to stop them outside the wall, the resulting gunfire would have alerted the entire fortress and destroyed the element of surprise. Surprise which allowed them the swift defeat of the soldiers and civilians encamped there. But the tracker never figured that these fugitives would be so difficult to follow. Luck led to the river current's slow progress, leaving the trace elements,— a murky cloud of mud stirred from the rocky bottom of the river marking the direction of the hunteds' flight. Trichanantu followed the river, watching for the point where the enemy left the water; but not finding any sign, crossed at the last safest place. He was determined to work back down the opposite bank and continue the search to find where they left the stream; but to his surprise found water splashed upon the smooth flat granite shore telling of his game's departure from the river and their course

118

moving up the steep cliffs, amid the incline of the valley's eastern mountain range. Again time was the deciding factor: the heavy amount of water spilled out on the round stone surface from the many horses exiting the stream would have dissipated in the porous rock and been indeterminate with the passing of another half hour. The blessing of The Seer was on his quest and he knew the Great Spirit had fated his catching of this enemy: ultimately, stopping the dreaded plague that his leader and childhood friend had foreseen.

The trading post was but a small infestation. If any escaped who were infected, death and carnage would sweep across the land and consume all like locust: without thought or mercy. The Seer's talk had enlivened the visions upon Trichanantu's mind and at the massacre, he himself had witnessed the strange deformation of bone as some of the men were already transforming. The mutilation of the dead, per The Seer's instructions, was necessary to kill the death walk growing inside those soldiers. Any doubt of the impending plague by the warriors that had chosen to follow The Seer were washed away at the sight of those grotesque aberrations. The men infected would have given birth to the Black Death, and that had to be stopped. The Seer's crusade was the only thing standing in opposition until the coming of the Messiah. The Mountains would call this one, who would lead their people from the plague spreading across their land. The visions of the yellow hair to come were confusing, even contradictory; but Trichanantu trusted The Seer and would follow his command: waiting for the Mountain Calling and the ultimate war to follow.

For now his orders were simple, to catch the escaped ones. Thus far the task had proved anything but simple. Trichanantu had almost lost a brave on the shards of slate on the eastern cliffs. The enemy had used the dangerous path to hide their trail instead of going around and the tracker followed suit, but Chic-car-ree's horse lost its footing on the unstable ground and nearly pulled the man to his death as the animal fell down the slope and over a cliff. Without a mount Chic-car-ree would only slow them down and so was sent back to The Seer horseless. But the distraction of the fall and saving of the warrior's life by the men of the hunting party brought the attention of the group back to the river, where, by the light of the bright moon they saw that their quarry had circled back and were again crossing its slow moving water. If the accident hadn't happened their game probably would have slipped away, but fate was with their every move. It was like the Great Spirit was watching over their trial and helping them to stop the Black Death.

Trichanantu had immediately turned around and made his way back to the river by the way they had come. It was safer than the course his enemy had taken and after clearing the shards of slate, he had his warriors cover the lamps with leather bags to conceal their light from the quarry.

They found the narrow pass up the northeastern mountain slope and made good time on the climb, without the burden of a long pack train to contend with. The fugitive's supply animals were a liability slowing their escape and the young Cheyenne brave guessed right: by first light they would catch up with them.

When Trichanantu reached the top ridge of the narrow cliff pass he guessed the quarry would make a run for it. Being familiar with the plateau he set a course paralleling the deep canyon to their right and charged across the spacious vista. Somewhere ahead the enemy would be hiding, knowing they had lost the game. Somewhere ahead they would be plotting an ambush, but Trichanantu knew the most likely place for a stand.

When the hunting party reached the crest of the rocky high ground, the tracker called his warriors' to a silent stop. From here on the game would change. The chase had ended and the battle would begin.

The warriors left one of their younger members to watch the horses and slipped silently through the underbrush concealing their approach. Trichanantu sent four of their number to try and sneak up the rock face amid the boulders and scrubby brush while he and three others kept the enemy occupied. Bullets whistled by his head as he fired back. The braves began shouting their war cries and slanderous challenges to the squaws hiding in the rocks, but the enemy was well concealed and shot back with amazing accuracy. Ka-ee-tun-ka was hit in the shoulder, but appeared OK as Trichanantu again fired his carbine at the bobbing head partially exposed above the smooth granite hill. As he went to reload a movement caught his eye distracting him momentarily.

Was someone lurking in the nearby trees and brush? The warrior ducked low and strained to find the enemy. There it was again... a flicker of light distorting the leaves and small branches as if a wind had stirred up a small amount of dust, clouding a patch of brush; but there was no breeze. The mystery had no form at first, just an out of focus space amid the background of green, frozen still amid the scrubs. Trichanantu blinked to clear his vision when the appearance moved. It was ghostly as it drifted with purpose like a haunting shadow floating along the tree line. Then the warrior saw branches part — becoming one with the distortion for but a moment and then snapped back into clarity. Something had passed through that undergrowth and was moving his way. The silhouette suddenly took form to Trichanantu's perception as the phantom had the outline of a man, but this ghost was a giant.

"Demons!" Trichanantu cried out in the Cheyenne language. "We have entered the Kie-tung's domain."

The two warriors close by Trichanantu looked at him questioningly as the young leader fired his rifle at the invisible enemy, but before the bullet could even leave the chamber the giant distortion was on him and the weapon discharged uselessly in the air. "Kie-tung!" he screamed again as he was lifted from the ground and tossed hard against the trunk of a dead tree.

Ka-ee-tun-ka dropped the leather bandage he was trying to tie to his shoulder as he watched in horror as his friend literally flew thirty feet and smashed into the wooden obstruction and fell lifelessly to the earth. Picking up his rifle, he raised it one handed; but silver lightning shot out from the silhouette burning his wrist and breaking the stock of the gun, while knocking the weapon clear.

The third warrior heard the call of "Kie-tung," and saw parts of the conflict through the brush, yet could not see the enemy. Why was Trichanantu calling out the name of demons.

The Kie-tung were a mystic tribe of warriors said to come from the sky. According to Cheyenne and Sioux legend they were cannibals that could transform into any animal of the forest or blend into the surrounding woods like ghosts, waiting to kill all that would enter their realm. And then the brave saw the searing flame strike Ka-ee-tun-ka.

Yelling for the warriors charging the hill to return, he moved in to support his friends, pulling a tomahawk from his belt while yelling his war cry. Bullets tore through the trees around him from those pinned down on the ridge, but he continued his charge toward Trichanantu. Behind he could hear his comrades working their way back for support as he entered the small clearing his fallen companions were in. Trichanantu laid lifeless and Ka-ee-tun-ka was groaning on his side, but the brave saw no enemy. Turning slowly as he looked around, he was grabbed from the back and slammed against a tree. His tomahawk was pulled from his hand as he was struck across the face causing him to drop his rifle. From the ground he looked to his attacker, but could only see a strange distortion of light as he reached for his gun. The brave shook his head when a giant suddenly appeared stepping down on the weapon forcing it from his hand. The warrior knew his death was imminent as he gazed on the stone still features of the demon god before him. The giant held a lance in one hand, his thick black jointed and corded locks hanging stiff around the massive reflective eyes that burned with an inner fire.

The brave tried to crawl away as the giant raised a hand pointing as it spoke, "We have entered the Kie-tung's domain."

The words were Trichanantu's, but an eerie clicking and popping followed the words. The warrior looked in the direction of the creature's indication, the direction from which they had come, but when he turned back to the demon it was gone. From a branch behind, where the monster had been standing a hawk screeched and took flight disappearing into the trees.

The four other warriors entered the clearing, coming to their comrades aid as the young brave scrambled to his feet and cried out, "Kie-tung is here, we must leave."

Trichanantu sat up, still shaken from the impact with the tree, then struggled to his feet. He had been unconscious, but on gaining his equilibrium he ordered the warriors a swift retreat.

Chapter Seventeen

The Long Lost?

Rider's Dispatch

Sir:

The Forks was hit by a war party, about thirty strong; it was a massacre. Casualties totaled Captain Oswalt and company, with civilians including women, children and a sizable body of men. All corpses were mutilated in the worst way. Have dispatched men following renegades and a sizable contingent of remaining forces to occupy post and take care of dead. All provisions either damaged or stolen. Enemy now armed with requisitioned repeaters. Request supplies to rendezvous two days ride north with company at Hollow's to continue pursuit. Awaiting your further orders.

Your obt. Servant

J.R. Erwing

Captain, 27th Cavalry

*   *   *

The company arrived at the forks at first sun. The entrance was open; black birds and ravens covered the grounds revealing a lack of a human presence at the site, or rather — living human presence. The scavengers could be seen feeding on a couple of bodies at the big wood gate left unguarded at the front of the stockade. Zeb immediately took control telling the captain his men would have to make camp outside for a few hours while they learned what they could from the scene. The captain considered the suggestion for a moment and gave the order to make camp.

Dismounting about a half mile from the trading post while the encampment was being established, Zeb, Claude and Titus walked their horses slowly to the fort, watching the ground so as not to disturb any sign that would tell what happened. The birds swarmed around numerous corpses, feasting on the scattered remains; relenting their meal with squawks of complaint as the scouts approached the first dead on their course. Hopping like a wave from the intruders as the men ambled carefully up to the lifeless guards, the birds stayed close protesting the disruption, but refused to leave the banquet area, almost bold in their defiance.

The earth was littered with the small trails of the feathered feeders destroying much of the evidence that would have explained what had happened, but the arrows in the backs of the men by the front door left little doubt as to how the men died. The mutilation of the chest cavities and decapitation was disturbing to Zeb. He knew the birds didn't open the wounds; but only fed after someone had inflicted the savageries to the dead men's upper torsos and the numerous headless corpse reminded him of the massacre of his own parents years earlier.

"Whad ya makes of dat carvin'?" Claude asked scratching his chin. "Awful pekular."

"They opened 'um up after they was dead," Zeb replied over the volume of their audience as Titus contemplated silently what the two bounty hunters were discussing.

"Makin' id easy fer them scav's?" The older man looked at the unwanted feathered guests.

"I don't rightly know," Zeb stood and began walking around the area looking for undisturbed sign — circling the bodies in an ever widening pattern. He found Sioux moccasin prints where he guessed they'd be from where the men had fallen and the depth of the arrows in their targets. What didn't make sense was the imprint of the soldier's rifles dropped by the fort door.

"Zeb,— dakes a gander ad dis." Opposite the Indian's tracks, Claude pointed to the large padded paw of a mountain lion left undisturbed in the soft dirt. "Why'd he'd leave da vittles."

"She was here before they died."

"How ya knows dat?"

"Just a guess." Zeb followed the cat's trail for a short distance; it paralleled two Indian ponies out to the woods. At the entrance Zeb found the same horse prints and the smaller tracks of a woman that walked them through the trading post's gate. "These here's Crow moccasin."

Claude followed his companion around, but wasn't as skilled as Zeb when it came to reading sign, but he could tell by his friends demeanor something was troubling him "Whads ya dinkin'?"

"How many Crows you know, travel with a big cat?"

"Ya dink Ben was here?"

"You know the ones that butchered these men?" Titus interrupted, intrigued by the trackers abilities to read sign, perhaps even better than his own skill.

Zeb's gaze focused on the big black man. "Sioux arrows killed these men: not Crow."

The mountain man then looked off to the trees where the ponies' trail disappeared. "I can't say for sure, but I be willin' to bet good money that these men died chasing after those two Indian ponies. One ridden by a Crow Indian woman the other, a man wearin' Crow moccasins and followed by a large cat. These poor boys here," pointing at the corpses, "got arrows in their backs fer their trouble." Zeb licked his lips then wiped the corners of his mouth with his thumb and index finger while bringing his attention to Claude. "What do you think?"

Claude nodded in approval.

Titus remained silent, but secretly believed the man was probably right.

As they continued the search inside the fort, Zeb was startled to find a dead body deformed down to the bone. It looked inhuman, unlike any he had ever seen before, yet it wore the uniform of a soldier. The skull near the body was elongated grossly as the skin had begun to fall away from the bone. It appeared as if one of the birds had dragged the skull to its present location. From what he could tell it had no injuries, not scalped, as he prodded it to see if all the skin would fall away. Drawing his knife from his boot he tried to cut into the bone of the skull, but his knife had little effect on the hard plating protecting its elongated form. Zeb pulled his short sword taken in a hand-to-hand battle with one of the demon hunters some fifty years earlier. The blade was made of a metal with amazing properties. It held an edge like none other and could cut through almost anything. As he sawed it into the hard shell casing of the brain cavity he found the steel cut through the tough armor with some effort, but the fluid that spilled out of the pocket smoked and bubbled as it hit the moist air.

The men backed away as Zeb's eyes cleared. The brain cavity had drained completely, but the earth still foamed from the fluid. Zeb looked at his short sword and was pleased to find it unharmed by the unusual blood. He wiped it off on the ground and re-sheathed it; taking his other knife from his boot, moved back to the skull. Poking the sharp point into the end of the opened half of the skull, he pick it up and carried it to a horse trough to wash off the unusual find. To his surprise, the body fluid began to boil when it came in contact with the water as the head dropped off his blade onto the ground. The stiletto, shaped blade, thinned from years of sharpening, caused more smoke and simply melted away as he drew back the shortened stub remaining on the hilt.

"What the hell?" Zeb stumbled backward as the acidic fumes teared his eyes and stung his lungs. Dropping to his knees he rubbed his face trying desperately to clear his vision.

"Whad's wrong?" Claude barked, spooked running to his friend's side.

"Feels like I just peeled me a nasty smellin' onion."

Titus watched in amazement as the black ooze seeped into a foaming puddle on the ground feeding the acidic action as it dissolved the soil like a hot coal dropped in a bucket of grease. "That sure would make diggin' fence post holes easier."

Claude settled his hand on Zeb's shoulders to steady him, "Woo,— doggie. Dat's some of da harshest wind I'z ever par dook of's. Whad's ya makes of dat?" Claude laughed in disbelief.

Zeb studied his ruined weapon in awe. "Think what would happen ifin' that critter's blood splattered on ya. Or worse yet, ifin' its innards spilled out on ya."

"I'd reckon it could burn clean though ya ifin' you was wet."

"Think a rattlers bad — I's suspect we should keep our

distance ifin' we's runs into any more of these deformed men." Zeb looked down at the groove cut in the soft dirt where the skull had originally laid. He followed the blood trail where it appeared a raven had dragged the deformed head through the soft soil from the correct corpse, "I think this critter was this man. A sergeant."

Titus scratched his head as he studied these strange clues revealed by his companions: Indian massacre, previous Crow acquaintances of the two men here and these haunting unnatural bodies— the likes of he'd never heard of or seen before; he needed time to think and perhaps gather his thoughts. Moving back to the entrance of the fort he decided to look more closely for anything missed.

Claude's attention was drawn to another body and also left Zeb. The carcass he walked to had also been mutilated and as he squatted, he spotted the ribcage's strange deformation, not cause by the attack of an assailant. The bones were black and spread protruding from the gaping wound in the soldier's chest. Examining closely the remains, sure enough the skin was separating from the skeleton. Claude pulled his knife and prodded the body, but it remained motionless. Re-sheathing his blade the man spotted a track of another visitor that had stopped for a look by this body.

"This is really peculiar," Zeb called out from the other side of the compound.

Claude stood and approached his friend, shaking his attention from his new find. "Whad's dat?"

"You tell me?" Zeb nudged the head of the body with a captain's uniform on: the only victim that had retained its head, but was scalped.

Claude scratched his head, then looked at his friend with real concern, "Waid dill ya see's dis."

Zeb watched questioning after his friend who began walking across the dirt road back to the other corpse, then followed. Claude pointed to the ground as a shocked expression melted over Zeb's features, "We've got's company."

The older man rubbed his chin, with concern, "Ya dink dat varmit did dis and made its look like ah ambush?"

"Did Titus see this?"

"No's he's headed back frond."

Zeb rested his hand on his short sword: his only trophy taken from the mystic god-like demons that hunted these lands fifty years ago. He knew the creatures of legend weren't from around here. They had come from some distance place — hunting... killing , but Zeb had tracked, stalked and observed these unusual visitors and learned much of their behavior. "It's not this one's way," was his simple reply. He then knelt down lightly touching the print: distorted from the trails of many small feathered scavengers. "This is a very fresh print."

"Dat buzzards probable gawkin' ad us rid now."

Zeb scanned his surroundings then found the rest of the trail. Not full prints: a heel mark here, a faint claw there. Most men would have missed these insignificant little details, but Zeb was too in-tune with his surroundings. He could read the story played out in the trail as easy as we might read a page in a book. To him the sign was a book and he could read it all — as he studied the atlas following its course and applying his experience to the map. The demon had taken note of all the victims. Six bodies in total had the telltale signs of a transformation, but the demon simply observed the dead and moved on. Zeb followed the creatures trail throughout the compound as Claude followed close behind, but Zeb paid little attention to his friend until they came again to the entrance of the post. "He was just like us,— passin' through fer a look-see."

"Why?"

"Curiosity?" Zeb recognized the direction the creature took from the front of the fort: ignoring all the possible game that had traveled different directions from the post and the sport it offered, the Demon moved north. "His next victim... or perhaps just in a hurry to get somewhere else."

Claude noticed Titus mulling around the trees beside the fort: searching, but averted back to Zeb. "We need us a meedin' with dat Captain. Gots ta warns Ben,— and mazbe..." His eyes squinted as he peered at the big black man and pointed with a thumb, "and have a talks with da new scout dare. Dink he'll be believing'?"

"We won't find Ben. Trails too cold and he would of made it hard to follow anyway. I don't think it'ull do any good to go about bringin' up Broken-Toe either. No-body's to believin' us anyhow. Spittin' noise about Indian's myths will just label us as loonies,— but that war party. We do need a talk with that Cap about them." Zeb glanced over at Titus, watching him check out the outside grounds to the west of the gate. "He seems capable enough. Let's hint around about some Indian hoopla and see how he responds."

Claude nodded, with a smile. "Just like da good old days,— singin' and servin' da mindless milidary."

*　　*　　*

Captain Erwing entered the post's officer's quarters followed by a lieutenant, Sergeant Lloyd and the scouts. The minimal amount of furnishings were in disarray with papers containing mundane records of the post flung haphazardly about the floor. The captain grunted in disgust as the men righted a simple desk and chairs.

Sergeant Lloyd picked up a few of the sheets and scratched his head, "What interest does some Injuns have with meaningless files?"

"More pleasant than leaves on the back side," Zeb snickered, as the sergeant stacked them on a corner of the desk with a frown.

Claude smiled, "I'd use a fer number of 'em if ya poind me tda latrine."

Titus started, "Oh it's behind..."

The captain rested both hands on the makeshift desk and interrupted in a commanding voice, "Gentlemen, we have business to attend to... if you don't mind."

"Sir!" The sergeant snapped back to the front of the desk in line with the scouts as the lieutenant stood at ease against the side wall.

Claude whispered to Zeb, "I'z was dalkin' business," as the younger man tried to suppress his smile.

"I don't think this is funny. We have over forty butchered. What can you tell me?"

"Sioux and I suspect Cheyenne hit the post shortly after dark," Zeb was the first to answer. "I would guess about thirty braves. After they finished here, eight headed southeast toward the river and the remaining moved northwest."

"Sergeant," the Captain's level gaze switched focus. "Was the deserter's... Clintlock? Was his body among the deceased?"

"No Sir, but there did appear to be a jail break last night."

"Could the Indians have been here to free the prisoner?"

Titus chimed in, "Sir, I don't think the prisoner was the scout."

"Why is that Sergeant?"

Titus was surprised the captain referred to him by his old rank. He had served as a sergeant under the captain when the officer was but a lieutenant with the 10th Cavalry. Most of the white officers deplored the command over a black unit, but the fact that Captain Erwing remembered him by rank and showed him a measure of respect, spoke well of the man in the scout's eyes. "Seven military shod horses left here about two days ago. Six of them returned late yesterday. I believe the seventh was the scout. It didn't return with them,— Sir."

"Do we have any idea who was in the stockade?"

Titus looked at Zeb and Claude, but the two bounty hunters remained silent. He wondered why they were quiet about the Crows that had been present at the gate the previous night, but decided to leave the matter with them.

But the captain noticed the black scouts query, "Mr. Titus do you have something to add?"

"No sir."

"Gentlemen are we holding something back?" The captain's icy stare locked on the two bounty hunters.

Claude averted his eyes meandering around the room, but Zeb took the officer's peering command without a waver. He pondered the consequences and guessed that somewhere in that stack of papers would be the record, or a log detailing the imprisonment; but names might not have been gathered. He decided to drop what was minimal and leave it at that. "Two Crow appear to have left the post before the attack."

"Crow?" The captain began to pace for a moment thinking. "Could the Indians have come to free the Crows?"

"Sir." Titus intervened, "They left before the attack. Probably came for whisky and had a little too much and then were released."

The captain sat down in his chair, considering all that had been reported. It was obvious these men were extremely capable at reading sign. Perhaps some of the best he had ever had contact with. They would prove very useful if they could be trusted. "Gentlemen, reports have been growing regarding a renegade some are calling The Seer. Some kind of Cheyenne War Medicine Man with a growing reputation among the Sioux and Cheyenne tribes. Hostilities have increased as of late and I believe if left unchecked we could have a major Indian uprising if we're not careful. Have any of you heard talk?"

"The Indian attacks are no secret to any of the settlements, or settlers, Captain." Zeb's matter of fact answer was not what the officer was looking for.

"Right..., but have any of you heard about this Seer?"

Sergeant Lloyd cleared his throat and filled his lungs.

"Yes Sergeant?"

"Sir, talk is he's some kind of prophet. Sees the future and such."

"Thank you Sergeant. I believe this Seer was the culprit in last nights attack." His voice, a measure of confidence,— softened. "Do you think with enough men, you could follow their trail and catch these renegades before they kill again?" The captain never wavered as he watched the two bounty hunters carefully, to render judgment on their response.

Claude muttered quietly as Zeb answered, "We can follow the trail, but it might take some time to catch them."

The older man whispered, "We'rn lookin' fer dis job here."

"Shi..." Zeb quipped back.

"Is there a problem?"

Claude could no longer keep quiet, "We's hired fer some deserder,— no Injuns."

"Well,— I need your help. These renegades must be stopped."

Sergeant Lloyd asked, "Sir, what about the deserter? It's bad for the men ifin' we let him go."

"I could track him down Sir," Titus said stepping forward.

The captain was silent for a moment then stood, "Very well, Titus, good luck, you're dismissed."

"Yes Sir," the scout saluted and left.

"Lieutenant, take the sergeant and get a detachment ready to go after the renegades.— You men," the captain's clear command and his affirming gaze returned to the two bounty hunters, "will accompany our troops and track down these renegades. No mistakes gentlemen, I want these hostiles captured:— Dismissed."

The soldiers saluted turning to leave as Claude scratched his head and gave Zeb a look to kill. Zeb humbly shook his head no as the men then quietly moved to the door.

"Damn military,— always changin' da rules," Claude

muttered as they left the office.

*   *   *

Chapter Eighteen

Kidnapped

"If an injury has to be done to a man

it should be so severe

that his vengeance not be feared."

Niccolo Machiavelli (1469 - 1527)

*   *   *

The scar-faced southern captain pulled up just short of the town, stopping his men after successfully losing the cavalry's pursuit. His cursing was directed at no one in particular as he swore at their bad luck. "Where's Benny?" he barked in his raspy voice after looking over his troops now numbering eleven. Benny and five others had been out scouting the area when they first hit the sheriff's office, but now he was missing.

"Them's bastards done dropped him at that Cradle Cap."

"Just like the Union to step in where they're not wanted and kill good boys."

"What do we do now Cap?"

"We get even."

"Cap," spoke up Johnny, his wild eyes flashing in the bright light of the moon. "From the window I heard them two bounties talkin' about one of them whores.— Robin they said. She's some relation."

The older man paused, pondering the revelation; his wrinkled and scarred features twisting at the plan formulating in his mind. "Well then, maybe we'll pay this whore a visit," he whispered, but the deep grating coo perked the southerners as laughing gripped his men.

* * *

Morning found six homeless women of pleasure wrapped in blankets and sitting around a potbelly stove warming the airy interior, rank with the smell of whiskey and tobacco smoke. No other patrons were present as the burly owner poured coffee for the ladies and tried to cheer their dampened spirits. Women were not usually allowed through the doors of the saloon, but the cavalry officer in charge ordered the accommodations be made available. Mr. Huskin, the owner, at first outraged by the intrusion, softened as his keen business sense and entrepreneurial spirit pondered the prospect of a new arrangement for his enterprise. 'With the madam Inez gone and the Cradle in ashes, his rooms upstairs could do no more than just house these fine women. After all — the army officer said he was to care for these ladies needs, but if he made a little money on the side while fulfilling his obligation — what was the harm?'

The owner's hairless dome turned a shade rosier as he

poured a second cup to a young thankful recipient, whose soft smile tantalized him even though her face was blackened with ash and her hair was tossed about in a most disheveled, un-kempt way. Her dainty white arm slipped out from under the heavy wool army blanket as she touched the mug to her lips, but her eyes never wavered in her hypnotic stare. Feminine wiles played her will upon most men she encountered and Daisy was a master at enticement. The blue cuff of an extra large cavalry blouse dropped through the folds of her blanket as her grip with the opposite hand on the covering slackened revealing the unbuttoned shirt and pale white skin of her scantily clothed, shapely figure.

Mr. Huskin's attention was drawn to the alluring partial exposure. He knew that money would have to be spent to lavish this young flower. After all — better attire would be required to present the right image to his patrons. "I was thinking..." The bald man said as he turned his attention to another of the ladies who extended her mug for a refill. "With Inez's passing and the Cradle gone you all might be needing a place to continue your work." A sheepish smile cracked his lips as all eyes in the room focused on his offer and he saw not one objection to his suggestion. This was going to be easier than he thought. "You need a place — and I'm sure I'll have willing patrons. Why don't we pool our resources? I think we could all prosper." His last expression almost echoed as the glint in his eye beamed from success.

A couple of the women were giggling as the man continued to lay out his thoughts on the partnership, of which he would be taking the lions share among other privileges, when the doors to the saloon opened and a number of trail beatened roughnecks entered disrupting the informal business meeting. Mr. Haskin, angered by the disturbance and distraction called out to the unwanted guests, "We're not open," but a pistol shot catching him in the left shoulder and pitching him to the ground said different. Daisy and Robin dropped their blankets and jumped to the bartender's aid as several of the others screamed and scrambled to their feet.

The men quickly circled the room blocking any exit as a man with a scarlet scar down his cheek, still holding his smoking pistol, stepped in close to the scared women. His deep raspy voice, that added a measure of fear and an image of hate to the coarse man's persona, stilled the room as his guttural question, almost whispered, transfixed the helpless. "Which one of you is Robin?"

No one responded. The abrasive man re-cocked his pistol and aimed it at the wounded man on the floor. "Must I kill this man?"

Daisy, dressed only in the partially buttoned cavalry blouse was kneeling next to the bartender, holding him across her lap. She tried to shield him as Robin stood, blocking the intention. "What do you men want?"

The pistol pulled back. "Are you Robin?" Jeered the evil man, his grating tone strangely soothing.

The young woman nodded, "What do you want?"

"Revenge."

Two of the men stepped forward grabbing the defenders, dragging them aside as the wounded man dropped back to the floor with a thud and a groan. The deafening 45 caliber handgun pumped another ball into the bartender's chest.

"You bastard!" Robin screamed as she pulled at her captor, but the heavy hand of the scar faced man struck her, knocking her to the ground.

"Shut up woman,— or you're next."

"You bastard," she repeated from her knees as she rubbed her hand across the corner of her mouth. Blood smeared the back side of her palm, but she paid it little heed.

"Cap," Johnny said as Daisy struggled. "What we going to do with the rest of these girls?" The wild eyed man wrapped one arm around the woman's waist he was contending with and grabbed her throat with the other. "Stop struggling or I'll kill you right now."

Daisy was able to turn her head slightly in the new grip and spat in the man's face. Johnny let go of her waist and struck her with a closed left fist. Dazed the woman fell, sprawled out over the dying bartender as the enraged man drew his pistol. To his embarrassment his companions were laughing as the scar faced man stayed Johnny's hand.

"Tie them up. We're taking them with."

Robin again stood protesting, "You came for me. You don't need them."

The captain raised his armed hand to pistol whip the woman, but Robin's defiant unyielding stance glimmered without fear to the man's threat of force. For some reason the scar down his cheek turned a deeper shade of crimson, but he stopped short of striking her. "I need you, but my men will have use of your friends."

The men laughed with glee as they secured their hostages.

137

Chapter Nineteen

Loner

Excerpts of a scout's log

Nov. 1871

Twenty years ago my friend and mentor told me a strange tale of magical creatures that roamed the world hunting men. Written off as myth I laughed at the story sworn as truth and chose to ignore the warnings that one day they would return. With his passing so I thought the legend would die until the glossy black beast that now haunts my dreams sprung from the realms below. Savage and dark the giant now chases my soul, seizing my unrest and consuming my will. When doubt gives way and reality takes hold the last words of his tale echoes in a plea as sincere as his petition.

YOU MUST STOP THEM!

*　　　*　　　*

Dusk seemed early as the young scout walked his mount down a narrow valley lined with pines. The cold night air whisked at his back and bit at his cheeks as the man lifted the collar of his black leather riding coat to block the wind. Like a shadow, the man blended into his surroundings almost invisible in the gloomy woodland,— resisting the soft light of the fading sunset. Titus had taken to the trees following the same course the scout Jake had traversed four days earlier, and although the trail was cold the newly recruited soldier had little trouble tracking the man who had taken no precautions avoiding pursuit. What did surprise Titus was the fresher trail he happened on where Jake had circled back over his old trail and then moved north. Titus was now two days closer to his quarry and hoping to catch the man soon.

What a strange turn of events, the young man thought to himself as he eased Sam down the steep incline. Working for the military, even though it was a temporary assignment, wasn't where Titus wanted to be: his mine was resting un-worked, his deputy friend killed by the very men that had stolen his horse (Sam) two days earlier, Indian hostilities had increased to the point of a massacre, and somehow he had been sucked back in with the cavalry tracking an deserter due to the pleadings of a friendly sergeant. Meanwhile the very men that had killed Blake were roaming about free and unmolested. Life somehow never seemed fair.

As the young man reached the bottom of the ridge he heard yelling and what sounded like a woman's scream to his right. Silently he slipped off Sam pulling his rifle from its boot. "You stay here," he whispered, patting his animal gentle on the neck. Dropping the reins Titus moved off quietly toward the commotion. Like a specter, the young man melted into the trees along the break in the valley floor that was devoid of foliage. The basin appeared to be a well traveled trail and Titus worked the tree line following its course. Patches of snow dotted the landscape and as the scout passed a narrowing channel he noticed the fresh print of a wagon amid the newly formed slush the wheels had caused. Titus paused and focused his attention up the mountain road. He could hear voices ahead and pinpointing their location he crept silently to a better vantage point.

Twelve men were standing about a wagon with a busted axle as two of their number were busy with repairs. The scout knew one of the men from the horse theft encounter a couple days earlier when he recovered Sam with the help of the two bounty hunters.

Five women sat huddled in blankets under guard nearby the wreck; but one woman, very scantily dressed considering the weather, and apparently having resisted the advances of her captors, was being dragged forcibly back to her companions. Titus recognized the woman. She was from The Cradle and it didn't appear she was under new employ by her own choosing. Titus had never frequented the house. As a black man to be seen with a white woman, even a prostitute, could bring a neck stretching by some unscrupulous men; but the scout had seen these women around town and had heard talk.

Titus couldn't understand why women for hire would be taken against their will into the wilderness when for the right price they would have probably gone by choice. *Why would men kidnap these ladies?* Titus considered the odds — Twelve-to-one, *not too favorable.* Help was at least a days ride. He was under orders right now. *What about the deserter Jake?* That mission seemed secondary now. *These men were tied to the murder of the sheriff and Blake,— horse thieves,— kidnappers,— these were dangerous men.* Titus decided the Captain would understand a slight detour. *Besides the Captain had seen to the safety of these women before we left town. Surely the welfare of civilians would come first.*

Titus hid quiet and watched the men repair the wagon for several hours. Just before they were done the party began preparing camp for the night. With the advent of holding up for the evening, the scout slipped away to recover his horse and rest until morning. The trail would be easy to follow tomorrow since the wagon would have to stick to the mountain road so Titus had little fear of losing his quarry.

Before dawn Titus was up again trailing the men to a high mountain path that dropped into a deep canyon. From overhead the scout could see the large encampment that appeared to be the extension of an immense mining operation. The women were nowhere to be seen, but Titus was sure they were being held probably somewhere within the mine. After a thorough study of the minimal defenses the man considered his options: town was more than a days ride and he doubted that anyone there would offer assistance anyway, The Forks although closer was still a full day's ride and because of the recent massacre and small contingent there he doubted the captain would be able to offer any help either; but

Zeb and Claude were scouting the area, looking for the renegades, southwest of his current position. He figured he could find them by midafternoon. Captain Erwing had dispatched a letter requesting troops and supplies to rendezvous at Hollow's: that's where he'd find the help he needed the quickest. Careful to avoid detection Titus backed away from the top of the canyon and moved quietly into the cover of the rocky terrain. The scout had deduced the men from the mining operation had a military background from his run in when Sam was stolen. He guessed there was a high probability of patrols or maybe even a few scouts so Titus used the natural cover afforded by the brush filled hilly landscape. He had come to the mine following the well worn valley trail, but decided it would be too dangerous to retrace his steps over the steep canyon ridges so close to that busy wagon path. Moving in a northwesterly line he pushed through the harsh country finally coming to a heavily wooded hillside circling the rough and rocky mountainous area. Traveling became easier as the pine trees were big enough to prevent the heavy growth of underbrush and the soft blanket of needles cushioned each footfall of Sam's shod hoofs. Outcroppings of rock in random patterns prevented Titus from holding a straight path down the gradual slope, but the scout weaved through the unmarked trail blazing his course without map or compass.

The leisure gait of Sam was suddenly interrupted as the horse froze with its ears alert to danger ahead.

"What is it boy?" Titus whispered patting the animals neck and leaning low trying to see what had spooked his horse.

Sam nickered and started to backup, but Titus used soothing words, holding his animal in place, while he stared through the grove of pines that appeared void of any threat. A slight breeze picked up as the icy wind carried with it a pungent odor unfamiliar to the man, but the smell of rotting flesh mixed with it was unmistakable. Although little snow had fallen this year the temperature had been below freezing for days. Titus wondered how something dead in this cold could smell so bad. "Feewooo...I agree Sam. That's some nasty wind." It was difficult, but the scout got his horse to continue down the hill approaching a large rocky outcropping. The smell was stronger and as the man came around a bend he spotted a cave mouth hidden among the boulders. Sam would go no closer so Titus dismounted dropping his reins and moved toward the opening covering his mouth with a scarf. The odor was almost acidic emanating from the tunnel as the man entered the dark entrance. It took his eyes a minute to adjust as he worked his way deeper into the confines of the cavern which was much warmer than the temperature outside. Stumbling over something, Titus knelt recognizing the source of the pungent aroma. A pile of rotting flesh and organs laid blocking his path. Examining the find, the skin of a man, mangled and rendered, was sprawled out on the floor. The face, with eyes still in place, rested blankly like a mask discarded after a costume ball. A massive chest wound appeared to be the cause of death, or perhaps some animal fed on the remains. But not one bone was in the grotesque dump.

Titus noticed and picked up the dead man's rifle lying nearby, then grabbed the man's limp arm and began pulling the body back to the opening of the cave. From the markings on the repeater and the description of the scout, Jake, Titus guessed he had found the deserter. What he didn't understand was the skin, muscle, and organs, minus the skeleton. The way the ribs had been pushed through the skin it appeared the bones had exploded away from all tissue,— *or literally walked out of the skin.* Titus remembered the strange bone deformations in the chest cavities of some of the men butchered at The Forks.

Could this man have been infected also and then escaped? Titus' eyes watered as he tried to wipe the tearing away. The strong acidic smell was beginning to overpower him. He backed away from the body concentrating his attention on the cave. *Could the strange disease be hiding in there?* Titus pulled the dead man's coat free of the nasty pile and cut off a sleeve. Wrapping the leather around a stick he moved over to Sam.

The horse was agitated, but remained standing as Titus secured the scout's rifle to his saddle and retrieved some oil from his saddlebags, dousing the makeshift torch. Lighting the end he reentered the cave and ventured to where he had found the body. In the soft dirt of the cavern floor he spotted the trail of a bony foot. "Damn," he mumbled in amazement. He started to follow the sign when a noise distracted him from deeper in the recess of the dark haunts; an eerie, shrill cry,— unlike anything he had ever heard before.

Titus pulled his pistol and started moving back out of the cave. Whatever was down there didn't sound small. He heard a shuffling sound of many feet as he stumbled dropping the torch. As he fumbled for the light a black ball with wings landed on a rock nearby. Titus shot the creature as it screeched jumping at him. The thick tar blood splattered on the wall behind and smoked as it began to congeal back together. "What the hell?" The scout blurted out as he scrambled to his feet. A second bird like creature darted out of the depths of the dark tunnel and Titus turned and ran. Looking back the creature was chasing him. Titus spun and fired his pistol again. The small beast flew backwards at the impact and withered in the soft wet soil, sizzling in a pool of mud and its own body fluid. Titus was shaken. "What the hell are you?" He cried out.

The shrill cry trumped again, this time closer from somewhere deep in the tunnel. Titus left the cavern and ran to Sam. The horse was spooked and it took the scout a moment to get into the saddle, but as he reined the animal around for one last look at the cave a giant emerged from the opening. Glossy black limbs seemed to reflect the light of day as the creature lifted its large domed head and screamed. Titus didn't even have to spur Sam as his horse bolted down the pine covered hillside. Branches raked the man's face and slapped his coat as he hung on to his frantic animal. Behind the trumpeting call and crashing sound of the monster revealed the worst; Titus feared Sam would not be able to outrun this enemy.

Chapter Twenty

Unexpected Welcome

$1000 REWARD
Wanted Dead or Alive!
Arthur McCray

For the murder of a US marshal and his deputy. Last seen in the Dakota territory. McCray is about fifty and carries a scar down his left cheek. Goes by Captain and wears confederate gray, although there is no confirmation he served as a legitimate soldier during the war. This paper is offering in addition to the foregoing—$200 for the capture of this dangerous man.

News excerpts

*   *   *

Midmorning found Reuben and Isaac scanning a snow laden valley void of trees. Past experience with creatures like Broken-Toe left Isaac with doubt about crossing the barren landscape ahead.

"Uncle there are at least thirty of us. Surely this critter would think twice about attacking us. After all — he's wounded."

Isaac shook his head, then rubbed his right hand over his forehead and down the side of his face. "You don't understand this creature. If it wants to hide — you won't find it. If he sees us following; it will melt into the woods without a trace." The blonde studied his younger counterpart with concern. "It can transform — turn invisible in a blink. This creature could take us down one-by-one and we won't even see him coming." Isaac rested his hand on Reuben's shoulder as his tone transferred to compassion: almost pleading, "Surprise is the only tool we have fighting this enemy."

"What would you have us do?" Reuben's face wrinkled with doubt. "Turn around with our tail between our legs?" The young man paused with intensity of eye. "Uncle, you are one of the bravest men I have ever met. I've never seen you like this." Reuben was almost yelling in his excited frame of mind, "This critter has a good eight hour lead on us. We've closed the gap by only an hour. We need! — to get across this clearing quickly and move on."

"He could be waiting — resting on that side," Isaac pointed across the clearing, shaking his hand, but was interrupted.

"This creature has been on a course with purpose. I assure you we need not waste time: trust me." Reuben smiled, patting Isaac's hand gripping his shoulder as he calmed himself down. "If we want to catch this creature, we need to move... now."

Isaac's concern didn't diminish, but he acquiesced to his close friend with a final plea that availed nothing. The party then mounted up and moved over the clearing swiftly, continuing pursuit without delay. Reuben smiled at his uncle as they reached the relative safety of the forest, but Isaac sullenly ignored the gesture, knowing his friend's zeal for this quest was suppressing his better judgment. Luck was a temptress that Isaac had learned from experience was fickle at best. Better to play your cards with experience than hope when dealing with life's strange twists. The golden haired mountain man knew this was an ill-fated journey. Every fiber in his soul was telling him to stop. Disaster lay ahead if they continued and none but Isaac understood what was at stake, but the entire party seemed intent on finding this demon.

"Reuben... what do you plan to do once we catch this creature?"

The young looking Crow chuckled, "There's thirty of us Uncle."

"Don't underestimate this critter."

"I'm not." Reuben suddenly turned very serious. "As we close the distance we'll get a feel for how best to trap him. Don't worry Uncle,— when the time comes the ambush will present itself."

"You got that right," Isaac smirked.

Reuben caught the sarcasm and shook his head. "Uncle if you don't wish to continue, return to your wife. I understand. You've had your shot at these creatures," the younger man locked eyes with his companion's. "It's my turn now."

Isaac thought hard about the young man's demeanor. He couldn't abandon his friend. They had been through too much together. The blonde sighed and resigned himself to the fact Reuben's mind was set. Looking up the trail he contemplated what the future would bring.

The other warriors listening to the continuing banter of Golden Hair and his Crow brother heightened their curiosity. The thrill of finding proof of such a being was there imprinted in the trail they followed. The large foot with talons that seemed to grip the earth with each passing stride. A monster that towered over a man and lived to kill was somewhere ahead, wounded and traveling alone. To be a part of the hunt to catch and slaughter one of the hard shells touched the fantasies of superstition and the glory of such a quest in each one of the braves that followed the tracker, Reuben. Few were the men that could dream of such an honor or challenge, and now they found themselves on the trail of such a beast... ready to kill or be killed.

Legends of the past, deemed not much more than myths, glorified warriors that hunted down and slayed such demons: *"The Haunting Ghosts of the Woods that delivered death to all that crossed their path."* Such stories were vivid in the minds of each man. The strange tribe of giants were no fiction; the tracks they followed laid to rest any doubt. Therefore, all the tales of the past were true. Each story carried with it the hint of big magic and the prestige that would pass to any warrior that was party to bringing one of the War Gods down. All had heard the legends, recounted numerous times, down through generations of Sioux. The magical beings traveling the land hunting and murdering men of valor in their wake. What glory awaited them? What honor was in store?

As the party traveled they came across a river near a familiar white man's trading post. They crossed the ice water swiftly taking note that the creature's trail did not deviate from its course. Sifting through the trees that stood like a tangled wall the warriors pushed through the underbrush and in moments broke into a large clearing before the tall stockade that fortressed a white settlement. The young Crow warrior stopped following the faint trail that looked to continue right up to the double doors of the post. Reuben held up his hand to stop his companions and turned to Isaac. "Uncle... why would that critter walk right up to the front opening of a human settlement?"

Isaac rubbed his face, then shook his head, "Don't know... but it would have been night, right?"

"Yes."

"Probably doin' a check-it-out thing."

"Wouldn't the guards have seen him?"

"Nobody would have seen him if he didn't want to be seen."

"Oh yeh.— It's invisible."

Reuben's words carried a note of sarcasm that Isaac for the first time realized meant the younger man didn't totally believe the stories surrounding these creatures. "That's right... It can turn invisible. And..." Isaac never finished his sentence. The sound of gunfire ripped through the still morning air as two of their number dropped from the saddle never to stir again.

"Hostiles!" Came the repeated cry from behind the walls of the fort. More shots whistled through the air and cut the trees and branches behind the party. Chaos scattered the Sioux into the cover of the woods as a hail of bullets cracked the brush and shattered limbs following the retreat.

"Uncle!" Reuben barked, almost thrown from his horse as the animal pitched; a bullet winging the animal's mane, tearing the flesh just above the withers and another shattering a neck vertebra a little further up. Reuben slipped his stirrup easily as the animal hit the dirt, simultaneously pulling his rifle from its boot as he dropped the reins, straddling his fallen ride. "What's happening?" He shouted cocking his weapon in defiance of the attack while watching the big doors of the stockade swing open. Several more bullets popped into the carcass of his dead animal before Reuben spotted a detachment of his enemies riding out of the fort. "Why are they shooting at us?"

Isaac was busy reining his startled horse into a small circle trying desperately to regain control of his spooked animal, then spurred his mount to save his friend. Extending his arm as his animal jumped the lifeless form, Reuben turned and pushing off the belly of his horse with his left foot, took hold of the offer with his free hand and spun into the saddle behind his companion with the momentum gained in the action. Isaac's large mare, with minor hesitation, took flight over a smattering of heavy brush, but both men appeared as one with the horse as it disappeared among the heavily wooded tree line as a bugle behind echoed the call to arms.

"What did we do?" Reuben cried out, looking behind. "I had just traded there last week without a hitch!"

"They've confused us with a recent problem,— apparently."

"Do we shoot back?"

"I think that would just add to the problem. We need to straighten this out quickly."

"How do we go about doing that with a trigger happy army shooting our tails?"

Branches wiped Isaac's face, one almost knocking him from the saddle as his animal pushed on through the heavy brush. The horse then jumped a small ravine and charged into a thicket in their path and down into the icy water of the river. Ahead the Sioux had converged in the small clearing ready to mount an offensive. Most with bow, they sounded their war cries building courage for the coming battle. Isaac knew the cavalry armed with rifles and sabers would make short work of any offensive. "My brother's — we must scatter!" He called out in the Sioux language. "We must divide their forces and fight them in the trees. Not in the open!" But his call fell on deaf ears. Charging his mount right through the middle of their line breaking up their numbers, he continued, "Scatter... take them in the trees." Isaac never slowed his steed, his course continuing past his companions and into the trees beyond. Several warriors disrupted in his passing took up pursuit as others now hesitant on what action to take watched their friends leaving the battle line.

The sound of the cavalry pushing through the brush ready to converge on the warriors reduced numbers and the retreat behind triggered the last of the defiant to turn on their heels for the woods to the rear. Taking Isaac's advice they scattered, changing the direct confrontation and advantage of the military approach to war to one of chase and ambush — a form perfected by the Indians and more suited to the weaponry they carried.

Isaac and Reuben came out of the woods with five other warriors close behind. They heard gunshots to their left so changed course to the right, out across the meadow and up a sharp ridge. A portion of the detachment broke through the tree line behind in hot pursuit; the bugle still sounding the call to arms. A heavily wooded ravine carved down the face of the ridge parted the incline as Isaac charged his steed into the canyon, disappearing from the view of the gaining military. The rock wash forked; Isaac took the left wing which angled back toward the pursuit: viewed by him as the less likely path of escape. The gravel bottom of the wash left no trail and the small party quickly melted into the cover afforded by the brush and trees. The cavalry hit the fork a few minuets later, but mistakenly took the more obvious course of escape, losing their quarry.

Chapter Twenty-one

The Drone

The Merging

The shadow sat upon its perch unmoving

The danger of the beings before it caused pause

For a good deal of time the black creature was moving

The leather eggs that it held to keep them from harm

Indian song: Excerpts

*   *   *

The silhouette moved through the darkness of the forest like it was the night itself; its black body nothing but a shadow amidst many. It drove itself through the trees toward a distant target. Nothing would stop it; nothing could distract it from its goal. The moon's light blocked by a distant summit proved no hindrance to the sightless creature. It knew where to go without eyes. Guided by a sense we couldn't begin to understand; it slipped through the night in this alien world bound to The Call sung like music directing its steps. A type of radar passed images of its surroundings to its head but The Call echoed and beckoned it forward through the woods. This trek it did not understand nor did it have the ability to comprehend. Driven by an inner force greater than instinct,— greater than reason: in the deeper recesses of thought the creature was commanded what to do,— what to think.

Its chief purpose was survival. Not survival of self, but survival of the hive and most importantly a queen. Although not born of her embryos, it could feel her growing presence on this foreign world. Linked by a mental connection the drone would change. Without descent from royalty of its own presence, The Call would bring about transformation, a mutation. The synaptic bond would grow and its DNA would alter; it would become part of her. Like an extension, a mindless appendage directed by nerves stimulated by the center. The adoption would be complete, and the drone would come to serve. Its life unquestionably to act. Bound to its new queen it would live for the hive; live for its queen. And so it continued on its journey, silently plodding along on its quest. Toting the gelatinous shells of the unborn in its clutches. Bringing abandoned orphans to their new nest.

Two drones had sprung from the carnage of the downed ship. Wounded pirates dying in the wake of the crash had hosted their beginning, but the remaining larvae were in danger. They needed the protection of the mother. The younger of the drones stayed behind to guard the clutch while the firstborn began the migration. The queen mother while still small had commanded it, and the children could not resist. Already the drone had made the trip once, but its entry to the nursery was hindered. A viable host had entered the hive's opening on its first run, but the prey had escaped easily with the aid of another large animal. With the firstborn not yet fully grown and the remaining eggs still hours away, the queen did not wish pursuit but now the task was nearly complete. One more trip, and the remaining embryos would be safe. Down into the cavern it followed the twisting path. Through the silent maze it carried out its task. The nursery was nearing completion. The firstborn deposited its clutch amid the growing numbers of clustered young spilling from the queen hump. Sorting the harvest the firstborn moved the stores about the chamber; then, molted its exoskeleton and added it to the structure housing the children. Tirelessly it worked at the behest of the mother. Endlessly it would slave never questioning the demands willed by the mind. Never doubting the direction of The Call. Suddenly the creature stopped its work. In its pause it scanned the room then disappeared down a dark corridor.

Danger, — this was the gist of the message but the danger was not to self. Deep within the cavern life-forms were detected: the synaptic signals of energy, the warm presence of hosts. Quietly the creature moved, melting into the black recesses of the hidden maze. To gather now The Call.

*   *   *

"Get the hell away from me with that pick you idiot!" Yelled the rotund man as he wiped sweat from his brow; but the dirty, and tattered sleeve covering a massive forearm served little aid to relief.

"I'm sorry Frankie," cried the thin rail in fear of retribution.

"Damnation Kenny, you nick me one more time and I'll bury this in yer head," Frankie barked waving his own ax in a fearful act of aggression.

"I,—I tripped," stuttered the thin man as he backed away stumbling over a pile of rock and debris landing hard on his backside; the handle of his pick-ax catching him across the face.

The rotund man chuckled at the thin man's misfortune. "Serves ya right ya dangerous pup."

Kenny scrambled to his feet; then, paused rubbing his forehead. A knot was already lifting as he felt the injury. "It's not funny!" He winced then spotting an opening in the wall that wasn't present prior to his last swing. Picking up his dropped ax the thin man moved to the large hole peering into the darkness beyond. "Hey Frankie, look at this."

The heavyset man pushed his companion out of the way for

a look. Nothing could be determined about the opening as Frankie stepped away pointing to an oil lantern pegged to the dirt wall a few paces away. "Get me that lamp," barked the round man as he knocked the little guy in the direction of the light.

Kenny obeyed without question, handing the lantern over as he tried to get a better look. "What do you think we've found?"

Frankie climbed into the opening; his rotund shape filling the space and blocking the lamplight, leaving Kenny in the dark.

"What is it?" The thin man asked excitedly, but was either ignored or not heard. Kenny stepped closer pulling himself up by means of a massive leg extending from the fissure ready to follow Frankie through the opening when to the thin man's surprise the rotund form filling the gap shot through the opening like he was pulled. "Frankie?" The dim light of the lantern lit the opening, but Kenny's large companion didn't respond. The thin man peered in through the small passageway when steely fingers latched onto his arm pulling him into the opening. Kenny froze in fear at the black glossy features of the fanged monster holding him. Salivating fluid drooled around the snarling canines as the monster's grip tightened. Empty eye sockets of a grotesque deformed skull dragged him closer as the ghostly beast's jaw rippled toward Kenny's face. The man screamed, but the sound was cut short as darkness blanketed the tunnel.

Chapter Twenty-two

Armed for the Hunt

12 April, 1842

Untitled

Legends speak of a mystic race
that died out long ago
Of giants that hunt and cannibals that ruled
whose ghosts still roam alone
They walk the earth in search of souls
gathering to fill a need
The tales they speak and whisper at night
do frighten their youth's before sleep.

Trapper's Poem

*   *   *

Ben watched the enemy retreat, questioningly. "What's in the hell got into them?"

Aiyana popped up over her cover and saw the warriors running back to the trees. "Think they're regrouping?"

"No reason to. They had us."

Both stood slowly, still staying well hidden to get a better look. The four warriors that were charging the hill disappeared in the brush and thick smattering of trees. An unnatural silence fell over the woods as the two strained to see what was happening. "You think they're trying to draw us out?"

"Don't make no sense," Ben muttered as he studied the encampment below. After several minutes the tracking party departed, making a speedy retreat back across the mountain plateau. "Why would a war party dog us all night and then just leave?"

Missy growled as a heavy thud sounded within the natural rock fortress. Ben and Aiyana spun around coming face-to-face with a giant Sky Demon in full armor. Ben raised his rifle in defense, but had to step back in order for the barrel to have space between him and his new antagonist.

"Wait!" Aiyana cried out placing her hand on Ben's arm to stop him. "He's not here as an enemy."

Missy paced, skirting the fortress of rock, obviously upset at the present company.

Ben pulled his arm free, poised and ready to kill the giant before him, but the creature stood as if frozen in time. "What are you talking about... this critter 'ull peel us just as to look at us."

"No, — no... He's here to help," Aiyana yelled, re-grabbing Ben's knife arm. "My father spoke of his return. I've dreamt it. It's the time of the Calling.... Two brothers at war; one a god, the other a Crow. I felt the signs at the post. The Black Death is here." Aiyana tried to get her husband's full attention as she pulled at his sleeve and laced her left fingers around Ben's wrist. "If he wanted us dead we'd be already."

Ben relaxed some as he stared at the monster standing motionless before him; the expressionless mask hiding the feature of the ghoulish face that still haunted his dreams,— always chasing him,— always hunting. Could this beast be an ally? Ben's left hand reached up to the medallion around his neck and felt its irregular shape through the heavy leathers of his buckskins. Broken-Toe, so named by Grizz in his logs because of the peculiar twisted dew-claw like appendage of his right foot, had rewarded Ben the trinket at the same time he had given the mountain man the strange bow with pulleys as a trophy after the Battle of the Fire Bird. Ben knew these creatures to be hunters. They stalked their game, but some were ruthless sadists. Others seemed to follow some type of code. *Were there rules?* Maybe it revolved around challenge; the skill involved in the hunt, but these demons also hunted each other. *Were they of different tribes,— like men? How many were there this time?*

Ben was perplexed. Here stood this mystic creature: viewed as a god to the Indians, or perhaps more like a demon haunting the woodlands; but whichever the monster turned out to be, right now he was here, and he wasn't attacking nor was he antagonizing. Ben's gaze drifted over the giant and fell upon the monster's right foot. Recognition of who this creature was melted over his features at the realization that here stood the same Sky Demon that had given him the medallion he was fondling. The same monster that Ben assumed had stalked and killed the legendary trapper, Grizz. The same giant that almost killed his wife, but now standing motionless before him as a statue. Broken-Toe was here to talk. The monster wanted something from Ben, but what?

Ben dropped his rifle muzzle low then rested the butt of the weapon on the ground. Aiyana let go of his sleeve as the mountain man waited for some type of action from this new friend,— or menace?

Broken-Toe extended his right hand with the palm open then closed his fist and struck his chest. The motion was slow and deliberate. Then he rocked the lance in his left hand with its butt planted in the earth toward the man in a gesture of peace.

Ben nodded and pushed the weapon back, "Okay,— we've established you mean us no harm but why are you here?"

"Join me," echoed the strange offer in an emotionless voice, followed by a rhythmic clicking and chirping of an alien nature. The words sounded completely human except for the pattern of noise that trailed the English.

Did the monster understand what it was saying? Was it ordering submission as it led a quest, or was it the haunting call for a joint venture?

"To the death," the chirping followed. "Click, click, click ," like the rolling of the tongue, yet containing a metallic quality. Steal grated, as blades appeared from the wrist band around the creature's left arm. Like the multiple feathering of an insect's legs the numerous sharp objects laced the arm porcupine quill style.

Ben jumped at the noise as Missy stepped forward and growled, but Broken-Toe simply let his lance fall against his chest and dragged one sharp edge of the exposed knifes across his right palm. purple phosphorous fluid spilled out through the wound as the creature then extended the hand to Ben.

The mountain man examined the proposition studying his nemesis with an eye of confusion. Here was a savage creature, bent on death and destruction? The hand was dripping as it hung still in the air waiting for a response. Ben looked hard at the long digits, like clawed talons, of murder. But then Ben noticed them shaking. Not from fear, but injury. Ben could see the stiffness of the joints. The swelling around the knuckles. Most of his fingers had been broken, and recently. The creature was standing in such a way that it was favoring its left side. And it was then Ben noticed the wound in Broken-Toe's abdomen. It looked to be a savage wound as a patch of burned flesh was exposed from behind the shielding armor of the beast's protective gear. What had happened to this god; this giant who lived to kill?

Ben unsheathed his knife and slowly followed Broken-Toe's course: passing his blade across his own right palm. Crimson coated his skin as Ben pressured the cut, then clasped the self-inflicted, wounded hand on Broken's offer.

The giant gripped the bargain sealing the pact then turned and motioned his students to follow. The Yet-Tat lay ahead; the vow had been sealed. The infestation was well on its way and the weapons suitable for battle would be needed. Broken flipped open a panel on his belt band and set his bearings. The pirate ship would carry the needed supplies and any eggs still present would need to be destroyed. The queen's larvae by this time would have found a host and could be anywhere. The massacre Broken-Toe had examined at the post, revealed the larvae of six drones. The infestation had begun, but the queen's seed was not among them. Somewhere in this vast wilderness she had awakened. Within hours she would mature and begin her nesting. A cycle of carnage would follow as more hosts for her young would be gathered and her drones would then continue to spread out in search of yet more of the living for incubation. The ship would be the starting point. A focal to begin the hunt and gather supplies, but the nest could be anywhere and hopefully the trail had not grown cold. With any luck there would be signs that would lead them to the hive.

And so the quest began as Broken-Toe turned up the hill and started the climb. Ben and Aiyana quickly turned to their pack animals and made preparations, taking up pursuit of the giant not knowing what lay ahead. The most unlikely of a gathering: one demigod, a trapper with his woman, and a cougar; bent on a path for survival. Each following the trail fate had arranged.

*   *   *

It was dusk when the strange companions reached the Valley of the Star. They lost most of the daylight hours backtracking and then detouring around the deep canyon that formed an unrelenting barrier to their course over the mountains. As the party topped the eastern ridge of the valley basin and scanned the devastation below, Ben marveled at the wreckage wrought by yet another metal bird. The scorched earth and burned trees revealed a massive path that had been carved by the immense object that cleared a wide channel down the distant slope and burrowed itself deep at the bottom of the dale.

Ben knew one of the Sky Hunter's ships had crashed again, but why would Broken-Toe lead them to this fallen vessel? For what purpose did this creature change his nature and draw him and his wife along, when the last time these giants hunted and killed men seemingly for pleasure? Aiyana's father, a great Crow medicine man, had told Ben the creatures would return to stop a great disaster; but Ben never considered these monsters as protectors. The prophecies just didn't fit what Ben understood and knew about these demons, yet here he was standing beside one and looking over a valley marking the means of their return.

Without a sound the giant continued down the hill for the epicenter of the ship's final resting point. The deep carved canyon revealed a dull green hue at the end of its course guiding them. The party tracked its base along the soft dirt path while the last rays of daylight gave way to a large moon casting its silvery tint to the shadowed haunt of night. The eerie swells of the unknown gripped Ben's soul as Broken-Toe disappeared through the mouth of the cavern with its unusual beacon beckoning the mountain man to follow suit.

Was this the entrance to hell itself? Ben dismounted and

dropped his reins stepping through the door and scanned the large chamber under the soft glow of various objects, diffusing their rays from panels, and walls around the interior. The first thing Ben noticed was the disarray of the chamber, reminding him of a cargo hold after a battle at sea.

Missy growled; but stayed by the entryway as Aiyana stepped up beside him and whispered, "What is this place?"

"We're in the belly of a fire bird,—buried in this mountain."

Aiyana's eyes went wide as she took in the chamber. "Is this its womb, where she carries her children?"

"Most likely," The mountain man replied as he watched the giant rummaging about the cavern, squatting by what looked like a few broken pieces of pottery. "Wait here."

"Like hell!"

Ben looked at his wife and smiled. "Be careful then,— we have no idea about this place."

Broken was crouched examining something as Ben stepped up beside him. On the floor sprawled out and covered in a purple gelatinous fluid was another Sky Demon. Its busted and contorted body looked as though it had fallen a great distance, but the final cause of death appeared to be the immense opening in the chest cavity. Deep stab wounds mutilated the rib cage and gashed the throat.

"Someone did a might bit of carvin' on this un," The mountain man said; but the giant ignored him. Ben scanned the floor and spotted the weapon some distance away as Broken-Toe rose and moved deeper into the chamber.

The mountain man discerned the blade was a green river design with a deer antler hilt as he worked his way over to the knife. Placing the butt of his rifle on the ground for support, he knelt to examine the find coated in the dead creature's purple blood. Picking up the weapon with his right hand he noticed that part of the blade had been eaten away somehow. "Now that's mighty peculiar?" As he studied the weapon he turned to look at the dead creature and wondered how the blade in its current condition could have pierced the thick hide of a Sky Demon... and for that matter who had wielded it. "What a strange place."

Aiyana had moved off to Ben's left on entering the room, but at her husband's mutterings approached to see what he had found. "What's that?" She exclaimed pointing at a strange object near Ben's position.

Ben turned to look at the gelatinous goo's quivering while it took shape causing him to jump, somewhat startled.

"I've seen things like that come to life and attack men in my dreams."

The mountain man poked at it with his rifle muzzle and deciding it was a harmless blob, he went ahead and picked it up.

While a young man serving in the Kentucky militia during the war, Ben had once seen an object pulled from the ocean with the same consistency brought into a seaside market by some fishermen. Amazed by the gelatinous mass and the memory it called back to mind of that strange squiggly creature; although, that life form had tentacles with suckers and eyes. This new thing was plain black and sightless. A quivering globule, *maybe some type of egg.*

Shooo...wack, burst forth a sound that echoed throughout the chamber causing Ben to drop the gelatin sack and spun, raising his rifle to ready. An eerie shriek erupted as Broken-Toe charging through the interior fired his shoulder cannon again, — *shooo...wack...shooo...wack.*

Ben spotted the target screeching, and fluttering over a large metal crate, trying to avoid the well paced shots by the giant. The mountain man joined in with a quick cock of his repeater as the creature jumped at him. The bullet hit the small body and deflected its path momentarily, knocking it against the nearby wall. Black fluid spilled, and smoked from one wing; but in seconds it was up again and ready to spring. *Shooo...wack,* Broken's last shot struck center and smeared the small beast's gooey body fluids across the steel frame support of the interior, right next to Ben, as the quivering mass of remaining flesh dropped on a shelf at Ben's waist and ignited. The mountain man stepped away from the burning heap as the bag at his feet formed wings. Broken-Toe still running reached the man and pushed him out of the way and shot the thing before it took flight. Ben picked himself up off the floor and looked questioningly at the giant, then relaxed. The shot engulfed the egg-sacks in flames.

Broken-Toe spotted the damaged knife Ben had dropped in the ruckus and picking it up dipped the blade in a nearby puddle of water and then stuck the weapon in the flaming goo, residue. Smoke spewed forth as he then pulled it free. Ben's jaw dropped when he saw the steel bubbling and melting before his eyes.

"I owe you one," the man said in appreciation as he stared at the blob. "What kind of critter's flaming blood boils metal?"

Broken-Toe, not interested in small talk, turned back to the dark interior and disappeared.

"The kind my father talked of, and I've seen in my dreams." Aiyana came near and wrapped her arm around her husband's. "He brought us here to stop these things."

"Why does he need us? He looks perfectly capable."

"These are the first to come. I saw them swarming over the bodies of men, bears, cats. Then the real monsters come. Huge things that burst out of the living and grow into giants. Walking skeletons. Bigger than Broken-Toe, bigger than this room." She pointed at the ceiling.

"So you've seen the varmints? The Gathers,— they look like bones?"

"I don't know how to explain. The visions are scattered... no order to them."

"Well what did you see?"

"A cave,— it was dark. They moved in the shadows."

Ben could tell his wife was shook up. Even the thought of the dreams disturbed her deeply. She was usually a tower of strength, but just the mention of the creatures seemed to be transforming her into a little child. "It's okay honey." Ben embraced Aiyana tenderly while running a hand through her long black hair. "It'll be okay."

"I saw men hanging all over the walls of a cave,— the long knives, deer,— Missy. There were so many of them. The Walking Dead, hideous monsters, drooling like rabid animals watching over the cache. Swarming like ants over a hill. Like locusts they'll venture forth turning the land black as they grow like the sands. And the sightless birds will lead them. Burning the flesh of their victims. Turning all they touch into The Walking Dead." Aiyana shuddered as she explained the depth of her visions. She had seen her own demise in that dream. The reality of the future placed her there in her mind. She stared at that cold mask of death holding her motionless while the winged plague sought her soul. "It was so vivid, so real — as though it was really happening."

"Let's go," Ben dropped the embrace and took his wife's hand pulling her back to the entrance.

"What?" Aiyana held back stopping them.

"I'm getting you away from here... now," Ben's icy stare

was firm with determination as he looked back at his wife.

"We can't leave." Aiyana pulled her hand free. Her husband's expression was one dumbfounded.

"And why not?"

"Because the mountain has called.— We must stop this plague." Aiyana's voice transformed into a confirmation of strength. "The winds have led us here. My father told me of it and I have seen it. If we don't,— our world will end anyway. Don't you see my husband?" Aiyana stepped close and ran her palm tenderly down her man's cheek and onto his heart. Her words pleaded gently. "These creatures will overrun us all... and in the end they will kill me anyway. The mountains have called.... The Great Spirit demands it.... We must act."

Ben didn't know how to respond, but didn't have to. Broken-Toe approached as if wanting something. "What!... It would be nice if you spoke English."

"Come." The word was deep and followed by a chirping and clicking noise that sounded unnatural.

"Does it know what it's saying?" Ben laughed, an uncomfortable snicker.

"Come," then the giant turned back down what looked like a corridor.

Ben raised his eyebrows, but started to follow. At the entrance to the tunnel he noticed more of what looked like puddles of fire by an opened steel box that hummed while giving off a faint blue glow. "I wonder what was stored in these cases?" he said as he stepped over the small burning tar pits.

"Eggs," Aiyana replied as she too walked by the fires and moved down the tunnel.

Another Sky Demon's body was draped over a crate with a massive wound in its chest. But the pile of flesh and skin lacked form. On closer inspection it was missing bone. Ben jabbed his rifle muzzle into the mass, but not one inkling of the skeletal structure remained to support the carcass.

Ben looked puzzled momentarily back at his wife; but continued, "This place doesn't look like that cave in your dreams does it?"

"No."

The mountain man felt a little relief as he reached another opening that Broken-Toe disappeared through. As he entered he noticed it looked very much like the first. The giant was standing by another of the crates as he motioned the humans to move a good distance from the box. Ben readied his rifle in anticipation of anything as the giant hit a lever and a side lid popped open. Two of the gelatinous spheres were floating in a stasis field unlike anything Ben had seen before. Three red lights flicked on, centered of Broken's forehead and the horns on either side of his head seemed to follow the light. The same triangular dotted pattern appeared on one of the eggs,— then closed into a single spot. Shooo...wack! sounded the weapon as the horns erupted and an egg burst into flames, but the second sprung wings and a sightless creature sprung from the casing. Ben and Aiyana both shot the thing knocking it back into the box, but their bullets didn't appear to kill it.

Shooo...wack, cracked the giant's cannon again splattering the beasts center as it quivered and ignited into a mass sprawled and burning in the crate.

Broken held up two fingers and motioned around the interior of the large room. Ben shook his head: "I take it there's two more of these somewhere in this ship,"

Aiyana nodded, "Let's help him find them."

As they were rummaging around the cluttered compartment Broken-Toe came upon a storage locker of weapons. He began examining its contents and found some of the gear to be substandard in size. Looking at his companions he contemplated the possibility of them being able to do battle with a queen without armor or even with their weapons that were useless against the monsters. But, to give Guardian technology to a sub species was against code. *Hadn't these proven their worth before?* Broken-Toe had offered the Sentient a trophy in their first encounter when the Sentient had defeated his fellow Marshal in hand-to-hand combat. And this was an exceptional circumstance: Broken-Toe was weakened from injuries sustained in the crash and it would be years before another ship of his clan entered this remote solar system. The infestation had to be stopped and the giant knew he couldn't do it alone. The whole reason he brought them here was to help.

The Guardian stared at the stores. *Could they be trained to use them*? The giant scanned the room.

Ben and Aiyana were wandering about the chamber looking for additional stasis chambers. The storage units had been damaged in the crash. It was a wonder the creatures inside survived without injury; although, Broken had noticed one of the parasites did have a defect. Probably a malfunctioning chamber. Systems failures were ship wide during the plummet.

He looked back at Ben. *Wasn't this Sentient honorable? It was certainly skilled with his own weapons.* It could hunt and track better than many Marshals of his own species, and it had followed him here to this ship like it knew it served a greater purpose.

The giant again turned his attention to the stores. If he could find a tooling laser he could make the needed alteration; *then I will see how fast the Sentient can learn.*

Chapter Twenty-three

The Hunted?

Excerpts from: A Mountain Man's Log

The old medicine man had talked before of the ghost tribe of the north that could walk unseen and stalked men alone. Murder followed the trail of the cannibal giants. Monsters that roamed and haunted the dreams of the impressionable and lived in the myths of men aforetime — bent on trickery and the game of death. I put little stock in the rantings of the aged, until I came face to face with the phantom itself and the truth of a power that hunts the realm invisible to this world. Man has called them devils, the religionist, fallen angels. But the Gatherers, the old man whispered, "...would return." The plague that would follow would mean the end if not stopped and the trail of the known would be hidden to all but few. I have come knowing the truth and witnessing the track. Death has a name and it has returned, but for what purpose the old man's mortality has concealed.

12th Nov. 1871

*   *   *

By midmorning, clouds moved in shielding the bright rays of sunshine, setting the ominous mood for 25 men dressed in blue, and two in buckskin. They exited The Forks, heading northwest under the command of Lieutenant Braves, with orders to find the hostiles accountable for the butchery of the previous night. The gloomy responsibility set before the troop was enhanced by the danger imposed by an enemy currently equipped with the stores of repeaters acquired from the post's trade supplies: arming them better than the very soldiers ordered to bring the renegades to justice. The trail followed: the smaller tributary of the river's fork, crossing before the incline of the range behind, and crossed over the open plain of a high mountain meadow, amid the shadow of the stone face peak to the distant north.

Zeb was well acquainted with the surrounding landscape having ventured the immediate territory in years past, and knew the most probable place of encampment for the adversaries. It was part of a scout's job to not only read the trail, but to interpret the moves of the stalked and predict the nature of the hunted under normal circumstance of which Zeb was a master. Having lived as an Indian in his early years, he was well acquainted, not only with their habits, and lifestyle; but with their battle strategies, which would prove invaluable while tracking a rogue medicine man on the war path.

Zeb was still troubled by the grotesquely deformed skeletal remains of several mutilated soldiers found at the Forks.

The strange mutations were brought to the attention of the commander by the men burying the dead; but the captain refused to entertain any theories on the unusual nature of some of the bodies, other than the savageries preformed on the victims. He was convinced the brutality was the work of The Seer, placing the entire occurrence under the realm of Indian witchery, and mysticism.

Zeb felt it best not to mention the acidic blood boiling episode, or the return of Broken-Toe to the unbelieving commander, guessing the loss of all credibility incurred by revealing the arrival of legendary ghostly hunters endowed with magic, and the simple tracks — indeterminate by the untrained eye — would prove nothing to such a man: educated to ignore anything that even touched on the supernatural. The fact that Broken-Toe appeared to have had nothing to do with the butchery; nor looked to be stalking any of the human game, did leave the tracker with serious questions about what was happening.

The significance of a Sky Demon that lived to kill, suddenly acting in total opposition to its norm and ignoring opportunity was telling; but to understand why would take time and deep consideration that Zeb felt must be tied somehow to the deformed skeletons hidden amidst the dead. The more Zeb thought about it; the more he wondered how the mutation began inside those soldiers, and for that matter how The Seer knew of the small infestation that had plagued the fort. He reasoned that the dead were mutilated because of those grotesquely, misshaped bones; but the only way to find the truth would be to catch The Seer, and question him personally.

The dangers involved in tracking an enemy such as The Seer posed immediate problems that could not be underscored: ambush was the most probable as a leader with just the smallest inkling that he was being followed would lead the unsuspecting into a trap; or at least take an around-about trail back to their home village, careful to keep the women, and children safe. Just west of the troop's current position, a half day's ride, was a prime camping area on the length of a beautiful river with plenty of grazing for a tribe's horses. To Zeb, it was the most likely point to continue the search. Without conferring with the lieutenant in charge of his plan, the mountain man deviated from the trail of the enemy; and set a westerly course that would put them south of the river where he and Claude could scout out the tribe's lodging unencumbered by the military.

Claude took notice of the change from pursuit; but said nothing and nodded in accord after leaving the last inspection of tracks, knowing what his partner was planning. The pace set by the scouts placed them at the mouth of the river by midafternoon where Zeb and Claude encouraged encampment, while they worked their way up the smaller tributary to try and find the village in secret; but the lieutenant, in defiance of the offered advice, gave the scouts a fifteen minute lead and then followed, taking up the rear guard so as not to alert the enemy of their advance.

The officer explained to the men, "Once the camp is found, a quicker response will be imposed. You boys won't have to backtrack and find us. We'll already be in position."

Zeb would have liked more time to spy out the territory before the cavalry acted; but acknowledged the command decision with a disapproving grunt. Recognizing the man's green nature as to the enemy and what his zeal for vengeance might invoke; perhaps, hitting an innocent party,— many tribes lodged along this quiet stream this time of year,— Zeb and Claude would have to act swiftly in determining if in fact any villages found were The Seer's, considering the military's efforts of late to move all tribes to the appropriate reservations, and most Indian refusals to relocate were being met with a stiff no tolerance, "Act-by-Force," issued direct from The White House.

Carefully working their way along the heavy brush by the river, Zeb and Claude walked their animals, concealed by the terrain and ground cover of the shore with all senses alert for signs of encampment. The November air was brisk with a soft breeze that after an hour of search carried with it the scent of smoke telling of the nearness of a village. Reaching a glen nestled by the watery rest, amid the wooded retreat, the two scouts spied the clearing with a sparse number of lodges revealing the congregation of a tribe of small account. For late afternoon there appeared no activity as the two scouts studied their surroundings wondering at the lifeless nature of a village where the women should have been busy with the cares of the mundane evening rituals.

It didn't take the men in buckskin long to determine something was seriously wrong. Tying off their horses the two carefully worked their way closer: Zeb being the first to see the peeled carcass of a human, secured upside down with rope inside a teepee by means of the tripod shaped lodge poles. A large hole had burned through the heavy buffalo skin cover exposing one entire side of the shelter to the elements and revealing the butchered body hanging like a meat store for the winter.

"It's been a few years since we seen the likes of that," Zeb whispered directing Claude's attention to the site.

Claude eyed the exposed lodge and ducked a little lower in the brush. "I'z thought dat cridder wen north?"

"Not like him to hit a village."

Claude parted some branches to get a better look. "Ya dink he's lingerin' some?"

Zeb studied his companion with a smile, "Only ifin he's just finished."

The older man shook his head in doubt. "I'z hates geddin' caught with my'z britches down dwice in as many days." He turned to his friend, "I'z says we'z hang a bits. Waits and sees."

"That lieutenant's going to hit here in a minute," Zeb replied with grim determination. "Won't do no good to wait."

"Bedder him'z den us."

Zeb cocked his rifle with a smile while shaking his head and crept low through the remaining ground cover, moving into the village. The ghostly quiet was unnerving as the man scanned the devastation of the small Indian camp ravaged by some, as of yet, unknown visitor. Except for the sound of Claude coming up behind, the mountain man heard nothing as he began looking for sign. The Sky Demons' tracks were everywhere and it didn't take the younger scout long to determine that three of the giants had hit the village, but Broken-Toe's print was nowhere to be found. By careful examination Zeb and Claude walked through the carnage, determining that most of the bodies were women: some very young, perhaps children.

"This doesn't make sense," Zeb mumbled as they stood by the last body, flung over a meat drying rack next to a dying fire. "These critters hunt for sport. I don't remember them ever hitting a village like this before."

Claude planted the butt of his rifle on the ground and rested both hands on the barrel. "Da're killers. Makes no never mind why."

Zeb began to poke at the body with the muzzle of his gun. "Maybe those transforming bones were happening to these people too?"

"Ya dinkin' dat's why da butchery?"

Zeb pulled his long knife and knelt by the rack. "Maybe,— only one way to find out."

The older man put one hand on Zeb's shoulder to stop him, "I ain't bein' no party to carvin' on no dead Injin squaw. Makin's fer bad blood. Just ain't right."

"I ain't lookin' forward to this none neither," Zeb replied with a dropped chin as he stared at his friend. "There's no other way."

Claude removed his fur hat and scratched his head. "We'z be lucky da hold our top-notch after dissin'," he muttered back with a frown.

None of the mutated bones were in any of the bodies the two autopsied, but the lieutenant was none to pleased upon arriving and finding the scouts opening up the corpses. After a few stern words and threats of chains from the officer the two men in buckskin were discharged from further service: the lieutenant unable to justify the ghoulish behavior of the pair. Zeb tried to explain they weren't mutilating the bodies, but any words spoken in defense seemed to make the officer more angry and even when the younger scout pointed out a clear track of one of the creatures, the lieutenant simply kicked dirt over it and called the sergeant to arrest them if they didn't leave.

As the pair walked back to the trees to gather their horses Claude turned to his friend, "Whad's now genius?"

"What are you upset about?" Zeb spat. "You didn't want no military career any-who."

"Do...n likes no threats of stocks." Claude shook his head mumbling, "runned off likes some damn un·die·zi·ra·bles."

Zeb untied his horse and stepped into the saddle. "Well,— we needed to know."

Claude followed suit, reining his animal around in front of his friend. "So — Whad now?"

"I say we track us down one of them vermin."

"Goin' afder more of dat bread from heaven?"

"Say what?"

Claude went silent. He had never mentioned what he had learned that fateful day at the hot pool when he had killed his first Sky Demon. The creature had been stalking him for days after a battle with a Blackfoot war party. The older man never forgot the image of that demon; an invisible ghostly shadow moving across the meadow after him. Claude had inadvertently shot the silhouette, striking what he later learned was some kind weapon that appeared as horns on a mask. The explosion that ensued injured the creature and at the same time caused it to appear in flashing waves of sparks and lightning that enveloped the body and quaked over the giant.

At the pool the monster was fully visible, but this time the mountain man was hidden by the waves of hot water that shielded his presence from the creatures' vision: who see by means of infrared. The mountain man had plunged his knife into the neck of his wounded enemy when it entered the pool to soak its wounds; its pasty blood flowed into the pond coating Claude's skin and healing his flesh burned by some type of acid in the hot natural cauldron hidden among the mysterious land of spewing waters and boiling streams. The man later, at the killing of other creatures, skinned and gutted the vanquished under the pretence of vengeance; but secretly saved key organs in a leather bag. He had fed a heart to Missy, Ben's cat, and when the animal appeared unaffected, jerked the livers and slipped it into the food supplies of his friends.

He also added blood from one of the creatures to a water skin containing whiskey, and found the healing properties unmatched by anything doctors of the day were using in their meager practice of health care. Claude well knew, *"the bread from heaven,"* had extended their lives, and maintained their age; but he had no answer for how long the effects would continue. Here was a chance to harvest more of the reservoirs of a fountain of youth; but he decided to still his true motives, less his companions learned the truth.

The Indians called the giants,— cannibals, although there was no evidence the monsters ever ate any of their human kills; but considering their remarkable human persona and intelligence, Claude still had difficulty rectifying his actions after the fact. At first he had just viewed the beings as beasts: creatures as wild and savage as the grizzly bear, but the more he was exposed to their skill and technology the more he questioned the dilemma; reasoning it was best not to tell the secret and be labeled a cannibal himself. "Gonna afder dem critters again are we?"

"They each went their own way after that village." Zeb's eyes drifted off to the west. "And I'll bet they'll be huntin' us before long anyway."

Chapter Twenty-four

Massacre

Sioux Song

Blood has been spilled

    from the ground cries carry the wind

Earth covers the tears

    but the mountain's rumbling never rests

The children silenced

    the desperate song lonely weeps its loss

The seasons will change

    but hatred's ax will not be quenched

Chant of the Lost

*   *   *

The heavily lathered mount entered the camp as its rider guided his animal directly to the command tent. Slipping from the saddle as the horse slid to a stop, the corporal saluted the officers stepping out to meet him. "Colonel Blanchet,— Captain Erwing sends word.... The Sioux hit the Forks, killed everyone. Captain Oswalt was there with his men. It was a massacre, Sir." The messenger took a deep breath, and exhaled.

Colonel Blanchet's long thin face was emotionless as the news settled in. His tall lanky form lacked the powerful stature one would assume dictated command, but the grim stone features of his narrow weathered face spoke of a man hardened by years in the service. Salty gray tinted the bushy dark mustache, curled at both corners of his thin lips; yet his thick black eyebrows, connected above the bridge of his button nose showed none of the tell-tale signs of age. Icy blue eyes observed every detail of the rider, exhausted from his compelling journey; but the commander said nothing as he weighed the implications just delivered.

The lieutenant with the colonel, also a thin man, nodded at the news and turned to his commander in a slurred tongue; but not from alcohol, "Sir, our scouts reported a village only about twenty miles from our present location. It can't be a coincidence."

Colonel Blanchet's gaze never faltered from the courier. "It was Sioux,— are they sure, Corporal?"

"Yes Sir. They believe it's The Seer, and the Sioux have joined him,— about thirty total."

The colonel shook his head with doubt wrinkling his brow.

"This uprising must be stopped before any more join this lunatic," barked the Lieutenant in his lazy drawl that deceptively hid a sharp but cruel mind.

"And what would you have us do Lieutenant? We already have our forces divided chasing this ghost and General James has requested an escort for the 25th and their supplies including that new Gatling gun."

"Sir, give me fifty men and two of the Indian scouts and I'll hit his village before first light. We'll catch this Seer at his own game."

The colonel thought about his young officer's proposal as he scratched his leathery chin amid the heavy stubble of late afternoon growth, shadowing his features. The raspy scrapings of his white glove against the bristles appeared to help him think as he pondered the plan. "I want you to bring me this Seer — Lieutenant. Do what you must, but I would like The Seer alive — if possible."

The officer saluted and was dismissed, leaving the colonel to again focus on the courier. "Walk with me Corporal and tell me what they've learned of this Seer."

*   *   *

Sashtee awoke to the sounds of the tribe's horses under duress. In the distance a wolf sang his lonely cry amid the barking of a few dogs, but the horses were on the move. Running from one side of the makeshift pen to the other while baying and snorting at some invisible ghost disturbing their nights slumber.

Moonlight filtered down through the narrow aperture at the pinnacle of the buffalo skin lodge revealing the hour was still early, but Sashtee slipped from the warmth of her heavy fur bed roll and crawled to the entrance of her tepee to see the cause of the commotion. A light snow had dusted the landscape reflecting the silver glow of the near full moon making the shadowy world around the village deceptively peaceful. She could see the horses' erratic behavior, but it didn't appear they were being chased and the dogs that were barking weren't facing the pen, but were poised opposite the flank more the direction of the wolf crying in the distance. Something unnerved her, but she saw nothing causing the disturbance as she ducked back into the comfort of the lodge and pondered what to do. Her husband, Isaac, along with all the younger men of the tribe were on the hunt, leaving only the very old or the really young to care for the village.

She guessed the boy watching over the horses must have fallen asleep and the dogs were just answering the wolf's serenade. Sashtee decided to check on the young charge of the pen. She slipped her moccasins on and wrapped herself in the thick fur of a soft sheepskin robe, stepping moments later out onto the fresh dusting of white powder. The brisk early morning air was still as she walked quietly toward the restless animals; her breath visible with each exhale as she trudged across the unmolested path marking the first trail on the fresh frozen fall.

A flap of a nearby lodge opened and Tashawnnay stepped out, apparently with the same resolution: to check on her brother appointed to watch the animals. Sashtee waited for her friend who

174

quickly ran to her side.

"What's happening?" The young girl asked in the Sioux dialect while pulling her robe tighter around her small frame.

"I don't know."

Both walked quietly to the grove of trees near the horses, but saw no sign of Tashawnnay's brother. The rope corral was still intact as the women strode beside it and tried to talk to the animals in soft cooing to calm them, but to no avail.

As Sashtee reached the island of trees her attention was drawn to something moving in the shadows of the brush. Guessing some predator was hiding in the bushes, scaring the horses, the woman picked up a large rock and moved closer to find the creature.

Tashawnnay saw her friend's actions and pulled a skinning blade from her belt. Swiftly she darted after Sashtee following her into the brush. As they walked, Isaac's wife found a trail where something was dragged through the soft snow. Blood discolored the white cover along the sign: the predator must have made its kill and dragged its meal to the security of the dense brush. The women huddled closer; but continued to follow the path when ahead, lying in the snow, was a buckskin covered leg resting motionless—the rest of the body hidden behind the trunk of a large tree.

"Ta-who!" Tashawnnay cried out running toward her brother. Sashtee tried to stop her, but the girl pulled free and fell at the side of the young boy. Blood covered his face; the white crown on the top of his skull exposed, his scalp pulled from its rest.

Sashtee spun at the crack of a twig behind her when she was struck in the face by the butt of a rifle. The blow glanced across her cheek knocking her down, but was of insufficient force to cause her to lose all consciousness.

Tashawnnay screamed and charged the assailant with raised knife; but, with the loud report of a gunshot, she dropped her in her tracks.

Sashtee groaned and tried to sit up as she felt something grab hold of her clothing. Dragged by her leather garb she could feel herself being pulled through the snow. Gradually she became more alert as rifles could now be heard in the distance amid the yells and screams of her people. The village had fallen under attack, but her delirium was more like a dream. The force-induced trance refused to release its hold, her muscles not responding as she fought to awake. Her head struck the ground hard as she was dropped. She moaned and tried to struggle as she could feel her clothes being cut off. The icy cold of the fresh snow chilled her bare skin as she rolled free of her garments onto the freezing earth. She could hear the distant battle: defenseless women, children, and old men—weak— weaponless—yelling in futility. And she could feel the presence of her assailant as he drew close. Then she awoke, with a scream. A soldier was bent over her with an evil grin. She swung her weak right arm at the man dragging her fingernails across her attacker's face. He cursed and struck her with a closed fist—and Sashtee— lost consciousness.

*   *   *

Twenty-eight trail weary warriors topped the ridge near their village returning empty handed. The hunt had proved less than successful. First—not finding any game, second—side tracked they took the trail of a mystic demon which led them to The Forks Trading Post, where they were fired on by soldiers, killing two of their number. The military had taken up pursuit of the braves playing a cat and mouse chase through the northern landscape for the better part of the day, but the Indians eluded the green trackers in the rocky hills skirting the creeks and stony washes where the Calvary scouts lost their trail.

Not knowing why they were fired on, or the reason for the pursuit, all decided to return to the village as soon as possible to move it to a safer location. When they topped the ridge, the entire party noticed something was wrong, even at the great distance separating them from home. Spurred to speed, they galloped across the meadow over the melting snow to the site of bloody bodies scattered around the camp. Tepee poles still smoldered—the skins covering them long since turned to ash and the remainder of their small herd of horses shot dead. Devastated by the scene, the party separated and wandered independently through the remains, searching the carnage for lost loved ones and clues to the enemy. Women and children had been shot and butchered along with the older men of the tribe. Stripped and scalped the victims were shown no mercy as the warriors tried to come to terms with the evil that had desecrated their home and land.

Isaac searched in vain around the burned remains of his lodge with hope his wife had escaped. Her body was nowhere to be found, but neither could he make any immediate conclusions for the ground was a maze of tracks so numerous it was almost unreadable.

Reuben was the first to notice the horses of the attackers were shod.

"The US Calvary did this," he spit in anger. "Why would they butcher women and children?

"I don't know." Tears welled in Isaac's eyes as he scanned the slaughter. "Have you found Tashawnnay?"

"No — Maybe they got away. Do you think they could have gotten to the horses?"

Isaac looked to the pen grounds riddled with dead animals; without a word he made his way to the site. Reuben followed close behind. "Why'd they shoot the ponies?"

"I don't know." Isaac stopped and surveyed. "If they wanted us to believe it was an enemy tribe they would have stolen the horses."

The blond warrior moved along the rope fence. "Left some false sign, but ..." The man spotted some bodies hidden among the trees. "Nooo...!" Running to the butchery, his wife lay naked and bloody in the shadows of a large trunk. Blue from loss of blood and cold she was scalped and stabbed in the abdomen: left to die a slow and painful death. Isaac dropped to her side in tears and lifted the limp form, brushing the matted remains of some hair, clotted by dried blood, from her bruised and battered face. Her skin was freezing as he rocked her in his arms crying, "No,—No,— Please— No."

She opened her eyes. Clouded and yellowed, her black orbs lacking their vibrant luster that always seemed to read all. She whispered. Isaac leaned close. "My love...I asked the Great Spirit to see you once more." She coughed, then groaned, fading in his arms.

Isaac wept long and hard.

Reuben patted his blond haired companion softly on the shoulder, "I'm sorry uncle." He hesitated with a helpless feeling then spied another body nearby. Leaving his friend to mourn, Reuben found Tashawnnay's body close to her murdered brother. He lifted her carefully from the frozen earth and carried her corpse to her father and helped the man with the winter burial of his family.

Chants of the bereavement echoed long into the night. A large fire was started by a few of the braves as a gathering point after taking care of their dead, but most danced death chants and carved on themselves in grief.

It was in early morning hours before Isaac joined the solemn assembly. Mourning had given way to rage and after concealing his wife's remains in the trees by the horse pen, he swore an oath of vengeance, unable to quench the pain in his heart; he finally took a seat by the fire. As he watched his brothers lament, the mountain man removed from his pouch the bear-claw necklace given to him by Jon when he was just a green newcomer to this northern land. It was a trophy, a badge of honor, gifted after the young man had dropped a charging grizzly with one shot. He clutched the band with his two hands and rubbed the demon finger that hung in the center like a charm with his right thumb and index, pondering his next move.

Across the fire was Reuben sitting next to Tashawnnay's father — accepted now as a belated son. The young Crow and Isaac where somewhat outcasts of the tribe, especially to Tunkanayhautue who looked at them as strangers; but after the recent events: death of his wife, daughter, and his only male child (killed in the massacre while watching the horses) the father recognized the young Crow half-breed as a man of honor. He deeply regretted his former rejection of this Crow warrior, genuinely pained at his daughter's death. They talked in whispers, exchanging glances between the fire and each other. Tunkanayhautue was a man who spoke with his hands, gesturing as he talked, telling a story or lamenting the winds of change. Reuben listened intently and said little as Isaac watched somewhat disassociated with the events happening around him. His mind adrift amid the agony of loss.

As the moon slowly settled in the west, Isaac placed the bear-claw trophy over his head and stood. The warriors sitting quietly by the fire glanced up at the golden haired mountain man and watched as he rubbed the mummified taloned finger that hung as a center piece like it was a lucky rabbit's foot. Isaac had shot that finger off one of the Demon-Gods at his first encounter with the species during the river battle against the Rees Indians his first year trapping. The irony of the conflict was that he had fought side by side with the Sioux in that small war and now circumstance had come full circle. With the return of the Demons From The Sky a quest again would begin, but this time his path was not with the magical creatures, or so he thought. Today his trail was pointing to the white man. The cavalry that had stolen his happiness and taken his reason for life. His ardor was now hardened to the point of breaking.

Isaac's horse, still saddled with the heavy buffalo riding pad, was busy grazing the wet meadow grass no longer covered by snow. He moved to the animal with purpose as others of the tribe paused and considered his actions. Isaac picked up the reins of his horse dragging on the ground and swung into the saddle. Silence fell over the crowd as the whispering stopped. The Golden One turned his mount facing the fire and stroked the necklace dangling high on his chest. "I ride to kill the white vermin that killed my wife and the families of my brothers."

A chorus of whoops and war cries broke the dirges as men took to the saddle in response to the warrior's call for vengeance.

"Reuben, do you know which way the enemy fled?"

"The main company went west uncle," Reuben called out as he ran to his horse, and leapt from behind to the animal's back, "but a small contingent of about thirty are headed east."

"Those headed east will be returning to the forces north of here. Let's hit them before they reach their reinforcements."

As one united throng the small number of Sioux joined for battle against an enemy they had long tried to stay at peace with, although, hostilities had increased among others of the Sioux nation. This first confrontation for this limited war party promised a challenge. The force they pursued were well armed, seasoned troops. If they reached the northern support their numbers could increase tenfold, but Isaac was determined to hit them before that happened.

The tribe knew the territory well and the terrain was turned to their advantage. The party cantered across the meadow and cut north, heading to a narrow valley that would cut hours off the trail. They would find the enemy. Revenge would echo throughout the hills and the hot blood of cowards, killers of women and children, would paint the mountains red, answering its call for vengeance.

Chapter Twenty-five

Bait

TELEGRAPH

TO ROBIN CLEVENGER. STOP.   DAD HAD NO BROTHER, BUT TELLS ME HIS GRANDFATHER HAD A HALF BROTHER NAMED   CLAUDE. STOP. I DOUBT IT COULD BE THE SAME MAN, HE WOULD BE OVER A HUNDRED YEARS OLD.   STOP. GRANDPA LOST TOUCH WITH HIM OVER THIRTY YEARS AGO. STOP.   DAD BELIEVES HE WAS KILLED BY INDIANS SO BE CAREFUL. STOP.

*   *   *

"Them damn lazy no-goods! Where'd Frankie and Kenny get off to?" McCray's savage scar turned crimson under his increased blood pressure. His temperament raged easily when orders were ignored. His plans always centered on obedience and the men stationed around him were expected to follow his decisions to the letter.

Bob, the unhappy messenger,— a mouse of a man trembling at the repercussion envisioned by the wrath that might be unleashed in a wisp,— shuttered at the commander's tone directed without mercy. "They were diggin' the south tunnel earlier, but no one's seen hide nor hair of um. No dirt's come up the tunnel for over an hour neither." Bob wiped sweat from his brow even though the subterranean shaft was a cool 68 degrees. "James took the buckets down with the mules to bring up the load and said their picks were just left at the bottom of the run and the carts were full; but pushed over,— right off the tracks."

"Frankie might be big, but I don't think even he could of toppled a full bucket." McCray calmed some, scratching his bristly chin as he thought. "Someone's had ta see where they got off to. I'll skin them no-goods ifin' them stole from me."

"You thinkin' they found themselves some color and ran?"

"There's only one way out-eh that shaft. The overturned buckets could be a ploy. Send Jimmy down there and see what he can tell. That boy's part blood hound." McCray turned to look at the women dirty from the trail and tired from lack of sleep, sitting quietly in a dark recess in the main chamber, watching their captors.

"What you want us to do with the whores?" Bob whispered as a crooked smile broke his cowering face.

"Tell the boys, they can have their pick after each shift," McCray answered back loud enough for the women to hear; his scarlet scar turning back to its natural pink hue. "Want to keep our workers happy."

"Yes sir Cap.," Bob snapped back with a brisk salute and took-off for the tunnel opening. Huddled in the corner of the large chamber Robin eyed the kidnappers with disdain. She heard McCray and watched as the little man ran out of the cave giggling to himself. "You're not our madam, nor do we work for you!" Robin yelled as she stood defiant with poise. She then turned her head and spit, finishing the gesture with a scowl.

McCray walked over unmoved by the action and smiled. In

an unexpected flash he backhanded Robin then grabbed her arm and threw her to the ground. Several of Robin's friends stood startled as a couple crawled to her side. McCray pulled his pistol and waved it at the defenseless women. "You'll do what your told or I'll put a bullet in all your pretty faces."

Robin again spit this time at his feet. "Go ahead you coward."

McCray stepped in closer and struck Robin again, this time with the barrel of his pistol. She fell back unconscious into Daisy's lap, a gaping wound split across her left cheek. McCray pointed his pistol at the young beautiful brunette cradling her fallen comrade. "Back off."

Daisy let Robin's head settle softly to the cave floor and crawled backwards, away in fear. McCray then grabbed Robin's arm and dragged the limp form out from under her heavy blanket down deeper into the dark tunnels of her new hell.

*   *   *

Bob returned a short time later with a tall, thin man, who continued by himself down the shaft while Bob approached the women and asked, "Where'd da boss go?"

Daisy stood and turned on her charms. She was tired and dirty from the trail, wrap in a tattered horse blanket; but the light from the single lamp in the chamber cast a mesmerizing hue to her deep blue eyes, enchanting the weak-minded-soul, falling victim to her wiles. Daisy let the well soiled blanket fall to the floor exposing her only garment; a loose fitting cavalry shirt missing several strategically important buttons. Her well contoured form enhanced the gaps in the simple piece of cloth conforming its parts and folds into a tool that accentuated every curve of her shapely figure. She sauntered closer to the man brushing some unruly hairs lightly away from his forehead. "He chose his companion," she purred, whispering softly as she brushed against him, her warm breath caressing his cheek. "Perhaps we could find a quiet place?"

"I'm,— suppose to wait here. I'm on duty," the man stuttered weakly. "The captain wouldn't like that."

"Sh...." Daisy continued while running her left hand down the man's shirt and along the man's waist until she found the object she was looking for. Her eyes glimmered with luster as she met his.

"Who's to know?" She whispered tenderly kissing him on the lips as she pulled his knife from his belt and plunged it to the hilt in the man's abdomen.

Bob crumpled to his knees bewildered as he looked up at his assailant while clutching his own blade buried in his flesh.

"What are you doing?" Screamed a taller brunette as she panicked, running and kneeling by the dying man. "They'll kill us all now for sure."

"They weren't plannin' to treat us with any favors," Daisy spit angrily pushing by her weaker companion. "We're on our own and going to have ta defend ourselves." Daisy bent over enough to grab one of the man's pistols.

Bob weakly tried to stop her, but Daisy put her right foot on his chest and pushed him backwards on the cave floor. Bob groaned, gasping for air, as Daisy knelt by him and pulled the knife from his abdomen, wiping the man's blood on his left thigh as he passed out.

"So what do we do now?" Protested the taller brunette.

"Quit your whining Shay and get his other pistol. Girls get over here and help us drag the body behind that pile."

"How are we supposes to git out of here Miss brains?" Shay smirked as the women worked together dragging the unconscious man behind the pile of mining residue. "If you haven't noticed the camp out there is teeming with men."

"You heard those two talking same as me. Take the girls down that tunnel," she motioned down the corridor the tracker took. "There must be a way out of this mine from that section. Otherwise they wouldn't of sent that thin guy down there lookin' fer their friends."

"But what if we run into that tracker?"

"You're half dressed women. I'm sure you'll think of something."

"You want us to kill that guy like you killed him?" Shay snapped back kicking the man at their feet. Bob groaned at the strike as all the women looked down at the dying man.

"You think these men would have any reservations about killing us?" Daisy began unbuckling the man's holster and moved to his feet to pull off his boots.

Bob weakly lifted his head, regaining consciousness. "What are you doing?" He whimpered then groaned at the agonizing pain of his wound as Daisy tugged unsympathically at his footwear.

"I need his clothes!" Daisy barked.

With little hesitation, her companions fell on the man, stripping him of his dirty garments and then finished by hiding the dying man behind the pile of mining waste.

Daisy slipped the cloth britches over her bare legs and pulled the man's boots on her tiny feet. Bob's shirt was a bloody mess; casting it aside, Daisy grabbed his leather vest and found it hung comfortably, but seductively over her feminine wiles, parting ever so gracefully yet concealing her shapely features. The desired look was to blend in: not stand out — so she retrieved her wool horse blanket and cut a slit at its center and then dropped the makeshift poncho over her head. Strapping Bob's holster to her slim waist under the cover of the wool drape she completed her masquerade by tucking her long dark hair under the man's hat. The transformation of her feminine allure behind the facade of a masculine wardrobe created the desired illusion for her plan and she took a deep breath of satisfaction. Luckily, Bob was a small man and his clothes, although loose, were adequate. "We must hurry!" Her companions stared dumbfounded as Daisy grabbed Shay's arm and pushed her toward the tunnel and handed her Bob's second pistol. "Take them and hurry. I'll get Robin and come up behind."

The younger woman took the weapon hesitantly resisting Daisy's efforts. "What are you going to do?"

"Shoot the bastard."

"Where'd you learn to shoot a gun?"

"I had three brothers — remember?" Daisy smiled. "Competition works wonders in honing your talents."

Shay dutifully snickered as Daisy broke the eye contact and lifted a lantern hanging on a wooden peg driven into the cave wall. With one last look and a nod to the women to move down the mine Daisy disappeared on her trek after Robin.

Shay and the girls watched momentarily, then followed the oldest's instructions. Clutching the cold steel of the Colt to her bosom under the cover of her wool horse blanket she led the way down the dimly lit passage. Strength is a virtue forged by necessity and Shay demonstrated her new found leadership with confidence that belied her fears. The unexpected demands of command forced her into an unforeseen position of poise and self-control as she stifled the self-doubt of her companions.

About fifty rods down the mining tunnel was a narrow

corridor that turned off to the left and ran at a steady incline up as far as they could see. After a moment of indecision Shay instructed the women that they would follow the smaller passage which appeared to be some type of airway. A stiff breeze pushed through the tunnel at this point leaving a sense of freedom ahead, but the wind whistling by carried an eerie scent of musk that could not be placed. Shay took the lead up the new trail, but no light marked their course forward — only the strange odor. The strong smell became nauseating as the passageway narrowed to where they had to crawl on hands and knees as a feeling of claustrophobia overtook a few of the women.

"Quiet,— they'll hear us." Shay snapped unable to turn around when the ground gave way underneath her and she slipped with a scream through the gaping rupture and splashed into the icy waters of a subterranean pool. Slapping the surface and kicking free of her blanket while trying to gain her equilibrium she coughed and choked after her belly-flop as one-by-one her companions followed her plunge; the weak roof of the chamber giving way to their combined weight.

Shay got her bearings and her breath as she dogpaddled with her left hand while retaining her grip on the revolver as portions of the ceiling dropped into the water around her. Her friends were screaming and splashing as the last one fell through the new opening above and gradually they all gathered composure in the chilly underground pond that had cushioned their fall. Shay was the first to study the haunting surroundings. The far walls and high ceiling seeming to glow with an eerie blue hue amid the blackness of the large domed amphitheater.

"What is this place?" cried out one of the girls as Shay noticed the water ripple around her.

"Ahh...," screamed another splashing the water in front of her as she tried desperately to push a hidden enemy away. "There's something in here with us!"

Shay felt a brush against her right leg and kicked vigorously then began swimming for what looked to be the underground shoreline. Her friends followed suit when one suddenly spasmed and disappeared under the surface. Shay turned to watch as she walked up onto the shore. The girl sprang to the surface screaming and choking, then again sank under the icy chill of the subterranean pool.

"Help her," Shay screamed pointing at her drowning companion when a second girl disappeared under the surface. Shay started back for the water's edge when a ghostly black skeletal form stepped from the shadows. Shay tried to run, but the fleshless frame cleared the short distance between and pushed her hard to the ground under its immense weight.

The woman rolled to her back and tried to crawl away as the smooth grinning nightmare bared down, grabbing her pale bare legs. Choking on the stench of rotting flesh, hanging uselessly like tattered clothes from a dead corpse, Shay's eyes began to water. Still holding her pistol she cocked the weapon, point blank, and pulled the trigger in the face of the walking bones; but the round was a dud and the hammer clicked uselessly on the worthless shell. Shay panicked, whimpering; but managed to pull the trigger twice more without reward as the giant twisted, stabbing the end of a protruding rib into her hip.

She cried out in agony and swung the pistol trying to bat the monster away, but its long bony fingers wrapped around her hand. She screamed and dropped the colt as the steely appendages tightened on her arm sending immense bolts of shooting pains up to her arm, tearing at the socked joint of her shoulder. She grabbed at the beast with her free hand, but the thing latched onto the new offering and then almost laughing stabbed her in the opposite hip. Shay couldn't move her legs or even feel them as she dropped backwards her muscles spasming. Gagging, the putrid odor cut off her wind as the poison from the rib barbs swiftly surged through her heart pounding soul. Shay passed struggling into unconsciousness.

Chapter Twenty-six

Legend

The Seer's Chant

The winds of change, the desert will come

Death has a name, but the warning will call

Who has heard, the message, the song

The vision is clear, will the daughter respond

Record of the Following

*　　*　　*

Broken-Toe picked up a mask smaller than the norm for an adult Guardian. *This ship must have carried young.* A Marshal's ship seldom allowed children on board, but apparently the pirates trained their youth differently. Broken turned the helmet examining its properties and possibilities. The mask had muscle sensors around the interior cheek pads for the operation of the controls: sighting laser, the horn cannon trigger, and atmospheric filters. A Guardian could manipulate the switches with its facial features: winking, twitching its cheeks, and tensioning its jaw muscles. *Could a Sentient trigger it?*

The Marshal picked up a liquid metal ionization rifle and checked the charges. The fluid cartridges were missing as the giant dug through the pile looking for the ammo. If he could find the supplies, the Sentients could make use of these weapons. The Guardian gear was somewhat bulkier than the Sentients' current gas propelled projectile arms: arms that would prove useless against the armored skin of the parasites. He could embed Icon shrapnel in the soft metal of the projectiles, but that would take time. Again a tooling laser would be needed. The giant continued digging and found a charged cartridge when his attention was disrupted by a faint sound picked up in his COM headset. Danger was lurking and death would come swift.

*   *   *

Aiyana had worked her way to the far corner of the chamber, finding a dark corridor almost hidden in the shadows of the partially lit room. She readied her rifle and moved forward at a small sound emanating ahead. If one of those bugs jumped from the gloom she would plug the critter. Moving into the tunnel the contours of the smooth rounded walls were remarkably different than the rest of the ship. This section seemed out of place, but strangely familiar. The walls glowed in a dull hue, that cast a dim perspective to the long walkway. Aiyana reached out and felt the smooth texture of the moist substance coating the surface. It seemed sticky after she pulled her hand away and the residue lingered on her fingers. Aiyana shook off the strange sensation and continued down the tube like structure. A large room opened up at the end of the shaft as water dripped from overhead and pooled on the floor draining into a shimmering basin storing runoff from surrounding tunnels. A rhythmic hum resonated in the chamber amid the sound of cascading water as the woman stepped onto a grated platform that spanned a large portion of the new compartment.

Aiyana marveled at the transparent beauty of the subterranean pool. It changed colors corresponding to a glistening tube deep within the unnatural pond formed from an underground spring leaking into the ship. Waves of red, green, blue and yellow cycled up the clear sleeve as the steady vibration echoed with each undulating flash of light. Aiyana was mesmerized by the phenomenon. Nothing in her experience compared to the strange sun pounding deep within its watery confines. So focused was Aiyana that she didn't hear the movement of a glossy black creature dropping from the railings above. Quietly the beast slipped closer inching its way nearer the unsuspecting woman. Aiyana suddenly turned when the creature's tail raked a loose deck plate. The large eyeless head drooled as the beast snarled, its canines, protruding slowly like tusks ready to seize the woman. Aiyana screamed, but was too close to the creature to target the muzzle effectively so she swung the butt of her rifle striking the creature hard across its bony jaw.

The parasite growth screeched in anger and grabbed the woman; steely fingers locking with such pressure on her arms that the repeater dropped uselessly to the grated plating of the metal platform. Aiyana tried to pull free as the almost spider like skeletal frame twisted, driving a pointed spur extending from a back vertebra into her thigh. The malformed rib then extracted quickly. The helpless woman shrieked in pain as the stinging burned deep within her muscle numbing its function. The poison slipped into the artery in her leg spreading quickly as nausea swept over her: clouding her vision and weakening her resolve.

Broken-Toe stepped through the portal and fired his mask cannon, but the creature had heard him coming and spun, dodging the first missiles of molten ionized metal, and dropping his victim, dove into the glowing pool. The warm water splashed onto the decking, drenching the Marshal momentarily blinding him as his visor flushed red with the sudden wash of heat. Broken fired again blind into the pool as Ben entered the room and saw the target slithering away like a lizard into the depths of the subterranean pond. Aiyana sighed and Ben's attention was immediately drawn to his wife, whose loosening grip on a nearby railing failed. She collapsed weakly to the deck.

"Noooo...." he cried out as he pushed by Broken and knelt by his wife taking her in his arms.

Aiyana's limp form shuddered briefly then she opened her eyes, gazing into her lover's. "My husband," she whispered weakly, "I saw my death coming,— but...."

"Aiyana? please..." Ben cried as she quietly slipped away.

*   *   *

"Aiyana," echoed the haunting call as the woman melted into a heavy fog. White clouds billowed at her feet as the sound chanted,— beckoning softly. "Aiyana, — you have been chosen," the words whispered in her native Crow language.

"Father? — is that you?" Aiyana cried out as the familiar voice resonated in the empty void.

"You have been chosen," Whispered, the echoing as if in a tunnel. Somewhere in the shifting mist Eyes-of-an-Owl drifted; Aiyana glimpsing his weathered features as the image appeared then faded.

"Come to me," commanded the words, but they weren't her father's.

"Who are you? What do you want?"

"You have been chosen," Eyes-of-an-Owl said, sitting next to a fire. Her father raised a pipe to the four winds and exhaled smoke. A stiff breeze followed the breath clearing the mist as the woman found herself in a beautiful valley with blue shaded mountains in the background. Her father motioned her to sit as he whispered, "You have been chosen." He waved his hands over the fire and blew and Aiyana was suddenly in a desert. Sand whipped at her face, blinding her momentarily. She cleared the dust and shielded her eyes when the same valley she had been in with her father was now void of trees and water and masked in the rippled parched land of sand dunes.

"Come to me," commanded a voice,— the chilling female tone haunting in its demand.

Her father took her arm, "It has fallen to you."

"What?" Aiyana cried out as his steely grip buried into her flesh and his jaw extended transforming his features into the black shadowy creature that had pierced her leg.

Drool covered fangs, inches from Aiyana's face, mimicked speech. The chilling words called deep within her soul, "You are mine,— come to me," beckoned the female song.

Aiyana pulled away from the nauseating breath. She crumpled to the ground in labor pains. Her chest contorted as she screamed in agony. Suddenly the pain stopped and flames lit the creature, the heat searing her flesh.

The monster screeched in pain; the torch surrounding its form billowed, then shrunk as Eyes-of-an-Owl inhaled the small flames into his pipe. The old man's features twisted in anger then blew the soot forth scorching a valley's trees, exposing a cave hidden in the rocks. "You have been chosen my daughter," he whispered, smiling, then disappeared.

Aiyana felt weak as she sat up.

"Wake up my love," came a soothing call from out in the void. Ben's features flickered in the fog then faded away. "Come back to me," pleaded the soft cry of her lover.

"My husband?"

Aiyana felt herself being lifted as her body felt drained.

"My God,— I thought I'd lost you."

Aiyana opened her eyes, the dim interior revealing little. "What happened?" Her husband's face was close, relieved.

"You were attacked by some kind of monster. I thought you were dead." Tears welled in Ben's eyes as he pulled the weak form of his wife closer. "I don't know what I'd done if I'd lost you," and he kissed her tenderly on the lips.

Aiyana felt peace in the embrace. Taking almost all her strength she ran her hand through her husband's hair.

Ben leaned back and smiled, looking deep within her piercing black orbs, "That was the longest couple hours of my life."

"What do you mean?"

"You've been still for hours. I wasn't sure if you'd ever wake up."

Aiyana sighed, and lay in the comfort of her husbands arms. "It wasn't my time. I have more to do," and she told Ben the strange vision: the plague that her father warned of years ago, the dreams of the creatures that had to be stopped, the message that warned of the growing danger, and the link that now tied her to the mind of the parasite queen.

Chapter Twenty-seven

Cursed

Log Entry: Mountain Man's Poem

The trail speaks of monsters. Legends that walk by night. Ghosts that hunt for souls. Indian myths that haunt and fright. Cannibal giants that live to hunt. From the distant north they arrived. A tribe driven deep to the icy cold. Their return would mark the time. Who will stop forever? Who will answer the song? The Mountain Calling whispers. "Stop the endless swarm!"

Nov. 17, 1871

*   *   *

"Is something wrong Sergeant?" The lieutenant asked, standing in the center of the devastated village holding the reins of his horse while watching his men pass throughout the burned lodges and skinned bodies, searching the carnage for clues.

Lloyd saluted his superior, then let his vision drift behind his commander, watching the two men in buckskin moving toward the trees. "Permission to speak,— freely,— Sir?"

"Yes, yes — what is it?"

"It's about the scouts Sir." The soldier stuttered trying to find the right words.

"Sergeant — we are trying to avert war." The lieutenant almost growled as he cocked his head in an appalled fashion and snarled at his subordinate. "Those damn — uncouth backwoodsmen are no better than the savages we're searching for. They were desecrating the dead for God's sakes." The officer paused then whispered, "There's no telling what they're capable of, let on the loose."

"Sir — I know... but they did get us here, and they're the best trackers I've ever seen. I believe we need to give them another chance." Lloyd met his commander's gaze and cleared his throat. "We're in a harsh land and those men know this territory and the enemy — probably better than anyone. They've spent their lives out here among the Indians so no doubt they've adopted other uncivilized practices; but Sir, we don't know who butchered these people in the first place or why.— We need them Sir."

The lieutenant paused and grunted. He again scanned the savagery shaking his head, then turned to Lloyd. "Very well Sergeant,— retrieve them,— but know this," the officer lowered his voice to a whisper and stepped in close to his subordinate. "I hold you personally responsible for those two backwoodsmen. One more escapade and you'll be on latrine duty for the next month. Do we have an understanding?"

"Yes Sir," the Sergeant saluted. Dismissed, he ran out after the scouts finding them as they were about to ride off. "Zeb,— Claude,—wait!"

The two riders were busy talking and seemed disturbed by the interruption, watching with distaste as the soldier stumbled through the brush.

"The lieutenant's had a change of heart.— wait!"

"We'z had our full of ya'z boys," Claude spat, then ran the

thumb side of his palm over the corners of his mouth.

"The lieutenant regrets his hasty decision and requests..." Lloyd paused while trying to catch his breath. "He needs you gentlemen to help him find The Seer."

"Tell the lieutenant we've lost interest in searchin' fer that critter," Zeb reined his horse around, aiming him up the river. "We've got more important vermin to hunt down now."

Claude smiled and followed suit, but Lloyd pressed on coming up beside Zeb and resting his hand on the man's saddle, "Please,— Zeb,— I know the lieutenant is a self-righteous ass, but that Indian killed innocents and needs to be stopped."

Zeb stared at the sad faced man and grunted. "There's something bigger going on here than a renegade chief and a few ragged Indians." Looking up the river the younger mountain man seemed to focus on nothing in particular and paused for a long moment. "Indian prophecy spoke of this time and I'm now convinced that if we don't stop the power behind the current chain of events,— more's gonna be dead than a few blues and a couple settlers." Zeb,— real serious, his icy glare centered on the sergeant. "There's a plague coming. It's gonna sweep across this land like locust. Nothing will survive. I now know the visions were true and that vermin was inside the dead soldiers at the fort deforming them." Zeb spit, not taking his eye off the sergeant. "The harvest has arrived."

"What are you talking about?"

"Who do you think killed those people in that village?" Zeb was pointing as his voice quaked with anger.

"Probably savages,— enemies from another...."

"No." The last sharp bark dropped like a hammer with an affirmed spark of hatred that cut Lloyd's reply short. Zeb turned in the saddle to Claude; his face crinkled into a serious quest of affirmation. "Show him the skin."

The older man paused for a moment, then reached back into his saddlebags and pulled out what looked like a huge mass of gnarly black, multiple jointed spider legs, protruding from a leather hide. Claude handed the mess to Zeb who fumbled with it, then spread the skin: opening it up into what looked like a mask.

The sergeant studied the ghoulish features of the eyeless face and was taken aback. Heavy cords crowned the scaled leathery attributes of a ghoul,— a creature that lived in the nightmares and stories of the supernatural. It seemed to stare at him; the empty sockets — like a vanquished soul ready to haunt his dreams. The upper jaw bone was still attached allowing jagged tusks, like that of a saber tooth tiger, to extended from where a small mouth gaped; a mouth that probably sucked the blood of the living and lavished in the flesh still pulsating in its death throes. "What in hell is that?"

"These critters came a few years back;— hunted and killed without mercy. They roamed these very woods," Zeb scanned the surrounding trees then turned back to Lloyd, "and we hunted them until they left. Well,— they're back." The mountain man slapped the mask into the sergeant's chest. "With them has come some damn plague and we need to stop them."

Lloyd fumbled with the skin and took one last look before he handed it back to Zeb. "What can we do?"

"Believe."

*   *   *

The two mountain men returned to the village with Lloyd, but said nothing to the lieutenant as the troop assembled to depart. Zeb told the sergeant they needed to head up river and Lloyd conveyed the message as the scouts preceded the assembly, working the brush and following the trail of one of the Sky Demons along the icy waterway. Hours passed, but as night approached the scouts came upon another site where bodies were killed and skinned. Three men with pack horses carrying supplies for a small mining operation had been hit by a demon. The entrepreneurs were traveling up the river on their way to the Black Hills. The lieutenant believed Indians were responsible, blaming The Seer for the assault on the miners, regardless of anything Zeb and Claude argued. The butchery and apparent torture were a new expression of Indian's hostilities, but the officer had seen such killing before and was set in his opinion.

The Sioux had been given the Dakota territory in a treaty by the US government, but with the rumor of gold in the northern hills, white men: drawn by greed and the call for wealth spilled out over the coarse terrain; eager for the precious ore resting free for the pickin's to any with the fortitude to endure the climate and the possible conflict with the native inhabitants. All, driven by lust, literally swarmed northward in the quest for the yellow metal. The trespassing by these numerous infiltrators was met by an increasingly

195

hostile measure of violence, meted out by a people tired of their treatment by the white man and sick of the encroachment on their deeded lands. The US government had no control over its populace and the temperament of all involved was reaching a boiling point, but little could be done to curb the lust or quench the anger. For now the lieutenant simply ordered camp; the troop settled in and the bodies were pulled from their butchering posts and buried under piles of rock before taps was sounded.

Zeb and Claude encouraged a cold camp, but again the suggestion fell on deaf ears. By dark, a stark meadow near the river was dotted with the fires of numerous small camps. The men established friendly individual groups with associated cooking pits for the evening meals and warmth. Bed rolls covered the area's frozen ground and most of the troop found solace in the wrap of army issue blankets as the starry cloudless sky turned icy under a cold, northern wind.

Resigning themselves to the ignorance of the military, Zeb and Claude skirted the outer ridge of the encampment knowing if the Sky Demons were still present the fires would be like a beacon directing the beasts right to them, whether they personally had a fire or not. Creatures that could see the body heat of a man in almost any temperature would be able to see the flames from the pits from miles away, and these new visitors didn't seem too particular in the manner in which they killed game in their lust for blood.

As silence drifted over the base camp Zeb and Claude remained vigilant, unable to sleep; more and more of the small fires burned into coals, emitting the orange amber glow to the chilly dotted landscape, casting a restful somber mood to the icy windswept plain as the entire troop huddled in the only smattering of trees. Tonight would be a long one, but the two mountain men sat quietly on their watch; each wondering if it was to be their last.

Chapter Twenty-eight

Myth?

Sir:

The requested provisions for rendezvous at snake junction never arrived, nor did Corporal Wiggins return with news. We have determined the renegades have moved south. Troop is under supplied and out of food for horses. Our Osage scouts believe we can acquire some staples at The Hollows. The situation is desperate. Request fresh horses and provision for rendezvous at The Hollows on Monday.

Your obt. servant

Jeffery Kain

1st Lieutenant

*   *   *

Branches slapped the scout's face as his horse pounded through the pine forest. Titus could hear the monster gaining behind, the eerie trumpeting call growing louder as the creature raced after him.

Sam snorted and stumbled, going down onto his belly, sliding into a maze of brush; but blew through the tangled brittle branches, the gnarly saplings almost ripping Titus from the saddle. With a burst of energy the horse sprang back into a run as the man pulled himself center, stable on his mount. A small clearing gave a reprieve to the constant battering the rider was receiving. Titus looked back, catching a glimpse of the threat, thundering through the maze of trees. The beast was huge. The scout recognized the similarity to the deformities of the skeletal remains of the people butchered back at the massacre; yet this creature was not dead bone, but living,—a massive exoskeleton with powerful legs and contorted features. The man turned his attention back to Sam, "Did we just find the parent of them bodies at The Forks?"

Sam snorted as Titus braced himself. A large fallen pine blocked their course standing almost five foot high with a low hanging branch from a nearby tree obstructing the space above. Titus ducked low in the saddle as Sam took flight. The horse cleared the obstacle easily, slipping under the overhead timber; but the thick limb raked the man's back almost knocking the wind out of him. An unexpected ridge dropped off on the opposite side of the downed trunk and Sam hit the steep incline with a grunt, sliding down the ravine on his belly until he reached the bottom. Titus held on almost going over the top of his animal, but by grabbing the saddle horn he maintained his balance, pulling himself upright as Sam came to his feet running. With unbelievable power the horse climbed the soft dirt of the opposite bank and cleared the brush lining the ridge as Titus snuck a look back. The creature had paused at the fallen tree as the man watched it scream in anger at its lost quarry. With a sigh of relief Titus spurred Sam on, but the heavily lathered mount needed no additional encouragement to continue its flight.

After a lengthy run, assuring the scout they were safe, Titus eased Sam to a walk.

Sam reluctantly complied, but remained agitated by the near death experience.

For about a mile the scout continued the pace then dismounted and walked, cooling his animal down in the brisk mountain air. From here he traversed another couple of miles on foot beside Sam.

In a small glen Titus spotted what he thought was perhaps a resting elk; hunger was gnawing at his gut. Quietly he pulled his Henry rifle and approached with Sam blocking the advance. It was peculiar, but as he neared he noticed an unusual odor in the air. It seemed too cold for meat to rot, but the rancid smell contained a sickly nauseating punch that burned his sinuses and pasted his throat. Sam stopped and would go no further; Titus dropped the reins deciding not to force his animal against its better instincts and pressed on alone. On closer inspection the resting elk turned out to be a dead horse; its chest cavity was ripped out and not a bone remained among the putrid flesh. It didn't appear to Titus that an animal feeding was the culprit. The massive wound had pushed through the ribs seemed to peel the very skeleton from the tearing muscle and tissue. It was the same type of wound he saw exhibited by the dead scout in the mouth of the cave. The cave where that strange monster was.

Titus continued his examination. An abandoned fire pit revealed it as a previous campsite, but what sent shivers up his spine was the scorched earth and lifeless ash from bones resting burnt near the pit. Similar to the creature in the cave, pieces remained of the blackened skull that looked similar to parts of a horse or perhaps like the corpses back at The Forks.

"What the hell are these things?"

Poking the hard shell with the muzzle of his rifle he assured himself it was completely sterilized from the torching. Then returning and kneeling by the cold pit, examining the ash he determined the campsite was about a week old. Curiosity got the better of him, overcoming his reluctance he went back and lifted the empty shell, studying it more closely. The skull pieces were much thicker than anything he had seen before. The fire had either boiled the innards out or simply consumed everything from within. Titus was scratching his chin when he spotted a man's finger in the snow. He thought back to the body in the cave; it was missing a finger. Titus began to put it together. *The dead horse was Jake's. The very bones had come to life, ripping free of the animal's flesh and Jake had killed it, burning it in the fire. The scout then ran to that cave and died. But how did the two get infected?* Titus pondered the conclusion. If he backtracked the scout's course, maybe he could find where these creatures came from. Then take the military back to the cave and kill the creature. *But what about the women?* The situation was troubling.

First thing first,— find the trail. The scout began scouring the site when a new track caught his attention. It was the full print of a creature that stood upright, on two legs. Titus had seen a partial back at The Forks, but here was the whole foot,— the mark of a giant. Taloned claws, that seemed to grip the snow, spanned the ground in such a fashion that told of an inquisitive visitor. Titus had never seen evidence of such an animal before, but he remembered the tales told by his mentor James. Stories of creatures that came from the sky and hunted men. The former slave thought the rantings,— a vivid imagination; but James described the tracks in great detail. Here was the evidence voicing the truth. Everything the old Iroquois had told him wasn't fantasy.

Titus examined the trail and quickly realized the new visitor must have arrived at a similar conclusion. Jake's trail was almost a week cold, but this new visitor took off on a parallel course backtracking the dead scouts path. The funny thing was the frozen print left by The Stone Giant (as James referred to them) appeared older than Jakes', but the evidence spoke differently. This puzzle troubled Titus, but the clues leading to the truth were there to follow. The scout was determined to find the answers.

Sam snorted and backed away as Titus approached lifting his head, but the animal stepped on its reins stopping him as the scout cooed his ride. The horse relaxed and Titus grabbed the bridle and patted Sam on the whither. "We have work to do."

Swinging easily into the saddle the man nudged the horse into a trot. The trail was cold and Titus needed to eat up the miles fast.

Chapter Twenty-nine

A Good Host

Retrospect

" The power of hiding ourselves from one another

is mercifully given,

for men are wild beasts,

and would devour one another but for this protection. "

Henry Ward Beecher (1813 - 1887)

*   *   *

Robin came to slowly, her head pounding from the pistol whipping to her cheek. She could feel herself being dragged over the cold dirt floor of the dark tunnel, but the reality of her plight was still lost in the haze of semi-consciousness. Her shoulder socket was burning from the rough handling of her captor and her hip was searing with pain. Her undergarments at her right side had given way to the raspy nature of the stone floor leaving a bloody trail of cloth from the torn and fraying friction of her torturous journey that rubbed her skin into a mass of scraped and bleeding flesh.

Robin opened her eyes slowly and looked down the dark corridor. The dim light of a lantern cast its glow deep within the subterranean passage like a beacon calling to the lost, but the distant flame did little to brighten her cramped surroundings. Behind was only darkness that seemed to obscure any hope of escape or succor.

Robin tried to regain her strength and rolled slightly to her back to relieve the scorching wound burning her hip. She supported her held arm with her left hand and tugged to free herself, but her captor just jerked her sharply, pulling her off the ground and dumping her with a thud to the hard stone floor ahead of him. Robin moaned under the new bruising, but the slight pause in the man's forward movement allowed her to spin to her knees and then to her feet. She staggered as the man jerked her off balance, but she maintained her footing. He shoved her with his free hand; she stepped to keep her balance, then followed the asserted direction, reluctantly.

"That's better," came the raspy response from her captor. "We can either make this easy or we can make it real hard," and he kicked her forward while letting go of her arm, pushing her toward the light. "Now walk."

Robin fell against the wall of the tunnel catching herself as McCray pushed her again. Stumbling, she braced herself on the wall and took a few steps; but was very weak and felt dizzy. McCray barked something at her that she could not understand, but she continued forward anyway feeling her cheek and the already crusting blood clotting her wound. As she got closer to the light she was regaining her composure and the reality of her situation.

Robin worked at Momma's Cradle, but not as one of the ladies. She ran the bath and shaved the patrons, but her Aunt Inez, the madam, had protected her from the more ravenous endeavors of the house's occupation. Robin had never been with a man and now fate was quickly revealing the gravity of her situation. She looked back at the burly McCray and his twisted smile, feeling a wave of nausea consume her soul. The man was armed and much stronger than her, but she was determined to put up a fight.

She began to examine her surroundings. The tunnel was a barren corridor. No rocks that could be used as weapons; not even loose dirt to throw in the face of her enemy. Robin winced as McCray's boot landed squarely on her backside and propelled her through the opening of a small chamber where the lantern hung on a peg in the far wall.

Robin scrambled to her feet as McCray jumped to her side and grabbed her bodice at the sleeve; pulling he ripped the heavy cloth, simultaneously spinning her around to face him.

The woman clutched at her falling apparel and spit in the man's face.

McCray backhanded Robin knocking her against the wall and reached out grabbing at her midsection. The petticoat, torn and frayed on the right hip, ripped free unexpectedly as the man tried to pull her back, causing McCray to stumble slightly still clutching the cloth.

Robin kicked hard, catching the grizzly rapist in his groin.

The man sucked in with the sudden shock falling to his knees clutching himself.

The woman pushed by, but McCray swung his free arm taking Robin's legs out from under her. She scrambled away picking up a rock and stood spinning to face her attacker.

McCray pulled his pistol and pointed it at the panting woman. "Drop the stone or I'll drop you."

"Go ahead and shoot you bastard, but I'll not give into you."

McCray cocked his pistol as a sudden look of fear contorted Robin's face; she backed toward the entryway. McCray smiled and fired at the tunnel's mouth causing the woman to jump back near the lantern. With a laugh he mumbled, "I thought so," as he re-cocked his colt.

His attention was drawn to a sound behind. Turning, the man felt steely fingers grip his weaponless arm as the smooth ebony head of an eyeless creature encapsulated his view. The salivating mouth hissed, as large fangs neared. The putrid smell of rotting flesh burned McCray's lungs as its hot breath choked his wind. Somewhere behind he heard Robin scream, but McCray was no longer aware of anything but the icy chill of his impending death. Bringing his pistol to bare on this new antagonist he fired point blank, but the bullet deflected off the face of the creature as vice like talons disarmed him.

Robin backed against the wall as the man yelled in pain. She watched in horror as what looked to be one of the creatures ribs stabbed her would-be rapist in the chest. McCray went limp as the monster dropped the body and turned its attention to her. Robin covered her mouth with her right hand and made a break, running for the exit of the chamber; but the monster cut her off. She moved to the left; a bat fluttered by her head and flew into McCray's face. Robin screamed again and tried to run by the man's body when a second winged thing jumped onto a broken stalagmite, blocking her path. She froze; with blinding speed the bird sprang through the air, slamming into her face. She wiped at the gooey tar smeared across her cheek. The fluid burned. Gagging, Robin choked some of the mess down her throat. She staggered and fell as the monster straddled her. Robin tried to cry out one last time, a silent scream, then slipped into unconsciousness.

*   *   *

Daisy could hear the confrontation somewhere in the darkness ahead, gunshots echoing down the narrow passage. She increased her pace; the smooth hard stone surface of the tunnel containing no obstacles as she felt her way along the walls. The long maze she traversed contained a few lamps, but she opted to leave them to secure her stealthy approach on her quarry; now she almost regretted her last decision after traveling almost a mile along the dark corridor.

Catching a glimmer of light off in the distance, a ray of hope launched her straight for the glowing flame, but the weapon's fire just minutes earlier suppressed her hopeful outlook. Now she forgot about stealth and pulled her pistol, breaking into a run. Her friend needed succor and she would provide deliverance; killing the animal that carried her off.

She entered the subterranean chamber, empty, except for the lantern casting its yellow light about the small room. Frayed bloody cloth dotted the floor like breadcrumbs; portions of Robin's garments laid scattered where they were dropped by the opposite exit. Daisy feared the worst, but still hoping Robin escaped her attacker, *Perhaps she ran deeper into the maze ahead.* Checking her weapon Daisy was determined not to be in the dark again and lifted the lantern from its post. The far opening looked like a cave-in. Daisy stepped over the rubble and scanned the next interior.

From the small entryway forward the mine took on a different appearance. *This is no man dug tunnel;* but a cave, hidden deep within the earth's crust. Daisy held the light up studying her surroundings. A waterfall dropped from a distant wall filling a stream that flowed along the far side of the chamber, *Perhaps a quarter mile away.* Large stalactites hung from the high ceiling, like icicles, in a beautiful array of white, green and differing shades of blue, reflecting the light of the lantern in glossy hues of brilliant color.

Daisy marveled at the beauty of the hidden chamber and stepped softly into the still tomb. She moved briskly to the slow stream and followed the water course a short distance, spotting more of the tattered cloth marking the trail. Daisy picked up a big piece of the ripped clothing, dropped at the edge of the water. She squatted, and held up her lamp up to see what was on the other side of the stream: a narrow incline, and a low ledge bridged over a dark chasm. Daisy guessed her quarry crossed the river at this point and disappeared in the dark aperture—beckoning her on.

Placing her hand in the water she pulled it back quickly. "Damn that's cold," she muttered and shivered at the thought of swimming in the icy stream. She looked at the distant crevice and then at the rag in her hand. Her friend needed her help and no one else could come to Robin's aid. Daisy thought how uncomfortable it would be in this cold dark cavern if she swam the course in her clothes. *How deep was this river?* The cave was damp; *would her clothes even dry?*

Quickly she disrobed, bundling her wardrobe into a ball and tied it together with the gun belt—buckling it snugly. Placing the pistol in its holster, she hoisted the package to her shoulder and checked to make sure the gun was in easy reach, pulling it out twice and replaced it with ease each time.

Picking up the lantern she stepped into the current amazed at the force exerted at her feet. The waterway was deceptively peaceful from the shore; but as she moved deeper, up to her waist, the water worked hard to take her feet out from under her. Daisy stepped slowly forward, feeling the bottom of the river carefully with each step; planting each foot solidly before dragging the other in her forward motion. Water lapped at her waist. She shivered under its icy spray. Goosebumps danced across skin. The cold was robbing her strength; her outer extremities turned blue. Her blood slowed. She lurched, and stumbled, as the ground gave-way under her feet. Dropping neck deep, she drifted quickly down stream, losing control, while the natural forces pummeled and choked her effort to survive. Sucking in sharply at the icy chill, she gasped for air and bobbed, trying desperately to regain her balance and keep her clothes and lantern out of the wet that was stealing her life.

The current slammed her up against a large rock and Daisy grunted at the impact. Struggling against the relentless power of the stream, she rolled, facing the outcropping; but the water pulled at her body in a continuous effort to take her life. She gasped and climbed the slippery surface, knowing if she held on to her bundle she would die, but the fear of severe exposure without clothes kept her hands locked to the gun belt supporting her meager possessions.

Shifting her weight, she lost her grip on the slick stone and was pushed into a pocket between a second rock. The power of the river was winning. Daisy's fight was slipping away.

Chapter Thirty

Battle

Sioux Legend

The ax has fallen
>*the lance is free*
The enemy has awakened
>*vengeance's decree*
There is no rest
>*for that of the wicked*
A messiah has risen
>*coming forth is the call*
Take Your Possession
>*In The Shadow's Rising*

*   *   *

Thirty enraged Indian braves and one golden haired mountain man hid in the trees watching the hated enemy approach the river. The cavalry's numbers had increased by about twenty-five; probably joined by the patrol from The Forks, chasing the Sioux most of the previous day. Why the US cavalry declared war on Isaac's tribe no longer mattered to the warriors ready to ambush the soldiers coming to water their horses. What did matter,— the Sioux were thirsty for blood. Vengeance fused this small, once peaceful branch of the Sioux tribe,— reluctant for war, into a dangerous band of merciless killers bent on the destruction of anyone associated with the US government. Death would come swiftly to the fools riding into a firestorm of men the golden haired warrior positioned to take the best advantage of the natural cover afforded by the trees and tall ridges, guarding the seemingly safest coarse to the river.

The green commander of the troop was oblivious to the danger, probably feeling safe in their numbers and training: armed with carbines and sabers, still toting the memories of their recent victory against the helpless victims of yesterdays offensive: the elderly too old to fight and the wives and children of Isaac and Reuben's adopted tribe.

Isaac's plan was simple: line up along the ridges on either side, wait until the enemy columns had made their way into the small valley, don't fire until they're so close no one would miss. In the first wave they would catch the soldiers by surprise and the numbers should swing closer to the tribe's favor. Resist the first impulse to charge, but reload and shoot again from the cover of tree, hill, or natural rock bulwark. The startled soldiers will then call a retreat to regroup; but as they try and run, a rear guard—that let them pass at first, would make as much noise as possible and open fire in an effort to turn them back to the river. Undoubtedly by that time the Sioux would have the advantage and any survivors of the cavalry would feel the wrath of men outraged by the unthinkable and forged into a force with one purpose in life—to avenge.

Isaac's pistol rested on a rock ledge by his side within easy reach as he stood poised with grim determination; his muzzleloader trained on the captain near the head of the column. His shot would signal the attack as Reuben sat ready to then take out the lieutenant. Any other men of rank would be their next targets as the two marksmen would try and eliminate the command structure.

The golden haired mountain man took two deep deliberate

breaths; exhaling them slowly as he calmed his nerves and steadied his muscles. With the ball at the muzzle end of his rifle resting smooth in the forked cradle of his sight he followed the captain's head effortlessly as the unsuspecting target moved closer. Suddenly the officer reined his mount to a stop raising his arm to halt his command. The silent order spoke of trouble and although the enemy was farther away then Isaac had hoped he squeezed his trigger smoothly. The report of the weapon echoed over the small valley as a cloud billowed forth momentarily blocking the mountain man's view, but the impact struck the intended man in the forehead, taking out half of the back of his skull as the ball exited, spinning the captain off the rear of his horse.

Almost simultaneously, Reuben shot the lieutenant in the chest. The man slumped forward in the saddle and then slid from his mount, his left foot still stuck in the stirrup as the horse bolted. The Sioux war cries and multiple rifle fire told the battle was in full swing within moments. Isaac and Reuben mechanically reloaded.

The golden-haired warrior shot a sergeant yelling commands as he tried to organize the chaos and Reuben dropped the bugler amidst a hail of lead aimed at his position. Both men ducked the onslaught and reloaded as the cavalry un-expectantly charged the ridges, taking the offensive to the enemy.

Isaac popped up over his natural rock battlement to shoot again and met a mounted soldier with pistol drawn and aimed at him. The horse reared, startled at the sudden appearance of the blond and Isaac stumbled, avoiding the hooves and fell back to his left hip. Swinging the muzzle of his rifle upward toward his antagonist, he instantaneously pulled the trigger. The bullet struck the soldier in the chest causing him to jerk back and drop his Colt. The horse's hooves hit the dirt to Isaac's left as the golden haired warrior rolled away from the danger, picked up his enemy's fallen pistol, shooting two more soldiers in quick succession from his prone position.

The charge quickly lost focus as some of the cavalry broke rank and bolted for the river. Reuben dropped the one leading the retreat and spun to the brush behind to recover his horse for pursuit.

Isaac scrambled to retrieve his own pistol from the rock ledge by his initial perch while the horse of the man he had shot with his rifle was still pounding the earth and striking the air with its front legs as the mortally wounded rider was fighting desperately to stay on. Isaac grabbed the reins to the rearing horse and swung into the saddle pulling the rider from his perch, then spurred the animal into a charge of the retreating enemy making a break for the river. The acquired cavalry pistol in his left hand clicked on an empty chamber as Isaac tried to fire the weapon so he threw it aside and pulled his revolver which he had tucked in his belt and shot into the fleeing soldiers.

Behind, his victorious brethren were also gathering up their horses to take up pursuit as ten yelling riders led by Reuben joined Isaac in his attack. About fifteen surviving soldiers regrouped at the river's edge and turned to charge,— to the Indians' surprise.

The blond mountain man noticing one of the men, with four crusted red marks down his left cheek, was flanking his companions nearer the river's edge. Sashtee had skin and blood under her right fingernails; Isaac assumed she had clawed the flesh of an assailant during her fight for life. Now the vengeful husband felt sure he had found the very man that assaulted his wife and left her and his unborn child to die. His rage surged as he thought of his beautiful Sashtee slipping away in his arms.

Gut-shot was a slow, unbearable way to die in itself, but this animal in his merciless assault had put a bullet in her stomach and left her to lie naked and alone on an icy snow bank in agony for hours before death finally claimed her. Isaac's soul screamed for revenge; to feel this man's life drain under his hand sucked all reason. He dashed his mount in a direct line of attack on the man to the right of the regrouped offensive. Pounding down the ridge on a course undeterred by the shower of lead, Isaac saw nothing but the single target of his retribution.

Isaac emptied his pistol in the direction of the advancing enemy then tossed the useless weapon aside and pulled his Bowie knife from its sheath. The soldiers drew saber to meet the onslaught of Indians as Isaac drove his animal into the charging scar-faced soldier's mount. Both horses stumbled at the collision, but Isaac sprang over his saddle at impact, hitting the soldier in the chest, forcing the enemy from the saddle and causing the soldier to land with a thud on his back. Isaac came up grabbing the solder's throat with his left hand and stuck his blade into the man's abdomen while spitting in the vanquished's face. Leaning down over the defeated, Isaac whispered in the helpless man's ear, "After I kill your comrades, I'll be back to peel ya slow." Then he twisted the blade as the man screamed out in agony. Grabbing the man's topknot, Isaac cut to the bone, tugging with his left hand as he drove his right knee into the man's shoulder, shoving the limp body to the earth. The scalp snapped free with a pop. With the Sioux war cry on his lips, the enraged mountain man rose off the defeated and pounded his chest in fury. Spotting the soldier's sword in the grass by the bank, Isaac lunged after the weapon and picking up the fallen saber with his left hand, ran to meet the next enemy.

Clashing sword, knife, war-axe and lance echoed over the rivers surface as the battle pushed into the swift water.

In the distance a bugle sounded announcing the near approach of support coming to the cavalry's aid.

Reuben flew off his horse and landed behind the saddle of a fighting soldier. Wrapping his left arm around the man's neck he plunged his knife into the soldier's kidney and pulled the man from his mount when the bugle's call caught his attention. A large force was pressing their way from the opposite side of the river. The young looking Crow brave scanned the battle, spotting his uncle pushing waist deep into the river after a soldier who had fallen from his mount. The chase through the splashing barrier would lead the two into the path of the advancing support. Panic melted over Reuben's features. "Uncle we must fall back!" He screamed, but Isaac was blinded by revenge and oblivious to danger's swift approach.

Reuben seized the reins of his acquired mount and turned, charging his ride into the river after Isaac as a hail of bullets whistled over the banks of the channel. The first volley had little effect other than warn the Sioux of the advancing reserves and the sudden reversal of their victory, but the warriors refused to yield and continued to press on over the vanquished to the other side of the water, misinterpreting Reuben's course as a continuing offensive.

Isaac caught his prey and drove the saber into the man's back then looked up to face the oncoming onslaught. With only a knife in his belt and sword in his hand he cursed. Taking no heed of his tribe's following him into death's jaws; he continued his path to the opposite bank. Resigning his mortality, Isaac would surrender his soul; with grim determination, he faced the well-armed reinforcements as the survivors of his band came up behind.

The cavalry was almost upon them when a Sioux war cry echoed from the sparse trees around the approaching fresh soldiers. Gunfire erupted from the hidden crags and brush of an almost barren landscape. As if from nowhere a party of Sioux and Cheyenne warriors intercepted the enemy, catching them off guard. The battle immediately turned in the Indians favor as The Seer's band, armed with repeating rifles, laid waste to the unsuspecting enemy.

Isaac's tribe charged into the fray with sword, lance and powder.

"Uncle!" Reuben called out as his mount splashed out of the river on the opposite bank beside Isaac and extended his hand to his golden haired brother.

The mountain man grasped the offer, and swung easily into the saddle behind the Crow warrior. Together, with war cries on their lips they attacked. Isaac again pulled his knife, as Reuben shot an acquired colt pistol at the enemy, hitting his first target square in the chest.

Isaac simultaneously launched himself from the back of the horse striking two soldiers off balance and taking one out of the saddle. He plunged his blade deep into the man's side. The other soldier struck by the blond's jump, regained his saddle and leveled his pistol at Isaac; but Reuben fired twice, the third trigger pull falling on an empty chamber; but the two bullets sufficed, as the enemy slumped over his horse's neck.

The animal reared spinning the dead man backwards as two other soldiers, now horseless charged Isaac. The mountain man grabbed the sword from the dying man under him and stood in time to parry the saber blow of his first assailant and blocked the second's jab with his long knife. Clashing metal echoed over the river valley as the two assailants pressed their advantage driving the mountain man back to the water's edge.

Reuben, under attack by another rider dropped the pistol and pulled his war axe and charged. The steeds collided as saber and tomahawk missed their intended targets, but the close quarter limited the sword's usefulness and the Crow brave caught the enemy with his next effort under the chin as the warrior's horse regained its footing. The soldier's busted jaw stunned his attack as Reuben then swung a savage backhanded blow, driving the blunt end of the ax into the man's temple knocking the man cold.

Isaac, grappling in close conflict with one of the assailants, as the other had tripped, kicked his enemy in his manhood then plunged his blade into the soldier's abdomen. With a cough the man spit up blood dropping to his knees as Isaac deflected another blow from the second man, intended to decapitate him. The mountain man ducked and spun, kicking at the soldier's knee with his left foot. The strike landed against the joint as a thunderous crack sounded and the man's leg buckled backward. The pain caused the saber to drop as the Isaac plunged his sword into the fallen's chest. The mountain man pulled his weapon free then scanned the battlefield. As the last soldier fell, the victorious Indians whooped and cheered their triumph.

Isaac fell back against a boulder catching his breath and scrutinized the devastation rent on the cavalry. An unknown tribe had come to their aid. How they got there, the blond had no idea but as the mountain man caught his breath he noticed a short warrior walking toward him with purpose. With steely eyes locked on the small Cheyenne, Isaac took a deep breath and stood up, not sure of the man's intentions.

Others of the short warrior's tribe gathered around, but the blond remained undaunted at the unnerving assembly. Isaac,—the only white man still standing on the battlefield and perhaps viewed as an enemy by this new group of Indians at war with the whites,— felt alone among this new throng.

Silence fell over the once chanting victor's as the apparent leader of the Cheyenne and Sioux war party stopped in front of the golden haired mountain man.

The men from Isaac's tribe gathered to their adopted brother's side, uncertain of this new leader's intentions.

The two men studied each other with a long pause then the eyes of The Seer dropped to the bear claw adornment around Isaac's neck. The mummified finger of The War God's hand rested center on the mountain man's chest and an expression of wonderment melted over the stone features of The Seer. The leader slowly reached out and touched the digit, taking it between his thumb and index finger and began to gently rub the token just as Isaac often did out of habit, then let go and stepped back. Turning to his men he cried out in the Cheyenne language, *"Behold! The one who is to come!"* The medicine man looked skyward then back to his tribe. *"The Great Spirit has heard the cry of his children and sent us a brother not of our flesh. A warrior forged by his battle with the gods. It marks the time of our end. A time of change... The gods have demanded sacrifice."* The warrior paused for a long moment, then shouted. *"The time of the calling has arrived."*

The gathered men began to mutter. Questioning looks passed

among the warriors,— one to the other. The braves of Isaac's tribe were bewildered as they watched in confusion the events unfolding. With the skill of a practiced orator the medicine man had the full attention of all.

The throng stared in amazement at the golden haired mountain man standing like a statue before the gestures of The Seer.

The preacher's voice dropped to a whisper, as he looked back to Isaac. *"We must join under The War God's lead."* Pounding his chest, his words then lifted in tempo to a rhythm of poetry. *"We must kill the hated enemy,"* and in a crescendo he cried, *"we must finish the task the heavens have loosened on our land."*

The Seer turned back to Isaac with his last word and pulled a knife from his belt.

The mountain man stood unwavering as the small man lifted the blade. *Am I the sacrifice the gods were calling for? What prophecy was this medicine man referring to?* Isaac met the steely gaze of The Seer. Any fear the blond had of death, washed away with the passing of his wife but Isaac felt he had more to do.

The short warrior unflinchingly dragged the edge of his blade across his own palm while his gaze never faltered from the mountain man's. *"You are the warrior who is young, but old. A brother, yet not. To death I pledge my life to you,—* Pu-na.*"—* (the Golden One) The Seer handed the knife to Isaac. *"May our mingled blood seal my loyalty."*

Pu-na took the offered steel and passed the fluid tarnished weapon into the flesh of his own left hand. *"May death not break our bond that war has sealed this day. In death I pledge my soul. May the Great Spirit not forsake our pact and grant us victory on the trail of vengeance we must walk together."*

The Seer smiled, *"But this path is one of deliverance."*

"Each man chooses his own destiny. But the goal acquired will only be victory if viewed by The One, based on his will." Isaac frowned, *"My choice is vengeance."*

The Seer turned to the throng, *"Deliverance!"*

And the mixed throng cheered.

Chapter Thirty-one

Ghost Tracking

The Song of the Priestess

The spirits have warned, of the trial to come

The winds of change, mother's children gone

Bleached as bones dried on the desert sands

parched is the message, a land stripped and dead

*   *   *

Aiyana sat up as Broken-Toe handed an altered headgear to Ben. The giant squatted and set a second helmet on the ground next to her. The Marshal had worked on the armaments the entire time Aiyana was unconscious.

Opening a compartment on the left side of his wide belt band, Broken-Toe removed a small rectangular box and pushed a few flickering buttons. The horns on Ben's mask moved, then swung in sequence and locked. The giant then motioned to Ben, pointing out the altered triggering mechanisms in the cheek pads and directed the mask in Ben's hands at a distant wall. Pushing the left cheek sensor with his hand a bright green laser turned on over the right eye of the mask and the horns pivoted in the direction the beam was pointing. The arming device normally sighted by calculating eye movements with the beam, but almost instantaneously on the wall marked by the laser, the horns fired a flaming ball of liquid metal. The Guardian then let go of the reconfigured helmet with a nod to Ben, *You understand?*

The mountain man smiled, "No wonder you critter's shoot so good. All you have to do is look and wink at a target."

Retrieving two fine-meshed, mail-coats, from the surplus armaments, Broken-Toe showed the humans how to put on the gear and helped fit the customized armor and masks to their person.

Ben was amazed at how light the metal felt as the giant worked the final fitting and then helped Aiyana. The mountain man stood clear of his companions scanning the surface of the wall finding an appropriate mark and triggered the left cheek sensor of the mask by a single blink. He could see the beams target the wall as his visor focused, triangulating the position by scanning his pupils, then fired. The erupting blast startled him at first, but there was almost no recoil to the weapon. Examining his target he was astounded at the accuracy. By winking his right eye the targeting laser sighted, but the weapon didn't fire. Ben right winked again and the distant wall enlarged as the mask visor zoomed in on the laser's location. Blinking both eyes did nothing.

Aiyana stepped over to her husband, still a little weak from her ordeal; but immediately targeted, shooting the same spot.

"Could this get any easier?" Ben laughed.

"No wonder these creatures are so powerful."

Aiyana's voice came over Ben's COM system. The man was amazed at the clarity of the words.

Broken-Toe interrupted with a few chirps and clicks and handed the humans two large gloves with a protective extension that ran all the way to the elbow. They recognized the items as smaller versions of what the giant was wearing and slipped them on. Broken took Ben's hand and forearm and forced a movement twisting the wrist and then motioned Ben to make a fist.

Ben complied and blades extended up and down the gauntlet, like curved razor hooks. As jagged burs on an insect's legs, the numerous knives could lacerate a man's flesh with one swipe. Repeating the motion disengaged the razors.

The giant then wrapped a thick belt around the mountain man's waist, opened a compartment on the wide band and showed him a series of buttons. As the Marshal tapped the controls the man's visor changed perspectives of vision from telescoping normal sight to changes in heat and night vision. The giant then cupped the center buckle which appeared to be a large oval crystal and the small hairs on Ben's body tingled as the mountain man disappeared. The polarized-transmuting field, transposed the light around Ben's aurora, bending the visual perception of an onlooker's optic nerves, hiding any morphed object. In this case the mountain man. Broken then tapped the field off.

Ben continued tinkering with the new controls while the giant instructed his wife.

While the two humans were busy playing with their new toys, Broken-Toe retrieved one of their rifles and unloaded the bullets. Taking his tooling laser the giant altered the head of the shell and pushed what looked like a tack in the newly formed hole. The metal rivet snapped into place with a pop as the Marshal started the process on the next bullet.

Ben was momentarily distracted from his practice, spotting the giant messing with his rifle. "What do you suppose that critter's up to now?"

"Let's find out."

The two humans approached watching the giant work. After about a minute Ben tapped him on the shoulder and pointed to his rifle, "What are you doing?"

Broken-Toe grabbed a piece of loose armor from the supply pile and tossed it a short distance away. He then showed one of the unaltered shells to the man, and loading it into the weapon shot the armor. The metal bounced at the impact. The Marshal then motioned

Ben to retrieve it. The man noticed as he picked up the breast mesh, *No damaged*. "No wonder your kind's so hard to kill." Ben meandered back to the giant.

Broken grabbed the armament from Ben and tossed it back where it was. At first Ben thought he had misinterpreted what the instructor wanted from him, but the giant continued by showing the humans one of the altered bullets; loading it into the rifle he again shot at the armor, demonstrating a remarkable amount of skill with the repeater.

"Damnation!" Ben muttered, picking up the protective armor with a large hole ripped through its center. "Metal piercing bullets," Ben nodded in approval, showing the target to his wife.

Broken-Toe went back to work on the ammunition available as the humans joined him. He showed them how to push the studs into place and while he drilled they assembled. After all the bullets present were altered, Broken-Toe put the remainder of the studs in belt pouches and handed the articles to his recruits, along with their rifles.

Ben and Aiyana strapped the supplies around their waists and stood almost at attention before the giant as they readied their weapons. Pointing to the tunnel where Aiyana was attacked, Broken-Toe made a fist in the air and motioned to the corridor.

"I guess we're goin' in there," Ben said with grim determination.

"I think we'll fare much better this time," Aiyana laughed.

A few clicks and chirps came over the COM and Ben got the distinct impression the giant was being short with him. "I don't think our leader is very patient."

"No sense of humor either," Aiyana giggled.

As they worked their way down the corridor Aiyana felt fear taking hold. Still a little weak from her ordeal she remembered how silently the creature had moved,— coming up behind her. Aiyana shuddered and froze.

"Everything okay?" Ben asked concerned as he noticed his wife had stopped behind him.

Aiyana took a deep breath and tried to calm her pounding heart, "I just need a minute."

"I understand."

Suddenly Aiyana was in darkness. She felt neither cold nor hot. There was a presence, but she could hear nothing. Images transposed to her mind of a room, much different than the corridor she was standing in moments ago. "Ben,— are you there?"

"*Come to me*," beckoned a voiceless urging, like a mental summons—pleading. A strange sense of comfort and well being drifted over her soul. The room seemed familiar, even soothing as a palm ran through her hair. She felt passive to the touch and gave in to the stroke. "*Come to me*," again whispered the voiceless thought. Aiyana looked up to the source of the call as a huge black taloned hand of the nightmarish skeleton cradled her head softly.

"Are you okay?" Ben asked, resting his hand on her shoulder.

Aiyana pulled away knocking her husband's hand off as she gasped.

Broken-Toe exited the opposite end of the tunnel ignoring the humans as Aiyana regained her composure.

"Do you want to wait out by the horses?"

"No,—" Aiyana barked in disgust, "I'm fine,— let's go."

Ben smiled as his wife pushed by him, guessing she was probably embarrassed at her slight show of weakness.

The room with the subterranean pool was warm as the two humans stepped onto the steel grated decking. The water level had risen, but the rhythmic pulsing of the undulating light was unchanged as it kept the compartment aglow with radiant colors. Broken-Toe had already worked his way around the platform skirting the pond and disappeared through a dark passageway on the far side. Ben and Aiyana followed.

The hallway they entered was larger than any other corridor on the ship and circular in shape, but less light was available. Dark crevices and hidden shadows lined the walls as the two humans scanned the interior. The marshal had disappeared somewhere within.

Ben and Aiyana made their way into the tunnel, rifles ready. Each step echoed as they ducked obstacles and downed girders. Small rooms lined the walkway as they explored the section that appeared to have taken more damage than any other part of the downed frigate. Water dripped and puddled making sections of the floor slick and mud spilled out over the expanse from ruptures in the exterior shell of the frigate.

"Does any of this look familiar?" Ben asked as they stumbled through the maze.

"Say what?"

"In your dreams,— anything familiar?"

"Oh,— no."

"Well I got some bad feelin's."

"Keep 'um to yerself," Aiyana mumbled.

A few faint clicks came over their COM's and Ben tapped his wife on the shoulder whispering, "You think he's trying to tell us something?"

"Probably to shut-up," Aiyana seemed annoyed,— different. Ben couldn't put his finger on it, but his wife was acting peculiar. He was wondering if the creature's attack was affecting her disposition. She was always a strong willed person, but this was strange.

More clicks and chirps resonated softly amid intermittent static.

"I wish I could understand — critter," Ben chuckled.

"That's not Broken-Toe," Aiyana whispered.

"You think that black varmint speaks their lingo?"

"No,— it doesn't."

Ben didn't bother to ask how she knew, but as he listened to the static he noticed multiple chirping, some overlapping others. "It sounds like a conversation."

"I think we're hearing the sounds from up ahead."

Ben thought about what his wife said and tilted and turned his head slightly. The strange dialect seemed to always be ahead of him, but Aiyana's voice came directly to his ears.

"Great,— we've got visitors to our party and we don't know if their friend or foe." Ben knelt and crawled forward past his wife to a natural bunker of downed structure and dirt, peering over it as his wife followed suit. Standing in the corridor were two Sky Demons. Broken-Toe wasn't with them.

"Who are these guys?" Came Aiyana's voice over the COMs.

"I don't know," whispered Ben.

"I didn't say that," Aiyana responded.

The mountain man looked back at his wife. "What?"

Ben's voice came over the COM system: "I don't know, but it looks like we're gonna have to make a stand." Broken-Toe's clicks and chirps came clearly to the ear followed by: "Ain't like no other soldier boys I've come across before."

Aiyana tapped her husband, "The renegades chasing us.

That's the conversation we had."

"Is Broken-Toe telling us these are enemies?"

"That was a discussion about enemies," Aiyana whispered back, as one of the Sky Demons turned their way.

"Damn!— they've seen us," Ben said as he froze.

The Sky Demon stared at Ben getting the attention of his companion, recognizing the mask as one of their young ones. The giant then motioned for the youth to come forward and turned the sights on his mask to zoom in his vision.

From the shadows and out of sight Aiyana took the action as an act of aggression and raised her rifle shooting her husband's antagonist in the chest. The shrapnel reinforced bullet ripped through the creature's body armor and knocked him back against his companion as the victim's mask cannon fired wildly into the air.

Ben triggered his mask's targeting switch and shot the second Sky Demon within seconds as a third enemy ran out of a hidden compartment and fired on the two humans. Shooo...wack, resounded the impact as debris flew. Ben ducked the shot as Broken-Toe stepped out of hiding and struck the enemy with a quarter-staff, knocking him off his feet. The Demon hit the ship floor with a thud as the Broken's gauntlet blades engaged and dropping to one knee the giant drove the multiple knives into the creature's chest and raked them down the abdomen.

Ben and Aiyana stepped out from behind the makeshift bunker as the demon Aiyana had shot groaned and his targeting laser came back online. Broken-Toe spun and kicked the creature's head, dislodging it from its mount and then stood over the enemy. The two humans arrived at his side as the giant drove the blade on the end of the war-lance, twisting it. The vanquished jerked in spasm then went still.

"I take it *prisoner's,* not in your vocabulary."

"Quiet Ben," Aiyana snapped as she slapped her husband on the back.

"What?" Ben flinched with a smile then turned back to Broken-Toe, "Friend of yours?"

"Friend," sounded an imitation of Ben's voice followed by a click.

The mountain man realized his mistake as his wife hit him again. Ben knelt by the body and triggered his wrist blades in a mock stabbing, "Enemy."

Broken parroted the dialogue and Ben responded by pointing at his wife and himself, "Friend."

The giant seemed to lose interest and turned his attention to an opening in the floor like a trapdoor that Ben hadn't noticed before. The Demons were apparently examining the opening when the two humans happened on them.

On closer inspection water had filled the compartment below, but what seemed the most curious to Broken-Toe was the damage to the floor around the hole. It looked like something punched and burned the metal.

Ben immediately reflected back on the acidic blood of the sightless birds and how it reacted when it came into contact with water. *Did that giant black varmint have the same type of blood? Broken-Toe must of injured it back at the pool.*

"What is it?" Aiyana asked as she joined her companions.

"I think that critter that attacked you came out here," Ben pointed at the floor. "It must bleed the same juice, as those winged vermin."

Broken-Toe raised a hand in the air and closed his fist with a small shake. Ben shook his head positively as Aiyana rested her palm on her husband's shoulder. "What's it mean?" She asked.

"The hunt has begun," Bed replied, with a grim smile.

*   *   *

Ben studied the unusual blood trail. The strange footprints burned into the floor of the ship. The creature's acidic fluid had undoubtedly run down its leg and mixed with the water from the pool, outlining its own instep permanently into the steel decking. The tracks were unlike anything the man had seen before, but he immediately began mentally cataloging the new find for future reference in stalking this prey.

The mountain man was amazed at the distance covered by the creature with each step as he followed the trail.

Broken-Toe watched with keen interest his student's uncanny ability to identify each sign and interpret almost immediately where the next track would fall as the party almost ran down the narrow corridor. The trail led through the bowels of the ship and exited at a breach in the outer hull opposite the cargo hole where they had entered. Earth filled the opening making the gap difficult to climb through but Broken-Toe led the way, almost getting stuck in the hole.

The loose dirt filled in behind the giant, narrowing the aperture as Ben dug his way through. The man remembered the size of the skeletal creature and questioned how it got through the opening, but crawling and digging he finally pushed his way clear, then helped his wife over the loose dirt and gravel.

The air outside was a refreshing change as the party gathered and paused; the humans filling their lungs with the clean oxygen after the lengthy stay in the musty chambers of the downed frigate.

"Feels good to have air again," Ben muttered, and then set about finding the trail.

Missy came over a low ridge growling, not sure of who these new trespassers were; but Aiyana lifted off her mask and called to the big cat who came purring and rubbing on her long lost companion.

Broken-Toe working with Ben on the trail, pointed in the direction the creature had fled and then disappeared over the knoll taking chase.

Ben and Aiyana followed shortly, after gathering their horses and preparing for the long night ahead. The Guardian was moving fast, but his trail was purposefully,— easy to track. Ben took to the sign unsure of what was in store for their future; although, Aiyana had already lived it,— in a dream.

Chapter Thirty-two

Butchery

12 April, 1842

The Preacher

His words still echo in my soul, but the impact has wilted with age. From the confines of a weathered wagon he spoke his sermon, pounding the Bible as his voice crescendoed like a chorus in song. "Go west, I was told,— to a land void of morals. Go west with the message of hope. Shed light to those in darkness, preach release to the savage heart."

But the void stole my dreams. My hopes became shattered. Love was lost to the darkness, and my heart released its rage.

"Brethren, the words from our Lord are clear: 'Vengeance is mine;' saith our God!" — But, I will repay. Therefore, I seek vengeance and his wrath. But the obedient only desire justice! Whose justice? Is the hand of divine retribution within the heart of one man? Or is the executioner forever lost? Will my peace be found by the edge of the sword? Or is destruction, alone, the road I walk?

Excerpts, trapper's journal

*   *   *

The victors cheered as The Seer raised his hands to the heavens and cried out, "The Great Spirit has rewarded his faithful children. Today the spoils of war are ours!"

Screams disrupted the gathered throng as the warriors began plundering the dead.

The Seer nodded a smile of approval. The warrior's call was answered as he scanned the battlefield. *They would meet the long knives with lance and tomahawk. The Great Spirit would reward his children.* Glancing over at the reaction of the golden-haired, white man with the trinket, *a finger of gods,* around his neck, he was amazed to see him standing idle. *This man is a chosen vessel, a leader, why would he not celebrate the victory?* The Seer shook off his question and joined the others in looting the fallen.

Isaac watched him go and leaned up again against the large rock by the bank of the river. His grim expression showed little emotion, but he scanned the devastation with mixed feelings. The almost lifeless body of the man with the fingernail scratches on his cheek was on the opposite bank, resting against a dead horse. He would die slow from the gut wound Isaac had inflicted.

Golden-Hair's gaze drifted back to the river; floating face down in the water was the last man he had fought. On both shores and beyond were the dead and dying. *These men killed my wife,— my family.* All around him were fallen cavalry; men that had butchered the innocent, murdered women and children. His hatred burned, but there was no solace in revenge. No comfort was easing his pain.

Tears filled his eyes as pictures of his wife flashed in his memory: her smile, the way her soft black hair framed the beautiful contours of her features. Then she slipped away as he held her one last time.

Isaac pushed off the rock and waded back into the river. Pulling his Bowie he grabbed the man floating face down by the hair and severed the dead man's scalp.

Isaac had changed. Forged by anger,— hate,— revenge,— his grim features turned to stone as he focused his attention on his wife's murderer. With purpose Pu-na continued toward the dying man. Wading through the deep stream he staggered out onto the shore, his buckskins heavy with water weighing him down.

The scar scratched man shuddered as Golden-Hair approach. "What'cha'ya gonna do?" He cried out, trying to move and winced at the pain from his gut wound. Blood dribbled down his face from his missing scalp.

The mountain man stopped and spit on the soldier.

"What do you want?" the dying man whimpered.

"You butchered innocence,— now it's your turn."

"What are you talking about?"

"The village you men massacred."

"We were only following orders."

Isaac grabbed the man by the remaining hair at the side of his face and twisted the dying man's head for a better look at the fingernail scratches down his cheek. "Is that what you told yourself when you butchered the woman that did this?"

"She was just an Injun. What would it matter to you,— you're a white man?" he sneered.

"She was my wife!" Isaac put his Bowie to the man's left ear. Reuben and The Seer came up as Golden-Hair carved deep into the tissue, removing the appendage under screams of agony.

The Seer nodded in approval as Reuben placed his hand on Isaac's arm. "Do you wish me to kill him uncle?"

"No,— he's goanna die," and placing a boot to the man's chest, he kicked the man to his back. "He's going to lie here." Isaac's expression turned ugly as he spoke through grinding teeth. "The coyotes will feed on his flesh while he watches helpless. Then the buzzards will feast." Isaac knelt and pried the point of his knife under the man's chin, pushing the soldier's head back. "You're going to die just like you left her,— but no one will mourn your passing. No one will know. Your bones will bleach, and the scavengers will grind them into droppings and no one will care." Isaac spat on the man again then stuck the blade into the man's thigh as the soldier cried out. "Just in case you're thinkin' of crawlin' out of here."

"Uncle we must go. More patrols are in the area and the sound of battle can carry large distances in these mountains."

"Please..." the dying man whimpered.

"My village is not far from here. We will head there, and rest." The Seer stepped forward putting his hand on Isaac's shoulder. "Come my brother."

Isaac stood amid the pleadings of the dying soldier, but the cries of mercy fell on deaf ears.

It was a half a days ride to the river where The Seer's people had made camp. Most of the warriors were excited about the victory over superior numbers and much talk was whispered about the new members: chiefly the white man, and The Seer's words about this messiah. Even Isaac's own tribe were curious, but Pu-na was lost to any conversation as he rode somewhat separated and quiet.

Snow blanketed the area near the village, but the warriors saw no smoke from fires as they approached the camp. Silence stilled the war party as they reached a crest in the rolling plain and came to a stop in full view of the carnage by a small river in a little clearing. The camp had been hit and Isaac could feel the pain and deep anxiety of helplessness. Like a replay of the events of a day ago, Pu-na rode into the village with his devastated, adopted brothers as they waded through the agony of loss. The men of the tribe wept and cared for the fallen as the mourning process started anew.

Isaac and Reuben helped where they could then explored the scene for clues, but this raid was different than the massacre of their home village. Shod horse tracks of the cavalry blanketed the area along with the boots of soldiers who had walked through the camp, but what was most shocking was that some of the dead had been skinned.

"Uncle,— why would the soldiers skin them like animals?"

The golden haired mountain man paused for a long time then shook his head. "This doesn't make sense." Isaac stroked the finger of the necklace resting on his chest.

Reuben watched questioningly, "Do you think the creature we were tracking the other day did this?"

"It's not his way. Broken-Toe was a hunter, he don't kill the helpless."

"Maybe he's changed."

Isaac scanned the village almost panicked, "We need to see if we can find some other tracks. There were others,—less—honorable,— true butchers."

As the men searched, Reuben found a few signs that the Sky Demons had come through, but nothing conclusive. The cavalry's walk through had almost obliterated everything except a random print here and there.

"Uncle, the cavalry was here yesterday as was this creature," the Crow warrior said pointing to a single print.

"That doesn't look like Broken-Toe's."

"It's not the same creature we tracked to The Forks, but it is the same kind and just as big."

"Did it kill these people?"

"I don't know. The wounds look like knife wounds." The younger man paused and pondered. "The soldiers might have used their long knives."

"Do you know where they went?"

"The soldiers went upriver.— I would have to scout around outside the village to see if any tracks of these creatures are there, or whatever else I can find."

"Creatures?" Isaac studied his younger companion. "Was there more than one here?"

"There's at least two, possibly three. The cavalry destroyed most all the sign."

"Maybe three of those critters,—" Isaac trailed off as The Seer approached with some of the Sioux from Golden-Hair's tribe.

"Your brothers have agreed to go after the men responsible for this slaughter while my people take care of their dead. We must move before the trail grows too cold."

Reuben looked questioningly at his uncle then turned to The Seer, "We tracked a creature,— a giant the other day, the same type as this track here." Reuben directed the medicine man's attention to the icy taloned print embedded in the soft blanket of snow.

"What kind of animal is this?"

Isaac took his necklace in hand, presenting the finger. "The creature like these left that track."

The Seer knelt and examined the strange print pressing his hand into the frozen contours of its icy shape. "Your coming has brought with it The Destroyer." He looked up with all seriousness. "We tried to stop the plague, but —" his gaze returned to the track. "Death's Shadow will cover the land."

"You think this creature killed your people?" Isaac asked.

"The Destroyer is here to help."

Isaac and Reuben didn't grasp the cryptic message.

"The Destroyer will find us when it's time,— for now the blue coats must die." The words were spoken with a finality.

The trail was a day old, but the enemy was moving slow. Outnumbered again, the battle would require tactics to disadvantage the enemy. Isaac considered the road ahead, but it appeared his path was already chosen.

Chapter Thirty-three

Campaign

Retrospect

" Numerical superiority is of no consequence.

In battle, victory will go to the best tactician."

George Custer (1839-1876)

*   *   *

Dawn came early as the troop broke camp on the slow trail to The Hollows. The winds of an early winter rustled the surrounding trees, high up on the valley's ridge. The weather pattern was changing with the rising sun; but on the valley floor, shielded behind a blanket of early morning fog, the men were quiet as they continued their duties on empty stomachs. The camps gray surroundings looked ominous, an omen,— gloomy as the desperation the men felt packing their animals without even benefit of coffee,— their remaining meager supplies, after an accident, had dwindled out the previous day. The company's scouts never returned from the last night's reconnaissance, perhaps abandoning them to a fate of starvation, lost among the rocky hills of this empty wilderness.

Late for their rendezvous and without escort, the commander was determined to valiantly continue the journey, but unfamiliar with the territory and without the benefit of a guide, the Captain was in a precarious position.

The Gatling gun they were moving was awkward for the hilly terrain; a .30 caliber ten barrel design, that could shoot up to 1200 times a minute, won the approval of the Ordnance Department in 1866 as a weapon of promise,— an improvement over Dr. Richard Gatling's 1862 model,— a .58 caliber hand crank machine gun that had only six revolving barrels and fired on average, about 400 rounds a minute. The earlier version never won acquisition by the U.S. Government because of numerous problems; but in the post war era, Richard's later achievement was adopted officially and deemed a valuable asset in the continuingly, increasing conflicts with hostile Native Americans.

Captain Jenkins was a man of moderate temperament and a stiff manner of control that held an unnerving power over the men under his command. He was under strict orders to move into the Northwestern region with his small contingent and support the failing efforts of the cavalry to suppress the escalating skirmishes.

The Gatling was the pride of his company, but after a week of pulling the weapon over the rocky terrain, limiting their advancement to a mere 20 miles a day, the men longed to dump the wagon wheeled monstrosity,— wishing they had dropped it over the narrow gorge where they lost the chuck wagon the previous week.

Captain Jenkins was of a different mindset and ordered the riggings set for another day when a call went out, and a panic erupted throughout the camp. Two men on horses thundered into the site yelling, "They're dead,— they got um... they're dead."

At first, because of the fog, it could not even be determined where the riders were coming from. Men scrambled to their horses not sure if the enemy was advancing, when Captain Jenkins' strong voice of authority resounded over the chaos, assembling the men in a large circle: a man about every ten yards apart, each with his animal by his side. A crew of four men wheeled the Gatling to the center on the higher ground, and prepared the magazine.

The riders broke the line, turning the heads of the nearby linemen and dismounted by the captain; their horses agitated and lathered, pulling at the reins wanting to continue their flight. With a quick salute, both men spoke at the same time in a panic, struggling to control their mounts.

"Gentlemen! One at a time," exclaimed Jenkins. "One at a time."

Corporal Sandgum, a small mouse of a man looked at his companion and nodded, quelling his excitement as best he could and reported: "Sir... we found the scouts on our recognizance this morning not a mile from here." Sandgum took a deep breath and expelled it quickly. "Someone skinned them,— Sir."

"What!" the commander barked in disbelief.

"Kettle and Oggal are hanging in a tree just over the next set of ridges dressed out like a shot deer," squeaked the man, pointing in the direction they had just come from.

"Was it hostiles?"

"Sir,— I'm not a tracker. We found them fellers and broke it fer here."

Suddenly, all the horses in the configuration spooked. Their charges, distracted by the confusion, broke formation when a crack like thunder erupted; and one of the men at the Gatling slumped over the axle.

"Corporal, man the gun!" The Captain directed, while placing his left hand on his saber. Turning his attention to his command he paced the top of the ridge and yelled, "Mount up."

A second crack dropped a horse soldier.

"Watch the left flank," Jenkins barked in a manner of full control while drawing his sword.

Sandgum and his crew spun the weapon preparing for a charge.

"Blanket that pocket Corporal!"

The Gatling exploded into operation, showering lead over the left bank as an almost white flame whistled from the opposite side dropping another warrior.

"We're surrounded men,— fire at will!"

Carbines spit and popped, but the fog limited even the simplest sighting of their attackers.

Two more soldiers were cut down by streaks of white lightning when the silhouette of a giant slammed through the lines and a private's head spun to the ground at the commander's feet. The ghostly form faded in and out with wisps of fog, rendering death in its wake.

The captain tried to understand the nature of the attack. In disbelief he watched as a second phantom breached his left flank amid the hand-cranked, rapid fire of his company's pride.

The outlined form that appeared without substance danced along the borders of the cavalry's resistance, then disappeared completely, only to spring back into view as the heavy moisture of the lowland cloud seemed to condensate about the specter's features.

The captain drew his pistol and fired instantaneously at the seemingly substance-less form which sprung lightly away, only to reappear behind Corporal Sandgum. The little man never knew what hit him as he slumped over the revolving barrels and was thrown into the spokes of the wooden wheels of the weapon. Horses bolted from their dead charges as the Gatling went quiet.

The captain called for his men to regroup, but an eerie silence dispelled any hope as the commander walked along the top ridge of his last stand. An unknown enemy had leveled his forces in mere seconds; and now he stood alone amid an invisible death that appeared to haunt this wilderness like a ghostly pack of ravenousness demons, bent on war with flesh-and-blood. *Could these wraiths even be killed?*

"Show yourselves you bastards!" The captain screamed as he stumbled over his fallen. "Cowards,— show yourselves!"

Jenkins spun as a glimmer of movement raked his right field of vision. He raised his sword and parried a savage blow. The clashing of metal resounded over the lonely hill, but the man could see no physical form; only the empty shadow of an outlined embodiment. *Strange that a ghost could exert such force against a steel blade.*

The captain raised his pistol shooting center of the shape and the specter lurched backward with the impact of the bullet, but immediately sprang to its feet apparently unharmed. The silhouette crackled, as a blue web of netted light, etched around its giant frame and in a twinkling of an eye the monster appeared,— dressed in what the officer guessed was battle armor. Bulging eyes with a deep red glow, burned behind the stone features of the insect shaped head. Curved horns pointed at the officer like Lucifer himself selecting a soul for special torment.

"What manner of demon are you?" screamed the captain taking a savage swing with his saber.

The beast jumped to the side and deflected the blow against a stout gauntlet with multiple blades that extended, forming hooks down its entire forearm. As it spun, it twisted sideways, backhanding as it moved.

The punch went wide as the officer ducked the sweeping swing, and locating a gap in the armor of his enemy lifted his colt and shot.

His opponent reeled under the impact, as a purple phosphorous fluid splattered from the wound and the creature howled in pain.

Captain Jenkins stabbed at the beast with his sword, but his antagonist easily rolled away and sprang back to its feet.

Two more of the creatures appeared as spectators around the life and death match, standing like chiseled forms of stone.

The commander was startled by their appearance and staggered backward to brace himself for a charge, but the enemy just looked on. The captain raised his pistol when his wounded enemy's forehead lit up with a small red light and the horns on the creature's head sprang to life spitting a streak of white flame that struck the commander's left hand taking it off at the wrist; his pistol dropping to the ground a few yards away.

In shock, the captain stared at his injury when the beast unexpectedly charged, swinging a brutal blow with its strange bladed arm. Jenkins, with the grace of a skilled swordsmen, parried the strike which deflected off to his right, dropped to one knee and plunged his saber into the soft tissue of the creature's left thigh, just behind its armor. Howling his enemy spun and swung again, but the captain stepped back as he pulled his sword free and easily dodged the mindless attack, again stabbing his enemy in a gap of its armor at its right side.

Bewildered, the creature paused with some distance between his opponent seeming to examine its wounds as its pasty phosphorous blood flowed over its battle garb.

The captain took advantage of the break and looked at his own injury. It was strange to him. The initial impact felt like a hammer had smashed his hand, but now there was no pain or blood. In fact the captain wasn't even sure if the events happening were real because it still seemed like the appendage was there,— just invisible and he was controlling and moving his fingers at will.

Noise interrupted the commander's inspection as he raised his eyes back to his assailant. The creature was lifting off its headpiece, amid hissing gas, and dropped the mask unceremoniously to the ground. The giant was the ugliest thing the captain had ever seen. Wiry locks of stiff black rope that looked like a tangled weave of disjointed black widow legs. The matted and twisted jumble draped the contours of the small head exaggerating the appearance of the limited forehead. Its eyes were unusually large under the deep brow of a steep ridge that conveyed the thought of evil to the mind of Jenkins. But the most unnerving thing about the creature's appearance was the tusks that lanced downward from the beast's mouth. Like a saber tooth tiger's fangs, the dagger like appendages, dripping with foam, seemed to salivated like a disembodied soul hungry for blood.

"What manner of demon are you?" Jenkins spat with disgust.

"What manner of demon are you?" echoed back from the creature's position, mimicking exactly the captain's voice, followed by an eerie clicking and chirping.

Jenkins snarled and readied himself for attack. "Let's finish this!"

The monster raised its left hand as the second gauntlet's set of blades engaged with the grating sound of metal on metal. Then the creature paused crossing his weapon bearing arms over his chest and then dropped them to his side.

"Let's finish this!" Repeated the captain's words from the creature's position and the demon charged.

The captain backed up gracefully dodging and parrying every blow even catching his enemy twice more with stabs in the right arm and left abdomen, but the creature seemed unaffected by the injuries and kept up its onslaught of blows in a mastery of a controlled attack. The commander was quickly learning his opponents moves, gauging his strikes and understanding his defenses when he tripped over the body of one of his fallen men. The blunder was disastrous. The creature jumped in for a final strike. The captain was able to jab his saber into the back of his enemies left ankle severing its large tendon, but as the demon fell it pinned the commander's sword arm to the ground and plunged its right forearm into the man's chest.

Captain Jenkins lurched foreword staring at his conqueror for but a moment, spit in the demon's face, then fell back weakened and gasping for air.

The giant then peeled the vanquished's flesh under the agonizing screams of the torture. The fiendish mouth seemed to revel in the atrocity. The demon's fangs dripped of froth, as if salivating in the helpless terror in the dying man's eyes.

Chapter Thirty-four

Trapped

Retrospect of 18 April, 1842 :

Blood covered his hands as the preacher wept over a glass of whisky. Tears of remorse over past sins haunting his soul diminished as the liquor washed away the stains only he could see; scars burnt deep that would return after the comatose slumber of overindulgence. Regret is a mask that remorse won't shield with the passage of time. An act of vengeance only resurrects pain over loss and the inability to right two wrongs; but words won't heal the deeds performed without reason, nor aid the soul to redeem its deepest desire. Can good deeds buy release of the curse? As he confided in me his story of woe over the shared bottle, I couldn't help but reflect on my own youth and its cry for justice. The road often traveled by humanity plays on, but to find one's self as the object of retribution will scorch the trail to friend and family, rendering peace a distant memory. Didn't I learn anything in my life's experience? The trail may be cold, but my longing lives on amid the demons of the glass, which,— in the end, — only nurtures sorrow.

Nov. 18, 1871 **Excerpts**

*   *   *

The trail circled north into the higher altitude then vanished in the wake of a wet snow that blanketed the landscape. Zeb and Claude's worst fears about the monster they chased turning on them,— unfulfilled; but now even the security of knowing the course of the creature,— masked by nature's white cover, leaving them blind to the whereabouts of a virtually invisible enemy.

Already late for the rendezvous at The Hollows and short on supplies, the lieutenant had grown increasingly hostile to the scout's: "inept chasings of a phantom." He felt the real threat from, The Seer was going to continue unchallenged, stabbing at his pride. In a loss of composure the lieutenant ordered a return to, "…The Forks in the morning," and as dawn approached the company was preparing its humiliating homecoming.

"I says we make's a break, wize we'z sill godz our hair," Claude said as he swung his saddle onto his mare.

Zeb seemed preoccupied and didn't respond as he bridled his mount while watching a stand of trees in an unobtrusive manner.

"Whad's godz yer dander?" The older man snapped at the lack of interest by his friend.

"Shhh...." Zeb continued quietly readying his horse, but his eyes never faltered from the shadowed foliage of the not too distant pines. "We're being watched," he whispered.

Claude strapped his saddle tight and moved in close to his animal. "How many?" He mumbled.

"Can't tell."

"Injun or demon?"

"None that neither."

"Damn yer sixth sense," Claude grunted displeased, "needs a better readin'."

The two scouts were interrupted by a private moving near the enemy by the creek to fill a canteen.

"I suspect we're about to find out."

Zeb made an unnecessary adjustment to his saddle and slipped his rifle from its boot as Claude moved his mare between the trees and Zeb's animal, pulling his weapon, out of sight of the enemy.

"Ifin's idz be one of dose beasdies aim fer dat horned mask," the older man whispered.

"Ya read my mind."

The gray hue of dawn passed its filtered glow over the

shadowed terrain as an eerie calm quieted even the birds in the surrounding trees, but the private was oblivious to any danger and squatted, filling his canteen. The icy runoff was the only sound, gurgling as its continuous flow passed over the many obstacles of tree roots, rock, and brush nature had placed in its path. The man rinsed out his container slopping the cold fluid haphazardly then repeated the process as Zeb and Claude under the cover of branches and horses trained their weapons in support of the ignorant soldier.

A single rifle shot broke the silence of the morning as a Cheyenne warrior toppled from a secured brush ledge hidden among a rock outcropping overlooking the creek. The brave hit the water at the private's feet as the man scrambled backward dropping his canteen.

"That's another gold coin fer the purse ya owes me," Zeb chuckled, re-cocking his repeater.

"Damn yer eyes," Claude barked back as the valley clearing erupted into a war zone.

Indian braves surrounding the encampment opened fire as their war cries resounded across the glen.

The lieutenant ran from his command tent shouting orders, and his well trained troops responded quickly, spreading out in a circle around the camp, taking position on one knee to defend the field base.

The Indians' normal battle strategy included the theft of horses, but in this attack the cavalry animals took the brunt of the early assault. Within 15 minutes the company had taken heavy losses and with no mounts to escape on, the lieutenant ordered a retreat as his men began to fall back moving slowly while repeatedly interrupting the withdrawal by dropping to a knee and firing a carefully aimed deterrent at the enemy. The cautiously executed abandonment of the camp prevented a charge from the antagonists as the soldiers were able to regroup on a small sheltered plateau that stood almost as an island amid the surrounding terrain.

The two scouts pinned down by the waterway watched in desperation at the gallant defense and withdrew, but were cut off from the troop, and unable to join the effort. Staying well concealed in the heavy brush by the creek, they offered support in the only way they could, — firing at the enemy at every opportunity when an unwary brave exposed himself to the crack shot expertise of the two buckskinned scouts.

Zeb spotted movement coming their way and warned his partner when recognition of the antagonist stayed his hand. As he dropped his rifle to get a better look a bullet struck the tree right next to his head throwing bark dust into his eyes. "Damn!" He yelled ducking low, but reached out with his hand and grabbed Claude's shoulder.

"Is ya nicked?"

"My eyes,— dust."

"Well ged yer hands off me unless you'z wan'z dem Injun's dakin' our hair!"

"I saw Reuben."

"Whad?"

"My nephew."

"I'z know'z who Reuben is," Claude barked back disgusted. "Whad would he be doin' runnin' with a bunch of red butchers?"

Zeb's eyes watered as he struggled to open them. "I don't know, but the warrior coming this way is Reuben."

"Well call out to him, dad blame ya."

"Reuben!" Zeb shouted. "Reuben it's your Uncle Zeb,— Zeb and Claude."

The gunfire stopped around their position after a few random volleys. The scouts' eyes had watered enough to flush the debris clear, but his vision was still clouding as he poked his head up above the heavy branch offering most of the cover. "Reuben did you hear me? It's me Zeb."

"What are you doing here uncle?" Came the familiar voice of Ben and Aiyana's son.

"We are working as scouts. We're tracking a Sky Demon. You remember the stories we told you about the hunting demons?"

"Why did you butcher the people of that village?"

"We didn't,— three Demons did."

"They don't hunt like that."

"Well these did."

"Soldiers hit a village three days ago near the crest. Do you know anything about that?" Came a second voice calling from a well hidden post.

"Isaac,— is that you?"

"What do you know of that massacre?"

"We were hired four days ago and taken to The Forks. Everyone there had been butchered by a renegade band of Sioux.

We were hired to find that band, but you know we would not have been party to any massacre, nor was that our orders."

"What was your orders?"

"To find the leader. They call him The Seer,— and bring him in. Nothing more."

"Then why are you tracking a Sky Demon?" Reuben's voice again interjected.

"While tracking the renegades, I guessed where they would camp and found the village and everybody dead. We then followed one of the Demons up river, but lost his trail in the snow yesterday."

Zeb and Claude were suddenly surrounded by five warriors with repeating rifles trained on them. The scouts set their weapons down reluctantly and stood surrendering quietly. The gunfire near the cavalry was still going strong, but the small group capturing the trackers seemed oblivious to the battle.

Reuben and Isaac approached quickly accompanied by a short Cheyenne brave.

"I'm glad to see you're doing well," Zeb said with a smile directed at Reuben, then turned his gaze to the short warrior. "but I question the company you've chosen as of late? The Seer, I would guess?"

Isaac ignored Zeb's quip stepping close into the bigger man's space. "Some of those bodies you say were butchered by the Demons were carved on by a white man's blade. You want to explain that?"

Zeb cleared his throat and hesitated as Claude turn away, and looked at the ground.

Isaac understood the guilty body language as anger hardened his voice. "Why were the dead desecrated after death?"

Zeb took a deep breath and started his defense. "At The Forks massacre, all the bodies were mutilated by the killers. We found distortions in the skeletal structure. Some kind of metamorphosis was taking place.

"Meta-a what?" Reuben spit.

"A changing,— like the caterpillar that turns to a butterfly. But this change was more a disrupting of the bones. Big medicine that appeared to be growing in some of the dead. Some type of infestation,— disease. By killing the men infected the growth inside them had also died. Claude and I thought maybe the Demons had wiped out that village to stop a similar infestation. We had no evil intent."

The Seer was suddenly enthralled by the tall man's words. He knew the big medicine was real.

"Liar!" Isaac screamed as he raised his hand to strike Zeb, but The Seer swiftly stayed his hand in mid-swing. Isaac's anger blazed uncontrolled as Reuben stepped in-between trying to calm Isaac, but the enraged man spat in Zeb's face. "You ride with the very men that butchered my wife," he screamed struggling with his companions holding him back.

Zeb wiped the hocker off his cheek, but remained calm. "I am truly sorry for your loss, but neither I, nor the men I'm riding with had anything to do with her death. I swear under pain of death,— none of us had anything to do with either massacre."

Isaac settled some as Zeb stepped forward placing his hand on Isaac's shoulder. "You know me, brother." His voice was soothing and compassionate. "We've traveled together, and hunted together,— you know I would have had no part in murdering innocent women. And I pledge my life to you. I will help you find the guilty, and see that they pay for the crime committed against you and avenge the victims."

Reuben too, holding Isaac's right arm, placed his right hand on Isaac's chest. "I believe him Uncle. Uncle Zeb would have never killed innocent women and children. You know this."

Isaac pulled free still hot with anger, but the hostility seemed no longer directed at his past companions. He looked over where the battle was still raging and motioned with his thumb. "You're sure they had no part in the massacre?"

"They couldn't have, but we could question the lieutenant and maybe learn what company was patrolling in the area where your village was. Call your men off and let's learn what we can."

The Seer nodded and sent one of his warriors in the direction of the conflict. Within minutes the gunfire diminished as the Indians withdrew, but still kept the soldiers pinned down.

Zeb was then sent in to negotiate the commander's surrender, but sadly the lieutenant had been killed. Zeb had quite a bit of pull with the next man in charge.

As the lone scout neared, one of the trapped stepped out waving a white cloth.

Sergeant Lloyd was eager to agree to a truce and followed the private up the incline. The two men waited on the ridge in awe as

Zeb rode in to discuss the situation. Lloyd knew nothing of the previous campaigns, but following the advice of the scout, whom he deeply respected; the man that had somehow managed to stop the Indian attack single-handedly; he returned with Zeb to meet with the enemy and workout a compromise.

Chapter Thirty-five

Lost and Found

Journal Entry: (1870 - 1873)

"Raging as eternal fire,

a woman's soul — contempt to burn.

Do not dare the viper's venom,

her fangs exposed — you'll not endure."

Titus Brown (1851-1922)

*   *   *

Water splashed over her face choking her in a merciless barrage, but still Daisy hung on, wedged securely in the pocket holding her from being swept away. Bracing herself and gauging the opposite shore, she reacted with the last of her strength. She was about to lose both her wardrobe and her light. In a decision without any doubt, she lunged forward with all her might, jumping as high as she could, tossing her bundle, hoping it wouldn't fall short and disappear in the wake of the swift water. Falling back into the stream away from the rocks, she struggled to keep the light high above her head. Pushing off the bottom of the river, she filled her lungs as her head cleared the surface. In a panic, she looked for her garments and spotted them a foot up on the opposite shore. Relieved, she dove toward the beach now using her right arm to guide and paddle.

Swimming proved easier than walking and in minutes she crawled up on the opposite bank shaking, and exhausted. Huddling close to the lamp she turned the flame up and tried desperately to gain its warmth. It helped some as she took the piece of cloth left behind from Robin's garment, wrapped in her bundle, and dried herself as best she could. Dressing slowly as her teeth chattered, she found herself unable to think clearly.

It's so cold, she thought as she struggled to keep conscious. Her clothing was damp in places, but surprisingly dry considering her ordeal. She finished pulling on the heavy wardrobe and then sat holding the lamp on her lap, basking in the small amount of heat generating from the kerosene flame. It was going to take some time for her to recuperate.

Daisy sat huddling the lamp unable to concentrate for the better part of an hour. Lost to the darkness around her, she shivered and quaked, but not out of fear. Hypothermia had taken its toll, but the small wick burning brightly on her lap was gradually erasing the chill. Her teeth chattered endlessly to the point where her jaw hurt from the strain. Finally, her body temperature started to rise, easing the pain.

Daisy's mental acuity began to stir and she lifted the lantern eyeing her surroundings. Her view locked on the underground river knowing how close she had come to death. There was no going back.

Standing on trembling feet, the woman turned to the crevice above, following the perceived course of her friend. Little did she know that the trail she longed to follow had ended at the river through an underwater cavern. If Daisy knew how close she had come to being sucked down its twisting vortex, the thought of saving her friend would have long diminished; but Daisy pressed on.

It was dusk before she had followed the twisting maze of narrow passages and panoramic rooms to a small light aperture, peeking through a high wall in a domed chamber. The compartment smelled heavy of ammonia, to the point of nausea, as Daisy came to the edge of a black pond blocking her way. She scanned her barrier, an inclined ledge wrapped the pool with the only crossing,— a stalagmite bridge to her far left that arched and twisted in a spiraling glossy trail that was both mesmerizing and functional.

Daisy made her way to the architectural marvel formed by mother nature over millions of years. Its colors were a blend of beauty that looked coated by glass and reflected the light of her lamp in an array of the rainbow. She stepped lightly on its smooth structure careful not to slip on the slick bat guano painting the more level surfaces of the gateway.

Small creatures watched, their eyes twinkling in the glow of the fiery wick. Daisy noticed the high ceiling above alive with movement from the tiny winged mammals. Catching her balance she placed her hand on the wall and immediately pulled it away with a stifled scream. A bat squeaked and scampered along the hard surface, clinging easily to the stone surface. Daisy covered her mouth and continued briskly, making it to the ledge and started up the walk way.

The shelf narrowed at one point and with her back to the cavern wall she inched across the narrow precipice arriving at her destination. It was a good thing Daisy was thin. The crevice was even smaller than it looked below, but Daisy managed to crawl through the opening and out into the night air. With a deep sigh of relief, she sat back against the stone outcropping hiding the entrance to the cave.

Freedom: how good it felt. Her thoughts returned to her friends trapped below. What could she do now? They needed help.

Daisy stood when she was almost knocked down by an array of life pushing their way through the crevice and into the night. Thousands of bats swept by, some colliding with her clothing as she screamed and fell, rolling down the rocky hillside. Standing and brushing herself in a panic she tried desperately to knock any still clinging creatures from her person.

Her composure gone she ducked, watching the multitude of

winged flight billowing from the dark opening. The lantern was on its side near the entrance. Fear gripped the woman. If the lamp went out so would her chances for a fire and warmth.

Crawling up the incline, Daisy reached her prize and still the seeming endless cloud of life fluttered in an appearance of chaos. Turning and moving down the hill the woman made it to a cluster of trees. Chilled from her ordeal and the cold night air, her mind no longer feared the men from the mining operation; Daisy went to work gathering wood and built a small fire. Its warmth brought peace and her exhaustion brought sleep. She curled up by the flames and dropped into unconsciousness.

Noise pulled her from her slumber, the noonday sun beating down on her exhausted frame. Daisy opened her eye spotting a saddled horse grazing a few feet from her position. The woman sat up startled, but the animal ignored the disturbance. Snorting from dust it walked a few paces away still munching on the limited grass dotting the landscape.

The woman looked around the hillside and noticed several more saddled horses feeding. *Was her enemies nearby?* Daisy stood quietly and approached the horse who showed little interest in the invasion. She picked up the reins dragging the ground with her right hand, and gently felt the brand on the animals hip. A cavalry insignia was burned into the saddle as she carefully inspected the smooth leather of the well maintained gear. *Were her captors horse thieves also?*

Daisy slipped into the saddle gracefully and eyed the other animals. If she could rescue her friends they would also need rides.

*   *   *

It's uncanny how easily a trail can go cold and be lost to the winds of change, Titus thought as he knelt in a rocky ravine trying to find evidence of passage. Somewhere the creature he was stalking, *had to of left sign, when it exited the dry river bed,* but Titus found nothing.

Sam snorted and tugged at the reins, then nibbled at a tuff of grass peeking out from under a wash of dead wood and matted debris. The horse had worked hard with little maintenance over the last few days and Titus regretted his neglect. Here was a good supply of winter greens, so the man dropped the reins, letting his animal feast as he continued to explore.

Titus had lost the trail the previous evening before dusk. Several hours elapsed before he gave up for the night and bedded down in a small cottonwood grove about a mile from his current position. Sleep had come easy, but this morning he fared no better on his trek. The creature was a mystery: circling back, moving for hours in one direction, then shifting for no apparent reason at right angles to its previous course. After a day of travel Titus was sure he was only a few miles from where he had started the day before. The zigzag path had led him in a big circle and now the man believed the creature was either lost himself, or trying to double back in case it was being followed. *Perhaps this was just the creature's hunting grounds.*

Sam nickered and lifted his head looking south. Titus heard the sound too; and ran to the steep ridge of the wash, and peeked over the high embankment. Something was coming his way. Titus crawled up into the brush by the shoreline, working his way cautiously toward the approaching enemy. Surprise was on his side.

The unsuspecting intruder was working along an animal trail through the dense foliage when Titus sprang on the enemy. Grabbing an arm and a woolen poncho, he dragged his hostage from the saddle, slamming the victim to the hard ground. A small struggle ensued when to Titus' surprise his opponent's hat fell off and he found himself holding a young white woman. "Who the hell are you," he barked as she continued to fight. "Hold still woman."

"Let go of me you bastard!" The woman cried out; pulling a pistol from under her wool drape, and cocked it in the man's face.

"Woe there missy!" Titus not wanting to hurt the woman any further let go and backed away. "This wilderness is filled with bad men, I was just watchin' my backside."

The woman sat up and gracefully spun to a knee continuing her bead on her attacker. "As you can see I'm not a man."

"Can you put the gun down? I ain't going to hurt you."

"You can bet you're not."

The words barely left her lips as Titus' right hand shot out, wrapping the revolver's cylinder, freezing the firing mechanism. The scout then pried the weapon from her hand, spinning it briskly and covered her with her own pistol; although the barrel was upside down, and his pinky was on the trigger.

The woman cried out startled and backed away.

"You a horse thief?"

"What?" the woman exclaimed perturbed. "How did you do that?"

"What are you doing with cavalry horses?"

"I found them."

"What are you doing out here?"

"I won't give in to you without a fight," the woman snarled standing and bracing herself for an attack.

"What are you,— a lone woman, doing out here?" The large black man demanded.

"What's it to you?"

"I'm an inquiring mind."

"I was kidnapped, but I escaped." The woman shifted on her feet, ready to run, or fight. "You won't be able to hold me either."

Titus spun the weapon once more and handed the pistol back, butt first. "What's your name?"

"Daisy," she replied, taking the colt carefully, still fearful that it might be a ploy to get her in closer.

"You're one of the women from town that was kidnapped? Did any of the others escape with you?"

Daisy for the first time noticed the man was dressed in military pants, although his coat was buckskin. "I don't think so. Were you sent out here looking for us?" Recognition suddenly dawned on the woman. "I remember you. You were at The Cradle the night of the fire with all those soldiers." Daisy holstered her weapon and picked up her hat, brushing debris from its brim. "Where's the rest of your men? We'll need them to free my friends."

Titus took Daisy by the wrist and stopped her. "Hold on there girl."

Daisy stared at the man angrily and pulled her hand free.

"There are no men,— just me."

Sam nickered down in the dry bed and then Titus' tone trailed off. "We have bigger problems right now." Titus whispered the last sentence and began listening intently to his surroundings.

"What!"

Titus held a finger to his lips and taking Daisy's hand softly, muttered, "I've been tracking a killer, and I think it's found us."

Chapter Thirty-Six

Into the Fire

Retrospect

"A timid person is frightened before a danger,

A coward during the time,

And a courageous person afterward."

Jean Paul Richter (1763 - 1825)

*   *   *

Titus led Daisy quietly into the brush with hardly a sound considering the woman's inexperience with the woodland arts. Her heart started racing. *Who is this man leading me into the brush? Can I trust him?* Then she reflected on how easily he had disarmed her. *Surely if he wanted to hurt me, he would have already done it.*

Branches scratched her arm as they crept along. Titus paused and motioned her to get low. He then knelt and peered through a break in their cover, out into a rolling plain beyond. "Did you bring any other horses with you?" The scout whispered to his companion without a glance, "I heard at least three."

Daisy leaned close over his shoulder, behind him. "Two, besides the one I was riding. I left them in the meadow to graze. It looked like a river ran through here and I wanted a drink. The brush was too heavy to pull the horses through." Daisy squinted trying to see what the scout was looking at. "What is it?"

"There's somethin' moving out there, but I can't quite make it out."

Daisy strained, but saw nothing. "I don't see anything,— and why are we whispering?"

Titus pointed, "By that rocky ridge,— over there."

This time Daisy saw the movement. It was eerie. A pocket of the landscape appeared out of focus. There was no dust or wind, but the scenery was distorted. Gradually the form took shape to her vision. "I see it,— what is it?"

Titus didn't take his eye's off the ghost, "A long time ago, a good friend of mine told me about magical creatures that roamed these woods. He said they could turn invisible and they tortured,— killed for sport. I thought they were just tales until yesterday when I happened on an unusual track. I believe I was following one. Then you barreled in here. Now, I think now he's found us."

"Can you kill it?"

"James told me they were no easy kill."

"They can be killed though?— Why don't you just shoot it?"

"I don't know what I'm shooting at. If I miss it, it will know right where we are." Titus looked at his companion with serious eyes. "They're very hard to keep track of."

Daisy stared back out to the glen, but the silhouette was gone.

"Damn,— we lost it." Titus studied his surroundings. The

brush was heavy, affording good cover, but it was going to be difficult to get back to Sam quietly. "I think we should try to get back to my horse."

"What about mine?"

"We'll come back for it later. Those creatures have no use for horses." Titus carefully moved away from the clearing with barely a sound. It was slow going, but he moved each branch they passed gently and seemed to always find the easiest path, yet with plenty of cover.

Daisy felt bad as the only noise emanating from their position was from her. He held plants out of her way, yet she still somehow managed to step on a dry twig or stumble on a small rock. It was nerve-racking that she was going to be the reason for their demise, when she suddenly realized she didn't even know the man's name she was going to die with. *Maybe this isn't the best time.*

Titus stopped when they reached the wash. The only movement he saw was Sam still grazing on the young greens. The scout put his hands to his mouth and made a call; the bark of a squirrel.

The horse lifted his head then started across the dry gorge.

"When Sam gets here we'll make a break up stream," Titus pointed. "If anything happens just get on that horse and ride."

"Sir,— I didn't get your name."

"I ain't no sir, ma'am."

"Your name?" Daisy insisted.

The scout smiled. "Titus,— the name's Titus."

The young brunette extended her hand. "Nice to meet you Titus," while taking the man's palm softly. Gently she shook and then lingered, holding the offering. "Thank you."

The man almost blushed, then stuttered, "Let's just get out of here safe."

Daisy suddenly felt an amazing sense of well being. This man, this stranger, had a way about him that radiated security. As a protector, the woman knew Titus was the caliber of man that would surrender his soul to save any in his care. And now she was under his protection. She placed her hand tenderly on the powerful man's shoulder as he turned back to watch the horse's progress. "We will," she whispered, brushing close to his ear.

Titus tried to ignore the sudden familiarity, but the woman's caressing voice beckoned to his soul. A bond had just developed, but the man struggled to keep his mind clear.

Sam stopped before reaching his charges and tossing his head in the air nickered. Titus knew the animal would come no farther and reached back taking Daisy's arm. "Let's go."

Making a break, they jumped out together and ran the twenty feet to the horse. Titus reached for the reins and grabbing Daisy around the waist, almost tossed her into the saddle. Taking his turn to swing on behind the girl, he put his foot in the stirrup when he was pulled off balance and stumbled to the dirt. Springing to his feet he drew his pistol only to have it batted out of his hand. A glimmer of light brushed by his right then the transparent silhouette unexpectedly took form.

Titus dove for his pistol as a streak of light cracked through the air and struck a dead pile of wood by his head. Within seconds a full scale battle erupted as the wash became a maze of gunshots and streaking flames, that ripped the air and exploded on impact over the maze of scattered timbers left behind by the receding waters.

The shadowy transparency by the scout was hit and thrown over the heap of debris as blue lightning rippled over its body. The dying hulk, now fully visible, quaked in its death throes, its chest ripped open from a savage weapon.

Titus' pistol was shot from his hand as he stood and a second silhouette charged his position. "Go," Titus screamed as he swung a fist at the monster, but the blow was easily deflected and a heavy rod struck the scout in the chest, knocking him back to the ground.

Daisy tried to pull the rifle in the saddle boot under her leg free as a hail of weapons' fire showered about her; but Sam reared changing her priorities.

A third creature shot, but due to the woman's wild ride the trajectory merely grazed her arm. Daisy lost her balance, but managed to hang onto the horn as Sam continued to buck and kick; a random hoof hitting the new adversary.

Titus coughed, under strain from his knees and saw Daisy's dilemma, "Sam Go!" But the horse was too spooked by fear.

The creature in front of Titus raised its weapon for a final blow when the crack of a repeater sounded and the monster simply dropped to its knees and then fell face first in the dirt. Titus looked around for his savior, but saw nothing. Picking up his pistol, it was hot; but he holstered it then tried to cool his hand moving it briskly.

The creature kicked by Sam had disappeared and Daisy was

doing her best to hold on to the bronc trying to unload its passenger as Titus dashed over the wash, calling to his animal to calm it. The horse was responding when the man was interrupted by a creature in his path. Out of nowhere the monster appeared. Titus drew his pistol, although it was scorching his hand and started to pull the trigger while at a dead run; but the creature shoved a quarterstaff into his legs and stepped aside as the man went down. The giant stood over the scout pinning his arm to the ground with its rod. Titus called out, "Sam go!" But two more creatures appeared, surrounding the animal. The man's pleading glare met Daisy's, "Run for it!" But Daisy just shook her head.

"Why haven't you killed us?" Titus asked clutching his chest as he stared at the giant in front of him. Turning his head he spat in defiance when a mountain lion jumped out of the nearby brush from the opposite shore and circled growling, then rubbed up next to one of the adversaries. The scout was dumbfounded. "What the hell?"

The shortest of the monsters bent over and stroked the big cat while pulling her horned mask off. A beautiful young crow woman shook her hair out, cupping the helmet under her arm. "We're not here to harm you."

Titus was flabbergasted. A second creature removed its mask and Titus noticed an amazing resemblance to Zeb, one of the scouts he worked with earlier in the week.

"Who are you?"

"The name's Ben, friend." The man stepped forward and extended a hand helping the scout up. "We couldn't help but notice you were trackin' the same critters we're after."

"What?"

"We've been watching you."

"I heard ya. How long?"

"Came upon you this morning. Placed some sign to help you along." Ben retained Titus' hand and shook.

Titus pushed the offer away in disgust. "You mean bait?"

Ben ignored the hostility. "You got's an uncanny talent son.— We simply tagged along on your aim."

The scout was mad. Turning his back on Ben, Titus stepped over to Sam and patted the animal. "Who's the mountain?" He mumbled and pointed a thumb back at the still masked giant.

"Oh,— he's one of them,— but he's with us."

Titus studied the big creature, and then looked at the dead monsters around the wash. "What are they?" His gaze fell to the taloned feet of the statue standing near him. "What?"

"Visitors you could say," Ben said with a chuckle. "It's a long story, so why don't we talk over some food."

Daisy chimed in interrupting, "I haven't eaten in days."

Titus was determined to part company, but Daisy pleaded that they at least stay long enough to eat. "And besides, there's safety in numbers."

Reluctantly the man acquiesced, and the group set about making a fire. Aiyana mentioned briefly a few choice tidbits of their journeys,— their quest.

The conversation got Titus thinking and he spoke of: the strange trumpeting creature that chased him from the cave, the dead scout, the horse with its bones ripped out and flesh left behind in a heap. And then mentioned the mine with the kidnapped women. Ben's interest peaked when Titus spoke referring to the trackers at the fort and the unusual skeletal distortions.

Daisy begged their new associates to join them to help her save her friends; but Ben and Aiyana suddenly withdrew changing the subject and prodded Titus a little more.

"What fort was that?" Ben redirected back to Titus.

"The Forks."

Aiyana and Ben looked at each other startled. "And where might this cave be?" Ben asked.

Titus was sparked by his new company's deep interest in the site's location. "I guess I could take you there."

"Well,— ifin' we's going to head into hell itself you two would probably be needin' the proper gear."

Titus and Daisy looked questioningly at each other.

"But we need to help my friends!" Daisy pleaded.

Ben stared over at the dead Sky Demons. "First things first." His mind was already plotting the next move. He knew Titus would be an asset. Ben saw the big scout in action, but the girl troubled him. She could hinder their progress, even endanger them all. The man's view dropped to the ground, then drifted to his wife. Aiyana had already began preparations to leave. A smile crept over his face, *but then again people have a way of surprising you.*

Chapter Thirty-seven

Encounter

Log Entry: *Mountain Man's Poem*

History would warrant by its passage of time
the edicts spoken
veracity masked to the blind
Fate has a way of playing its tune
but ears deaf to the concerto
will miss the song's truth

*   *   *

It was an unusual mixed company of riders that topped the ridge overlooking the bodies of fallen soldiers scattered about the rise in a bloody death shroud. Former enemies, the party of Sioux, Cheyenne, cavalry, and mountain men looked on in stone silence respectively imagining the stand the cavalry had fought against its unknown adversary.

Zeb dismounted and approached the knoll on foot scanning the carnage. He had tracked three Guardians to this point and knew what forces the company had met up with only a few days earlier. Three Sky Demons had killed everyone. Death came in an invisible wave of confusion as the military took its stand against its unseen foe. Zeb read the signs and interpret how the battle played out as if he had watched it. Most were killed in hand-to-hand combat, probably unaware of even who the force was that was crushing them; then he spotted the phosphorous glow of inhuman blood. A purple film glistened in the sun, smeared over a long blade of steel lying in the grass by one body, splattered by the unnatural pasty fluid. The only body on the field that was skinned and missing its skull. *A tortured kill,* Zeb thought to himself. This man had fought the creatures valiantly; but in the end his reward was a live peeling, and body parts strung out somewhere in the cosmos. Zeb was angered by the irony. Life and death reduced to a game: a game he had played often, but now brought sorrow as he viewed the battlefield and the waste of good young men.

The Seer approached Zeb silently and stood resting his hands on his rifle butt planted firmly to the earth. Compassionate eyes overlooked the site as he whispered in Cheyenne, "It seems our enemy bares no preferences."

Zeb answered, "Yes,— they any… all the same," shaking his head.

Soldiers walked the solemn hill and paid respects to the fallen, and the dangerous nature of their adversaries became more real. Talk passed through the gathering, whispers of disbelief. "Only three had wreaked this havoc?" Fear gripped some of the less hardened as superstition transfixed their souls. Their future, and the danger of their quest vividly spilled out over the bloody scene, was telling. Fate was an un-wielding adversary leading them down a narrow road. Survival was an optimism that carried little weight right now.

Zeb picked up the sword doused with Sky Demon blood and

examined its balance. Suddenly he froze. A transparent silhouette distorted the landscape on the next ridge. The enemy had returned. Zeb's mind raced. He read quickly the terrain: no cover, no way to hide and nowhere to run. "Sergeant," Zeb whispered with authority, "do you know how to operate that Gatling?"

Lloyd looked dumbfounded. "Sir?— Yes, I've been briefed."

"We've got company, quietly, and casually take a few men with you and get it operational."

"How long we got?"

"Probable,— less than a minute."

"Shit,— I don't see anyone."

"Move."

The sergeant almost saluted, unfamiliar with taking orders from a scout. "Smith, Thomas, and Bennett,— come with me."

"Sir?"

"Now, gentlemen."

The Seer standing next to Zeb leaned over and whispered, this time in Sioux. "Should mount up."

"Get your horses and scatter over the hill. Make it look like helping with the dead."

The Seer moved without question, motioning his braves to follow.

"Sergeant, we'll need some men looking after these bodies to avert the enemy from our knowledge of them."

Lloyd acknowledged Zeb's ploy and quickly designated several of his remaining men to get busy, but to be prepared for attack.

Isaac, Reuben and Claude, standing some distance away, saw the sudden shift in activity. Without words they led out with their horses toward Zeb at a brisk walk, across the top of the last stand with five Sioux braves following on horseback. "What is it?" The blond asked as he neared.

"We got visitors."

"Where?"

"Left flank," Zeb whispered softly, nodding indirectly to the position. "Be prepared for anything."

Isaac spoke without any sight acknowledgement of Zeb's words. "We'll ride back the way we came and circle around the ridge behind. We'll hit it fast and hard."

"I don't think there's time. Besides,— I need your eyes on a rifle. You and Claude are among a few men here that could hit the damned horns, the canons they wear,— silhouetted and on the move." Zeb made eye contact with his nephew. "Reuben, Isaac's idea for a distraction is a good one. Be careful,— and hurry,— remember, they've changed their tactics. No telling how long they reconnaissance their prey before they'll hit."

"Yes Uncle."

"I'll go with him," The Seer stated in Cheyenne and then called to some of his braves.

"We'z be danglin' likes bare hooks here in da open," Claude mumbled, as Reuben swung into the saddle. With a wave Reuben's horse reared and spun, hitting the retreat in one fluid motion as five of his brothers followed in a cloud of dust. The Seer and his warriors followed close behind. "I dells ya we're buzzard picking's, ifin's..."

"Isaac,— Claude," Zeb's tone was deathly serious as he cut his older companion off. "They probably already know what's going on. You two get prepped and low."

Zeb barely finished his last word as a commotion broke out behind. Spinning, the mountain man caught sight of a giant, black, skeletal frame, that appeared as if out of nowhere; springing into a group of Indians, and soldiers it grabbed a hostage. A massive appendage knocked two other defenders out of the way, spilling their entrails with one crushing blow. Gunfire erupted in haphazard confusion. The giant ebony frame carried its prey with ease, charging through the battlegrounds, wreaking havoc among the solders, and civilians desperately trying to fend off the encounter.

A second giant creature, rose out of a low crevice in the knoll as the Gatling gun erupted in a cloud of sulfured smoke, and lead. Wave-upon-wave of projectiles slammed against the hard exoskeleton surface of the second creature; but did little to hinder the monster. Each slug that hit seemed to deflect, or was absorbed without any injury; some ricochets even striking fellow soldiers in the wake.

Claude swung into his saddle and raised his rifle charging the first creature as it neared.

Isaac stood shooting repeatedly, but watched in horror as his well aimed shots did little to impede the monsters' progress.

Claude fired once before his animal collided with the monster. The impact knocked all involved to the ground.

The giant lost its grip on the prey, rolled in the dirt trumpeting; but within seconds was back on its feet.

Claude dropped free of his animal and pumped two more shots into the creature as he circled his seemingly invincible foe before the thing turned on him.

Huge drool covered fangs seemed to salivate as an eerie cry called to the small nuisance, standing defiant before the creature's immense stone features.

Claude stood frozen, almost mesmerized by the daunting display, hypnotic as the creature virtually purred his attacker into submission.

Zeb, on Claude's charge, drew his short sword and followed his friend's blind attack without thought.

Claude's horse was scrambling to get up, and out of the way of the monster as the creature spun on its rider.

Zeb continued his race, jumping to the back of the rising horse, and using the animal as a spring board, propelled himself high over the Death-Bones-Walking. Swinging his blade, Zeb severed one of the monster's limbs, then hit the ground behind and rolled back to his feet.

The giant shrieked in pain, and anger. Black tar spewed from the injury hitting Claude's horse.

The animal, only halfway to its feet, winced disoriented. Scrambling in a panic to escape, it smashed into the soldier freed from the monster, knocking him to the ground. Then stumbling, the horse ran into the creature again.

The momentum pushed the alien off its feet.

The giant, viewing the horse as the culprit to its woes, trumpeted in anger, and drove a taloned stinger into the animal's midsection, pinning the horse to the earth. Steel shod hooves struck out in spasmodic death throes dislocating one of the monster's leg joints with a thunderous crack. The lower part of the limb contorted unnaturally. The creature spun uncontrolled, dropping onto the horse. Tar spewed from the injury, bathing the lathered equine. The sweat accelerated the acidic properties of the proteins, reducing the animal into a mass of quivering, twitching muscles.

Fumes from the caustic action of the horse mixed with the heavy sulfur, and carbon of the weapon's fire thickened the air into a putrid, eye-blinding gas. With the light breeze, the cloud drifted like a fog over the knoll, reducing vision as men's eyes watered, and burned from the unnaturally formed chemical weapon.

Reuben, The Seer, and the warriors charged back toward the battlefield, hearing the commotion. They found nothing on their flanking operation, but could now see the desperate battle. Helpless to give succor, they raced forward with war lance, and rifle ready.

The gas burned as Claude tried to wipe the tearing away, and shot two more times.

Zeb circled behind the monster that killed the horse. The second creature grabbed the soldier Claude tried to save, and disappeared over the ridge it appeared from. A streak of white light then screamed through the air; and the drone pinning Claude's horse to the earth flipped off the dying animal knocking Zeb off balance, and to the ground. Trumpeting, the giant rolled, then made a break for the same ridge as its companion, dragging its damaged limb with amazing agility. Two more streaks of white flame ripped through the air. One taking off another of the creature's limbs; but the second missed, striking a wheel of the Gatling. The weapon spun out of control as the drone plowed into the operators. Tar spewed over two of the men. Screams, blending with the shrieks of the monster, echoed over the knoll. The drone rolled free of the wreckage and grabbed a Sioux warrior, dropped over the nearby ridge, and disappeared.

Moments later an eerie silence fell over the battlefield. Zeb scrambled to the edge of the ridge, and looked over it at the small cave entrance hidden by the contours of the land as Reuben, and the braves charged back into the camp. With a curse of aggravation Zeb ducked low scanning the horizon for the source of the mask-cannon fire. "Get down,— we still have company!" Zeb couldn't help his sense of shock as he scanned the devastation brought on by only, *two of these,— these,—* "What the hell were those things?"

Claude almost crawled to Zeb's side, he was staying so low. "Never seen da likes. Black-walking-bones."

Zeb grabbed his friend in anger. "What the hell were you thinking?"

"Cain't sanz by watchin' while no cridder carries off our own."

"You old fool." Zeb let go spitting in disgust. Some of the men were beginning to meander around confused. Zeb almost shook with frustration. "This ain't over yet. Get you asses down if you want to keep um."

Reuben, and The Seer, at the edge of the battlefield scanned from horseback, but could see nothing.

"You dink dem varmints some kind of pets?" Claude whispered to Zeb.

"Hard tellin' what those beasties were, but I know what I saw before they hit."

Isaac overheard the conversation. He moved in closer to Zeb and Claude. "Why'd the demons shoot that critter ifin' their pets?"

"Maybe they was shootin' at us and missed."

"Dem boys don' play dat careless."

"Zebulan," cried out a familiar voice. Zeb's name floated over the knoll in a hauntingly detached, almost ghostly apparition. "Zeb don't shoot, it's us." The words had no focal point. They came from nowhere, yet seemed to be everywhere.

The translucent wave of an empty shadow melted low over the ridge and the three men watched in horror as it then disappeared again against the backdrop of the contoured prairie beyond. "Zeb, Claude, Isaac, Reuben— don't shoot, we've come to help."

"Mom?" Reuben was mystified and walked his mount over the ridge.

The Seer stayed back as warriors began mulling toward him.

"Id be a drick I'z dell ya."

"Aiyana?" Zeb cried out in desperation as something invisible jumped from the ridge below and landed softly on the ground next to the big mountain man. Zeb could hear the soft footfalls, but could see nothing as he scrambled backwards. The soothing purr of a gentle tabby disrupted the men as soft fur rubbed up against Zeb. "What the hell," Zeb exclaimed.

With a flicker of spasmodic shape, and a soft buzz a large mountain lion appeared, pushing its head into the man's chest affectionately. "Missy?" Zeb relaxed. He ran his hand over the animal feeling a collar, and a strange netting draped over the cat.

Lloyd, startled by the sudden arrival, picked up his rifle to save his friend; but a streak of white lightning smote the weapon from his hand. "We'll be having none of that." Barked a commanding male voice as Missy jerked at the sudden disruption and disappeared.

Seconds later a beautiful Crow women appeared in the same spot the cat stood moments earlier. She craddled a strange mask in her left hand and shook out her long black hair, after removing the unusual helmet. Extending a hand she helped her brother-in-law to his feet. Soldiers and Indians gathered around to marvel at the mysterious banshee that appeared from nowhere, and change form.

"Mom? What?— How?" Reuben moved closer and slipped off his animal, running to his mother.

"What is this? Witchcraft?" Lloyd cried out as he rubbed his hand softly, trying to ease the burning. A second form appeared from nowhere right next to him. The giant grabbed his hand roughly examining his injury. Lloyd shook with fear at the immense image holding him. Long taloned fingers twisted his arm as the stone features of the metallic face gave no inkling to the creature's purpose. Lloyd pulled to free his forearm, but the giant latched onto his bicep with his other hand, almost lifting him off the ground. A second form, much shorter then the first, appeared placing a hand on Lloyd's shoulder.

"Friend,— it's OK. Let Broken-Toe have a look-see."

"Ben is that you?" Zeb said leaving Aiyana's side as Reuben ran in and hugged his mother. "Why the hell is that thing with you?"

Aiyana kissed her son, but grabbed Zeb's arm stopping him. Isaac's features went stone cold as Claude looked on amazed. "He's here to help." She said softly.

Isaac stood pushing past while pulling his knife. "They killed my wife."

He would have stuck it in Broken's back, but Ben intervened. "He's been with us. Even killed his own kind."

"What?" Isaac cried out in disbelief.

Aiyana moved in, pulling away from her son. Softly resting her hand on Isaac's arm, "I'm sorry for your wife, but it's true. Broken-Toe is at war with his people and helping us." She let go and raised her hand upward. "The Great Spirit has sent him because of rebellion. My father spoke of it." Her dark eyes probed deep into the desperations of the blond's soul. "He is here to help us stop The Black Death. If it isn't stopped they will number greater than the buffalo and lay waste to everything."

The Seer, having pulled up short of the knoll, looked on in awe at the sudden turn of events. Dropping from his horse, and turning to his warriors he cried out in Cheyenne, "The priestess and the Destroyer have come as I told you. It's the time of The Gathering. Let your doubts fall. Death awaits our trail, but the brave will be remembered." He raised his rifle over his head and chanted.

All doubts wavered as his warriors joined in the death chant.

Claude stepped into the family reunion. "You mean dem black cridders?"

Broken-Toe opened a pouch at his side, dabbing an ointment retrieved from his medicine pocket on Lloyd's injury. At first it stung then the discoloration of the wound began to fade.

"Yes. Like locust they come," Aiyana replied nodding. "The Great Spirit let me see this."

Titus and a woman suddenly appeared among the group, startling almost all. Neither wore masks, but the strange netting that Missy had on, they also wore.

"Quit doing that," Zeb cried out in frustration.

Ben removed his mask and with sympathy tried to comfort Isaac. "We were tracking one of them black critters to here and along the way bumped into a few of Broken's friends. Two of'em won't be killin' again, but one got away. They're probably the one's responsible for your wife's death."

"It was soldiers that butchered my wife, but the Demon God's instigated it by their murderin' return."

"A great battle has taken place in the heavens. These warriors have fell from the sky. With them has come the horde,— the Black Death." Aiyana took Isaac's hand to comfort him. "Your wife's death pains us; but we must press on and stop this disease that infests the souls of men,— before it spreads. Before it can no longer be stopped." Aiyana looked over at Broken-Toe who was studying the Gatling. He obviously had plans for the weapon. "Broken comes this time as friend to stop a mutual enemy.— Join us.— Help us."

The Indian prophetess held great power in her pleadings. Isaac's head hung low. His heart had been forged. "I will join you. What must I do?"

"There's a cave not far from here," Ben injected. "Aiyana's seen it in a vision and Titus there," Ben pointed out the tall buffalo soldier, "told us about it."

"But first we need to save my friends." For the first time the brunette spoke, suddenly becoming the center of attention. She seemed vaguely familiar to Zeb and Claude, but they could not place where they had met.

"And who migh' your friends be?" Claude asked.

"We were kidnapped from town."

Titus broke in, "McCray and his men grabbed them."

Zeb, and Claude shook their heads understandingly. Then with sudden recognition Claude blurted out, "Was Robin grabbed?"

"Yes," Daisy covered her mouth. — "You were the men that pulled us out of the fire."

Claude was shaking with anger. "Ifin' dat coward lays a hand on my niece I'z dare 'im limbs from limbs."

Titus rubbed his jaw, shaking his head somewhat confused. "I saw the women at McCay's mine northeast of the cave. I was headed for you two,— you know traveling with the lieuten—ant—" the scout started scanning the battlefield realizing the lieutenant wasn't there — "and help when I bumped into the present company." Titus paused, "Where's the lieutenant?"

"He got himself killed." Lloyd had moved in closer to the people and away from the giant, but his expression showed little pleasure. "We were continuing pursuit of I guess," Lloyd pointed at Broken-Toe who was now examining the cartridge assembly of the Gatling, "more of them critters. There's some mighty strange goin's on here." Missy purred and rubbed up against Lloyd. "What the hell?" The sergeant jump in panic, seeing nothing.

Aiyana chuckled, tapping a device on her waist and the big cat appeared with a flicker and a buzz.

"Damn." Lloyd moved behind Zeb, but the cat followed.

"She ain't looking' to hurt ya." Ben laughed. "Must be some catnip on your legging's there."

Zeb reached down stroking the big animal. "How are you doin' old girl? It's been a long time."

Missy affectionately rubbed against the man's buckskins, like a contented tabby.

"We need to pow-wow boys." Ben got suddenly serious. "We've got us some critters to kill and some women to save."

With that a camp was organized. Lloyd stationed several men to keep an eye on the cave. Soldiers, and Indians together helped with the dead while plans were discussed about how best to proceed.

Chapter Thirty-eight

The Yet-Tat

Retrospect

" We 've caught them napping. "

"Let 's kick their ass and get the Hell out of here. "

George Custer (1839-1876)

*　　　*　　　*

The shadows of pre-twilight cast an eerie hue to the rugged landscape; blanketed with scattered boulders, brush, and barren trees; ravines that carved twisted veins throughout mountainous outcroppings; a wilderness of hills, and rolling prairies, of ragged cliffs, and scattered brambles.

Treacherous as the terrain, the path that lay ahead was fraught with danger. The ghost hour was upon them, foreboding as a dream; but the reality had already killed,— and would kill again. Like phantoms, the small party listlessly moved toward the hidden cave: the mouth of the hive; the entrance to, "The Shadows," death warren.

Somewhere deep in its bowels the queen was calling. The prophetess was being drawn, almost wooed by its pleadings. No words were spoken. No tune did it mimic; but like the rhythmic beat of a relentless song, it pulled at the soul of the infected.

The poison in Aiyana's veins opened the door to the hypnotic dictates the demon used to control its surroundings. The woman was resisting its influence, but could not deny the presence. Because of the messages, Aiyana could see the murky world below. Not as a human would see it, for darkness bathed this environment. She saw the black recesses as the queen perceived them: images, and pictures; shapes, and forms erupting from a colorless background.

Without eyes the creature viewed its world. A type of mental radar that transposed all substance into shapes. Form, and function dancing within the reality of its mind. And its perceptions were being passed on. In glimpses, and flashes Aiyana could interpret the queen's lair. She used it as a tool, guiding her to destiny. Like a path marked with signals, she walked the course of her vision. The hillside her father had shown her in a dream, under her feet. The place fate was calling her to war was before her. Nightmares that would haunt the minds of the weak pushed her forward. The future seemed certain, but it would not hinder her from her task. Those chosen for trial must not waver. The battle, no matter how desperate, must be fought. Grim determination was leading her on.

She wished the enemy ignorant of their plans, but the queen also knew they were coming. Aiyana saw the world of the hive, and the queen saw the prophetess's realm through the woman's mind. The alien watched their approach,— spied their every move: The War God, Ben, The Seer. The five Indian braves that chose to join their party. Missy, the big cat that stalked silently in the shadows near her companions. Aiyana knew she could not hide anything from the queen. Like a hovering demon the alien saw them reach the cave opening. And like a jealous mother she sent her horde to harvest the wealth: living, breathing hosts.

Broken-Toe was the first to enter the cave. Oblivious to the stench of rotting flesh, he stepped over the corpse guarding the entrance: a beacon marking the trail, a testimony to what lay ahead,— the warren.

The giant fiddled with his belt: controls to his mask, and his vision. Heat would no longer be the preferable way to see in the void beyond. Infra-red was at best useless when hunting the parasites. Broken-Toe channeled through the various settings. The visor would enhance the vision of the wearer. Like binoculars, or night vision goggles are tools of a hunter; The Guardian's mask had built in functions to aid in the hunt for criminals, and in this case,— disease.

Ben stepped in behind and paused. "Phew,— that would peel the linin' off the most undiscriminating sniffer."

Broken-Toe unceremoniously grabbed Ben's wrist and adjusted the setting on the man's mask. Ben watched with curiosity as his views changed with each tap of the Guardian's taloned finger.

The mountain man was just getting use to the unusual heat vision. The strange bright fiery colors of life that danced across the drab, shadowed backdrop,— as the mask revealed the world. Broken stopped on a setting that turned Ben's sight to a fuzzy, gloomy green. The giant appeared as a silhouette of ghostly white. The Marshal turned to help Aiyana, but the mountain man was unhappy with the new setting.

"Hey! Turn this thing back," Ben said as he pulled his mask off. He was amazed to find himself in complete darkness. Moments later the six Indian warriors traveling with them entered the cave mouth carrying torches they had made. Their small delay, balanced by the time it took to ignite the oiled wraps. The new light flickered haunting shadows over the caves interior. Ben put his mask back on, disgruntled. The dull green had become sharper with the new light, but the view was still extremely unappealing. He realized it would be best to keep the helmet on. If for any reason the torches went out he would find himself completely blind, but he didn't understand why the hunter had changed his view.

Missy ran in, jumping past the men, and pushed by Ben. The big cat paused by the carcass of the dead scout, and growled. Even to an animal the rancid meat was unappealing. It would be questionable if buzzards would choose to dine on the putrid mass of contaminated flesh.

The stench of ammonia and waste added to the nasty aroma as Ben pressed on deeper into the cave.

Missy started hissing and hacking as she stopped by a break in the wall, studying the crevice momentarily, then turned and darted deeper into the subterranean passages. The opening led into a large chamber off to the side of the main tunnel. Here the odor was strongest; again mixed with the putrid smell of rotting meat.

Ben looked in finding a pile of fur and mutilated flesh. Through the visor he could not determine the species, but they were big. Ben moved in closer and grabbed at a hide, but the fur just pulled out in his hand. He tried to shake off the clinging mass, but it stuck to his fingers like it had been glued.

"Shit," he wiped the mess on his pant's leg, regretting his ignorance as the fuzz adhered like a nasty clump of ill smelling lint. "Damn,— what the hell?" He left the chamber in disgust cursing his misfortune.

Leaning against the ragged opening he looked out into the tunnel. His companions were working their way down the passageway. The trail continued off to his left. He stepped out of the hole as Missy shot by like a bullet. She was looking to leave, and in a hurry. Ben studied her retreat spotting movement deep within the twisting maze below. "We've got company."

Missy stopped when she reached Aiyana, turned and snarled at the enemy coming their way.

"What did you see?" The woman asked, stroking the big cat. Looking down into the dark recesses she then called out, "How many?"

"I just see movement. The cave widens out ahead. We should make our stand there."

Broken-Toe walked by Ben, and continued down the tunnel. Either he didn't see the enemy, or he didn't care.

Ben decided the latter and followed with more confidence. The mountain man was no coward; but he had seen what these creatures were capable of, the mystery behind them. The way they moved. The nightmarish way they looked and fought. It played on his imagination and haunted his dreams. Ben faced death often in his world, but there's something about the unknown that casts a shroud over even the bravest of men. It allows the unexplainable fears we had as children to again find a foothold, twisting at our nerves, and weakening our resolve. Ben was struggling with the task ahead, and the danger it posed to his wife. Her courage in the face of the inevitable was amazing. He could not turn her from this course, but he would fight to protect her.

Ben stared at the giant leading the way. *Was he leading them to certain death? Why would this monster suddenly befriend them? Were we just the needed bait to enhance the game?* Ben pushed his doubts aside. *If that were true, Broken wouldn't have armed them.* Something bigger was happening here. Ben knew in his heart that this creature lived by some type of code. Broken-Toe had a sense of honor, and he had chosen his present company to help defend that principle. For whatever reason, the Sky Demon was not a sadistic killer like others of his kind. He had chosen his lot with humans. *Hunting with humans.* It was hard to comprehend.

The giant was the first to fire his mask cannon; but appeared to miss as the creatures stayed well hidden in the maze of stalagmites, rock, and fallen debris. Dark recesses, crevices, and chasms seemed everywhere. The amphitheater like room ahead opened into an arena of hidden catacombs, tunnels, and pits from where the enemy could hide, and strike. A huge slab that at one time belonged to part of the roof, stretched as a bridge, partitioning the room into two sections. The ceiling in this area looked like giant sheets of slate running at oblique angles with the floor. It was an architectural wonder. Natures advent of marvel, and mystery that added to the unreal setting. A place where the haunting illusions of the mind breed: the realm of the unknown; a world un-ventured, and out of place.

Aiyana adjusted her waist band, and engaged Missy's cloak. She didn't know if it would help, but she wanted the added protection for her companion. The same touch pad on her band controlled her own invisibility.

Ben was looking back as she slid her finger across the flickering hieroglyphs, and melted from the view of the warriors around her, but Ben saw no change. "Pick up the pace. We don't have all day."

The warriors, still mystified by the magic, panicked. Then the first wave hit. Over the dividing bridge the horde ambushed the party from the rear.

Broken spun as Ben fired at the enemy behind them.

Black gooey tar spewed over two of the warriors amid screams, and echoing gunfire.

The other braves shot their rifles.

Aiyana's mask cannon burst forth, but the mass of armored-exoskeletons overpowered the defense,— applied too little, too late.

Ben charged up the incline of the chasm, trying to help his companions; but unable to shoot because of the danger the walking bones' blood posed to his friends. He reached the battle site in seconds, but the war was already over. The stand was empty. Ben looked around in shock. "Ai...ya...na," he cried out, but nothing. Missy brushed by his leg startling him, then one of the adult parasites appeared in a narrow offshoot. Ben triggered his sights as the creature charged.

*   *   *

Chapter Thirty-nine

Assault

Lyrics: from an unknown tune

Yankee lift that glass, Judgment has arrived

Death will hold no quarter, The winepress vats are dry

*   *   *

Dusk was falling early as the strange mixed company slipped through the canyon, making use of every tree and bush to conceal their approach. A short distance behind a busted but functional buckboard, salvage from the previous battle site, brought up the rear. The Gatling was loaded on the back with Lloyd manning the weapon. A second soldier stood at his side for operational support. Titus and Daisy sat in the front guiding the team of four horses pulling the wagon. Surrounding the makeshift artillery chariot, Sioux and cavalry rode side-by-side; warriors riding paired in battle lines.

Once enemies, a cause greater than their own personal differences brought them together. An infestation was about to be unleashed on the world. A plague that would destroy all life. As the Sioux would later tell: *The Great Spirit would not leave his chosen ones to fight this battle alone.* Death was awaiting them, but they would face it as warriors, *"as saviors."* They had been brought together: at this time, at this place by a force almost too great to comprehend, — survival.

The scouts in the lead stealthily sought the best path. They had walked this trail often in the past. Mountain men stalking their adversaries. Using every avenue nature provided to conceal their approach. Practicing the deadly art of ambush against an enemy more numerous, but unaware.

Zeb, Reuben, Isaac, and Claude on foot, directed their small contingent of the most able marksmen. It was their responsibility to watch for the enemy and get the entire company in as close as possible to the mine without being discovered. After they freed the women being held hostages they were to work their way back to the cave and support the assault on the hive.

Isaac and Reuben slipped over a small crest and found cover behind a maze of rock and fallen trees. Zeb and Claude were higher on the hill having a good view of the grounds. The soldiers and warriors with the scouts melted into the surrounding natural bulwark and prepared for battle.

"Looks like dem buzzards flockin' around dry bones?"

"Somethin' sure don't seem right." Zeb pulled a spy glass and scanned the target. The mine ahead seemed in turmoil. "Titus said there were at least fifty men working, or mulling about the exterior of this mine."

"Don' look like dat feller had enough fingers."

"Maybe we've been spotted."

Isaac was also estimating a much smaller number. Something was happening. The Golden-One was under the impression the camp was run in a military fashion, but the hysteria ahead was totally out of character. There was no order to the chaos. "Now would be the perfect time to strike."

Reuben nodded and directed attention to a weak point in the enemies simple defenses.

Isaac agreed with the assessment and looked back at his artillery unit. It would take about three, or five minutes for the wagon to reach their position. Obstacles around them would prevent passage. He spied a break in the blockade at a road about thirty yards away. It was the trail used by the company to enter and leave the valley. Motioning to a nearby Sioux brave, Isaac pointed out the passageway below and directed the chosen one with signals to relay the message.

The warrior studied the best approach momentarily then quietly melted into the surrounding terrain without word or sound.

Isaac directed two more of his marksmen to move higher on the ridge to a natural crows nest above Zeb and Claude. Perched there overlooking the entire valley they could shoot right over the low dirt wall where the miners would most likely be making their stand. Reuben's eye for weakness would play an important role in the coming battle. The marksmen, from their new vantage, would be able to give full support to the attack.

"Let's get in a little closer."

"I'm right behind you uncle." The two warriors started slipping down the hill on their bellies as the rest of the men with them continued their stealthy approach on the mine.

"Dem blind vultures couldn' find dare butts with both hands. Look ad dem."

"Well somethin's got them pluckin' feathers in a bee hive."

Claude pointed out Isaac and Reuben. "Dem boys wants close up and personable. Should we'z join um?"

Zeb studied the terrain and took note of the artillery wagon. "I say we got good vantage here."

Titus paused the wagon before the entrance, out of sight. "We've got the element of surprise, but we'll need to get in that mine as quick as possible to save those girls."

Daisy's anxiety was building as she scratched her throat, "I shouldn't never left them."

"That's crazy talk girl," Lloyd blurted out. "Ifin' you hadn't come, we wouldn't be here."

Daisy looked deep into the eyes of the big buffalo soldier next to her. "You would have come for us?" She wrapped her hand over Titus' forearm, "Right?"

Titus felt uncomfortable, and not because of the impending battle. "I was on my way for help when I bumped into you."

Daisy gave a questioning glare back at Lloyd, who mumbled something incoherent.

Titus nudged the woman next to him. "Girl,— turn on that invisibility thing. If we get in close they won't be able to see you get in the mine,— and don't be afraid to use those six shooters."

Daisy sneered and then stopped short. This man was just trying to be helpful. "I'll do my best, but don't you think a seemingly driverless wagon might have an impact all its own?"

Titus smiled and engaged his cloaking device as did Daisy.

"Damnation, that's creepy," Lloyd jeered as Titus slapped the reins and the wagon lurched forward.

As the artillery and light cavalry hit the entrance of the operation, Isaac and Reuben reached the left flank and opened fire. The ghost driven wagon barreled down the narrow valley pathway. Men scattered as the horses thundered by, the reins floating magically in the air guiding the buckboard. Then the Gatling unleashed its hail of bullets. Lead pummeled the grounds in front of the mine as the light cavalry charged the stronghold amid a shower of return fire.

The battle took a sudden turn when the men defending the mine seemed without reason to leave the relative safety of the natural bulwark in and around the grounds and made a direct frontal assault on the aggressors. The attack was unorganized, but fierce. The reason for the change in tactics became amazingly clear when three monstrous black creatures emerged chasing the miners.

"Dem damn cridders are here," Claude barked as he dropped a miner.

Zeb began emptying his rifle. "Reload quickly with the rounds Broken changed fer us."

Titus spun the wagon in a narrow turn almost spilling the cart as the direction of the battle shifted to the new enemy. Lloyd used the fresh angle to his advantage and brought the Gatling to bare on one of the skeletal giants. This time the weapon had an effect.

Broken-Toe converted every third round with a metal piercing stud and the bullets ripped into the tough exo-skeletal-bone of the creature, spilling foul smelling tar in a wave of smoke and shrieks. The giant jumped at least thirty feet, clearing of the hail of lead, and hit a warrior on horseback. The brave was plucked from the saddle and pinned to the earth when an explosion rocked the valley.

A stray bullet struck a wagon loaded with nitroglycerin. The supply was brought in for use in the mining operation. The blast was devastating, leveling the battlefield nearest the eruption. Flames belched forth wood, rock, and metal. The shrapnel laid waste to the fighters, and a hail of fire smote the combatants. Kerosene barrels on the same supply cart burst into flaming bombs, adding to the unleashed chaos.

Isaac and Reuben were knocked senseless as the wave of the explosion threw them backwards, landing them in a pile of soft sand excavated from the mine.

Titus tried to control the horses; but the spooked animals, turned too sharp, dumping the buckboard and everyone in it. Amid the screams of men and animals, Titus looked up as he rolled clear and spotted one of the giants running from the burning maze. "They don't like fire!"

Lloyd was already trying to right the Gatling, but alone as the other soldier was pinned under the overturned wagon — his neck broken.

Titus couldn't see Daisy, but then remembered her cloak was on. "Daisy,— are you ok?" He cried out.

"I'm alright. Help Lloyd."

Titus ran to the sergeant and Daisy bolted for the mine. The smoke and fire were blinding, but Daisy charged through the maze confident of her secrecy when a mutant mass of walking bones hit the ground in front of her. She turned to avoid it, but the monster moved with her,— right in her path. "It can see me," she screamed.

Titus helping Lloyd stabilize the Gatling, turned in a panic, spotting the creature. "Shoot that damn thing," he yelled.

Lloyd spun the barrel, "Where's the girl?"

"Shoot or she's dead."

Titus grabbed the crank and Lloyd shook, gripping the rails, as the gun belched forth its thundering hail of 30 caliber rounds.

Zeb, catching a glimpse of the commotion below and the shimmering silhouette of Daisy's cloak cried out, "That critters on one of ours." Both men began to unload on the alien.

The creature fell backward at the combined force of the marksmen and the machine gun.

Daisy hit the ground crawling away from the storm.

The drone rolled into a puddle of flaming kerosene. The sudden splash shot a canopy of hot liquid fuel into the air, blanketing the creature, and dousing two miners just awakening from the onslaught of the earlier explosion. Unnatural shrieks, ear piercing at their decibels, emitted in an array of panic as the creature made a break for the mine. The men's screams joined in the chorus as one man rolled in the dirt trying to douse the flames, but the other ran in blind ignorance like a human torch, fighting the burning light.

Claude shot the running man, dropping him in his tracks.

"Whad ya waste a bullet on that one fer?" Zeb barked in disgust. "He was a dead man already."

"Dat poor man was a screamin'," Claude yelled while pointing at the body, "you heartless buzzard."

"Those rounds are for the critters,— not men."

"One bullet ain' goin' ta make no never mind."

Zeb turned away and drew a bead, nailing the burning miner rolling in the dirt.

"Hey,— you said dems fer da varmints."

Zeb smiled, "That one put you dead even of me."

"Damned pup I'z not payin' ya any coin on dis'un."

The Gatling jammed and Titus' hands slipped off the crank. "The damn thing's getting away."

Lloyd snapped the feed drum off the mount immediately spotting the problem. "We need another canister."

Both men looked back at the wreck and spied two more drums nearby, in the dirt.

Titus ran and retrieved one, but by the time he looked up two of the living bones had vanished. The third lay quivering; its limbs twisted in a mass that looked like a burning woodpile.

"We're too late." Lloyd barked as he watched the canister float into the air. His attention turned to scanning the devastation. Smoke spewed from innumeral fires. Bodies of men and horses laid everywhere. Havoc had been wreaked and survivors looked few. "I don't think we fared much the victory here."

"Daisy you alright?" Titus called out.

"I'm fine." The woman appeared next to the big buffalo

soldier. "I wasn't able to get into the mine." She then spotted a miner in the dirt coming to. Daisy ran over to the man pulling her six-gun. She spun him over. Dropping to her knees, she cocked the weapon and stuck it in his face. "Where's my friends."

"I don't know," the man muttered.

"What do you mean?" The enraged women shrieked as she shook her injured captive.

"They disappeared yesterday along with about half our crew," the man struggled to relay, gasping between burnt and parched lips.

"What?" Daisy screamed.

"The rest of us were just gettin' ready to leave." The man inhaled deeply then coughed. "Them monsters been killin'..." The man faded away.

Daisy's head dropped as she fought the tears.

Titus came up putting his hand on her shoulder. "You got out. Maybe your friends did too."

The words fell on deaf ears. "We got to find them." Tears choked further pleas.

Titus looked around and spotted Zeb and Claude helping Isaac and Reuben. The warriors were far enough away from the blast to escape serious injury. The only men from the offensive that survived were a few of the marksmen that stayed on the hill during the battle. The small victory had come at great cost. They had taken control of the entrance of the mine, but the effort still lacked closure. The women they came to save were still unaccounted for.

Lloyd stepped in close with his company. "Looks like that cave of yours must be connected to this here mine."

Titus thought about that as he helped Daisy off her knees. "Looks like we hit the hive from this end."

Lloyd scratched his chin as he stared at the entrance, "I was thinkin' the same thing."

Chapter Forty

The Gathering

Log Entry

Cut slices into the rump 2" deep, 1" apart, top and bottom, to allow juices to flow freely during cooking. Place in Dutch oven and add one jigger of whisky, Knife tip of salt, one quarter tin coffee mug of animal fat,— mule's quite lean,— plus any preferred seasonings. Line the oven with scallions. Topping the mule roast with wild berries if available,— preferably raspberries. Cook until meat separates freely with a fork. Bon appetit.

*　　*　　*

Aiyana came to plastered to a wall by some type of gelatinous goo. The mass was intermixed with stiff web-like fibers. She could see the hazy outline of the warriors around her through her visor and guessed they were trapped by the same substance. Two of the five men appeared conscious. The sharp green hue of the night vision mask dictated there was light present, but Aiyana could detect no source. She struggled to free herself, then spotted what looked like a swarm of bats moving toward her and the men to her left. The familiar voice of The Seer broke the silence. The Cheyenne language was spoken calm, but firm. "Pull your knife my brother. Don't allow the seed its planting."

"I can't get my blade free."

Aiyana could hear the struggling of the helpless victim. She triggered her laser sight on and tried to turn her head. The webbing hindered her movement. The mask cannon came online, but the gelatinous goo had locked the pivoting controls of the helmet. She could hear the magnetics strain as the guidance mechanism fought to respond. Aiyana had no idea what her weapon was trained on, but she flicked the firing, winking her left eye.

Sha—wack …

The blast burned through the fibrous netting around the cannon and cleared the web holding Aiyana's head. The main thrust of the shot struck a parasitic egg sack, obliterating the leathery casing and ignited the contents. Flaming tar splashed over a wide area of the nursery. It was then that the prophetess realized where she was: the nest. Hundreds of the gelatinous, almost amphibian looking, incubation-bubbles clustered all over the floor.

A commotion grew to her left. Aiyana strained, turning her head. The laser's familiar glow danced out across the cave's interior and found the winged infection agent almost on the warrior. Aiyana didn't hesitate. Sha—wack—.

The flaming parasitic body fluids spilled out over the webbing holding the man, and some hit his foot. Aiyana could hear the groans of agony, but the man did not cry out. The fluid burned through the warrior's leather moccasins and began eating flesh and bone.

More of the winged denizen morphed from their eggs. Aiyana aimed first at the fibrous mass holding her companions. *Shaa—wack,— shaa—wack,* the blast loosened the webbing partially, but she was cut short from completely freeing the third man yelling for help; forced to focus her attention on the growing swarm of flying bugs darting across the dark cave interior. Five,— ten,— she couldn't tell how many. The battle erupted swiftly. Two armed humans against the will of a mindless multitude of a flight enabled virus. Weapons fire lit the interior as the humans engaged the foe.

The Seer pulled his arm from the entanglement still holding his rifle. The dull hue of the blue phosphorous glowing walls, cast a canopy of light over the living ground. The horde weaved and fluttered, sightless, as they echoed out a type of radar looking for life, ever drawing nearer. With one arm swinging the repeater between shots, he cocked his weapon and fired, maintaining amazing accuracy in his trapped position. And still the wave pressed forward.

Aiyana's neck hurt from the continuous pounding of her cannon. The numerous relentless blasts generated heat that burned her temples and cooked her forehead. More of the creatures transformed from the eggs. She didn't know how much longer her weapon would last. "There's too many." *Sha—wack*, her shots continued,— *sha—wack*.

"We must hold on. Isaac will come." Bam, belched forth the repeater. "I have seen it." The Seer caught a glimpse of motion to his left. Straining he pivoted. The sightless bird stretched out swirling around and landed near the injured man next to him. He then spotted two more winged bugs very close, flanking him.

"What?"

The Seer cocked his rifle. "Don't give up," and his rifle thundered.

Aiyana didn't see the bobble to her right working out onto a nearby ledge. She heard the eerie shriek too late. Spinning her head, she saw the flight of the black-mass, like talons, reaching out to grab their host. *Click, — click*, her cannon didn't fire. The device had overheated. She felt the beast slam into her mask. A strong nasty smell clogged her sinuses, choking off her air as the visor went black. The mask ignited and Aiyana screamed as she felt the heat, like a shroud, tightening its grip, sealing off her last bit of remaining air.

*   *   *

"You alright?" Zeb asked as he helped Reuben to his feet. The younger man didn't respond.

280

Marksmen from the hill joined in helping the fallen.

Claude was supporting Isaac, who felt his forehead and moaned at the pounding. "What happened?"

"Plumb fools dancing' in da hornets face. Should jus leave you'uns where's ya dropped." The older man directed Isaac toward Titus and Lloyd. "Young pups never knows da smarts about dings."

"Reuben, you with us?" Zeb continued almost lifting his brother's son to his feet.

"I think so, Uncle," came the weary response.

"We was suppose ta drop dem buzzards from up in dares," pointing up the hill. "But no,— we'z gots da kiss da devil."

"Claude, that's enough," Zeb ordered as he began to lead his nephew toward the other survivors.

"Blame fools," Claude mumbled as he supported Isaac and fell in beside his companion.

Titus had turned his cloak off and was helping Lloyd with the Gatling as the party approached. The big black man paused in his assistance and looked up. "We figger this here mine is attached to the cave. We're goin' to hit it from this side and shove this Gatling down their throats."

"Your goin' to shove that Gatlin'?" Zeb asked. "And just how are we going to shove that Gatlin' in there?"

"We'll push it," Lloyd interjected. "It'll be slow goin', but them rounds altered by that critter worked on them bones." The sergeant pointed out two of the dead adult drones among the fallen. "They played havoc with us, but old Betsy here did the job." The man patted the weapon with a smile.

Claude gave Zeb a questioning look. "I don'wan' da be walkin' down dat dark belly withou's dat sifter-maker, watchin' my backsides."

Isaac rubbed his face and spotted tracks near the entrance of the mine as he dropped his hand. "Maybe we could use those," he pointed.

Zeb turned. The rails ended by a wooden sluice constructed for separating the gold from the dirt hauled out of the mine. "Let's find the cart that runs on those." Zeb let go of his nephew. "You good?"

"I'll manage."

Several of the party followed Zeb including Claude. Others helped Titus and Lloyd push the artillery toward the sluice.

Inside the mouth of the excavation a train of wagons filled with dirt rested: most overturned off the tracks. Zeb and Claude examined the scene. Two mules were probably sitting impatiently at the front of the buckets. They were used to haul the loads up the shaft, but then the attack of the walking skeletons. The harnesses were in shreds and the hoof tracks showed some panic, but little struggle.

"I think we found our war wagon," Zed smiled through the corner of his mouth.

"Dem beasdies, dinned nasdy on dem, parked dare lonely?" Looking at the hoof tracks.

"The poor packers probably never knew what hit them." Zeb waved to the other men loitering about as he stepped over to the first wagon. "Help us get this thing upright."

"I et mule onced. Damned foul smellin' bread fer sure. Coarse id been dead some four days in da deser'. I'd gone withou's prob'ly dwo." Claude's forehead crinkled up as he reminisced.

Zeb strained as he tried to flip one of the mining buckets by himself, "I found mule to be quite tasty. A little whiskey, some animal fat: it cooks up very tender."

"Blaw," Claude spit shaking his head. "I'z can s'ill smell da' rank buzzard fixin's."

Four soldiers joined in working on the cart as Zeb paused and stared at his friend. "You gonna help? We've got critters to squash."

*   *   *

Ben ran back to where his wife was standing a moment ago. Two drones lay crumpled and quivering in a pile of smoking refuse. The tar that burned with an almost blue flame had cooked into the limestone floor spreading a fog over the moist, motionless air of the musty interior. The unusual odor seared the lining of Ben's nasal passages. He sneezed, then coughed as Broken-Toe moved up beside him.

"If anything happens to her I'll kill you," he growled. "All this is your fault."

Broken-Toe ignored Ben's hostility. Probably unaware of what was said. He knelt examining the scene for clues on the direction the captives were taken. Numerous egg catches could be within the hive. They needed find the right hatchery and quickly.

The hard stone floor left no residue. No sign dictating a path through the abundant catacombs lining the walls opposite the natural bridge. Broken-Toe and Ben climbed the fallen barrier and studied the tunnels beyond. Ben was panicking, *where'd they take her?*

Missy jumped to Ben's side and growled. Ben turned as Broken-Toe shot. A drone trumpeted and splattered into a quivering mass. Two more charged out of the darkness and the warriors together pummeled their enemies.

"Come on down," Ben cried out. "We'll cook you mothers." A smile cracked his lips as he wasted one after another. Gooey body fluids spewed and ignited, and more charged, but the combined wave of cannon fire decimated the horde. As the smoke settled Broken-Toe tapped Ben on the shoulder and pointed to one tunnel, motioning, then turned to run down another. Ben stopped him, shaking his head: "no." He diverted his attention to the big cat. "Missy,— find Aiyana. Find her girl."

The cat purred then hissed at the crumpled mass of parasitic bones blockading the maze ahead. She then took an unexpected path.

Ben paused momentarily, but his doubt quickly subsided. "We need to follow her. Missy won't abandon my wife."

Broken-Toe acknowledged and fell in behind his student as they followed the bounding mountain lion. Missy was in a hurry. She could feel her connection with Aiyana slipping.

*　　　*　　　*

Shisss—ue,— the mask hissed as coolant spewed from ports dousing the flames. The chemicals thinned the tarry fluid from the visor, but Aiyana was slipping into unconsciousness.

She desperately triggered the firing mechanism again. Shu…wack, white flame rifled through the air hitting another winged menace as the sightless bird burst into a puddle of goo. More flaming tar spilled out over the mask and the webbing holding it. Aiyana's buckskin shirt was etched with holes. The splatter quickly burning through her leather garment; but the alien armor underneath protected her skin. Bug juice covering her visor still continued to blind her. She panicked. Struggling, she fought herself free of the weakened fibrous net holding her. The visor cleared and the woman saw more of the winged vermin coming her way.

"We've got to get out of here," she screamed and fired briskly at the wall supporting the gelatinous net holding The Seer. The fibers gave way as The Seer shot his last round.

"We can't leave my brothers."

Aiyana looked around as she helped pull the man from his confinement. All the other men were infected. Twitching from the black viral blanket that carried the spore, like a pathogen, planting its seeds deep within their souls.

"It's too late."

"No,— we must kill them. The walking death must not be allowed to grow."

Aiyana swallowed hard, then shot two more darting carriers on approach.

The Seer ran to his nearest companion and pulled the man's weapon from its entanglement. Aiyana defended the position as The Seer executed his friends. One-by-one he put a bullet in each chest as he said a prayer to the Great Spirit. *"Cursed were the chosen. Sacrifice, the only prize that could carry weight in the eyes of the damned. The trial has played out as seen. Death their only reward."*

Then long bony fingers latched onto The Seer's arm. The shrill scream of a miniature drone echoed. It was an enlarged, transformed raccoon. It lurched, then sprang for the man's head.

The Cheyenne medicine man wedged his rifle between the offending creature's body as the beast's grip cut off circulation: tightening its appendage on the man's bicep. Iron fingers of bone latched onto the rifle, endeavoring to pull it out of the way.

Aiyana jumped to the Seer's side, grabbing the resistive mass and tried to help, but the enlarged exoskeleton pressed closer.

*   *   *

The Gatling's wheels spanned the cart perfectly, wedging the weapon securely within its confines; but the men had strapped it down anyway to prevent shifting. Lloyd rode inside sitting on the back edge manning the gun, while four men pushed the trolley down the tracks deeper into the mine. The two kerosene lamps tied to the front handle of the wagon, mounted on either corner, rocked with the movements of the mobile, like ancient headlights blazing a dark road on a pitch night.

Titus stood on a baseboard at the side of the makeshift war

284

wagon, ready to operate the crank should the mutants attack. Daisy held on to the opposite side of the rectangular bucket, making use of the other running board. She was briefed on reloading the Gatling, the magazines were secured to the cart's rail within easy reach. Zeb, Claude, Isaac and Reuben were in the lead, lamps high and rifles ready, following a day old trail. Indians and cavalry made up the remainder of the infantry and the relief crew for the four men designated to push.

Daisy recognized the tunnel. She had escaped traversing its depths mere hours earlier.

Parasitic sign was everywhere and the men expected a strike at any moment, but they reached the end of the trolley's rails unmolested.

"What do we do now?" asked Titus,— angered. "We didn't think about running out of track."

"We push da damn ding."

"You act like that will be an easy job?" Barked one of the soldiers pushing the cart.

"What do you think we should do,— unload it?" Lloyd jumped out of the wagon and got in the face of his subordinate. "We have all our supplies and ammunition in this wagon. It would be too much to carry."

"I didn't sign up for this," argued another.

"You signed up to serve and take orders," Lloyd spit back.

"Not from you."

Zeb cocked his rifle then rested it menacingly across his left arm. "None of us signed up for this, but we're here now and damn it we'll finish this or I'll end it right now.

A Sioux brave moved in and grabbed the private's rifle. "I always knew the long knives were cowards," and spit in the man's face.

The soldier pulled his weapon free as two of his comrades stepped in training their weapons on the offending Indian. "Get back red boy or I'll pump one in your belly," one of the supporters barked.

Reuben disarmed the supporter laying him out on his back, as a rifle misfired in the commotion. Isaac jumped in breaking up the wayward parley. "We have a bigger battle than fighting amongst ourselves."

"Isaac's right," Zeb's commanding voice resonated throughout the narrow interior. "All life on this planet is at stake.

It's up to us to make a stand now. This plague will sweep across our land and take away everything we hold dear ifin' we…. "

"Zeb," Claude interrupted.

"don't….What?"

"We'z gots visitors."

"Damn." Zeb jumped to a position of oversight. "Lloyd take your position. You men take a knee and defend a frontal assault. The rest of you find cover and give support. Let's do this gentlemen."

In military fashion, the mixed contingent took up a defensive stand. Quiet fell over the entire body, then from somewhere deep in the mine a mule brayed. Men looked questioningly at each other as the gray pack animal stumbled up the corridor.

"Shit,— that's a blessing from above."

"Send someone to get a harness."

"I'll go," cried the coward.

The animal ran up to the men and hee-hawed twice more. The men pushing the trolley began to pet the mule. Without warning the mule dropped to the ground, kicking and crying. Its ribcage contorted as the humans gave it space: mystified.

"What the hell's wrong with it?"

"Shit,— look at that."

The breast bone ruptured; a thunderous crack and pushed through muscle and skin. Tissue fell from the bones like a shed coat as the skeleton of the mule stepped from its chrysalis.

"What in the world?"

"Kill it," someone yelled.

"It's already dead," cried another, when the skull tilted back and screamed. The tunnel erupted into a shooting gallery. The living skeleton sprang from its birthing, screeching as lead ricocheted: rifles belching forth their fury.

"Don't let the damn thing get away," Zeb yelled as his shot scored a hit. The impact pushed the creature against the dirt wall of the mine only grazing the tough outer exoskeleton.

Claude grabbed one of the lanterns at the fore of the mining cart, pulling it free, and tossed the canister in the path of the creature's flight. Kerosene spilled and ignited as the glass shattered on contact with the stone floor; the flames spread out blocking the tunnel. The monster bellowed and shot across the ground away from the flames as target practice resumed on the incredibly swift bones.

Bullets seemed to dance off its stone skin, although each strike did damage to its tough carapace shell.

"Wait," Lloyd cried out to Titus. "We'll hit someone." The sergeant continued to try to draw a bead, but the men dodging and shooting made it impossible.

In the panic, Titus, unable to fulfill his job, retrieved a bottle of kerosene from the wagon and pitched it at the critter. His aim was true and the unlit Molotov cocktail busted over the creature's back, dousing its outer shell.

Isaac stuck the butt of his rifle in a flaming pool of previously lit fluid and swept flames at the serpent, exploding a new puddle. The massive living torch ran screeching from the fire as Zeb pulled his short sword and swung severing the beast in two down its back. The creature's blood popped and crackled as it took to the flames, and Zeb raised his blade still on fire over his head and yelled, "Does anyone still have questions why we're here?"

Silence fell over the party.

"Someone get that ass out from the front of the cart."

Claude stepped over to the burning pile and pushed at it with the muzzle of his rifle. "And just how mights we to do dat?"

Isaac poked at the flaming refuse also. "How many of them bottles of kerosene did we bring?"

Zeb smiled looking down at the blond, "About twenty. We didn't know how long we'd be in here. Didn't want to run out of lamplight."

"I have an idea."

"I'z hope id involves fire," Claude snickered.

Isaac started to chuckle.

Claude kicked dirt on the dead mule's butt and sniffed the air, then focused on Zeb. "Smells abou' ripe. Should I'z slice ya's a wedge fer dinnin'?"

"Maybe later. Right now get that damn thing out of the way."

Claude chuckled to himself and waved some of the men his way. "Dinner has da wai' boys. Grab some shovels and picks and less git busy."

Chapter Forty-one

Duck, Duck,— Burn

Log Entry:

" Enemies come in many forms,

sometimes a man must fight the Evil within."

Isaac Gibson (1803 - ?)

*   *   *

Ben followed Missy deep into the catacombs. The cat's keen sense of smell and amazing night vision were not the only things guiding her. Missy had a sixth sense. A mystic awareness of her surroundings and her companion's peril. Like an extra-sensory link joining the cognizant with instinct, the big cat drew on an inner consciousness.

It's been noted that married couples, deep in love, have felt the danger or death of the loved one: far away. People have envisioned the demise of a soul, even picturing the place and type of fatality, without any physical link. And what of animals that seem to be able to detect the shake of a quake before it happens, even fleeing a tsunami before it strikes? Somewhere, deep in the souls of certain living beings, a power beyond the normal operates. Missy was drawing on this strength.

With powerful strides the lioness traversed the miles of underground passages with a confidence void of ego. She knew nothing of pride. She felt no remorse. Nor did the big cat love in the sense that humans do. What causes a mother in the animal kingdom to care for its young? What drives the big cats to defend their own? A similar motivation pushed Missy onward,— into the danger ahead. Against the fear of the unknown she was unwavering. Of the demons hiding in the shadow, she was wary but pressed on. She was on a mission, void of reason. Aiyana was in trouble, and Missy could feel her peril.

Ben was moved by an entirely different force. The mountain man was a hunter,— a tracker. In the Northern Territory, he trailed death itself and come off the victor. Man or beast, myth or demon: Ben had followed the most obscure sign and found his quarry. Neither rock nor water could cover his vigilance, snow nor rain the trail to hide. Legend said, *"He could stalk the wind on a cold night."* But here, Ben was out of his element. In the dark recesses of a limestone hole, his love was captive. In the underbelly of the earth itself, Ben was lost. A novice in a world as foreign to him as the planet the parasite sprung from.

But Ben trusted Missy. The cat was chiseled from an unmatched stone. A faithful companion more loyal than man's best friend. Years of traveling together had forged an alliance: animal and man joined into a family. Missy would not betray Aiyana, nor would she lead Ben false. Ben knew the only hope of finding his wife,— his lover, was the big cat. And because of this Ben had no doubt.

Broken-Toe followed close behind, not so sure why his student — whom he knew to be an accomplished tracker — was taking directions from an unintelligent beast. The giant understood the four footed creatures to be fierce hunters. As a predator it was one of the most fierce in this strange world. But it was a mindless beast. Broken-Toe had personally witnessed the loyalty that Sentients could display toward their own clan. They would fight to the death, sacrificing their own life to protect a fellow Sentient. And the Guardian knew Ben and Aiyana were closely linked. But this quadruped was just game. *Sentients sometimes used creatures for their own purposes. Like the big herbivores they rode on, or the small pack animals with teeth they hunt with.* But this species, from what Broken-Toe knew of this planet, was an independent creature. It normally traveled alone and hunted by itself. *Why was this creature even with the Sentients? Why would his student choose to follow it, rather than the more obvious tunnel near the abduction?*

Missy paused, looking back at her straggling pride. The rough terrain and narrow passages made it a difficult course for her two legged companions. She growled as if to say, *"Just a little further."* Or perhaps she was encouraging the bipeds to pick up the pace. But whatever the reason, Missy's attention was quickly diverted away. Jumping, the big cat avoided the long bony fingers endeavoring to gain a prize.

Broken-Toe spotted the mutant before Missy had. His laser nailed the target; it topped the stalagmite and his weapon splattered its hard carapace shell into a mass of tar and quivering limbs.

They were near the nursery.

The Marshal swiftly climbed to a narrow ledge as Ben reached Missy's side. From their respective vantage points, each overlooked the large room.

Ben could see men, women, and animals; pinned to the walls and hanging from stalactites. Most were dead. The same nasty piles of flesh and shed remains, left behind, he had witnessed aboard the downed spacecraft. The decimated boneless corpses, disfigured refuse: rendering the cave with the putrid smell of rotting organs and other unrecognizable odors. The acidic mass of foul air, hung heavy and was almost unbearable.

The inner structure of the cave was unnatural. Reinforced with glossy black carapaces and plastered with a gelatinous goo, the room was aglow with a living bacteria. Hauntingly, the contours of the bony embodiments of discarded exoskeletons lined the twisted confines of the giant chamber and warned of the danger of pressing forward.

Broken-Toe scanned the hive's birthing chamber. Missy had led them to the queen's lair. His amazement and respect for the lioness grew. *How did the big cat know*? But now he needed his full attention on the task ahead. Failure was unacceptable. One minor slip would mean certain death.

Broken-Toe took in the full panoramic view before him. He had seen similar nests at the infected colony on Sig-zaw. The harvest of the queen was abandoned there in favor of retrieving a sampling of the larva. Unfortunately that Yet-Tat failed due to the intervention of the pirates. But even that hive had not grown so big, so fast.

The original mission called for capturing the queen or securing the larva in the pursuit of an antidote. But, abandoned on this distant planet, lost to the empire made his original goal obsolete. He had no ship to contain her massive frame. No container to store her seed. Today he needed to kill the mother. It would be years before members of his clan would return to this planet. If left alone the parasite would spread like a virus, consuming this world,— overtaking all its treasures. They would absorb its spark of life and morph it into a travesty of innumerable living hives, each bent on pilfering hosts until the planet could breed no more. Nothing would survive the onslaught. Like a fire, the creatures would consume, until the planets emaciated resources, lay wasted.

The honor of the Marshal's code could never allow such a passing. No planet infected by the seeding could be allowed to be overrun. How could the empire continue if the parasite is not brought under control? No hive could be allowed to destroy all life on any planet. Broken-Toe mentally prepared his psyche. This queen had reached her end.

The Queen would be almost impossible to capture, but even harder to kill. Pulling a live mother out of a hive kept the drones at bay. But once its queen is gone, the hive would become an uncontrolled hornets nest. Each slave in turn would need to be destroyed. No egg could be left to continue the species. Broken-Toe's honor was at stake.

Ben knew Aiyana was somewhere near; inside one of the numerous chambers lining the walls of the dome shaped amphitheater. She was hidden away fighting her destiny. And Ben was fighting the urge to charge into the unknown, without plan or strategy. He needed to save her. To run to her side and fight the dream,— her curse,— her destiny. He didn't believe in fate. To Ben, Aiyana's vision was just one of any number of outcomes. Destiny is what each person makes of his road of choice. Ben had chosen Aiyana, or perhaps vice-a-versa, but in any case the mountain man was not going to spend his future without her.

Missy jumped off the ledge and dashed across the cave floor disappearing through a crack in the wall. Ben, ready to follow,— stopped. He spotted movement. Something was skipping erratically across the stone surface below, behind where the cat had just passed. Then the mountain man spotted the egg sacks. The same damn clutches they hunted aboard that downed ship, but this time the numbers dwarfed the paltry few found amid the crumpled wreckage.

A voice called out of the death warren, "Help me," the haunting plea. It was weak,— male,— but the words denoted life.

Ben jumped off the ledge and charged into the void below, weary of the blind birds. "Where are you?" Death would be swift if he wasn't careful.

The thunderous trumpet of an angry queen replied as the mother pulled herself from her station to face the intruder.

*   *   *

Fifteen men stood in the shadows of the numerous lamplights. Each lit wick cast its own perspective to the immense tunnel echoing the foreign movements of a party, lost, and half blind to their surroundings. Behind them a beautiful waterfall spit a fountain of cool spring water into a swift moving underground river, partitioning the cave into two distinct sections.

Daisy pointed to a sandy delta at the rivers edge. "I crossed right there. That tunnel over there leads out."

Zeb leaned over a scuff in the stone floor where he was standing and lifted his lamp to get a better look. "We ain't looking' to leave. We've got a hornet's nest to kill."

"What'ch see uncle?" Reuben asked, wondering about Zeb's discovery.

"We got critters that headed down that direction. Two I 'spect."

292

"How do you know that?" The coward spit nervously. "We ain't seen nothing' in over an hour."

"Shit for brains, keep your thoughts to yourself," Lloyd snapped back.

"Somebody's been here," a young soldier spoke standing near the water course. He lifted up the shreds of an undergarment hiding between two stalagmites. "This ain't no bat wing."

"Damn Charlie, I doubt you'z even knows what that's from."

"It's Robin's you assholes. Show a little respect," barked the brunette.

The soldiers ignored Daisy and got a good laugh, when the young man was ripped from the shore into the black depths of the swift water.

"What the hell?" One barked, running with another to the water's edge.

Frankie, carrying a lamp, held it high, looking for the boy from the shore.

The other pointed, "Is that him ?"

"Git back from dare you fools," Claude ordered, but it fell on deaf ears.

Lloyd swung the Gatling and prepared for the worst.

Titus jumped to the backend of the wagon to operate the crank.

Daisy climbed over the side and into the front end of the trolley and grabbed a bottle of kerosene. A wad of cloth was stuffed in the mouth — per Isaac's suggestion — and wet with the flammable liquid, forming a wicking. The woman then removed the glass shield around the lamp at the front of the cart.

"Right there, do you see him Frankie?"

The other held his lamp high scanning the river. "I don't see nothin', Tom."

Three warriors circled with rifles ready, supporting the pair.

"Get away from that water now," Zeb yelled, but it was too late.

An ebony, serrated tail shot out of the water transfixing Frankie as a second monster leaped into the startled mass of humans. Bone-hard-talons ripped into flesh. Drooling fangs, spit frothing saliva, amid the yells of agony. The warriors were brushed aside with one sweep of a giant arm. With blinding speed, the jaws shot downward and punched through Tom's skull with a crack that resounded over the crashing of the distant waterfall.

The three Indians scrambled for cover as Lloyd screamed, "Crank the damn thing!"

Titus wrenched the handle and the Gatling burst to life, spitting smoke and lead in a shower of death. Thirty caliber rounds, danced across the river then pummeled the black creature. Everyone joined in, training their rifles on the dark shadow, trumpeting in anger as the sudden fire power slammed into its hard bony exterior. Tarry goo, mixed with water splattered over the bodies crumpled at its feet. The stench of torched human flesh rose in a blinding cloud, with burnt sulfur, and carbon from the exploding gun powder.

"Aim for the head," Isaac yelled.

Daisy stuck the cloth end of the kerosene bottle into the flame of the lamp and stood, tossing the bomb at the lone enemy. The glass slammed into the beast's head and shattered, dousing the monster instantly, and transformed it into a blue burning torch.

The screeching intensified as the blazing skeleton pounced onto a nearby warrior, driving its talons into the man's chest. The monster lifted the victim into the air by the brave's organs and pitched the dying man into his fellows, then dropped backwards as the heavy artillery finished its life. Crumpling into a pile of twisted, twitching nerves, the creature's body fluids ignited as it reached critical mass and exploded.

Two more skeletal drones sprang from the river and Lloyd spun the Gatling, riddling the new attackers in a storm of lead.

The creatures seemed oblivious to the damage and charged into the defensive, trumpeting while rendering human flesh and bone into a mass of broken and busted bodies.

Isaac swung the butt of his empty rifle in desperation as Claude unloaded a bullet, point blank, into the beast's face.

Reuben dove out of the way of the deadly black fluid as the shock of the fatal injury stopped the giant-skeletal-frame in its tracks.

Zeb drew his short sword and jumped into the fray, swinging his blade, severing the drone's arm. He quickly twisted and plunged the blade parting the beast's head from its shoulders. Tar spewed, but he dodged the splatter and rolled from the conflict as the second monster grabbed a victim and disappeared beneath the murky waters of the cave's dark tomb.

The Gatling spun on empty chambers as Titus backed off on the crank,— the weapon depleted of its ammo.

"Get another drum," Lloyd yelled.

Daisy jumped to action with the command.

The decimated defensive scrambled, men running to new, safer positions while urgently reloading their empty weapons.

The heavy cloud of sulfured gas limited vision, adding to the shadows of the dim lantern light as men strained to see the dangers lurking,— real, or imaginary,— just beyond the shadows.
Panic began to set in as the tragedy of the recent battle sunk in.

"We gotta get out of here," screamed the coward. "We're all dead men."

"Shut up," Reuben barked, leveling his rifle at the man's neck.

"What's wrong with you man?"

"Quiet,— or I'll drop you right here."

"Look around man. Look what they've done to us. You think we stand a chance?"

Isaac stepped in and grabbed Reuben's barrel. "You want out? Leave," he spit between gritting teeth. Letting go of Reuben's rifle with a push he turned to the remainder of the party. "Any that want out, there's the tunnel." Isaac pointed back the way they had come. "The last thing we need to do is lose it: panic spreads. We've killed two of the damn things and we'll kill more. They're not invincible."

The coward was almost crying, but fear kept him where he was. To walk the dark tunnels alone was unthinkable. To leave by himself, scarier than the certain death they had just faced. The coward dropped to his knees and whimpered. He looked up through tears at the stiff faces of determination pitying his weakness. Worse now, no one cared. He had become insignificant.

Silence fell over the entire party as they stared, each one realizing, and resenting, what they didn't want to become.

Then the explosion of weapons' fire erupted from somewhere further down the dark abyss.

Zeb moved toward the sound searching for the source, then back to the men. "Our friends are in trouble. Let's move!"

*   *   *

Aiyana leaned back with all her might trying to pull the living skeleton free from its grip on The Seer, but the strength of the

295

bony fingers wrapped around the man's arm just drew tighter,— squeezing all mobility from the limb,— like a tourniquet cutting off the blood to an open wound.

"Shoot the thing," the medicine man screamed, but Aiyana hesitated.

"We're too close. The blood might kill us."

"We're dead anyway,— shoot."

Aiyana thought for a moment and engaged her gauntlet blades. Unaccustomed to their use she had forgotten about the weapon. With a *ching*, the hooked blades snapped into place and the woman swiftly, but carefully severed the arm bone of the hand latched onto the rifle. Black goo spilled out over the barrel onto the steel as it sizzled in the moist air.

The lost appendage was enough of an incentive and the creature let go screeching and jumped, pulling free to flee this unexpected attack.

The man spun, getting a small bit of strange blood on his foot; dropped his coated, weapon, and ignoring the pain, scrambled for another rifle — buried in the wall by a dead companion.

Aiyana simultaneously blasted the running drone, smearing the carapace across the very rock face the creature had made a break for.

Three more birds jumped on a nearby ledge ready to spring.

Light suddenly filled the chamber as the field of Aiyana's visor snapped to a sharper hue and she turned to face the new threat of alien parasites. On a high natural balcony across the room she saw the gray silhouette of a man transposed in the dark backdrop of the cave. "Help us," she screamed, but the words were drowned out in the thunder of her own mask cannon as it burst to life.

Isaac entered the room from above, dumbfounded at the array of egg sacks spread out over the vast floor, then spotted the commotion in a recess, cut into the far wall. Humans were fighting what he thought at first were giant grasshoppers. As he looked down into the nursery, the entire floor suddenly looked alive with movement.

"Quick," he screamed, "get the Gatlin'in here." Isaac ran back to help as the entire party began to push the wagon into the den ahead.

"What is it?" Zeb asked, leaning hard against the rail of the cart as the men virtually lifted the rolling artillery bin over an obstacle.

"More darget prac'ice?"

"Something new, and it needs killin'. We got people to save."

The wagon popped through the doorway and slammed into a rock ledge as the party paused, scanning the immensity of the plague below.

"Don't just sit there Lloyd,— shoot."

Titus grabbed the lever and the rain of lead spilled out over the nest of parasitic, egg clutches, that shattered in the wave of thundering rounds.

Daisy lit the home made fire bombs and pitched them into the fury as the men lined up on the walls, plugging the vermin the Gatling missed.

It is said, "war is hell," but this was a battle against the denizens of the abyss itself. 1200 rounds a minute, the rotary chambers of the early machine gun delivered. Smoke, sulfur and sweat poured; but the mass of scampering demons below, dodged and jumped, darted and transformed, climbing over the smashed and oozing puddles of the fallen, in their effort for flight and life.

Aiyana and The Seer climbed to a safer vantage point and joined the war. Mask cannon and repeater belched to life spitting death in a shower of light and lead.

Fire spread through the nest as kerosene and parasite blood mixed, producing an explosive combination that turned the floor into a living inferno. Scores of winged bugs popped and cracked, passing acidic fumes into the air that were almost as poisonous as the alien tar was deadly.

The Gatling spun empty and Daisy slapped another canister into place. The battle raged, at first appearing hopeless, but by the time Daisy clicked the next drum into place, the demise of the enemy below looked assured. Lloyd pumped another full artillery cartridge into the zone for good measure, then stopped and watched as his men finished with the stragglers. No mercy here, nothing could be left to haunt them again.

"Woo—who—," cried the coward. "Take that vermin," he laughed, hungry with the power he felt in the victory. "We showed them,—ye…s,"

The others began to cheer, joining in the elated revelry.

"Let's,—" the man froze. His face stretched into a freakish

grin then twisted. Blood ran from his mouth as his body spasmed; a serrated tail pushing a second thrust completely through his chest. Then the coward was ripped backward and disappeared through a gap in the wall. Moments later a drone jumped out the same opening and charged the survivors.

Daisy just finished slapping the next drum into position as the living bones slammed into a warrior, driving its fangs deep into the man's forehead; but Lloyd was unable to pivot the weapon.

Aiyana spotted the commotion from below while the pair were trying to work their way around the inferno — her and The Seer still popping winged enemies fighting the blaze.

The creature up by the men appeared like a beep on a radar screen on her visor and the Prophetess acted without hesitation, spinning her head as her laser sight locked onto the target in milliseconds of her recognition. The bolt from the blast plastered the mutants odd shaped cranium, killing the monster instantly.

Men on the shelf scrambled to avoid the enemies flaming blood, but the flow was minimal. The drone slipped off the ledge and fell into the fire below with a puff of sparks as its bodily fluid took to the flames. Zeb waved a thanks to Aiyana and then scanned the room for a way to the stranded pair.

The shelf the party stood on was like a natural path that wrapped the interior of the burning nursery. On their side of the wall, it tapered down to the floor of the chamber, at the opposite end from where Aiyana and The Seer were running.

Zeb waved and called out pointing, "We'll meet you at that end." It took several tries to get the pair to acknowledge the directions over the noise of the raging fire, but shortly all were working toward the common goal.

As the men neared the floor, the heavy smoke thinned. A draft blew from tunnels beyond the room, and like a natural flue, channeled the poisonous gas through the cracks in the ceiling above and vented the black fog up the mile high chimney.

With increased vision, the party spotted bodies imbedded in the walls and hanging from stalactites: men, women, a few animals. Tar covered some of the victims, but most bodies were decimated,— the residue of the abandonment of the host's infected skeleton.

Claude saw Robin and ran to her corpse, dropping to his knees.

Daisy leaped from the wagon and joined him.

"I dried da save her," he cried. "She was family."

Daisy put her hand on Claude's shoulder. "It's my fault. I should have never left them."

Claude composed himself and placed his palm over Daisy's. "No,— if you s'ayed, you'd been vermin food fer sure."

Daisy's attention was suddenly pulled to a man moving within the gelatinous goo of a parasitic web. The scar was unforgettable. The face etched in her mind forever.

One of the soldiers spotted the same movement and spoke up. "We got a live one here," and began pulling at the fibrous netting holding him prisoner.

Daisy leaped to the private's side and stopped him.

McCray's eyes opened weary and bloodshot. "Help me," the raspy voice pleaded, "help me please. It burns. It burns"

"We can't leave this man here." The soldier continued, fighting Daisy as he pulled at the goo.

Daisy spit on the pleading man over the private's shoulder. "He's why my friend is dead," she cried trying to push past her blocker. "Even this is too good for him."

Claude reached into a pocket and pulled out a piece of paper as he stood. Unrolling it, "Say'z here we git'z same coin ifin' he's dead or alive." The bounty hunter stuck the poster back in his shirt. "I'z vo'e dead."

"Nobody's executing anybody here," Zeb interceded as Aiyana and The Seer arrived.

"He's dead already," the Cheyenne visionary spoke in his native language. "Kill him now. He's infected."

"He's right, Zeb," Aiyana agreed.

Zeb shook his head no, but before he could stop her: Daisy drew a knife, pushed by the soldier, and stuck the blade in the man's chest, while spitting in his face. McCray's head sank to his chest as Isaac grabbed the woman's hand pulling her away.

"Let me go," she struggled.

Then McCray's chest began to contort like the mule's breast hours earlier. The men panicked, but Aiyana's mask cannon lit up frying the creature before it could emerge.

The Seer put his hand on Daisy's shoulder as she calmed down. "You just saved that man an agonizing death."

Daisy dropped to her knees and cried.

Men mulled around unsure of what to do.

"Hey,— what the hell." An invisible form brushed against one of the men and he stumbled on something underfoot. The savage growl of an angry mountain lion backed the man away from the mystery.

Aiyana saw Missy emerge from the hidden crevice because of her alien visor, but forgot her company was not so equipped. The feline just appeared when the soldier had stepped on the big cat's paw. "Missy," Aiyana moved quickly to avoid any misunderstanding and stroked the angry animal. "He didn't see you."

The cat calmed and purred.

"How'd you find us,— and where's Ben?"

Echoing up from the chasm beyond the room, the sound of a battle erupted.

Chapter Forty-two

Into the Queen's Lair

Trapper's Poem

Somewhere in, the northern winds, The Shadow
Stalkers hunt
Viewed by few, a fortress blind, as ghosts they walk
by moonlight
Ghouls that roam, as legends grow, their wish
an abomination.
The call to arms, but the voice is wrong, only one could be
The savior
If you listen long, in a hidden song, only she's the one that
heeds
The winds will hide, the treachery inside, the tune
a rhythmic plea,
Fear aside, it's do or die, the moment to press on
through
Do not seek, the demon's lair, dark shadows guard
the door,
The maiden seized, the maze, false leads, can she find
an opening to
The siege goes forth, as ramparts grow, fate leading to,
Eternity's Window.

*   *   *

Ben jumped into the shadows and fell into a narrow fissure as the queen's tail swung, striking the very footing where he had just stood. Rock and rubble flew as the earth shook under the force of the blow. The near miss shattered the edge of the fissure tossing stone and dirt, burying Ben. The mountain man crawled from the debris as the serpentine weapon stabbed into the cleft and parted the ground between his legs.

"Now that ain't friendly at all," Ben barked, skinning away from the failed attack.

Twisting, the man triggered his laser and locked on the swinging death spike as it was pulled from the gaping crevice. *Sha—wack,* spit the mask cannon severing the tip of the creature's extremity.

A dance of anger followed as the queen waved the spewing stub and pounded the soil, trumpeting in pain and frustration.

Ben crawled deeper into the fissure when something struck his helmet. The slithering bones of a snake,— like rope, wrapped around his neck and squeezed. The sinewed tentacle latched to his mask and blocked his visor. Ben choked at the pressure almost losing consciousness and grabbed for the thorn bleeding his life. The steely death grip was unmovable. "Damn little bastards," he coughed through gritted teeth. Ben engaged his right gauntlet blades, piercing the infected snake-bones as the hooked knives slammed into place.

Black goo spilled as the creature shrieked, a glob of tar hitting Ben's left hand. Water on the glove made the blood caustic, finding a weakness in the protective gear. The fluid burned into the gauntlet's polarized webbing, cooking off Ben's little finger."

The snake let go at the shock of its injury and tore free from the man with ease, slithering away.

Ben jerked, gasping for air, then "Son-of-a-bitch.— You little bastard," grabbing his hand, trying to ease the pain. He saw the fleeing source of his woes and, "Not so fast, you,—." The triggering, prevented further cursing as Ben sighted the moving bones, plastering it against the limestone lining the fissure's wall. The small body took to flame.

Broken-Toe watched the queen attack his student and felt a sense of pride as she drew her tip-less tail back from the hole she had so carelessly jammed it in. He jumped to the next ledge for a better vantage point, realizing that with the parasite distracted, he would have ample time to position himself for the best possible offensive.

Never underestimate these Sentients, Broken-Toe thought to himself. The Yet-Tat always showed the true nature of a guardian. And this test was proving his choice of team was not unfounded.

Going up against a hive was not a job for just any of his race. Under normal conditions no master would ever consider going up against a viral queen by himself. All Yet-Tats were carried out under the direction of the teacher, but this wasn't just any Right-of-Passage. And this wasn't just any queen. Broken-Toe was faced with a *Termination War* and abandoned to do the job alone. Such an extermination would have been impossible without help. And there fighting the queen was his selected warrior: a Sentient of another race. One that would dare face, not just drones,— but a *Queen-Mother*. The elite of the parasitic species. Like the nucleus of a one celled organism. Drones come and go. Hives were spreading across the empire. Some of the queen royalty killed in past encounters were not much more capable than a drone. But this Queen was something more. You could tell by her movement. Her control of her hive. This type was identified as a *Queen-Mother*: she was a queen beyond the norm. She could possibly be able to monitor an entire planet infested with almost unlimited hives. She would oversee it all. From the selection of sub-sisters, to the direction of a single drone against the order of its own sub-royalty. The Queen-Mother was the master of all in the dark parasitic realm.

How did this royalty happen to be here? It didn't matter: *focus.*

Few Guardians had ever seen one of this new development in this virus. Broken-Toe only fought one other in his missions to defend the empire. Back when the disease was in its inception. Now, here on a distant world, stripped of his crew, suffering injuries from a crash: death would play the coward, failure would smite the weak. Victory was the only option.

Broken-Toe positioned for his shot. The mutated elongated cranium was too thick even for his cannon to penetrate. A well placed salvo aimed at the base of the skull though,— that would disorient the queen, — weaken her abilities, allowing further bombardments to diffuse her life. But anything else — at first — would just aggravate her rage.

The target was pounding the cave floor, focused on its would-be assailant. She was oblivious to the Marshal ready to strike. The laser shot across the chamber's interior. The mask tracked the orientation of his pupils, aligning with the laser-sight: calculating distance, centering on the objective, triangulating the position in milliseconds. Broken-Toe had the lock and went to fire. Steely fingers grabbed his left ankle and the shot went wide striking a leathery shell: an egg sack embryo. The teacher engaged his Gauntlet blades on the way down and severed the appendage holding his leg.

The drone screamed, endeavoring to climb out of the fissure, a mere crack in the floor.

Broken-Toe laid the carapace head open with a powerful downward thrust, killing the beast instantly.

Rolling to his side the hunter saw the giant charge. He killed the young and the queen would avenge. Broken-Toe sprang to his knees, his second set of hooked blades sang, snapping into place, as the giant unleashed the fury of his mask cannon. White bolts of ionized liquid metal slammed into the black exoskeleton, breaking forth rivers of parasitic blood, but the queen was unwavering.

Ben felt the thunder of the Queen's power digging at his security for what seemed interminably, then suddenly the ground was shaking — heading away from him. He climbed up the narrow crevice and poked his head out the hole.

"Whoa," *she's huge, and leaving,— that's good.* Then the man saw the reason for his salvation. Without hesitation his weapon joined in the salvo. A well-aimed shot, nailed the joint at the back of the giant parasite's knee, sending the skeletal Queen crashing to the stone floor.

Broken-Toe jumped to the creature's back as it went down and punched his serrated gauntlet deep into the cranial armor slicing a savage gash in the protective plate.

The parasite mother reared then jerked, tossing the Marshal into the air and swatted the Guardian with a huge taloned hand.

Broken-Toe flew across most of the expanse of the chamber: his fall broken by a pile of discarded body parts. Winged infectors sprang from crevices ready to plant the seed. The hunter cut two in half with a swipe of his blades and shot another as he rolled from the pile. Hatchlings danced to the call as more popped from the clutch and the Marshal blasted them each in turn. The thunder of the Queen's voice raged as she scrambled to her feet and charged. When Broken-Toe looked up she was almost on him. A small outcropping was his only possible protection and he leaped for the limited cover as a light sharpened the field of his night vision.

*   *   *

"What in hell is going on in there," Zeb yelled as the men leaned into the wheeled mining bucket shoving it down the incline.

Titus was running along the side helping with the impetus. "I don't know,— but if we don't hurry, we'll miss it."

"That would probably be the smart thing," Reuben chuckled, somewhat winded.

"My husband is in there," Aiyana growled angrily.

"We're getting there," Isaac assured her.

The wagon cleared the opening into another nursery as Daisy laid on the brake lever and the men let go: the cart skidding to a stop. All attention was immediately focused on the massive moving behemoth coming parallel to their entrance.

"Ho—ly shit! What — the hell — is, that thing?"

Aiyana had already surveyed the battle and saw the cannon bolts pounding the giant parasite from behind. She triggered her weapon and unleashed its fury while running to the side of the hatchery, along the wall of the huge amphitheater.

"Crank, damn it,— Titus,— crank this damn thing now."

The scout stumbled getting to position, but instantly the Gatling belched and joined in spitting death in a spiral of repeating, pummeling lead.

"Spread out," Zeb ordered and the men united into the fray. Repeaters coughing fire, as the few remaining soldiers and Indians scattered about the interior, shooting as they ran.

Zeb spotted a black bird, "And watch out fer them flying vermin." He raised his rifle to shoot the thing when an infector slammed onto the Indian nearest him. The brave spun and hit the dirt grabbing at the tar locked to his chest. Kicking in panic the warrior was helpless.

Zeb dropped his rifle and wetting a leather hide from his belt in a puddle at his feet jumped to the man's side. Taking hold of the brave's forearm he scrubbed at the black goo, but the tar-ish blood sizzled and the warrior kicked more. The acidic action increased from the water as the ooz ran over the brave's throat and cooked through the unprotected tissue killing the hapless victim in a spasm of frenzied fighting.

Zeb stepped back panicked that he accidentally killed the

305

man. "Damn," he almost whimpered unsure of himself, probably for one of the first times in his life.

The Seer, catching sight of the incident and the big man's reaction, paused and yelled, "There was nothing you could have do—," in Cheyenne, but was cut short. Lifting his rifle he shot Zeb's direction as the scout saw the danger out the corner of his eye.

Ducking, the big man pulled and swung his blade, batting at the bird launched at his person. The bullet struck home as did the sword and the sightless monstrosity bounced backward; Zeb dodging the flying blood.

The winged menaces hit the ground with a flop and Zeb turned to retrieve his rifle and thank his protector, when the Indian medicine man was tackled by a half grown drone.

The mountain man scooped up his repeater in his left, hand and charged. Steely canines shot out biting down on the leader's forehead as Zeb slammed into the beast, shoving the sharp edge of his blade into the monster's side. The drone screamed as it rolled free of its attacker, but Zeb was already on his feet and swinging the rifle with his left hand — cocked and fired a metal piercing bullet deep in the critter's brain.

The Queen-mother slid to a stop, crashing into the rock outcropping Broken-Toe sought refuge behind, and then turned forgetting all about the Marshal. Running along the wall was a threat that dominated her entire being. A sub-sister had entered her domain. Aiyana's mental telepathy screamed to the mother in synaptic chants of hostility. The parasitic queen identified Aiyana as royalty trying to usurp her throne. The thunderous rage that shook the cave caused the structural dome ceiling rock to plummet to the stone floor as the giant disease leaped at her new adversary. The mother would defend her nest from this intrusion at all cost.

Broken-Toe poked his skull out the side of the pile somewhat startled at the sudden turn of events. *What would cause an attacking queen to stop in her tracks?*

Broken-Toe knew he'd been a goner. *Marked for death.* There was no-way he could have survived. He watched in amazement at her departure as he opened up on her fleeing backside. The wagon,— *the Sentients had joined the fray,—* a desperate fight; but, *this wasn't the focus of her vengeance.*

Then the Marshal spotted the crux of the Queen's wrath. For some reason the mother was after his other student: *"Yiannah,"*

Broken-Toe jumped to the top of the outcropping and locked his laser on the moving target. He would sever the *stick of a neck supporting that oversized head.*

Bolts like lightning itself whistled across the hatchery scoring home. Broken-Toe pummeled the weakest link on the creature's anatomy.

Daisy lit a cocktail as the monster approached and threw the bomb with all her might, then jumped screaming in fear. The bottle nailed the behemoth on the hip breaking. The fire spread down the creature's leg. Leaking parasitic blood mixed with kerosene increasing the flammability of the concoction and the blaze spread further.

Missy hissed at the immense charge and backed up into the tunnel unsure of what to do. Daisy bumped into the cat, but both parties were too distracted to care.

The mother roared in anger at the damaging onslaught and swung a savage clawed hand at the irritating man thing spitting its paltry nuisance at her as she passed. Like mosquitoes to an elephant the Gatling was nothing more than an annoyance that she swatted in passing.

Daisy made her way clear of the stroke.

Titus saw the attack coming and yelled, then jumped; but Lloyd was trapped sitting in the back of the cart and couldn't get out fast enough.

The metal bucket collapsed under the force of the giant palm as bottles shattered, spilling their fuel, igniting simultaneously by way of the busted lanterns. The wagon catapulted through the air like a paper box on fire with Lloyd wedged in his steel coffin, plummeting to his burial site. Lit kerosene rained out over the chamber. The trolley bounced and rolled coming to a rest as the helpless man, broken and bruised, still conscious, was paralyzed due to his injuries.

Unable to move his head Lloyd saw out of the corner of his eye his impending fate. The sightless bug hopped through the spreading fire as if aware his victim was defenseless. Long wings fanned out as Lloyd moaned, unable to fight or call out.

The body launched into the sergeant's face, shoving its black goo down the man's esophagus.

Lloyd coughed, gagged and then quietly,— helplessly, fell into unconsciousness.

Isaac picked up a rifle from a dead Indian and pitched it to Titus who caught it easily, "Kill some critters."

Reuben pointed at an increasingly growing area of the awakening vermin, when a drone pounced screaming at the young warrior.

Titus nodded a thanks to the blond and ran to defend Daisy from the horde emerging from the hatchery and took aim at the new intruder.

The brunette was already busy with her six shooters, an excellent shot. Missy guarding her backside.

Reuben ducked the drone's attack and blocked a savage swing with his rifle. Twisting, he kicked out with his right foot hitting the creature in the chest. The alien stumbled backward as Isaac swung the butt of his rifle at its neck.

Zeb threw his short sword sticking the drone in the chest. Tripping, it went down, and the big man charged slamming his boot against the grotesque head, pulled his weapon free and then severed the skull at the thickened vertebra.

"I had him," Reuben barked.

Isaac laughed as Zeb re-cocked his rifle with his left hand. "Your mother would never forgive me ifin' something happened."

The fire began spreading, taking advantage of accumulating parasitic blood and pools of stockpiled bat guano. Pockets of methane gas popped and spewed, as the natural gas vented through age old pores in the earth. Hell was lighting the way, or perhaps being lit.

Aiyana spotted Ben and made a break for her husband as the roar of the queen turned her way. She sprang across the open ground planting several well aimed bolts into the queen's midsection as well as juicing a few birds in her way. The mother was almost on her as she jumped into the fissure with her husband and hid as the monster slid over the top of the hole.

Ben took notice of Broken-Toe's shots and took stock in the Marshal's knowledge. Plugging three clean bolts into the parasite's neck, he caught his wife and dove for the bottom of the crag.

Claude was working his way to higher ground and reached Broken-Toe, climbing onto the rock face. Having depleted his rounds he was reloading as the Guardian took notice of his arrival. "Mighdee nice perch ya got's here friend.— Minds ifin' I joins ya?"

The hunter clicked and chirped something unrecognizable to

the man and then continued his assault on the queen and stray winged infecting agents.

Claude tipped his hat. "Obliged," and put his readied weapon to use on the increasing number of sightless birds spilling out because of the fire.

Broken-Toe suddenly grabbed the man and threw him backwards.

Claude slammed hard against the natural stone buttressing cursing, and scrambled back to his feet.

The Marshal was tackled, rolling over glossy jagged stalagmites, standing like stakes to a trapper's death pit. Arms and legs, blades and claws, flashed in the light of the roaring blaze. The two demons fought: twisting and kicking in the grips of a death match.

Claude drew a bead and pumped a metal piercing bullet through the armor of the drone's skull. Broken-Toe lashed out with both feet and the dead drone flew through the air landing on a burning pool of bat guano.

The Guardian jumped to its feet and in no uncertain terms directed Claude to the exit. *"Click-click-click, chirp-chirp,— *!/*\!#, "* Alien barking.

Claude got the idea. The man made a break for the mouth of the tunnel as Broken-Toe charged the Queen. She was weak now,— *time to bring her down.*

The Queen fell. Her left leg burned through as the nursery was consumed in the flames. Explosions and bursts of energy were erupting everywhere as the inferno licked the entire hatchery. The parasite mother's only fear was fire,— and now it was devouring her home. She trumpeted in anger and jumped using her arms and good leg to attack what was most desperate in this lost hour. The sub-sister beneath her somewhere. She was the cause of her pain. She was the demise of her realm.

Aiyana wedged herself deeper into the crevice, defending against the onslaught and avoiding the Queen-mother's hands as they pushed down into the narrow hole trying to crush her life. Bolts of blue flame pummeled the beast, that pounded the surface, digging at the barricade as dirt and debris filled the gap covering the couple.

Ben shot the steely digits and the behemoth would extract its appendages swiftly, screeching in pain and frustration, only to plunge its claws back into the fissure with renewed resolve.

Smoke from the fire was poisoning the air. Claude ran back to the opening by his friends yelling, "Le's go. Da demon say's go."

Coughing, the party resisted the suggestion.

"Ben and Aiyana or trapped in there. We can't leave," Zeb barked.

Claude stopped, panting and gagging in the limited air, as he reached the men and directed attention to Broken-Toe's charge across the nursery. "We're dead unless we've gone now. He'll dake cares of dem."

Zeb hesitated for a fraction of a second looking at Reuben and Isaac.

"He's right Uncle," Reuben confirmed.

"Let's go," and the remaining four took off to where Titus and Daisy were making their stand.

"Time to go."

"Just point the way," Titus spit between clenched teeth as he killed another infector.

Isaac looked down the passage: the tunnel they had entered from. Fire was blocking their exit. "We're trapped."

"Where's Missy?" Zeb cried out.

The big cat answered. Daisy reached down and touched the animal. "She's right here with me."

"Take hold of her collar. Missy get us out of here," Zeb ordered. "Now."

The lion snarled and hesitated. She wouldn't go.

Aiyana felt the anxiety, the doubt. She knew the fear. Understood the danger. The prophetess slapped her wrist controls turning off Missy's cloak. "Go baby," she cried out. "Save them."

Ben heard his wife, but was confused as he shot a finger off the raging monster above. "Yah-hah,— take that you bitch."

The mountain lion suddenly appeared, somewhat startling the on-lookers.

Zeb's attention became riveted on the big cat. "Go Missy. Get us out of here now," Zeb almost screamed, but this time the big cat listened. Down a side tunnel the lioness ran, and the human's followed.

"I don't think we're getting out of this one," Ben yelled over the raving of the monster above.

"She's dying," Aiyana landed two more shots and then her cannon locked up.

The noise above lessened and then moved away as the two humans acted on the retreat, and began climbing up the narrow crevice.

Broken-Toe ran to an overhanging ledge and jumped, landing cleanly on the Queen-mother's back at the shoulders. Ragged saw-toothed gauntlet blades plunged deep into the creature's armored skin anchoring the Marshal as he struck out with his other arm slashing at the parasite's vertebrae.

The Queen trumpeted and jumped trying to wrench its antagonist off, but the guardian clung on, cutting and pummeling the monster with its cannon until the last shot scored its hole.

The two humans popped up from the recess, Ben landing another bolt, then his weapon clicked empty. "Damn, you mean these things need loading?"

"We need to make it to that tunnel," Aiyana pointed and pulled herself from the fissure.

"What about him?"

"He'll be right behind us I'm sure."

The two humans made a break for the passageway to exit the warren as the Queen hit the dirt. Broken-Toe jumped from his perch as the mother tried to rise and then fell again. The entire chamber was on fire and it was difficult for the warriors to make their way through the maze. Broken-Toe, having traversed half the distance looked back, as the giant viral nucleus pulled herself to her good leg, and bounding on damaged arms started the chase.

Sparks flew as the monster splashed through the burning ash in its dying effort to avenge its home. Broken-Toe made it to the narrow retreat as the queen smashed into its surrounding wall. A clawed hand shot into the tunnel and the Marshal struck the intrusion with a gaping wound, tearing ligaments and muscle in the giant's carapace hand: a painful reward for its trouble. The mother staggered back and fell into a pit as the fire licked around her. She shook in her death throes as the flame comsumed her withering frame. She screeched and screamed, but remorse was unfelt as the pyre grew. The inferno was finishing her life and destroying the hatchery she failed to protect.

"I think it's time we blow this hell hole." Ben looked around, "Which way did they go? Which way do we go?"

Aiyana pointed down a side tunnel and the party all ran evading the smoke as quickly as possible. It took about an hour for the three stragglers to meet up with the remainder of their party at the waterfall room. Aiyana was relieved to see her son alive and ran embracing him. Ben slapped his brother, Zeb, on the back and shook Isaac's hand with a smile. Then he gave his son and wife a big hug.

Titus and Daisy watched smiling as the brunette wrapped her hand around the scout's waist. "Thank you," she whispered. The soldier almost blushed then responded in kind.

Missy pushed, purring into her family, and Broken-Toe looked-on at his new clan. He was going to be stuck on this world for quite some time, but his company would be an honored tribe. All of them Marshals. All of them Sentient Guardians. They would receive his mark. Together they had achieved the goal. The Queen was dead. The hive destroyed. Possible stragglers would force them to stay in the area for weeks to make sure nothing survived, but that was training. And after all, even seasoned Marshals could learn something new in the realm of possibilities.

Epilogue

Three-Spots slipped into the ravine on his left hand and knees. Hitting the bottom of the shallow crevice he rolled to his side, keeping his right arm pinned tight against his body. Consciousness was waning as his shoulder spasmed under the intense fervent agony. His mask cannon damaged in the battle, he gingerly unhooked its harness and peeled the useless helmet-weapon from his armor. *The Guardian clan will pay for this,* he thought as he looked at the indiscernible hunk of twisted and melted metal. A stray shot exploded the liquid metal in the horn reserve resulting in a massive explosion and a broken collar bone. The cannon's ionized, molten fuel spilled out causing serious lacerations to the pirate's skin. The heat of the blast had radiated through his protective armor causing third degree burns. He carefully removed his breast mesh, but the injured tissue stuck to the vest intensifying the pain as he fought to remain conscious.

He laid back for a moment to rest and to regain strength, but the voices of the enemy were just over the ridge. The danger of discovery was imminent. Three-Spots needed to distance himself from the area of his lost battle. *"Just like a Marshal.* What cowards,— *using pets to fight for them."*

The Sky Demon struggled to stand, then staggered down the natural cover as quietly as he could. He was alone now. The only survivor of his clan. Abandoned on this distant world and weaponless, except for his gauntlets,— vengeance was left to him; but he needed time,— time to recuperate,— *Time to heal.*

The creature looked up at the big star casting its light high in distant space. *Strange how parts of this world lay frozen and parts were always warm.*

Three-Spots had visited this planet once before. Back when he was part of the Guardian clan. He had stalked, side-by-side with the cowards. Learned their ways. Pursued their same enemies: criminals of the state. But, *after the injury, the battle where I fell so long ago defending the empire, I awoke in that cloned tank. Then they,— the noble guardians rejected me. Said I was weak. Said I would never police again; that something went wrong, that I was flawed. But I showed them… rework me,— ha!*

Three-Spots burned with hatred. *I will show them who's flawed,* "I will kill them all!"

The pirate gingerly touched his injury; but first, he needed to survive. The southern terrain of this planet was much more to his liking. Similar to his home world with its high humidity and marshy grounds. It was a haven compared to, *this worthless land of snow and endless ice.* Three-Spots knew he needed to recuperate, and in the deep south. There he could heal. *There, I will be home.*

A branch slapped his wound and sent him reeling. Weak and exhausted, he groaned and fell back against a large tree trunk. He needed rest. The Sky Demon took some deep breaths, then pushed himself away only to hear footfalls behind. The alien spun, but saw nothing. Picking up the pace he started to run.

The steps grew louder, like the heavy hand of a haunting shadow it dogged him. A phantom following relentlessly, casting a curse to the ground he trod. Three-Spots threw disparaging looks behind, but still the void revealed nothing. He was being stalked by a ghost. A specter drifting among the brush and trees seeking his soul.

Three-Spots stopped and engaged his gauntlet blades as he turned. He would make his stand.

Silence,— the pirate scanned his trail, but the ravine was empty. To his left a demon screamed; like the savage call of an angry panther. The pirate spun as the lingering crescendo pierced the still arena like a sudden wind lashing through the trees,— then nothing. No form backed the hollow call. No shape mimicked the ghastly banter. Three-Spots searched the backdrop with longing eyes, but the stalking death was hidden,— unrevealed.

Three-Spots ran. The delirium of his wounds were playing on his imagination. But fear of the unknown left him wanting. Desperate glances backward slowed his progress as he stumbled over the ragged terrain of the rocky wash. Footfalls to his right. The scream of a wraith and then an impact as the Sky Demon hit the ground, a snarling cat ripping into the tough flesh of his neck. Pain rifled through his shoulder as the alien rolled and slammed his antagonist into a boulder and swung his good arm knocking the creature away. Three-Spots prepared for a charge scrambling with the big rock at his back, but the ravine was empty. Stunned, the pirate struggled to his feet as the ghostly scream erupted to his right. The Sky Demon crouched when he spotted a padded paw print flatten a track into a patch of snow.

The pirate reacted without hesitation, swinging his left arm at the invisible charging enemy. The blow swiped empty air as the ghost landed against the pirate's chest, pushing him over the large rock. Three-Spots somersaulted over the obstacle and clambered to his feet. A snarl sounded from on top of the rock, but the pirate turned and ran unable to see his enemy. Four steps and something hit his legs taking him down face first in the bank of a stream. Taloned claws ripped at the back of his thighs when a savage jaw bit down at the base of his neck.

Three-Spots crawled into the edge of the water and fought to remove the vice grip latched to his back. Deeper into the river he dragged himself as the invisible mountain lion lacerated and mangled his flesh. Three-Spots plunged into the depths of the river and the unseen demon let go. Without his mask to filter and supply the needed atmosphere the Sky Demon held his breath and worked his way along with the current of the icy cold, fast moving waterway, pushing along the bottom of the swiftly increasing rapids. A sense of relief strengthened the alien's persona. The chill, numbed the pain of his damaged wounds. He would make good his flight. Apparently the stalking demon had a distaste for water. Three-Spots smiled. He would live and wreak revenge.

Drifting with the current he floated downstream under the depth of this new cover: hidden to the world, ready to be reborn. Carried by the whim of a powerful river, Three-Spots melted into the mythology of this foreign world. Into the legends of his new home.

Book Three
in the
Guardian Series

The Golden City

Carol Cole O'Dell

Prologue

Tawque sat like a bird of prey, perched on the stone cliff face, watching the ghostly apparition weaving its mystic dance over the sacred valley's moonlit sky. Vibrant hues of green, red and purple silhouetted in a streaming glory of colors; ribbons twisting and intertwining to a silent song calming the early winter winds to a whisper, marking the seasonal change to fall. The warrior had little knowledge of the science behind the phenomenon, but the strange occurrence appeared regularly at the full moon of the fall equinox every seven years after the "Battle of Flaming Eagle." The light-dance was a reminder to the Blackfoot people of that desperate day over twenty years earlier when his tribe battled The Sky Gods in this very valley. It was believed the glowing aurora was the souls of the lost trying to exit the confinement of the firebird's wrath.

To Tawque the reminders burned deep. He had become an outcast before the war, but fought with his brothers at the battle to rid the land of the strange warlike demons that plagued his people. Many of his tribe died when the winged goddess belched forth fire, striking mother earth. The ground shook with pain and the wound that was opened spewed forth winds leveling the plains, bringing a sudden end to the war.

Tawque didn't know about aliens, flying ships or understand the advanced weaponry of the visiting creature's technology. Few even in our day could explain how the explosion that ensued, fused the elements buried deep within the surrounding mountains, charging its resources like a battery, and acting against the magnetic fields of the iron rich soils surrounding the hills that opened a portal of mystery, deep within the confines of the hidden crater below. Every seven years the energy built up to a point that ionized the surrounding atmosphere as it discharged its capacitance in a show of colorful ribbons of light, but the magic behind the show touched the superstitious minds of Tawque's people and the valley was marked as sacred and off limits to all.

As self-proclaimed protectors of this secluded landmark the Blackfoot would kill any who entered its borders or encroached on its boundaries. But tonight Tawque eyed the marvel not as a sentry, but as an enemy. Somehow he was linked to the spectacle and its rhythmic silhouettes of dancing light; its beauty called to him like an evil mistress seducing his mind with pleadings of favor.

Tawque tried to resist. He was an appointed guardian of his people. Once an outcast he was now revered as a deliverer. Hadn't he fought hand-to-hand with the War Gods and been victorious? Hadn't he killed one with only knife and tomahawk, lifting its head as a prize? The Great Spirit, Tawque felt, rewarded his valor with eternal youth and strength. Tawque had not aged a day in twenty years, but the warrior had no knowledge of the chemistry behind the miracle. He did not understand how telomeres affect the number of times a cell will divide, or how enzymes from the aliens, masked and suppressed, the shrinkage of this control on aging. To Tawque it was a gift from the Great Spirit; same as the amazing strength imparted to his sinews by the alien fluid reacting with his hormones and enhancing his muscles in a powerful way; or the mighty bow he held in his left hand, gifted him by the white trapper, Ben.

It was a beautifully crafted weapon with the strange circles of a dream catcher at top and bottom of the elegant curvatures at each extremity. The unusual wheels (dream catchers) supported the bowstring. It operated on principles of physics, but to Tawque it was a reflection of his strength. It took him two years to develop the muscles to bend that mighty bow, but when he was finally rewarded by drawing it full, how amazed he was at the ease at which he could hold and aim. Big medicine worked its magic on the weapon as twenty years ago big medicine flowed with the coming of the sky demons. But this night, so long after the time of the gathering, the supernatural was at work again. Something was different about the shifting patterns of glowing colors and Tawque could no longer fight the urge heaving at his soul.

Silently the mystic warrior slipped from his perch and melted into the surrounding brush like a specter lost to the view of fleshly eyes.

Tawque was a master of stealth, but two young warriors took note of his departure. Although hidden in the dim silvery light of the sky's lonely monolith that cast its warming hue, the braves guessed a trespasser warranted the guardian's departure and took up pursuit as noiselessly as their predecessor. Tonight they were sure glory would follow as the deliverer was summoned to avenge their sacred lands.

Within minutes Tawque had made his way to the valley's floor and crossed to the opening of a small cave at the center of the vortex apparition. From this epicenter the mystic show emanated, affecting the surrounding land in a wave that spiraled forth as trees near the area grew twisted and gnarled in a fight against the unnatural, unseen forces pushing at their very existence. No animal would venture near this marvel. Not even a bird would tilt its wings in the direction of the cave. Void of the sounds of insects, the anomaly rested hauntingly amid the sacred grounds. Hidden among the dense brush of the tangled mass growing outward,— vegetation bent, appearing almost crawling in a silent plea, as if desperately trying to uproot and vacate an un-chosen home, —Tawque stood.

A hazy mist blocked the entrance, but light emanating from deep within the chamber's tunnels called hypnotically to the Guardian. The rays filtered through the thin veneer of fog, like a beacon,— very dissimilar to the aurora dancing in the night sky above. Tawque was captivated. The twirling show flashed and blinked without pattern as from deep within the tunnels the glow awakened the goose bumps on the brave warrior's arms. *Was this the called for Awakening... birth of The Swarm?* Fear gripped the Blackfoot's heart. The prophecy spoke of a passage opened. The blood of sacrifice. The feast of death.

Tawque could fight the urge no longer. Mindless: he stepped through the empty mist standing like a facade, blockading the widening chamber beyond. The Guardian felt dizzy as he almost collapsed. His skin suddenly froze as ice incrusted his eyelashes and moisture around his lips. The warrior fell to his knees, but he felt like he was moving deeper into the tunnel at a blinding speed. The sensation was but a moment, yet the struggling brave could not even breathe during the occurrence. Coughing and gagging Tawque's dizziness subsided as a numbness left his flesh and the tingling of a waking body part shook every inch of his muscular frame. He staggered to his feet, catching his wind and rubbing his freezing arms as he looked on in awe at the superlative room he had entered. A flashing glow from deep within the bowels of the twisting maze was his focal; but its radiant hues glimmered over the glossy rock and crystallized emeralds, encased in the chamber's inner walls in an ever widening amphitheater. A panorama of glistening colors and striking shades entranced the Guardian's mind and captivated his soul. The rays bounced over the cave's ragged structural anomalies, but the strange call that moved the warrior to enter the vortex in the first place again pulled at his very being as the marvel of the cave dissipated. Determined, his facial features turned to stone as his emotionless expression revealed he was unmoved by the display; his entire mind centered on the source radiating the magnificent light.

At the end of the large room the walls tapered down to the opening where the caves inner sun was emanating: a light beckoning entrance, a beacon drawing forth the fool. Tawque stepped through the passage and disappeared.

The two braves behind looked questioningly at each other, then fitted shafts in silent agreement to their heavy war bows. *Perhaps material weapon would be useless in the spirit realm?* And cautiously they followed.

Chapter One

The Search

The strange party moved through the foliage, most unaccustomed to the mysterious and gloomy haunts of the forbidden forest. Above,— the lofty canopy of green leafy giants blocked perpetually the sun's warming rays, allowing only the heartiest of vegetation to break through the mass of rotting compost cushioning the rich terrain. The soft carpet padded the foot falls of the ten experienced guides, dressed in heavy woolen skirts and arrayed with numerous trinkets of ivory and polished stones. Stout javelins with razor sharp flint tips balanced the decor of the men, accustomed to the riggers of the hunt within any shadowy woodland. With the skill and stealth of the big cats: they melted into their surroundings, silent as the dew forms in the early morning hours on the broad leaf grasses of the open prairies.

In stark contrast, the compliment of soldiers that followed, decked out with heavy leather girdles, shields and helmets were unsuitable to the task of woodcraft required for the mission. The oiled straps of their garb groaned under the stress of each movement. Shields, maces and spears seemed to thump and scrape against every branch of the relatively sparse undergrowth.

"How much longer are we going to stomp around this dreadful place before we accept the fact she's gone?" Whispered one of the ragged soldiers.

"Shut your tongue Kay-two, or the prince will have it served to you tonight for your meal."

"I speak only the truth, Tee-ah."

"Your mind lies."

"Listen,— any sign is long cold. The wind, weather and fallen leaves have covered all of our hopes. Her abductors probably had their way with her and cast her to the demons of this terrible place."

The older man gritted his teeth. "Speak such words again and I'll carve that wretched speech from your mouth myself." His seething words dripped with anger as he glared at his younger companion. "Our queen lives and our duty despite hardship is to save her. Cowering at our commission,— Why did you volunteer, anyway?" The disgust in Tee-ah's last statement attracted the attention of others nearby.

"I meant no disrespect, Tee-ah. You are older and wiser and have the strength of the musks. I was just speaking my mind. Forgive me. I came because rescuing our princess seemed plausible and noble at the time, but I truly believe after weeks and nothing,— Isn't it time to go home?"

The thick shaft of a lance slammed across the back of Kay-two. He almost stumbled to the ground under the blow.

"Quiet," barked the voice of authority, as the third party then grabbed Kay-two by the arm,— lifting him back stationary as easily as a father might adjust a young child. The voice of authority then whispered, "Do you wish to bring a whole horde of the Nephraceetans down upon us?"

The short fuse of the young warrior wanted to retaliate against the man dressed in the wool skirt, but the power in the man's grips and icy glare quickly humbled any thought of revenge. After all, the mammoth men were feared and respected, and Key-ol-te-ton was stronger than a musk oxen.

Kay-two pulled his arm free, but wavered from trying to stare his superior down. "We meant no harm," he spat.

"Speak again and you'll feel more than the butt of my lance."

*　　　*　　　*

326

Night was fast approaching and the entire party stopped to prepare for the long darkness in a literal primeval jungle, haunted by more than predators that merely feed on the flesh of their kills to survive. For this forest, this jungle, was dominated by the supernatural. Cannibal giants that wandered in the shadows without fear and hunted man without remorse. They stalked men for the pure pleasure of torture and murder.

The mammoth men, the noble masters of the plains and woodlands, who hunted for a brutal and dangerous living, feared to whisper of the magic of these demons of the Dark Forest. Fantastic stories and legends, perhaps with a taste of exaggeration, vilified the persona of the Nephraceetan, and rightly so. But the noble mammoth men knew the truth.

In setting up camp they always took the necessary precautions practiced throughout the ages since the first appearance of the cannibal giants after the confrontation with the dark gods who fell from the heavens. They learned through trial and error how to elude the monsters. And the gifts of this knowledge was handed down through the medicine men of each clan. The relative safety in numbers meant little to the mammoth men, but the magic of the circle would shield them, so the ritual was taught to the soldiers of the Golden City and was practiced nightly since the beginning of their arduous trek.

The soldiers preferred a large bonfire, the custom of the warrior. They believed it repelled the dangerous carnivores of the land, and struck fear in any enemy, symbolizing the presence of a large force. The camaraderie enjoyed around its roaring blaze also raised the spirits of the enlisted. But that practice was out of the question. It would attract the attention of the Nephraceetan.

So, in a small glen, hidden within the bordering walls of tall grass and brush the nightly sacrament was performed. A circular clearing was stamped out and numerous small fires were built in deep dug pits just within its boundaries. The flames were almost smothered with the roots of the cateruo plant: a flowery vine with dagger like thorns growing in abundance throughout the nomadic clansman's haunts. The black pungent smoke that arose from burning the root kept the larger predatorily animals at bay while simultaneously diminishing most of the light of the fires until just a bed of coals smoldered in the holes for cooking, warmth and the protective fumes.

Zee- ya, the clan's medicine man then blessed his sacred staff, his javelin, decorated with beautiful ivory inlays, and connected the pits by dragging the butt of the lance from hole to hole while uttering the prayer of poison. Then the author of the ritual plunged the staff within the northern most border of the protective barrier as the door.

"To desecrate this den brings a curse and death," the spiritualist muttered. "Do not cross its boundaries without breaking its walls with the blessed staff," and he placed his hand back on his lance. "To protect all, the staff must bar the door. If opened the door must be closed and can only be opened by the one who crossed over to the other side. Once one has defecated and the man is cleansed the door must be closed again on reentry."

The soldier Kay-two muttered to Tee-ah while listening to the nightly ritual, "This nonsense of the pagans is a waste of time," as he warmed his hands over his smoky hollow. "How I long for the blaze that warms the spirits and fosters strength."

"I would prefer our ways also, but the clan has lived among the terrors of this forest for a long time. It would probably do us well to accept the blessings of experience, rather than the will of custom."

"But the stench of this fire kills the taste of my meat, and what little warmth it casts,— I freeze at night. Why can't we build a central fire to cook and sleep by?"

"Because the light would attract the Nephraceetan or worse,— their children."

"More myths to scare the young. Stories to tell about the monsters that haunt men's dreams."

"The stories are true. The cannibal giants do roam this land. And their children, abominations.— Feral hybrids with a lust for blood. I fear for our princess,— for, woe to the woman unlucky enough to fall into their grasps. Beaten and degraded, she would live, but death would be preferred to the torturous life as a concubine to these monsters. An unwilling slave and vessel for the demons unholy offspring."

"Tell me it's not true. Tell me,— you,— Tee-ah,— the great warrior of many battles,— tell me you don't believe in these dream conjured ghosts."

"Oh my young friend,— these tales are true. Within these very borders the strange spirits of human form prey upon men and their flesh."

"What walks these woods are the big cats. This stinkin' pit and a few words spoken while drawing a line in the dirt won't keep them away."

"I'm not so sure. Have you noticed the lack of biting insects since we've practiced this ritual?"

Kay-two thought reflectively for a moment, then snarled, "Tee-ah, how can you believe a stick scratching the ground and a prayer could stop evil or even insects. It's just too cold for the bugs."

"The mammoth men are better in the ways of woodcraft than we. I have learned in my life to draw on the wisdom of others. No one is more skilled in the art of survival out here then the clansmen. I am a mere soldier. I bend to the dictates of my commander or those suited to lead. The clansmen, in this case, are our guides. We need to listen to them."

"Superstitious nonsense."

"Maybe, but what harm is there in going through the motions. It's just another drill and we are trained to obey for the good of all."

"Well, tell me this Tee-ah, if I were traveling alone how does digging one pit make a circle?"

"I asked about that myself. If a man travels at any time alone, a minimum of four pits must be dug to complete the sacred circle. Because we are a large party each man can dig his own fire pit."

Kay-two grunted and shook his head.

"Cook your meal Kay-two, and savor the belief we are on a sacred mission."

The full moon rose high casting its silvery light over the compliment of men as they ate, mostly in silence. Sentries were scheduled and few of the party whispered quietly long past the first posting.

Chapter Two

Prison Bonds

Bobby sat back clutching the gourd bowl drinking down the fatty slop that the lone guard passed through the wooden lashed bars of his dirty prison. The hard stone wall felt cold on his bare back, but the chill helped soothe the burn of his untreated injuries even as the gruel turned his stomach. Two days of drinking grease was paying a toll on the little man's digestive system, but sheer hunger drove the poor one to relish the single meal afforded the lonely prisoner.

Bobby awoke in his corner cell two days earlier to the stench of rotting flesh and human waste, unaware of why or how he came to be in the underground cage. His sentry appeared to be mute and his L—shaped cellblock revealed little signs of life as he looked up the long corridor lit by oil lamps set strategically on the walls of the narrow passageway. From his current vantage point against the back of his wall he couldn't see down the corridor his row faced.

Bobby leaned forward and cleared his throat. "Could I have some water please?"

If the guard heard the plea, he made no motion and showed no intention of giving succor.

"Water,—please."

Nothing.

A strange jumble of syllables sounded to his right. Bobby

pushed off the wall and crawled to the wooden poles lashed tightly with leather thongs,— the bars to his cell. "Is someone there?" He pushed his face through the thin partition with considerable effort and looked down to his right. "Hello?"

A woman's head popped out into the passage and seeing Bobby let out a flurry of garbled speech.

Bobby listened carefully to the dialect as he studied the smooth contours of her features. Her strong, high cheekbones and her dark eyebrows magnified the hazel of her irises. The gentle cresset of her button nose and small chin was pleasing. As her lips moved, Bobby found himself mesmerized. Her voice quality was almost musical. The dialect carried a measure of familiarity. Had he heard the language before? He couldn't make the connection.

When the woman paused, Bobby interrupted, pointing to himself. "Bah—bee. M—y na—me is Bah—bee. What is your name?" and he pointed to her.

The initial excitement melted from her delicate features and turned to one of disappointment. Then the lovely face disappeared from view.

"Wait,—wait,— come back. Please come back."

Bobby could see two hands grab the wooden lattice of her cell as the beautiful jaw line reappeared slowly, then the woman again peeked out from behind her bars. Tears had welled under her soft eyes as she peered at the little man.

"Please,—please,—stay with me." Bobby again pointed at himself, "Bobby,' he enunciated slowly. Then pointed at her. "Your name?"

"Boo—bee."

"Close enough," the little man muttered still pointing at her while he nodded in the affirmative.

The woman pointed to herself, speaking very slowly, "Ha-i-wi."

Bobby smiled, "Ha-i-wi, nice to make your acquaintance."

"Boobee."

"Yes,—yes," nodding his head, "Bobby. And you are Ha-i-wi."

The little man had heard that name before. It was like a heavy accent was depriving him of the meaning. He dug into the recesses of his memory. Then it hit him. It sounded like the first Native American language he learned in the Northwestern Territory,

Shoshone. She was of the Uto-Aztecan language group with a slight deviation to the phonetics. Bobby stuck his arms out from the bars and began flapping them like a bird, "Hai-wi, *you are Dove. A bird, the* Hai-wi.*"*

"Yes, yes, I am Dove."

Bobby had a way with language and now the dialect came flooding back, although, the accent made understanding a little slow, but the little man carefully pronounced each word. *"Where are we?"*

"We are prisoners of the Yak-a-taw-wee-kee-tuo, *The people of the* Inc-u-bison,— *the dragon. We both will probably be fed to their god come the new moon unless my father can save us."*

"Who is your father?"

Haiwi's chin lifted with a sense of dignity and pride, "Maa-toe-zun-na *is my father."*

The young woman looked for recognition of the name from her companion, but was startled that the little man appeared ignorant of her father or his position.

"Maa-toe-zun-na,— *your father will come for you?"*

Her eyes narrowed at the stupid question as confidence resonated in her voice. *"Yes, he will come. With a thousand warriors he will come, and the* Yak-a-taw-wee-kee-tuo *will quake with fear when he storms their city."*

"Maa-toe-zun-na *must be a powerful man. Is the Yak-a-taw-wee-kee-tuo's city big?"*

"Not as big as my city. The Golden City. You will see. When my father comes I will take you there. It's splendor is as radiant as the sun."

Bobby nodded with a smile, *"I hope we will see it soon."* The little man paused and looked at the sentry then down the long corridors. He could see other prisoners now bobbing out from various cells, watching and staring at him and his new friend. Bobby turned back to Haiwi, *"How long have you been a prisoner?"*

"I was captured yesterday."

"How did you get taken from the Golden City?"

"I wasn't in the city."

"Why did you leave the safety of your father's house?"

Haiwi's chin dropped with a blank stare as she pondered the question. Then she slipped silently back behind her bars.

"Wait,— Haiwi, *come back. I'm sorry. I didn't mean anything. Please come back."* The pretty face was gone and Bobby

was sure he heard some muffled sobs coming from Haiwi's cell. How he longed to see her pleasant features again and he waited a long time leaning on the wood lattice. "Haiwi, *I'm sorry,"* he mumbled, then pushed off his bars and moved back sitting against the hard stone wall.

He looked at his arms and rubbed them soothingly. Most of his skin was peeling miserably. First degree burns covered his body and the rags he wore were mere scorched and tattered remnants of his former wool and leather clothes James had given him after his rescue from the wilderness. Bobby tugged gently at his woolen shirt lifting it off his chest and then scratched lightly. *How did I get here,* he thought. Then smiled as he mused, *and where the hell is here?*

He remembered traveling up the Mississippi to the North Western Territory as part owner of a trade company. And that awful night at the fort when he was chased by an eerie demigod. Oh that creature was dreadful. It looked half insect with its big bulging eyes and the mask it wore, with its long curved antenna that reminded the little man of the horns on a buffalo. Hair, gnarled and twisted, draped the back of the stone features. And the teeth,— immense fangs that protruded down from the mouth to the scaly chest. Like twin daggers ready to bury themselves in the soft flesh of his neck.

Bobby shivered as he recalled that fateful night not so long ago. The devil stood over him with a bow at full draw aimed for his heart. But the weapon was unlike the recurves of the Native Americans. There was a graceful symmetry about the extensions and what looked like pulleys at top and bottom that supported the string. The little man closed his eyes and prayed, waiting for the blow that would pierce his heart; but it never came. He opened one eye then both, but the creature had vanished. Then he ran. Ran from that dreadful place. Ran from the demon. Ran for his life, but the haunting images of the ghost plagued his mind. He wandered for weeks almost dying of hunger when he was saved by James.

James, Bobby smiled. He looked down at the tattered remnants of his clothes. *We were returning somewhere? But somebody was coming.* Bobby paused trying to think. It was like the slate was wiped clean. *We were returning to the fort and then found that ship.* Now he remembered. *The demons were returning. We were planning something.* Bobby thought long and hard then dosed off. He awoke slowly hours later to a familiar voice. It was Haiwi, but he could not understand the words. Another voice, much deeper, responded as Bobby listened half asleep. Was he dreaming? The conversation was rather lengthy and finally Bobby opened his eyes. A new guard had been posted and he was talking with Haiwi.

Bobby stared at the sentry and the strange piercings of bone that riddled the stone like features, showing little emotion while he spoke. A simple headband with a circular medallion of copper held the long coarse hair back and out of the man's eyes. Centered on the headpiece, the round coin object tied in the middle of the forehead had an inlay of gold that sparkled in the flickering lantern light from the hall. Spiraling tattoos covered most of the muscular frame. An unusual breastplate that looked of virgin gold mesh protected the chest and the man was girded with a heavy leather belt and thong. He looked prepared for battle, yet his only weapon was a long spear he held in one hand with the butt resting statuesque on the hard stone floor by his feet. What a daunting figure the sentry posed.

Bobby looked away almost frightened by the stoic hindrance to his freedom but listened carefully to the garbled speech while resting his head on his arms and knees. Many of the sounds and syllables had a note of familiarity. The dialects were similar and every once in a while Bobby started to pick out Shoshone words.

The guard grunted and moved a short distance away. Haiwi continued to press the man, but he continued to ignore the woman.

"Boobee," came a soft sweet call.

The little man stood up and stumbled to the bars pushing his face through a narrow opening. *"Yes Haiwi?"*

The small face had a questioning appeal and one of worry. *"Who are you, Boo-Bee?"*

That is a strange question. "What do you mean?"

"Did you notice there is only one guard in this prison?"

Bobby looked at the sentry then up and down the passageways, *"Yes."*

"He is guarding you.—Who are you Boo-bee?"

"Whatever do you mean? I am nobody."

"Boo-bee no-body,—are you a god?"

"What?"

"The sentry said you just appeared in the cave by a group of the priest's honor guard a few days ago. The priest said you were sent to kill him and had you imprisoned. Did the gods send you to rescue me? Or are you here to kill me also?"

Bobby frowned, and his sad eyes telegraphed his full

intention. He studied the beautiful quizzical face and then whispered, *"I would never hurt you Haiwi and I would save you if I could, but I am nothing."* The little man wanted to tell her the truth. That he was a coward. That his whole life he was fearful, running, hiding. Did he once ever stand up and fight? Bobby stopped short then dropped his head staring at the ground. *"I wish,—"* he raised his eyes and looked into the soft features of Haiwi's wistful gaze, so full of hope, so graceful in her soft dignity,— and Bobby cowered within. *"I'm sorry."*

But Haiwi read what the man was afraid to say. *"Did the gods banish you here? Were you their messenger and you failed them? Or were you sent here to tell me, as my father has on many occasions, that I must accept my fate?"*

Bobby thought carefully about her question. Because of the superstitious mind of this woman any statement by him could be misinterpreted, perhaps to her detriment. Smiling, the little man whispered, *"Perhaps the gods did ban me here, but I would never tell Haiwi she should accept her fate. You deserve your freedom and if I can help I will die to save you. You must never give up."*

Haiwi smiled, *"Perhaps the Great Spirit will save us yet. He will send his warriors, for my father will come with many men to save us. I believe you Boo-bee No-body. You defy the gods with your words, but the Great Spirit loves his children and your true message comes from him, not the gods who are bitter and resentful. For your honor, standing up to the gods, I am sure you will also taste freedom."*

Bobby looked over to the guard and shook his head, *"You are right Haiwi. You will soon be free. But my guard will never let me go. He won't even acknowledge me."*

"Oh Boo-bee, he is not here to keep you prisoner. He is here to protect you from the treachery of the magi. To guard you from an assassination by the high priest slaves."

"What do you mean?"

"He is of the king's own guard."

"Then why am I a prisoner?"

"Powerful is the king, but fearful of the power of the magi. The priest ordered your death, but the king feared the wrath of the gods even over the magic of the priest. If you are a god, the king felt, then you will walk out of this prison; but if you are nothing to fear you will die here. Are you a god Boo-bee No-body, or are you their

messenger?"

"If I were a god don't you think I would lead us both out of here?"

"Even the gods work their purpose according to the winds. Time reveals the truth of all things. If you are not a god, yet you appeared by magic, then you are their messenger." Haiwi turned to the sentry and spoke the strange dialect to the man; but he ignored her, staring at the wall with indifference. She looked back to her cell mate, *"I told him you were the messenger from the gods and that you said the war god will come and deliver us both. He is afraid. He thinks you will cast a spell on him if he looks or talks to you. He believes you have already cast a spell on me with your devil tongue and strange sounds you utter."*

Bobby paused. *How did she know so much about this people?* *"You said you came from the Golden City and you are enemies?"*

"Yes."

"How is it you know so much about your adversaries?"

"It is wisdom to understand your enemy. How else will you defeat them?"

Bobby marveled at the intelligent and yet simplicity of her words. This girl, this woman, had a way of looking at things and read meanings that were well above her years. *"I hope we don't disappoint when we escape, but I am fearful."* Bobby looked at his captor. *"Same situation, different face."*

"What do you mean?"

"It seems like a dream now."

"What seemed like a dream?"

"I was running from a devil. Scarier than this fellow," pointing a thumb at the guard. *"Then I fell. It was hopeless. A demon was standing over me with his weapon ready to pierce my heart."*

"What happened?"

"He just disappeared."

"This is how the gods speak." Haiwi grinned from ear to ear. *"So in this vision you were sent on a mission of defiance. What's the truth in your heart that the gods couldn't pierce? Tell me Boo-bee No-body."* Her head slipped behind her cage and she pulled at her bars then reappeared. *"Hide the truth no longer. You were sent to me."*

Bobby smiled, but could say nothing.

Haiwi turned and barked gibberish at the guard then laughed. *"I know you can't tell me Boo-bee, but I know the truth in your heart."*

Then the little face slipped silently behind the wooden lattice of her confinement. Bobby pondered her wishful dream then scratched his raw forearm. *Maybe I will walk out of here. I have escaped worse.*

*   *   *

The weeks dragged on for Bobby, but the food didn't improve. Haiwi was generous with her prison fare though. She was being fattened as the offering to Incubison and was given more than she could eat. Bobby found his bondage bearable with the pleasant company she afforded, but he found the accommodations appalling. No sanitation, no water to wash with and although he had adjusted some to the offensive smell of waste and decomposition, ammonia still burned his eyes at times. How he longed for a razor, his scraggly beard itched horribly not to mention his backside and the small size of his cell magnified his misery. An accountant by nature, he was keeping track of his imprisonment by scratching markings on the wall when his meals were brought. The routine of the hospitality never changing until about three weeks into his imprisonment. Ten men dressed quite differently than his guard entered the passageway. Two stopped at the ingress holding what looked like lions held by chains. The cats were big. Bigger then any mountain lions Bobby had seen in the North Western Territory. And the fangs,— they were the teeth of the demon that had stood over him with drawn bow.

Where am I? he thought as he studied the magnificent animals. The soldiers marched down the corridor ignored by Bobby's sentry.

"Boo-bee, pray to your God now!"

"What is it Haiwi?*"*

"Don't let them take me. You are the messenger. Don't let them take me."

Haiwi fought as her captors dragged her from her from her cell. Like a tigress she scratched and clawed kicking and biting her assailants. She was a fighter and the much larger and stronger men

337

could barely manage to hold on to her.

"Leave her alone!" Bobby screamed as he reached through his bars trying to stop the attack.

"Boo-bee, help me," she cried as one of the men raised his spear and struck the beautiful face across the chin with the blunt end of the weapon. Haiwi fell limp.

The spear raked across Bobby's lattice and to the soldier's surprise, the little man grabbed the shaft and pulled it into his cell and spinning it in one quick motion shoved the sharp flint blade into the offender's ribs.

The soldier grunted opening his mouth without a scream. Bobby stepped back. The soldier snarled exposing his filed sharpened teeth, but his mouth was tongueless. Then the antagonist sank to the floor dead.

The others turned their attention to the little man. But his guard jumped between with spear ready and barked a warning.

Bobby was helpless as he backed further away from the bars. He stared down at the unconscious Haiwi, dressed only in a tattered loincloth as the soldiers grabbed her roughly and dragged her limp form and that of their fallen comrade down the hall. "Haiwi," he cried, running back to the bars shaking them. "Haiwi," he called out one more time as Bobby watched, but her long dark hair covered most of her face, hiding any revelation of consciousness. The poor little man didn't even get one last look at his friend's beautiful eyes that sparkled with life.

Bobby dropped to the floor as tears welled. And then he prayed. He prayed not for himself, but for Haiwi.— For the messenger would have gladly taken her place.

**Visit the
Warnock Press Web Site:**

www.warnockpress.com

And sign up for the
Guardian series
e-mail updates!

Coming in 2010

"The Witch, the Ghost, and the Demon"

Turn the page for an exciting excerpt….

The Witch, the Ghost, and the Demon

Giggling, a scantily clad woman stepped from behind an unlocked door into the hall.

"Get back here,— Rosy."

"I'll be right back," she whispered seductively pulling the knob closed. Shivering, the woman looked down the corridor as a draft ruffled the thin veneer trappings hanging from her shoulders.

The window at the end of the breezeway flew up with a bang as the wind and rain ripped through the opening, tossing the curtains into a billowing rage.

"What the hell?" Rosy crossed her arms to her breast for warmth and moved down the hall to shut the obtrusion. As she neared, the heavy downpour had already soaked the red carpet, puddling at the base of the opening. The woman looked at the mess with disgust.

Reaching for the sill, she paused when a footprint formed into the saturated material, squeezing water out around the compression of the track. She froze as the storm was momentarily blocked and something hit her hand. Rose backed away when the footprint shifted and a shadowy silhouette stood upright inside the hall. Streaks of netted lightning rippled over the ghostly form amid the crackling and popping of the blue glowing flames. A man appeared suddenly, then with a snap was gone; but Rosy couldn't move. She stared where the apparition appeared,— but nothing.

Turning to run, a steely grip locked onto her wrist and something covered her mouth and slammed her body face first against the wall. Rose tried to struggle, but was helpless as the invisible force pushed against her. She could feel the hot breath of her attacker next to her ear. The cold dampness of the winter storm from outside clung to the ghoul and transferred the wet to her thin garment, sending goose bumps down her spine.

Rosy whimpered.

"Where's Andrew Walkins?" whispered a deep guttural voice.

About the Authors

Glenwood "Carol" O'Dell

G.C. was born in the great state of South Dakota in the late 1950s. Growing up in the Midwest, he learned the joys of camping and the study of tracking and woodcraft in the Boy Scouts. He spent his teenage years trapping and hunting in the Missouri backwoods. Reaching the half century mark **G.C.** now lives in the California Sierras. An outdoor enthusiast, he still enjoys riding horses, hunting, fishing, and black-powder. As an avid reader of both history, science fiction and fantasy, he longs for the days of yore when hunter-gatherers ruled and life was simpler.

Jeremy "Cole" O'Dell

Spending most of his school recesses with his nose in novels, **J.C.** is a self-proclaimed, "Nerdy Intellectual." His love of reading reached new heights while reading Tarzan, by Edgar Rice Burroughs at age 10. He soon tore through the series and branched out in his love for other genres. When 18 he made a great discovery,— a folder full of stories his father had written. Asking his dad about the unfinished work, soon the two of them were writing books together. **J.C.** draws inspiration from his varied life experiences and interests: growing up on a small farm, hunting (both archery and rifle) old west reenacting and of course,— his reading. His favorite authors are Stephen King, Dean Koontz, Orson Scott Card, Jim Butcher, William R. Frostchen, and of course, the master,—Edgar Rice Burroughs.

WARNOCK PRESS

Keep up to date with the latest releases.

www.warnockpress.com

If you enjoyed this novel and would like to

order additional copies for yourself or friends:

check your local bookstore

Or

you can send your check or money order to:

Warnock Press
P.O. Box 846
Dept. BPV-2
North Fork, CA 93643

Priced for 2008

Mountain Calling $14.95 US
(CAN $18.70)

Please add the following for postage and handling:
$5.75 for priority mail, $4.75 for media mail,
Sales Tax (CA residents only) $1.16

All prices are subject to change without notice.

Printed in the United States
131060LV00001B/2/P